Praise for *The First Cut*

"*The First Cut* should immediately establish Dianne Emley in the front ranks of thriller writers. . . . A great read."

—MICHAEL CONNELLY

"Impressive . . . expertly plotted . . . Emley makes each gamble pay off."

—*Detroit Free Press*

"Guaranteed to keep readers at the edge of their seats until the final page."

—*Tucson Citizen*

"An edge-of-your-seat plot . . . Nicely developed characters and genuine suspense."

—*Kirkus Reviews*

Has all the makings of what promises to be a captivating and enduring series."

—newmysteryreader.com

Advance praise for *Cut to the Quick*

"*Cut to the Quick*'s razor-sharp pacing and twisted plot kept me on the edge of my chair from the first page to the last. Intense, smart, and relentless, Nan Vining is no run-of-the-mill cop."

—MARIAH STEWART, author of *Last Breath*

"Dianne Emley sets a cracking pace in this crime thriller, a follow-up novel to her blistering debut, *The First Cut*."

—*The Sunday Mail*

"Compelling. Readers will look forward to seeing more of this edgy, unpredictable heroine."

—*Publishers Weekly*

By Dianne Emley

THE FIRST CUT
CUT TO THE QUICK

DIANNE EMLEY

THE FIRST CUT

A NOVEL

BALLANTINE BOOKS • NEW YORK

2008 Ballantine Books Mass Market Edition

Copyright © 2006 by Emley and Co., LLC.
Excerpt from *Cut to the Quick* copyright © 2007 by Emley and Co., LLC.

Published in the United States by Ballantine Books, an imprint of The Random House Publishing Group, a division of Random House, Inc., New York.

BALLANTINE and colophon are registered trademarks of Random House, Inc.

Originally published in hardcover in the United States by Ballantine Books, an imprint of The Random House Publishing Group, a division of Random House, Inc., in 2006.

This book contains an excerpt from the forthcoming hardcover edition of *Cut to the Quick* by Dianne Emley. This excerpt has been set for this edition only and may not reflect the final content of the forthcoming edition.

ISBN 978-0-345-48618-9

Cover design and illustration: Tony Greco

Printed in the United States of America

www.ballantinebooks.com

OPM   9 8 7 6 5 4 3 2 1

For my husband,
Charles G. Emley, Jr.
Country walks in springtime . . .

ACKNOWLEDGMENTS

My heartfelt gratitude goes first to my brilliant editors and pals, Linda Marrow and Dana Isaacson. Thanks for your unwavering faith, never settling for less than my best, and demonstrating that an astute editor's guiding hand in a writer's career is not a relic of the distant past.

A great debt of thanks is owed to Gina Centrello and everyone on the Ballantine team, in particular Dan Mallory (fellow Highsmith fan), Kim Hovey, Cindy Murray, and Rachel Kind.

Huzzah to my wonderful agent and champion, Robin Rue, and everyone at Writer's House, especially Diana Fox.

Though the people and events depicted in this book are fictitious—the handiwork of my imagination—I could not have written this story without the generous assistance of many law and order professionals. Any errors in police procedure or criminal law are solely the fault of this author.

Officer Donna Cayson of the Pasadena Police Department was particularly helpful, taking time from her busy schedule to answer my questions. Thanks also to the PPD officers who graciously allowed me to ride along on their patrols: John Buchholz, Mary Hooker, and Gil Ortiz. You've given me an eye-opening appreciation for the tough and skillful work required to hold that thin blue line.

I am indebted to the Davidson brothers, retired Police Captain Steve Davidson and retired Sheriff's Office Lieutenant Herb Davidson, for their assistance. Special acknowledgment to Steve Davidson for his abundant and invaluable advice concerning the methodology, personalities, and politics of the police world.

The Tucson Police Department's Lieutenant Mark Napier and Lieutenant Mike Pryor were wonderfully hospitable in showing me their facility and answering questions.

Karla Kerlin, deputy district attorney, Los Angeles County, deserves hearty recognition for amiably answering scads of questions, usually posed by me in e-mails that naïvely began: "Here's a quick one for you." Thanks for giving me a crash course in Criminal Law 101.

On the other side of the legal fence, my appreciation to criminal defense attorney Dan Davis for his perspective.

Also of great help were my readers and amigas Jayne Anderson and Mary Goss. Your perceptive insight into plot quirks and ability to catch typos that everyone else missed saved my bacon. Cheers to my buddy Ann Escue for the psychologist's insight. *Chère amie* Leslie Pape for showing me the lesser-known corners of Tucson, *je t'embrasse.*

Last, but never least, thanks to my family, my constant supporters, who love me anyway. And of course, to my husband, Charlie, my safety net, my love.

ONE

No one knew her here. No one she knew would show up at this joint near LAX where the music was loud enough to muffle the roar of jets. There were usually no cops here. She could make a cop no matter how good the cover. She was an attractive female alone in a strip club but no one would bother her. Her uniform, gun, and badge repelled that sort of nonsense. A guy she figured for the manager asked if he could be of assistance. She said she was waiting for someone. She would only be there a couple of minutes. Thanks. He retreated to his stool at the bar and was giving her a dirty look. A police officer had a chilling effect on business. A female cop was especially vexing. Frankie Lynde enjoyed the power she had to disturb this tough guy and she kept on her game face, her take-no-prisoners face. It was fun. A prelude to the night of fun ahead.

It was midnight. She had finished her shift, letting the last guy she could have collared for solicitation go home with a warning because the arrest and the paperwork would have made her late. That was okay with her team. One was taking off the next morning for the Colorado River with his family. The others were just plain ready to resume their lives. The john was scared out of his wits anyway. He was a clean-cut family man kind of guy who probably had a job where people looked up to him. Frankie doubted he'd ever again seek action along that stretch of Sunset near Gower.

In the station locker room, she'd taken off the silver wig and leather miniskirt. She'd unzipped and peeled off the over-the-knee boots she'd bought at Frederick's purple flagship store on Hollywood Boulevard. She didn't have to go to such effort to costume herself. The other female undercover cops who posed as streetwalkers wore tight jeans and belly shirts, looking as if they could be waiting for their boyfriends to pick them up to go to the movies, like many whores working Sunset's east end. For the whores, their sexy-but-regular-girl clothing bolstered their innocent excuses when cops questioned them about why they were loitering. "My car broke down over there." "I had a fight with my boyfriend and he took off and I'm gonna see if he's at his mom's house over here. Around the corner. Up there."

Frankie liked to dress like a hooker. She had a dozen wigs and outfits. She told the other vice detectives that by changing her look, the hookers and johns wouldn't make her. She told about having picked up the same john three times, wearing three different wigs. There were rumors around the department that Frankie got into her role a little too much. She didn't deny it. It was pointless, made her look weak, and gave the rumors credibility. Her numbers spoke louder than talk. Any night she was on the street, she made three times as many collars as the other female officers. She knew how to stand with her legs apart, moving her hips back and forth as if she had an itch.

She was tall and good-looking. Too good-looking to be standing on a street corner. If she were a hooker for real, she'd be a highly paid call girl, not a streetwalker. The johns never put that together. They saw. They wanted. They pulled over. When they started talking specific fees for specific favors, she'd lean toward their car to give them a glimpse of her cleavage and yank the hem of her skirt with both hands, the signal for her backup to move in for the arrest.

Bottom line, she roped them in, that's all they needed to know at the station. They had no idea how much truth there was to the rumors. That was for Frankie to know and the others never to find out.

At home, she'd peeled off the metallic tube top that she had not removed in the locker room in front of the others. She didn't want glances and whispers about what she was hiding there. She'd scrubbed off the heavy makeup and shampooed and blow-dried her long, blond hair. She'd pinned it into a tight bun at the back of her head and applied conservative makeup. She wasn't conservative in her choice of earrings, selecting the diamond studs. *He'd asked her to wear them.* The large diamonds seemed to have inner life, radiating when touched by light. Most definitely not regulation.

She'd strapped on her Kevlar vest. One never knew. The last thing she needed was someone with a cop grudge taking a potshot at her. Finally, she'd put on her uniform, crisp and fresh from the dry cleaners. Flying the colors while not on police business was in violation of department policy. If caught, she'd be formally reprimanded and possibly suspended. It was worth the risk. She wasn't going to get caught.

Even with the bust-flattening vest, hip-obscuring slacks, and waist-eliminating equipment belt, Frankie knew she still looked hot. It was common cop knowledge that if a female managed to look hot in uniform, she'd look three times as hot in street clothes.

"What'll you have?" The bartender's surgically enhanced breasts ballooned from her tight, low-cut top.

"Diet Coke." That was part of the game. There would be plenty of drinks later.

From his seat at the end of the bar, the manager watched the bartender shoot cola into a glass from a nozzle.

Frankie set a five-dollar bill on the bar and turned to watch the stage, an oval set in an arena of chairs and small tables. Three women wearing only G-strings gyrated around poles, spinning, hanging upside down. Their enlarged boobs defied gravity. It was Friday night. The club was crowded with businessmen, guys with buddies, guys alone, and a few couples out to spice up their sex life.

Two men wearing dress shirts with the top buttons undone and no ties entered the club. They were loose and loud. They had started drinking somewhere else.

"Hey, hey . . . Lookie here. A po-leece woman. Howya doin', lady cop?"

"Fine. How are you?"

"Never better," reciting the mantra of the party guy.

The other one, unsteady on his feet, pointed at Frankie's chest, nearly touching her. "You wearing a bulletproof vest?"

"Please step away, sir."

"Oooh . . . Hey. Okay, officer, okay." He held up his fists, wrists together. "Arrest me."

That started them guffawing. The goofball closest to Frankie did not comply with her request. He looked like the kind of guy who took crap all week long. On the weekends, he got drunk and dished out some of his own. Some cop, sometime, somewhere had done something to piss him off and now Frankie had to deal with the residue.

She gave him her dead-eye gaze.

"You're kinda cute. I could maybe have a thing for a woman in uniform."

In the blink of an eye, she pulled her nightstick from its ring on her equipment belt, flipped it by the handle, and assumed an aggressive stance. The polished cherrywood was an old-time weapon passed to Frankie from her father, who'd received it from his father. It did the trick. If party boy moved an inch closer, she'd shove the rod into the soft spot below his rib cage.

He made a motion as if to grab the nightstick.

"Sir, I asked you to step away."

She kept her eyes on him as he tentatively backed off, reaching to slide his beer from the bar. Saying "Let's beat it" to his buddy, he moved toward the stage. She heard him mutter "Bitch" under his breath.

Frankie resisted smiling as she picked up her Diet Coke.

Customers eyed her uncomfortably. The manager dropped a foot from the stool rung and was about to step off when a young, attractive woman darted into the club.

She stopped short when she saw the nearly nude dancers, even though the club's giant sign, visible from the 105 freeway said "XXX Marks the Spot." She let out a yelp of surprise as she pressed the back of her hand against her mouth and whirled around. She spotted Officer Lynde.

"Oh, Officer, Officer. Help me, please."

She ran to Lynde, wringing her hands.

Frankie stepped forward, her feet shoulder distance apart in a ready position. "What's the problem, ma'am?"

The woman's demeanor was as oddball as her appearance. She was wearing a masculine pantsuit, a white button-down shirt, a rep tie, polished wingtips, and a billed chauffeur's cap. From beneath the cap, a platinum blond braid dropped to the middle of her back. White frosted lipstick set off a deep tan. Heart-shaped, red plastic sunglasses obscured her eyes.

"My boss was robbed. He was *robbed*," she wailed in a high-pitched voice. "A man, with a gun."

"Where?"

People turned their attention from the dancers to watch this show.

"Outside. In the parking lot. Please help us. *Please*."

"When?"

"Just now. Come out. I'll show you."

"Is the man with the gun still there?" Frankie's stoic demeanor cracked and she appeared bewildered.

"No, no. Just come out." The chauffeur didn't wait but bolted out the door.

Frankie jogged after her, quickly catching up. "My boss was robbed. What kind of crap is that, Pussycat?"

Still running, one hand holding her hat on her head, the other cradling her large breasts to keep them from bouncing, Pussycat let out a squeal. "Your acting stinks."

"I thought we were meeting inside."

"Change of plans."

Pussycat's voice was airy and her speech rapid.

Frankie couldn't see her eyes behind the heart-shaped sunglasses. "How high are we?"

Pussycat gave her a big, open-mouthed grin. "I'm having a real good time."

"Maybe a little over-amped, huh? You'd better check yourself."

"Oh, Officer Lynde. You just can't stop being a cop, can you?" She squealed as they approached a limousine that was parked in the farthest corner of the lot and laughed with abandon when the passenger door dropped open.

Panting from the run, Pussycat resumed the ruse. "He's in there, Officer. My boss is in there."

Frankie climbed into the back of the limo and the chauffeur, giggling, closed the door after her.

"Good evening, Officer Lynde."

He was immaculate in a white tuxedo with tails, a red rose in his lapel.

His wife climbed behind the wheel and pulled the limo into the street. The entrance to the 105 was less than a block away. She got on heading east.

He took Frankie's breath away. He always did, but tonight . . . Something was different tonight. Something was special. He had requested that she wear her uniform. The only other time she'd been with them in uniform was when they had first met.

John Lesley had walked into her life at the best and worst time for debauchery. She was in a moribund relationship, each waiting for the other to drive home a stake. She suspected her inamorato was covertly doing just that as she'd gotten wind that he was stepping out with someone else. This hurt and infuriated Frankie in equal measure. The SOB didn't have the balls to end it like a man. Prick bastard. While at an endless luncheon banquet, she'd received a text message from him canceling their date. CNT 2DAY. L8TR. She sought solace in a cigarette outside.

John Lesley was seated at a table on the hotel patio, drinking a glass of beer and smoking a cigar. She took note of him, as she did everything. She took in his expensive suit and the way his physique filled it just right, his stylish dark hair flecked with gray, and his profile, like that of a matinee idol from the days of black-and-white movies. She kept moving to the garden wall that bordered the pool and hiked her hip onto it.

She took out a cigarette and he was beside her, gold lighter in hand. She guided his hand with the flame and their eyes locked. They stood silently, smoking. She saw he was not wearing a wedding ring.

She held out her cigarette and turned it in front of her face. "We're a couple of outlaws."

"These days." Holding his beer, he raised it in a way that asked if she wanted one.

She declined.

He gave her a crooked smile and leisurely looked her over, returning to her eyes. "No drinking on duty."

"That's the rule."

"Do you always follow the rules?"

"When it works for me."

"You know what they say about rules."

She dragged on her cigarette. "I think I broke that one, too."

Standing too close, he sipped the beer and watched her, openly and unapologetically, with no attempt to hide his thoughts. She read his thoughts. His gaze alone made her tingle. She had no trouble imagining what his hands, mouth, and body would do.

She took the beer from him and finished it all at once. She handed the empty glass back to him and licked her lips. Walking back inside, she felt his eyes on her.

She took her seat at the banquet table. Shortly, he came in and sat a few tables away, next to a pretty woman with long hair dyed an assertive shade of auburn. He and the woman chatted in that casually intimate but disinterested way of old friends or married couples. They both gazed at her across the tables that separated them. The woman twirled a strand of hair and Frankie caught the glint cast by her wedding rings.

After a further exchange of disagreeable text messages with her lover, Frankie pushed aside her dessert plate and excused herself. She was staring into the restroom mirror, lip gloss poised in her hand, when the woman with auburn hair entered. She toured the room, glancing beneath stalls, and returned to stand beside her. She wore a simple black dress and understated, real jewelry, but she somehow made the ensemble look provocative and a whiff trashy. The two women fussed with their hair, neither speaking.

A toilet flushed. A woman emerged from a stall and washed her hands. Soon Frankie and the redhead were alone. She stepped close enough to fill Frankie's nostrils with an alluring mixture of delicate perfume and money. She came right to the point.

"I'm Pussycat. My husband and I like you. We want you to come with us. We'll have caviar and Champagne or cocaine or whatever the hell you want and we'll fuck you like you've never been fucked before."

Frankie had heard of Vice detectives who had become too close to the Job. When she'd first started working Vice, the thought was outrageous to her. She'd planned to do her year or so then work on moving into homicide. Three years later, she was still in vice and had no intention of leaving. The Job had worked on her. Made her see things about herself. It was tough, trying to keep people from pursuing their basic urges, restraining their unhealthy impulses when she was having the same struggle herself.

She'd met them later and they'd spent the weekend in the penthouse suite of an exclusive hotel. She'd gone lots of other nights, too. Mostly they went to the couple's home. It was big and private and perfect for their kind of partying. The sex slowly got rougher and the setup, disguises, and rules of the game more complex. John Lesley had a predator's instinct for luring her in. He stoked her confidence and dependence on him while, ever so slowly, they progressed from the erotic and experimental to the perverted. She once came home with bruises, nothing visible outside her clothes, and locks of hair yanked out. She refused to meet him again, but he wore her down. Near the first of the month, when things were tight and the mortgage on her tiny condo was due, a knock on her door brought a messenger with a robin's egg blue box from Tiffany's and a manila envelope crammed with crisp hundred-dollar bills. Not having to worry about money for the first time in her life was blissfully freeing. A natural aphrodisiac.

Didn't she deserve nice things? She'd busted her hump her whole life and was still on the outside looking in. She had also missed the sexy excitement of the tightrope walk he represented. Worse yet, she missed him. She'd fallen in love with him a little. That made her feel crazier than she wanted to accept.

What she was doing was immoral, but it wasn't illegal. She'd checked. She'd also checked them out. Knew everything about them. Knowledge was power and she made sure she was always in control. She told herself that the moment she stopped feeling in control, she'd walk away, keeping his gifts and money. She had told no one and made sure there were no traces between them. She had taken pains to avoid an ugly confrontation between her two lives. As for the Lesleys, they also held her at arm's length. Frankie flirted with worst-case scenarios, but the style suited her personal agenda. Their liaison would eventually end and no one wanted repercussions.

It was beyond dangerous. Every cop instinct in her body told her so. And it was thrilling.

Frankie said to him, "Sir, I understand you've been robbed."

At a stoplight, the smoked-glass partition rolled down and Pussycat grinned back at them, her teeth unnaturally white and her lips too full.

"I haven't been robbed yet, Officer Lynde, but I'm ready."

He pulled away his tuxedo jacket, exposing himself through his unzipped pants.

Pussycat let out a throaty laugh.

"I'll take your report now, sir."

Frankie lowered her head to his lap.

He stretched his arms across the seat back. "That's right, baby. That's it."

She felt his excitement building.

Grabbing her tightly pinned hair, he followed her up-and-down motion. Suddenly, he forced her head down and held it there. She began to choke and struggled to push away. He let go. She didn't like his smug expression.

She reached for the pepper spray on her equipment belt. "You prick. I warned you about that rough stuff."

She could tell he relished her distress.

There was a flicker of that look in his eyes. The look that betrayed his soul. It quickly passed, making Frankie wonder if she'd misjudged. He smiled and caressed her face between his hands. The smile of a charming man. She was still a sucker for it. She couldn't get past it. It had to do with not receiving enough attention from her father growing up and blah, blah, blah. She slid the pepper spray back into its sleeve.

"Aw, Officer Lynde, I didn't mean to hurt you."

"Could have fooled me."

"I have something for you."

"You already gave me something I didn't like." Lately she'd wondered if the party was coming to an end.

He took a small box from his inside jacket pocket and ceremoniously opened the hinged lid.

She drew in a sharp breath as he slipped the watch around her wrist. She caught the look in Pussycat's eyes in the rearview mirror and took pleasure in the hint of shock and hurt there. Maybe the wife was the one who was on the way out.

"Patek Philippe," he said. "Twenty-five grand."

"It's beautiful." The watch was gold and paper thin, lying nearly flush against her wrist. A line of diamonds around the face sparkled.

Pussycat kept driving, her shoulders stiff.

"I have something for you, too, my love," he told his wife.

"Really?"

"Yes, really. Something you want. It's at home." He rolled his eyes. "Women."

They had left the freeway and were heading up Mulholland Drive. Pussycat pulled off onto a lookout point. Twinkling lights blanketed the landscape to land's end. A classic L.A. postcard. No other cars were parked there. Pussycat got out and climbed into the back with them.

Frankie gulped the flute of Cristal that John Lesley gave her and closed her eyes as Pussycat massaged her shoulders, the watch issue forgotten.

"Poor Frankie. She works so hard." She began unbuttoning Frankie's shirt.

He refilled Frankie's glass, stuck his finger in the Champagne, and painted her lips. She sucked his finger. She threw the brimming glass to the floor and began kissing him and madly ripping at his clothes as Pussycat did the same to her. She felt her equipment belt fall away and raised her hips to allow Pussycat to pull off her slacks.

He gently guided her head to where he wanted her. Relaxed now and aroused, she started again. She couldn't wait.

This was her addiction, this feeling of wild abandon, of doing and having, wasting money and indulging every fantasy. They sometimes drove past MacArthur Park near downtown L.A. and let fistfuls of twenty-dollar bills flutter from the limo's moon roof just to laugh as the drug addicts and dealers chased and fought over the money. They rolled in sex for days on end. Later, at work or at home, the guilt would come and Frankie would ask herself why. But not now. The moment had taken hold. Why had no meaning here. Why was the lament of the weak and sleeping.

He was close. He was there.

He slid his hands around Frankie's throat and squeezed.

Frankie tried to pull away, but he wouldn't let her. This was too soon for the rough stuff. She flailed her arms and reached for her gun. This was over right now. Where was her gun?

She heard Pussycat jabbering incoherently and felt her trying to pry off his fingers.

Frankie reached up and jabbed her thumbs into his eyes. She bit down on him as hard as she could. He cried out, but it wasn't a cry of true, sustained pain and it sounded far away. Her thumbs and jaw had no force. There were spots in front of her eyes and a metallic taste in her mouth.

The last thing she saw before going out was his face. It was pure evil.

TWO

It was nearly a year since Officer Nan Vining had last walked up the six low steps that lead to the Pasadena Police Department on her way to work. She wanted to avoid returning so close to the one-year anniversary, but bureaucratic B.S. had interfered, postponing the end of her leave until then. She refused to see it as anything more than coincidence.

Officers generally came in by the back entrance through the garage, but that route would take her through the thick of the graveyard shift, officially called Morning Watch, waiting to go home and the Day Watch preparing to roll out. She needed to make this transition slowly. Ease back in. It had been a long journey. No one except her daughter, Emily, knew how far she had traveled.

At the top of the steps, a supporting post of the arcade bore four plaques commemorating officers killed in the line of duty since the city's incorporation in 1886. Sergeant Sebastian Crone, shot responding to a liquor store robbery in 1971, was the last. Vining reflected that she had nearly become the fifth name, beneath Crone's.

"Okay, Em," Vining whispered, imagining her fourteen-year-old standing beside her. "I'll be honest."

Em had insisted on Vining's respect for the journey, an incident that Vining dismissed as the fickle finger of fate, the cards she'd been dealt, how her cookie had crumbled, combined with a medically explainable neurological effect. For Em, it had been much more.

"I was the fifth. For two minutes and twelve seconds, I was the fifth."

Vining stood erect and snapped her hand to her forehead in a salute. People who passed looked, but she didn't care. Em was right about that. Vining had changed.

T. B. Mann had changed Emily, too. It was as if she and Em had been traveling down a road and someone had shoved them off. Now they were still traveling the same direction as the road, but walking in the brush and pebbles beside it. The road was right there, but damned if they knew how to get back on. But they were fine, she and Em. They were doing all right.

She entered the building into the records lobby.

The three-story Mission Revival structure was built in 1989. New, as police departments went. Nice, as police departments went. Virtually all the PPD's operations, other than the gun range, heliport, and a couple of substations in minimalls, were based in this building.

Pasadena, California, has a resident population of 135,000 that swells to 500,000 during the workweek.

With over 200 sworn officers, it has one of the largest police forces in the state but is dwarfed by that of Los Angeles, its neighbor to the west. LAPD has about 10,000 officers serving a population of 2.5 million.

The PPD is small enough to be family. The chief's office is in the same building from which the patrol cars roll out. The jail is in the basement.

Vining had been on the force for twelve years. Five were spent in various detective desks, the past three in Homicide. She included the previous year in the total. She had bled for it. She had earned it.

A short line had already formed behind the bulletproof glass that protected the cadets who staffed the two reception windows. The department had installed the glass after 9/11. A female and three males were sitting on the two wood benches in the lobby. Vining suspected they were waiting to be escorted to the jail downstairs. The female had a brown paper shopping bag that probably held the change of underwear, book, and few toiletries prisoners were allowed.

Outside one of the windows, a woman was reporting a stolen car to a cadet whom Vining didn't recognize. The stool next to him was empty.

Vining stood at the locked door that led to the main lobby and elevators and looked over at the cadet, waiting for him to unlock the door.

She was searching for her keys when he asked, "Ma'am, who are you here to see?"

The cadet was around nineteen years old. Vining guessed he was a student at Pasadena City College, nearly all the cadets were, but he already had acquired the unyielding, unhesitating demeanor of a cop. In a way Vining was glad he didn't know who she was. Maybe her story wasn't as notorious around the department as she thought.

She was about to pull her flat badge from her pocket when Rosalie, who had worked in the records department forever, spotted her from behind the windows, burst through the side door, and jogged across the fired tile floor. She enveloped Vining in a bear hug.

"Nan, you're back! Oh my gosh. It's so *good* to see you. They told me you were in last week; I was so sorry I missed you. How are you?" Rosalie held her at arm's length, her eyes glittering with tears.

"I'm good."

"You look terrific."

"Thank you. I feel good."

Vining had worked hard physically and mentally to prepare for this day. She wanted to obliterate the idea— the shadow of an idea—in anyone's mind that she was not capable of returning to her job. She'd struggled to convince her superiors that she was up to working at her old desk in Homicide. She'd lost. They'd offered her Residential Burglary. She'd be dealing with crimes against property, not persons. Nothing that bled. Detective Sergeant Kendra Early would no longer be her boss. Vining was philosophical. Among other things, she'd learned patience in the year she'd been gone. She'd get her old job back in time. After having nearly lost her future, she was calm with the knowledge that time was on her side.

She loved being a cop. She'd fallen into the career, but now saw it as destiny rather than happenstance. It had taken her tragedy to reveal to her the reason for her fervor, as if it had always been there but obscured. A shape behind a screen. There were people out there who needed to be put in prison. There was one man in particular. The man who had killed her. She and Emily had named him. T. B. Mann. The Bad Man.

"Come in this way." Rosalie pulled her inside through another door. "Say hi to Joanie and Ramon."

Others came to greet her. She felt eyes on the long scar on her neck and the smaller one on the back of her right hand. The scars had faded to pink. After much deliberation, Vining decided she wasn't going to cover them. They defined who she was now. But the attention made her uncomfortable in a way she hadn't anticipated.

"It was so horrible. We prayed for you every day, Nan. Every day. All of us."

"Thank you." She didn't believe in prayers, but neither did she feel they did any harm. It was nice that people had taken time out of their day to think of her. Many throughout Pasadena, across the country, and even around the world had done so. The department had received scads of cards and notes from well-wishers. Kind, heartfelt sentiments. One stood out. One was not nice. Camouflaged inside a cheery Hallmark card with a cartoon doctor and patient on the front, was this note: "You should have died, bitch."

She dismissed it as probably sent by someone still ticked off about the man she had shot and killed five years ago. The shooting was determined to have been in policy. A good shooting. Still, she'd received lots of hate mail. It eventually tapered off. Vining figured her appearance in the news this past year had fanned the last sparks of resentment about that incident. It was disturbing to think T. B. Mann might have sent the nasty greeting card, knowing he had fully intended for her to die.

"Nan, I can't believe he's still out there. That he got away with it."

"He hasn't gotten away with it. Not for long. Not for long." She repeated it, as if T. B. Mann could hear her.

"Look, thanks, everyone, for your kind calls and letters. They really cheered me up and kept me going, but I've got to get to work." She couldn't help but grin. Today was the day. She was back.

Vining took the elevator with two uniformed officers who were late for roll call. They nodded at her but didn't speak. The elevator opened on the second floor and the uniforms got off to head for the briefing room. Nan stepped out and turned in the other direction. She walked down the hallway past a display case with a collection of antique police badges donated by a retired officer. Framed newspaper pages showing the World Trade Center towers just after the attacks and patriotic posters lined the walls.

At the end of the hall was the Detectives Section. She punched in the access code and entered a large, open room filled with cubicles upholstered in pearl gray fabric, looking like cubes in an office anywhere. Affixed to the outside of each were computer-made signs printed on white paper in bold type: Missing Persons, Assaults, Residential Burglary, Commercial Burglary, Auto Theft, Financial Crimes, Robbery, Sex Assaults/Runaways, Domestic Violence, Homicide.

"Poison Ivy!" A nickname she hated boomed from a man who was not her ally.

"Hey, Picachu." It was the first time she'd ever called Tony Ruiz by his moniker. It was apt as he resembled the squat, rotund cartoon character, but she had found it mean, even if the department nicknames were presumably uttered with familial affection. Today she was trying to be game. The style didn't come naturally to her.

Most things about cop work did, but not the jiving, joking, buddy-making part. Ruiz wouldn't warm to her no matter what she did. His enmity wasn't caused by anything she had actively done. She was a victim of association. There was no love lost between Ruiz and Lieutenant Bill Gavigan, who had taken Vining under his wing from the time she was a rookie and he was a patrol sergeant. Sometimes Vining thought Ruiz disliked her simply because she was taller. He was having the last laugh. After years of trying, he finally had her job.

Ruiz had made the obligatory visit to her hospital room but hadn't contacted her after that. That was fine with her. She didn't find his presence particularly healing.

Heads began popping up like prairie dogs over the tops of cubicles.

"Look who's back."

"Ivy's here."

"Hey, Quick Draw. Howyadoin'?"

Vining cringed at that nickname, too, but took it in stride, slapping palms and accepting hugs.

"Heard they transferred you to Community Services, Vining."

"I couldn't get the stench of the second floor off me. I'm ruined for any other job."

"I hear that running the Citizen's Police Academy is very rewarding."

"So is teaching Sunday school. I haven't heard about you doing that."

Vining peeked into Jim Kissick's cubicle. He wasn't there.

"Kissick's probably in the can," Ruiz offered.

"Whoa. You've got a story to tell the grandkids,

huh?" A young man who looked vaguely familiar to Vining was pointing at her scar. Everyone else had the good manners to look without really looking.

"I don't believe we've met." Vining extended her hand over the cubicle, her gaze cool. She guessed he was in his twenties. She detected a callow cockiness that sometimes got young cops into trouble.

His eyes dropped from her scar to her bust.

Only the top button of her blouse was undone. The fabric was medium blue and not transparent. She was wearing a jacket and was lean anyway, so there was nothing to see. Vining pitied the women who stumbled across this scumbag.

He finished his once-over before grasping her palm. "Alex Caspers. Like the friendly ghost with an *s*."

"You can ignore him," one of the guys said. "He's rotating out of Residential Burglary at the end of this week. He can't wait. He doesn't like it up here with us."

The Department had four rotational spots in detectives for patrol officers. The positions lasted one year and were generally in property crimes.

"You detectives have too much paperwork," Caspers said. "I need to get back on the street where the action is, homes."

"She's ba-ack." Detective Sergeant Kendra Early rounded the corner and enveloped Vining in a bear hug. She was forty, African American, shorter than Vining, and more filled out. Vining had never seen her wearing makeup, and the persistent dark circles under her eyes made her always look tired. A habit of frequently rubbing her eyes added to her world-weary aura. Vining's nose brushed against her short, curly hair. She had liked working for Early and was going to miss it. Vining had been the sole female in Early's crew. Their relationship was not particularly friendly or warm, and neither of them felt a pressure to move beyond the professional. However, they understood each other, which made their working rapport the most uncomplicated that Vining had experienced.

"I *am* back."

"You look good, girl."

"Thanks. Feel good."

"Vining!" Ron Cho's voice bellowed.

A tiny waver of Early's eyebrow conveyed that she didn't think much of Cho's greeting.

Vining followed Early to the glassed-in room that she shared with the two other detective sergeants. Ernie Taylor's and Ron Cho's desks were side by side and held impressive piles of disorganized clutter. Early's desk was opposite Taylor's and looked like a place where one could work. Silver-framed photos of her extensive family spilled from a corner of her desk onto the empty desk beside her.

The windows faced Garfield Street and the courthouse, an unadorned concrete rectangle lined with soulless windows. Across the street to the south was City Hall, empty and encircled by temporary fencing while it underwent refurbishing and earthquake retrofitting. PPD shields bore a replica of its Spanish Baroque dome.

Vining shook the other two sergeants' hands and pulled a chair in front of Cho's desk. He wasn't a tall man but he had a massive upper body from daily workouts at the station gym. His mother was Latina and his father was Korean.

"What are you doing yellin' at the woman, Cho? First day back after IOD leave."

"The criminals weren't Injured on Duty. Judging from the pile of reports that came up last night, they're in fine shape. Vining is, too. Look at her. Bright-eyed, fit . . . Ready to go." Cho leered at Early. "You're just ticked off because your girl got blown out at Wimbledon."

"You go there and I'm going to have to talk about your Lakers."

"Just squeeze 'em till they hurt, Early."

Taylor snickered as he went through a stack of reports. He had piercing blue eyes and a crew cut that disguised thinning hair. He was wearing a holster over a dark gray dress shirt.

"What are you laughing at?" Early walked to him and brushed dandruff from his shoulders.

"The way you treat me, Kendra. It's hurtful."

"Making sure you're keeping up your appearance. That's all." Early sat at her desk.

"Seriously, Vining," Cho said. "How do you feel?"

"Great. Ready to get back to work."

This was not Vining's first official meeting discussing her injury. She'd met with Early and George Beltran, the lieutenant in charge of Detectives, before. She'd worked hard to make her case that she was ready to return to a desk in Crimes Against Persons. Wanting to look robust, strong, like a force to be reckoned with, she'd spent many hours at the gym, believing being fit and disciplined physically was a prelude to mental strength. Bit by bit, she built herself up. Each chest press and bicep curl brought her closer. Closer to catching him.

She also had to recertify with her firearms. That was no problem. During her leave, she'd gone back to the gun range as soon as she was able, honing her skills with her service Glock .40 and the 9mm that most PPD officers carried. She renewed her familiarity with the Remington 12 gauge that was standard in PPD patrol cars. She'd also built up her personal arsenal during her leave, adding a Winchester Model 70 Featherweight .30-06 high-powered rifle to the .223 she already owned, giving her additional range that could come in handy. She chose the Mossberg 500 as a good up-close-and-personal weapon that would stop anyone within twenty feet and would be easy for Emily to use under duress. She coaxed her ex-husband into buying that one.

Off-duty, she still carried a tiny, pearl-handled .22 in her purse, but now added a second weapon. She tried wearing a Smith & Wesson .38 in an ankle holster. Her mentor, retired lieutenant Bill Gavigan, had carried one as his sidearm throughout his career in the PPD. She loved the old-school aspect of the .38. Unlike the semi-automatics, it wouldn't jam or let you down. The short barrel gave less opportunity for someone to grab it away from you. But she found it too heavy and bulky for an ankle holster, so she settled for a .32 caliber Walther PPK.

Emily accompanied her to the gun range as she had done since she was a small child. Nan's girl had a proper respect for firearms. While other mothers and daughters went shopping, Vining and Emily shot guns, to the overheated angst of her ex-husband's newer wife, who had deemed Vining's entire lifestyle as corrupting to a young lady. These shrill objections only enhanced the fun of those mother-daughter shooting outings for both Vining and Emily.

Vining's work in getting herself mentally fit to return to duty hadn't been as easy to measure. She was here, so she must have done okay with the police-appointed shrink. That had been a challenge, revealing enough to sound credible yet holding back the critical flaw that could do her in. The panic attacks would remain her and Emily's secret.

Going inside houses set them off. Not every house, just certain ones. Old. New. Didn't matter. A certain unknown attribute of the house triggered them. Her chest constricted. Beads of perspiration bloomed on her face and down her spine. Her hands grew clammy. Sometimes she hyperventilated. Sometimes she fainted.

Being in the open didn't bother her. There she could see. There, there were no wood blocks filled with cutlery. No refrigerator magnets. No pantries with smeared trails of blood leading inside. Being in her own home didn't frighten her, or the homes of her mother, sister, or grandmother. She was okay in the home of her ex-husband and his wife. Supermarkets, malls, business offices, and movie theaters were no problem.

But going into strangers' homes was part of her job.

Home. So many warm connotations, turned rancid by T. B. Mann.

Vining knew there was no way to exorcise the panic attacks with words. She had to face her fears head-on. She and Emily devised a plan.

She started by accepting invitations from the parents of Emily's friends to come inside when she'd arrive to retrieve her daughter. At first, she could only walk a few steps down the front path before seeing spots and gasping for air. Eventually, she made it to the front door, then across the threshold, then farther inside. Finally, she was able to reach the kitchen—that cozy center of a home. The place where family and guests congregated, where food was prepared and consumed, stories told and traditions passed down. To Vining, a home kitchen had become an opening to an abyss filled with knives and her own blood. An abyss in which he waited. T. B. Mann waited.

Vining promoted herself to the homes of strangers. She made it through an hour at a cocktail party given by neighbors new to the street, her eyes darting to the hands of a grandfather clock, watching the minutes tick by, the hour chimes sounding like the recess bell at school. Finally, she attended realtor open houses. That "For Sale" placard in the front yard looked so innocuous, so inviting. Anyone and everyone can enter. T. B. Mann had.

Emily had a theory. "Houses have karma, Mom."

She argued that houses retained a residue of the events and emotions that had occurred within their walls. A permanent imprint. A burned-in brand. Invisible, except Vining could sense it. She could sense a house's karma, more psychic residue left by T. B. Mann. He had changed her.

"Mom, it's like your antenna's been retuned and you can pick up on these things now."

"That's something to think about, sweet pea." Vining then refused to think about it that way at all.

Emily tried to convince her that it was a gift. Vining didn't think so. She found it more like an embarrassing twitch that she couldn't stop. It had prompted Emily to take up a new hobby. The girl attempted to capture on audio and film the essence of places and people that Vining sensed.

The full-on panic attacks subsided. Vining felt she had got the demon under control. She had won this battle. Yes, she had. She was in control.

"I guess you can't go through something like that and

not feel you've been given a second chance," Sergeant Cho said.

Vining nodded. "Lots of things matter less and a few things matter more."

Cho watched Vining with eyes that revealed little. They all knew about the two-odd minutes when she'd flat-lined. No one at the department had yet asked her about that. She didn't know what she would say if they did. It felt too private to talk about. A lot of cops were religious, but they were still practical and grounded in reality. She believed in God in a general sort of way. She attributed little significance to the weird out-of-body experience she'd had when she was dead, even though Emily felt otherwise. All Vining knew was that she felt present in the world in a way she hadn't before. It was as if a door to a hidden room in her mind had been cracked and was waiting for something to blow it wide open. As if she'd turned a corner and had arrived on the other side of . . . what?

Yes, Emily, she had changed.

"Has he attempted to contact you?" Early asked.

Vining knew about whom she was speaking. "I should be so lucky."

It was tough talk and she knew it. She wanted desperately to get T. B. Mann, but the panic attacks betrayed her. Both her hate and fear of him were visceral.

"Working Burglary is a good move for you," Cho said. "The more cross-training you get, the better for your career advancement."

He had a misconception held by many at the department that Vining had ambitions to work on the third floor, where the department's top brass had their offices.

Vining did not consider herself ambitious. She was simply a single mother who needed to work. If an opportunity for promotion came, fine. She went for it. It meant more money and perks for her. Somehow she'd inadvertently earned a jacket that she was a political player, working the system, kissing behinds.

Vining had another jacket as a cowboy. A lone wolf. She'd earned that one after the fatal shooting five years before. She was found to have acted within policy, but some still had questions about what had gone on that night.

The events surrounding T. B. Mann's assault on her a year ago in the house at 835 El Alisal Road revived the gossip. There were officers on the force, and she'd heard that Ruiz was among them, who thought she'd been cocky that day, knew better than what procedure mandated, didn't need help, and consequently put other officers in danger along with her.

The investigating committee found she'd used proper judgment in the El Alisal Road incident, but commented that Vining's experience was a cautionary lesson about carelessness. Still, officers talked, and the talk had gotten back to her.

She'd worn both jackets for years before she was aware she had them. She'd also learned that once you had a jacket, it was harder than hell to get rid of it.

She'd made enemies along the way. Some female officers were cool to her. That started years ago when Lieutenant Gavigan singled her out, took her under his wing, and gave her primo assignments. Conversations still stopped when she entered the locker room. Women were hardest on one another. It was worse than high school.

That was okay with Nan. Making friends had never been her objective. She wanted to do her job, stay safe, and go home at the end of her shift.

She had one more jacket she would never take off. She was a mom, and that changed her view about everything.

"I'm just happy to get back to work." She tried to appear enthusiastic. She would get her old desk back. She didn't know when, but she would.

Cho picked up a stack of reports that had come up from the Records Section. The cases had initially been processed by the patrol sergeants after filtering up from the street cops on Morning Watch. He was about to hand them to her when they both turned at a slap on the doorjamb.

Jim Kissick strode in, smiled at Vining, and gave her a couple of pats on the shoulder.

"Hey, Partner. Good to see you."

She stood and shook his hand. "Nice to see you, too. Good to be back."

Their exchange was cordial, nothing more. Both were aware that the three sergeants in the room were watching them. There had been rumors about Vining and Kissick. No one but the two of them knew the truth and they weren't talking.

"Some Adam Henry dumped a body in the arroyo by the bridge," Kissick announced, using a polite term for "asshole." "A film crew arriving to make a car commercial spotted it. Nude female. White."

"She wasn't a jumper?"

"Appears her throat was slit. Folke is the officer in charge."

Pasadena averaged two or three murders a year, generally gang-related and occurring in the northwest part of the city. The Colorado Street Bridge spanned neighborhoods in the city's affluent southwest side. The PPD likely would not be jacking up the usual suspects in this investigation.

"Let's roll." Early grabbed her jacket. As she headed out the door, she said, "Cho, I'm going to need Vining."

He held his hand out to indicate the new cases he was about to hand over. "What the fuck, Early? Vining works for me now."

Sergeant Taylor returned his attention to his work, pointedly staying out of the dispute.

"Assume she's not back today and handle it from there."

"This was all decided."

"That was then. This is now. I'll deal with the L.T. Don't worry."

"Oh, I'm not worried."

Vining guessed that Cho would be in Lieutenant George Beltran's office as soon as Early was gone. She knew Early had predicted this, too, and had already worked out her argument. She wouldn't have made her move if she wasn't confident Beltran would agree with her.

Cho stared Early down before making a sweeping motion with his hand to Vining.

She bolted from the chair and followed Early and Kissick out the door.

THREE

The locals know the Colorado Street Bridge as Suicide Bridge. The elegant structure extends 1,468 feet in a slight S shape across the Arroyo Seco watershed, its curved structure resulting from the engineer's quandary over finding solid footing. The white concrete bridge's enormous double arches joined by columns create a delicate weblike effect that belies its notorious history. A hundred or so people had jumped from it since construction in 1913. Neither the police nor the fire department knew the exact count. The police were still called out to coax down would-be jumpers who managed to climb over the eight-foot iron protective fence that tops the bridge.

Vining had answered one such call early in her career. She was still a rookie on probation but had been cut loose to drive an L-car, meaning she was in a patrol car solo. She'd found a young woman, Tiffany Pearson, who had climbed outside the barrier and was pacing back and forth on the outside ledge. When Tiffany saw Vining roll up, she grabbed the bars behind her with both hands, her back bowed and her chest punched out, defiantly taking on the city.

Vining tried to calm her down and keep her talking.

"My old man ran off with some chick," Tiffany explained. "Left me with three babies and no money. What am I supposed to do?"

"I hear you, Tiffany. My husband did the same thing to me. Left me and my two-year-old daughter. Left me with no job and nothing but bills. But I got over it. It'll get better."

Tiffany just looked out and shook her head. Moonlight shone on the tears that moistened her face.

"Think about your kids, Tiffany. They need you."

Vining thought she was doing well, had made a connection with the woman and gained her trust. She still anxiously counted the minutes until the suicide prevention expert arrived. She was about to learn why the bars could only *discourage* jumpers. Seconds after saying she was fine, Tiffany let go, falling 150 feet to the dry ravine.

Whenever Vining was on the bridge, she imagined the ghost of Tiffany Pearson holding on to those bars, her body arched like a bow, her eyes not looking down, but straight out. Vining concluded that she had already jumped, she just hadn't let go.

All cops collect war stories. The more years, the more stories. Pasadena's twenty-three square miles were the repository for dozens of Vining's stories, from the ridiculous to the touching to the horrible, including her own bloody tragedy. As Early drove the Crown Victoria onto the bridge, Vining saw another story in the making in the twisted white figure that looked like a cast-off doll partway down the hillside. The PPD's small Forensic Services Unit was taking photographs and searching for evidence.

Vining was glad to see that Sergeant Terrence Folke was the officer on scene. He was African American, with an easy smile that masked how tough he could be. A seasoned veteran, he had taken the precaution of unrolling yellow crime scene tape around a large area of the wash.

The stretch of the Arroyo Seco that extended through Pasadena remained close to its natural state. Thick with trees, chaparral, and native plants and wildlife, it was a popular recreational spot where people jogged, walked dogs, and rode horses. Hiking trails crisscrossed the area.

Vining recognized Tara Khorsandi from FSU. Young and new with the PPD, she was intense and methodical about her job. She flapped open a white sheet and covered the body.

You've turned the corner of your life to find this woman, Vining told herself.

The bridge was crowded with people from the production company, police officers, reporters, and Lookie-Lous. Black-and-white PPD patrol cars were parked beside catering trucks and long trailers with "Star Waggons" painted on the outside. One van bore the insignia of the L.A. County coroner. On flatbed trailers were the stars of the commercials, new hybrid vehicles manufactured by Honda.

A young man who appeared to be from the production company was engaged in a heated discussion with Kissick, Ruiz, and Folke.

A PPD helicopter unit and three news helicopters circled the area. More patrol units rolled on scene. Officers were busy trying to maintain the integrity of the crime scene and keep the waves of reporters at bay.

Early parked the Crown Victoria as close as she could get to the action. She and Vining got out.

"I'll shut down production, but someone's going to pay for it." The young man was wearing an Oakland A's baseball cap backwards and a black T-shirt printed with the word "Feminist."

Kissick handed Early the guy's card. Vining glanced over her shoulder at it.

He was the location manager and he was heated when he told Kissick, "Your crime scene is down there, not up here. No one threw her off the bridge. She'd be closer. She'd be right beside it. Obviously she was rolled down the hill."

Kissick slid a glance at Vining and Early before asking the guy, "So you're the crime scene expert?"

"I worked a couple of *CSI* shows."

Folke and Ruiz laughed out loud. Kissick smirked and stared off at the commuters on the 210, known as the Foothill Freeway. Drivers traversing what locals called the new bridge slowed to look at the action on the old bridge that reached within fifty feet before the freeway veered off.

Kissick's pause was for effect. He wanted to make the guy wait for him to speak.

"Pal, we've got a show right here. It's called dead white female in the arroyo who's somebody's child, somebody's sister or mother or wife who deserves our respect and uninterrupted attention that's not diminished by you bozos up here making a frigging car commercial."

"I'm calling the mayor's office."

"Call Arnold Schwarzenegger while you're at it. You have ten minutes to clear these people out of my crime scene or I'm going to start making arrests for interfering with the duties of a police officer, and you'll be the first."

The A's fan marched off, barking to a younger man nearby, "Call the Pasadena film office and the mayor."

Kissick shook his head as he scribbled in his field notebook. "I worked on *CSI*, he says. Unbelievable."

Folke called over uniformed officers who were nearby. "Make sure these TV commercial people get their asses out of here ASAP. We've got the bridge shut down east of the crime scene. Shut it down on the west up to San Rafael."

He turned back to the detectives. "I probably cast a bigger net than we need, but better to be safe than sorry."

"Absolutely," Early said. "What do we have?"

"Female Caucasian. Twenty-five to thirty years old. Bruised up pretty bad. Throat slit. Coroner's tech estimates TOD between ten o'clock and midnight."

Folke took in a breath as if preparing himself.

"Whassup, T?" Kissick asked.

Folke looked around to make sure no one was within earshot. He took a step closer and they instinctively closed the circle. When he spoke, it was nearly a whisper.

"I didn't broadcast this over the radio because I didn't want it to leak out, but I think she might be Frank Lynde's daughter."

"Holy shit," Ruiz said.

Frank Lynde was a twenty-five-year PPD veteran. He'd spent most of his career riding a motorcycle and had recently resumed pushing a patrol car. He was a solid cop with no career aspirations beyond doing his job each day and retiring after thirty years.

Frances, nicknamed Frankie, was his only child. She had been missing for over two weeks and LAPD had been handling the case. Frankie had last been seen off-duty in uniform at a strip club near LAX. She'd left with a woman who was dressed in a suit and wearing a chauffeur's cap. Witnesses saw them laughing as they ran to a black Lincoln Town Car limo parked in a far corner of the club's lot. No one took note of the license plate.

During the ordeal, Frank had kept a stiff upper lip, but friends said he was getting more worn down with each passing day. The missing person flyer that LAPD had distributed was posted on a bulletin board in the PPD's report-writing room. Someone had tacked to it a yellow ribbon tied in a bow.

Early broke the group's stunned silence. "Folke, you did good to keep it under wraps. Last thing we want is Lynde coming down here and seeing his daughter laid out like that. Do the Field I.D. Techs know to keep it on the Q.T.?"

"I told them."

"Is Lynde on today?" Kissick asked.

"He just got off Morning Watch," Folke said. "Hopefully he's asleep."

Ruiz looked up at the news helicopters churning the sky. "My money's on somebody calling him after seeing this on T.V."

"Don't you socialize with Frank?" Kissick asked Ruiz.

"Yeah. He's in our monthly poker game."

"Folke, tell your team that if anyone comes around who's not supposed to be here, even if they're one of us, to let you know and not to let them in," Early said. "Poor bastard's going to find out sooner than later, but we can try to do it with dignity."

Folke took his cell phone from a pocket in his equipment belt, avoiding broadcasting through dispatch and risking the information being picked up by someone with a police scanner. He pressed a speed-dial number.

They walked to the end of the bridge. The scene there was frenzied as people and vehicles made their departure, clashing with uniformed officers who were attempting to control and expedite the process.

In the midst of the chaos, a pall had fallen over the group of detectives.

Vining decided to remain in the background. She wasn't sure she was even part of the team. If she was, she'd been demoted to junior member. Best to be seen and not heard, even though she knew a lot about the disappearance of Frankie Lynde, much more than any of the detectives there.

"Adult women missing for over two weeks don't usually show up alive," Kissick said. "Everyone knows that. But this . . ."

"Wonder if it was a vengeance move against Frank Lynde," Folke said.

"LAPD detective by the name of Schuyler is handling the M.P. case." Ruiz mopped perspiration from his forehead with a handkerchief. It was just after nine o'clock on an early June morning, but it was already hot. "Frank told me that he and Schuyler went through the arrests he's made over the past ten years, all the guys he's sent to jail, looking for someone with a motive. No one jumped out. Nothing that made any sense."

"She have a boyfriend?" Early asked.

"Frank said she never talked to him about her social life," Ruiz said. "Frankie had a reputation for partying a little too much. Pressing the envelope. Her best friend said she'd dated an LAPD lieutenant for a while. Schuyler told Frank he'd tracked down a dozen guys that Frankie'd been involved with to a greater or lesser degree. Said Frank flipped out. Said he didn't know anything and didn't want to know anything about that."

Kissick took off his jacket and tossed it over his shoulder. "Any of these guys suspects?"

"We'll find out."

Folke was walking ahead of them. "Why dump her body in Pasadena? If Frank's not the connection, what is?"

"Random?" Ruiz suggested.

"Vining, what do you think?"

Kissick was walking in front of her. She was thinking how nice his shoulders looked in his light blue dress shirt, a good color for him, when he drew her into the conversation.

"I doubt it's random."

She sensed Ruiz bristling when she challenged his view. "The bridge is a Pasadena icon. What better way to taint it? If we can figure out why Pasadena, we'll find him."

"Taint the Pasadena icon." Ruiz shot a glance at her over his shoulder. "Right. The asshole probably lives in Eagle Rock and drives across to go to work in Pasadena. Middle of the night, there's no traffic here. You can see headlights in the distance, to give you warning. Houses on the ridge are too far away. Can't see that spot from the freeway. Not a bad place to dump a body. Still, Angeles Crest would have been more remote. Roll the body into a canyon from up there, chances are it would never be found."

"Doesn't that prove Vining's point, Ruiz?" Sergeant Early said. "That scenario you outlined is not random."

Vining was pulling up the rear, so no one caught her small smile. Early's stock with her had always been favorable. Today it skyrocketed. It would be a Pyrrhic victory as Ruiz would certainly make Vining pay.

"I'm thinking out loud," Ruiz protested. "So, yes. Why the body was dumped here probably does not follow the precise definition of random. But I wouldn't go so far as to say he's making a statement, 'Screw Pasadena.' You know what I'm saying? All due respect."

"Point well taken," Early said.

"Pasadena icon. That's going out on a limb, in my view."

Ruiz, give it a rest, Vining thought.

"We've already agreed, best to cast a wide net." Early seemed determined to have the last word. "Whatever reason he dumped the body in Pasadena, one thing's for double damn sure. If she is Frank Lynde's daughter, even if she was last seen in L.A. and she was LAPD, this is our homicide investigation."

FOUR

They reached the western edge of the bridge and stood beside the steel railing off the end that inhibited wayward cars from plunging over.

The view was a favorite of local artists. To the south, a near-wild expanse of trees and brush stretched into the distance. To the north were Brookside Park and the Rose Bowl. Along the canyon's base, a few inches of water still flowed through the cement channel that constrained the Arroyo Seco watershed. A stately Moorish building that

had been the Vista del Arroyo Hotel in the 1920s dominated the canyon's eastern ridge. The former hotel was
now home to the U.S. Court of Appeals for the Ninth
Circuit. It had served as a military hospital during World
War II. The big homes flanking it were now used as offices. New town homes were under construction nearby.

Kissick expressed what Vining was thinking. "The opposite ridge is over a quarter of a mile away. It's unlikely
anyone was around in the middle of the night."

Vining turned to look in the other direction at the
mansions on the western side that overlooked the arroyo, tucked among dense trees and chaparral. Gated,
gigantic places along San Rafael Avenue meandered
along the ridge line. The closest was several hundred
yards from the bridge.

She said, "Those homes are too far away for anyone to
have seen anything without binoculars."

Still standing were the burnt-out, skeletal ruins of the
brick gothic-style mansion that had been used as Wayne
Manor in a Batman movie. It had been undergoing extensive renovations that were nearly complete when it
burned to the ground in a spectacular blaze battled by
firefighters from Pasadena and four neighboring cities.

A spark of light glimmered from a large Mediter-
ranean manse near it. Vining asked Kissick for his binoculars. The flash of light must have been a reflection of the
morning sun off the windows. The mansions were most
likely bustling with the activities of their rich owners and
their overscheduled children, not to mention the extensive household staffs required to keep them going. She
wondered why the grand homes always seemed empty.
She imagined what it would be like to walk through one,

opulent, cavernous, and still. She felt her lungs compress as if a hobgoblin had sucked the air from her.

She quickly returned the binoculars.

"Not hopeful that knocking on doors will turn up much," Early said.

A few yards past the end of the bridge was the spot where the body had been rolled downhill. Beyond the railing was a flat area of patchy wild wheat and grass, dried golden, and sun-hardened dirt before the ridge dropped steeply. The body was not visible from where they were standing in the street.

Field I.D. tech Tara Khorsandi was looking over the ground with a crime scene tech from the county. The PPD had a small forensics department that gathered and processed evidence, took photographs, and analyzed fingerprints. Anything beyond that was handled by the county crime lab.

"What's doin', Tara?" Folke asked.

Bent over with her hands on her thighs, she shook her head without looking up. "The ground is like cement. A car was driven up here, over the curb between that break in the railing. The weeds are packed down, but no tire marks." She straightened, rubbing her lower back and pointing. "Not finding much. A few blood drops here. Likely the victim's. We're about to go down and see what we can get off the body."

"Okay if we have a look?" Early asked.

"Sure." The tech placed a plastic marker imprinted with a number near the blood.

Ruiz drew their attention to a tall, halogen streetlamp several feet away on the other side of the street. "That should have concerned him."

Almost at once, the group looked back at the bridge. It

was lined with original lampposts with large, frosted-glass globes. The lampposts had been restored as part of the bridge's renovation and seismic retrofitting in the 1990s. It was closed for years after being severely damaged in the 1987 Whittier Narrows quake.

"Those lights on the bridge aren't bright at night," Early said. "Still, between them and the streetlight here, he didn't pick a dark spot to do his business."

She stepped over the railing, picked her way to the edge, and looked over. The sheet-draped body was about fifty feet down on the hillside.

"That's steep."

Vining came up beside her and had a look.

The songs of birds in the trees were barely audible above the roar of the freeway and helicopters. Bees buzzed around the last of the wild mustard blooms. The air was filled with the pungent, almost dusty aroma of eucalyptus trees. A thatch of wild grass sent up long, fuzzy, lavender-hued spears.

The body had made a trail in the dried brush as it rolled down.

"We don't all need to go down there," Early said. "Mess up the scene."

"I had that hip replaced," Ruiz said.

"I'll go," Vining said.

Kissick looked at her. "No. I'll go. I can head off at an angle and hang on to those bushes if I have to."

"I'm going, too." Vining took off her jacket and handed it to Folke.

"You don't need to," Kissick told her.

"Go ahead." She waved him on.

He headed over the edge and she followed. His stiff-soled shoes lost traction on the loose dirt and pebbles and he slipped, shouting "Whoa!" He skidded to a stop on the slope, pitching himself backward and grabbing a handful of slick, dried wild wheat that pulled free, dangling a dirt clod. He slid another foot before again stopping.

Vining nearly collided with him, falling onto her butt and scraping her palms.

Kissick recoiled when he caught sight of a snake lying on the ground in a loose pile. It was gold with brown stripes and nearly as big around as a fire hose.

It wasn't moving.

"I hate snakes," he said.

Vining tossed a stone and hit it. "Dead."

"You think?"

"All the noise we made coming down, it would have slithered into the brush."

"You had to use that word. Slither."

"Carry on, Daniel Boone."

Detouring away from the snake, Kissick crossed and switched back until he reached the body. He squatted beside it and waited for Vining before grabbing the sheet. He raised it.

The dead woman was tall and well-built. She was on her side, her face turned toward the bridge. Her head was lower than her feet, her legs splayed, her right arm tossed over her head. Locks of long, blond, blood-matted hair were twisted around her neck. Bruises mottled her face and torso. Her tumble down the hill had pulled open the deep knife wound to her throat. Weeds and dirt adhered to the dried blood and her hair. A crumpled In-N-Out Burger drink cup lay near her head.

While her body told a different story, her face seemed peaceful. Maybe at the end, she was glad it was over.

"Prick bastard." Kissick dropped the sheet. He partially stood, grabbing on to the branches of a nearby tree. "Head's almost cut off and he beat the crap out of her."

"Is it Lynde's daughter?" Ruiz asked.

The others peered down over the edge at them.

Kissick shook his head, his mouth drawn open in anguish. "Might be Frankie. Can't tell for sure." He rubbed his free hand over his face, mixing dirt with perspiration. "She's a mess."

Vining crept closer and picked up the sheet. She leaned in.

The dead woman's parted lips were blue-gray. Her eyes were clouded.

Her eyes sparked with life.

Vining started, nearly losing her balance on the hill. She blinked hard, not believing what she had seen.

The eyes shifted to her.

Vining began to feel that familiar and unwelcome tightness in her chest. The hobgoblin.

Oh no. Not here. Please. Not now.

Kissick and the others were talking across the expanse.

Vining drew in a wheezing breath.

The woman's chapped lips moved. She whispered, "I am you."

Vining dropped to her knees, clutching a thatch of weeds to keep from sliding. She struggled to breathe. She felt like ice, yet she was perspiring. She still held the sheet, unable to tear her eyes from the corpse.

The dead woman then whispered, "I am not you."

"Nan, you okay?" Early shouted down to her.

Adam, boy, Charles, David, Edward . . .

Vining murmured the phonetic alphabet, the device she'd adopted to focus on something else.

" 'M okay."

Still holding on to the weeds, she sat hard on the

ground, dropping the sheet and covering the battered face.

Frank, George, Henry, Ida, Ida . . . Come on . . . John, King, Lincoln, Mary . . .

She put her head between her knees, cupped a hand over her nose and mouth, and breathed through it, hoping her legs shielded what she was doing.

Kissick squatted beside her.

Nora, ocean, Paul . . . "Didn't have breakfast." She squeezed out the words and tried to smile. "I'm okay."

She could tell by Kissick's face that she looked like hell. She'd seen herself in a mirror after a panic attack. Her skin color was probably slightly warmer than that of the corpse on the ground.

"I'm okay," she insisted. "Tell them. Jim, tell them I'm okay."

Kissick touched her shoulder and yelled up to the ridge. "She's all right. Just a little low blood sugar."

Vining appreciated him going along with her lie. He'd worked with her enough to know she never skipped meals.

She again got to her knees, picked up the sheet, and leaned over the dead woman to make a point that the body hadn't gotten to her. The spell had lasted only a minute. The damage might be permanent. She forced herself to take a good look. She saw the face of a dead woman, the life gone from her eyes. Her lips were not about to whisper to Vining or anyone.

You were hallucinating.

The roar of a motorcycle engine cut through the din of helicopters and freeway traffic. Right on its heels was a patrol car with lights and siren. The motorcycle fell silent, the noise replaced by yelling.

Kissick and Vining looked at each other then at the top

of the hill. Everyone had moved away and they couldn't see what was going on. He started back up and held out his hand for her. She took it and scampered after him.

The crowd shuffled back to the edge. In the middle was Frank Lynde. He was a giant man, tall and heavyset, and it took all of them to keep him from heading down the slope.

"Is it her?" he wailed. "Is it Frankie?"

Kissick stepped back onto the flat area and reached to help Vining up.

Restrained by three men, Lynde still managed to take a step forward as Kissick approached.

"Is it her?" Lynde's normally ruddy complexion was bright pink, his cheeks streaked with tears. "Jim, is it her?"

Kissick put his hand on Lynde's shoulder. "Frank, I can't be sure."

Vining came up beside him. She said nothing, but couldn't avoid Lynde's eyes. The daughter was there, in the father.

Perhaps he was overcome by emotion or saw the truth in Vining's face. Lynde's knees buckled and he dropped to the ground.

FIVE

Vining knew the corpse was Frankie Lynde. She had been obsessed with the case since the police officer had gone missing, intrigued by the similarities with her own assault. A tall and fit female police officer was lured to a place where she was abducted. Lynde was twenty-eight. Vining was thirty-four. Now Vining learned they had both suffered knife wounds. But Vining was ambushed while on duty. Lynde had gone willingly into a situation that had called for elaborate preparation on her part and had reeked of danger.

Vining persisted in seeing more similarities than differences. T. B. Mann could have adapted his tactics to fit Lynde's circumstances. He could have studied her, learned her vulnerabilities, used them against her, and dumped her in the city where Vining worked close to the year anniversary of his attack on her.

Kissick, Ruiz, and Early took note of the parallels with Vining's attempted murder but saw them as curiosity rather than design. They didn't know the motive for the attack on her, but weren't convinced they should go the serial killer route. Vining didn't argue with them. Neither did she let on how much she knew about Frankie Lynde.

She had spent the last days of her leave investigating the case. She had her PPD shield and I.D. card, but tried to avoid using them as it could backfire on her. She went to XXX Marks the Spot and lied to the manager, telling him she was a friend of Frankie's. It would not be the first lie she'd tell in her quest to get closer to Lynde. Seeing the club in person told her volumes. It was no place for a woman to go alone, unless she was looking to be picked up. And Lynde had been picked up, by a woman after a silly bit of role-playing. Lynde wouldn't have been the first officer who answered the call of the dark side.

Vining called Steve Schuyler, the LAPD detective in charge of Lynde's missing person case. She again claimed to be a friend of Frankie's. He wouldn't give her information over the phone and told her to come in. She decided that would be really stepping over the line. She dropped it. Without proving her bona fides to Schuyler, she was just another wacko off the street. Besides, she was returning to duty shortly and could more legitimately follow up then.

She went around him and called a female LAPD sergeant she knew slightly. The sergeant didn't know Lynde personally but filled in the blanks of the media reports and gave her Lynde's home address. She said that Lynde had been good at her job in vice prostitution. Maybe too good.

Vining went to Frankie's home in Studio City on the southeastern edge of the San Fernando Valley. It was an older apartment building that had been converted to condominiums. A sign on the façade said "The Royal Palms" in wooden script. Two stories of stucco surrounded a courtyard with a swimming pool. Chaise longues were lined up like coffins on a battlefield. The earth-toned paint and palm trees were designed to make the place look upscale and resortlike, an effect that was undone by the 101 freeway that ran behind the complex.

Someone had left a stone propping open the locked front gate. Vining entered and walked upstairs where she found an elderly woman locking the door to Lynde's unit. Vining badged her.

"The police were here already." Her voice wavered but her gaze was clear and direct. The top of her stiff coiffure barely reached the middle of Vining's chest.

"I'm Detective Nan Vining and I'm investigating for the city of Pasadena. We've had leads on the case. We're assisting LAPD."

Vining knew she'd be toast if the woman checked out her story.

The woman introduced herself as Mrs. Bodek and said she was Lynde's neighbor across the walkway. She took care of Lynde's place, bringing in mail and newspapers, whenever Lynde was gone. She volunteered that this had happened a lot before Lynde disappeared.

"Could you let me inside?"

She felt a pang of guilt. Elderly people tended to trust others, especially authority figures, a trait that made Mrs. Bodek's generation a frequent victim of scams. Vining was taking advantage of that trust. Her guilt faded quickly. She had to see. She had to learn more about Frankie Lynde.

She learned the old lady was nobody's fool.

Mrs. Bodek narrowed her eyes at Vining. "Do you have another I.D.? I don't mean to be rude, but how do I know that badge isn't fake?"

Vining dug inside her handbag for her police I.D. card. Mrs. Bodek scrutinized it to her satisfaction, returned it, and unlocked the door.

Vining feared a panic attack upon entering Lynde's condo, but none came. Maybe she was cured or maybe the place felt like home.

"Did Officer Lynde have a boyfriend?" She was counting on Mrs. Bodek being the type who peeked out of her drapes at her neighbors' comings and goings.

"There was one who came around sometimes. Tall, dark man. Short hair. Like a crew cut. Kind of bad skin. Old acne scars. That policeman who's looking into Frankie's disappearance came one day with a picture."

"Detective Schuyler?"

"That sounds right. I looked at the picture and said, yeah, I think that's the one."

"Did he tell you who the man in the photograph was?"

"No. Wouldn't tell me anything. When Frankie's gentleman friend came by, I didn't get the idea it was a date, if you get my drift. He'd stay for a couple of hours during the day and then leave. If I was a betting woman, I'd bet he was married."

Mrs. Bodek squared her jaw. "I hate to talk about Frankie like this, but seeing as we don't know what happened to her, there's no point in keeping it to myself. If you ask me, she could have done a whole lot better."

I know the feeling, Vining thought.

"Lately, Frankie was gone overnight a lot. A couple days at a time, sometimes. Could have been working. Hard to tell because her schedule changed a lot. She wasn't one to talk much about her personal life. I like that in a person, especially a woman. Not a quality you see much anymore."

The condo was pleasantly but not lovingly decorated, with framed art prints on the walls and comfortable, mid-level furniture. Vining surmised her house would look the same if she didn't have Emily.

Vining guessed it was all about the job for Lynde. Male cops had wives and girlfriends to feather their nests and make a home. If they didn't, it was all about partying, and no one expected more than a grimy bachelor pad. If a female cop's job consumed her, the absence of an outside life was more obvious than it was for a man.

Thank goodness for Emily, her anchor.

Vining walked slowly through the small place. Whatever had happened to Lynde had not happened there. She hadn't brought it home with her. She hadn't opened her front door to it. The space felt empty but expectant. A life hovering on a knife edge. Running her hand over the officer's bed pillows, Vining sensed the unsettledness in Lynde's heart. There was trouble here. The opportunity for trouble. A crack in the armor.

Vining knew her perceptions were useless. There was nothing in them that could help anyone find Lynde.

She walked to a dresser and examined the bottles of fragrance on a glass round. Expensive brands. She couldn't recall the last time she'd spritzed on cologne. She still had the bottle of Chanel No. 5 that her ex-husband, Wes, had given her one Valentine's Day years ago.

She asked Mrs. Bodek, "Can you think of any reason she'd run away? Was she happy?"

"Happy? Who's happy? But we don't run away."

Vining looked at framed photographs on the dresser. She recognized Frank Lynde in his wedding photo and was surprised by how much hair he had. Frankie looked like her mother. All the others were current photos of Frankie with friends. Judging by the tabletop real estate devoted to family, Frankie didn't seem close to them.

A grammar school photo of Frankie was stuck into the mirror frame. It was a goofy, bucktoothed, preadolescent photo. A whimsical outline of the beauty that Frankie would become. Vining wondered why that photograph was significant to Frankie. Maybe she came upon it while looking through old papers and spontaneously planted it on the mirror. That explanation didn't satisfy Vining. People may not consciously be aware of the multitude of decisions they make each day, but they're often not the result of happenstance.

She made notes in a memo pad and took shots with

her digital camera—a birthday gift from her mother and grandmother, purchased with Emily's help.

She thanked Mrs. Bodek and was about to leave when the old woman touched her arm.

"Almost forgot. Week before last, I'd been out grocery shopping and came up the steps when I see this gal leaving Frankie's place. I think, what's this? I came right up to her and said, 'Hi. Can I help you?' She became very flustered. She was carrying this big handbag that was almost a suitcase. She drops it and I don't know what all. I can tell it's heavy. She says she's a friend of Frankie's from out of town and Frankie said she could stay with her for a few days.

"So I said, 'Oh?' Frankie wasn't missing yet. I'd just seen her the day before. Her paper was there that morning, but when she works late, she sometimes doesn't take it in until the evening. I figure I'll call Frankie's cell phone after this gal leaves. Her face was red and she was sniffing, like she'd been crying. So I ask her if she's all right. She says she's fine and the tears roll out from beneath these big sunglasses she has on. I ask her if she wants something to drink and she says no. She's having a hard time trying to turn the bolt lock and I notice she has Frankie's set of keys. Frankie had this key ring shaped like a tiny pistol. The little thing for the bullets rolled around and everything. Said her dad gave it to her. He's a police officer, too, you know."

"What did this woman look like?"

"I told Detective Schuyler about it and he showed me the drawing of the woman Frankie was seen with at that club by the airport. This could have been the same woman. Instead of the heart-shaped sunglasses, she had on these big square ones that covered half her face and she had black hair that went past her shoulders. Looked like a wig. I didn't pay that much attention to what she was wearing, you know how they dress these days, but when I thought about it later, it seems to me that she had on gloves. Leather gloves." Mrs. Bodek tilted her chin to make sure Vining got the significance.

"Then what?"

"She went down the stairs, muttering to herself, and out through the front gate. I called Frankie's cell phone and left her a message about it. A couple of days later, the police show up, telling me Frankie's gone missing."

"Thank you, Mrs. Bodek. You've been very helpful." Vining started heading down the stairs. She turned back. "Did you hear what the woman was muttering?"

Mrs. Bodek raised both hands. "Nonsense. Gibberish. Who can understand how they talk these days. She said, 'This is vujaday. This is seriously vujaday.' " She shrugged.

Vining shrugged as well.

SIX

R uiz drove Frank Lynde home.

Kissick coordinated patrol officers into teams for knock-and-talks around the neighborhood and interviews with the film production crew.

Vining thought she'd also be knocking on doors, one

more pair of feet on the street, but Early told her to get into the car, an indication that Early wanted to chat. Vining wasn't surprised.

They stopped at Goldstein's Bagels before returning to the station, going to the La Cañada Flintridge store since the Old Pasadena location had been forced to close.

"Raised their rent too high," Early said. "Had to make room for more high-end retailers. The city planners call it gentrification. I call it a shame that they're eroding the character of the city for the glory of people who max out their credit cards."

"Right."

"Best we grab something to eat while we can. Going to be a long day and night. Plus you're running on empty anyway." Early's small glance revealed to Vining what the sergeant had not said.

Cops notice everything. Even when they aren't looking, they're looking. Being watchful was second nature to a cop. That included watching one another, especially in a department the size of Pasadena's, where everyone knew everyone else, at least by sight. An officer who was having problems, showing signs of distress, would not go unnoticed for long. Everyone had a bad day. Most cops eventually burned out, either becoming apathetic, letting everything go, or becoming aggressive, refusing to take the smallest amount of crap. That was predictable, expected, and acceptable within a range. But for a cop who was going over the deep end big-time, who had gone from a known quantity to the X factor, the stakes were too high to do nothing.

Vining was holding to her story about feeling wobbly that morning because she hadn't eaten enough. She claimed she hadn't yet settled into her old routine. The story was flimsy. She knew it and Kissick knew it. Didn't matter. She was sticking to it and she knew he'd back her up for now. What could they do, call her a liar? Being a cop was all about putting up barriers—between the Job and home life, between one's emotions and the ugliness of what the Job brings day in and day out. There was no need for her to reveal the panic attacks to anyone in the department. There was no need for anyone, including her daughter, to know how much the attacks frightened her.

They made her feel damaged. Damaged beyond her control.

The panic attack today had taken her by surprise. She thought she had corralled her fear of being inside strange homes. Put it in a box. Tied it with a ribbon. Here it is, my phobia. And now I'm setting it on a shelf where it can't affect me. Today was the first time she'd seen a homicide victim since her assault. Had this phobia been hiding beneath her other, more obvious one? Would seeing any corpse provoke a panic attack or had the source of this one been more specific? A tortured and slaughtered female cop streaked with dried blood.

She couldn't shake the image of Frankie's dead eyes flashing to life and her chapped lips speaking to her. To her.

"I am you. I am not you."

Her rational mind insisted that the incident on the hillside had been pure hallucination. Fantasy. Imagination. Nothing more.

On the drive back to the station, Vining pursued something that Early had said.

"You said we're going to have a long day and night.

Thought I was Residential Burglary under Sergeant Cho."

"This is going to be a big investigation with all eyes on us. Not just L.A.; this will be news in Timbuktu, the way things go these days. It's more than Kissick and Ruiz can handle by themselves. You're the logical choice to be on the team and we'll need more than just you. I want to break this thing and fast, for our sake. For Frank Lynde's sake."

"Kissick wasn't sure she was Frank's daughter."

"That's Kissick's style. He was sure. He was just waiting. *You* were sure."

The searing look she gave Vining was a test to see if her opinion about the dead woman's identity was solid.

"It's Frankie Lynde," Vining said.

"The coroner will have a positive I.D. any time now. Detective Schuyler should have done a lot of our homework for us. Kissick's calling him to arrange a meeting."

"Now we have the body. Let's hope she gives up her secrets."

While Early waited for the gate to roll back at the Ramona Street garage entrance, several reporters who knew enough about the station to go there instead of the front entrance rushed the car. Early accelerated past them.

"So it starts."

Sitting at her new desk in the section of the cubicle Warren allocated to property crimes, Vining wrapped the remaining half of the bagel, cream cheese, turkey, and sprouts sandwich in wax paper and shoved it to the corner. She'd ordered something healthy-sounding only because Sergeant Early was with her. The bundle in wax paper was the sole item on her desk. The drawers held only pens and pads of paper. She'd neglected to bring a mug or any personal items. After she was injured, Kissick had boxed up the handful of things in her cubicle—drawings and crafts done by Emily and family photos—and delivered them to her house. For safekeeping, he'd said. After she'd pressed, he confessed that Ruiz had moved into her cubicle. The box was still unopened in a corner of her family room where he'd set it that day. She'd bring it back tomorrow.

Something made her look up. She saw Officer Alex Caspers peering at her over the top of the adjoining cubicle.

"Pretty fucked up, huh?"

"What's that?"

"Finding Frank Lynde's daughter nude and cut up."

"Where d'ya hear that?"

"Come on . . ." He made a sucking noise with his teeth. "Shame. She was real good lookin'. Tall, like you."

He was giving her the hungry-eye look like he'd done earlier that morning. She would like nothing better than for him to vacate the area and the planet, but she was intrigued.

"Did you know her?"

"Met her at the last service awards luncheon or whatever they call it. Frank got an award for twenty-five years on the force. He introduced Frankie to me. Real standup guy, Frank. I called Frankie at her precinct, but she and I couldn't find a time to connect."

I wonder why.

"I hear she was pretty wild."

Vining gave the woman credit for some discretion in her men. "We don't know for sure it's her. Whoever it is, that's a hell of a way to talk about the dead. A little respect?"

"How is that being disrespectful? She knew she was a piece of ass and liked hearing it."

Vining shook her head and stood. On her way to get coffee, Caspers answered his phone.

"Hey, peckerhead. You coming to the party tonight?"

She went to the coffee station on a table at the rear of the suite and pulled a Styrofoam cup from the stack. There was tension in the air. The calm before the storm. The investigation was in the works, but Vining was not privy to details. She was hanging around, waiting to be given something to do, as if it truly was her first day on the job. Kissick had returned and was busy on the phone. She knew he was waiting for Detective Schuyler to come up from Hollywood LAPD with materials from his missing person investigation. Ruiz was still with Frank Lynde off-site, waiting out the time until they had an official I.D. on the body.

She knew Lynde already suspected the worst. Adult women don't disappear of their own volition.

"But we don't run away."

The notification would be a strange relief for Lynde. It would end his time in purgatory.

Vining thought of the calls made to her family after she had been attacked, that ringing phone dreaded by loved ones of police officers. Kissick had made them, calling Vining's mother and her ex-husband, Wes.

"Nan's been hurt on the job. She's alive but her condition is serious."

It was a white lie. Her condition had been critical.

Emily claimed to know the moment of Vining's attack.

She was reading by the pool at her father's house when she felt coldness in her extremities and couldn't breathe.

After Vining had been resuscitated, she'd lain in a coma for three days.

Vining believed she wasn't T. B. Mann's first victim. The belief had no basis in fact, but she couldn't shake that deep-in-her-bones instinct. He had seemed so assured, intentionally coming close to getting caught. They had found a police radio scanner in the house on El Alisal Road. He had tracked her movements and the status of her backup. There had been a realtor's open house in that location the weekend before Vining was attacked. Kissick, who had handled the investigation, speculated that Vining's assailant entered the house then and unlocked a window through which he later returned. Vining had worked patrol in that neighborhood on Sundays for several weeks, picking up overtime. T. B. Mann couldn't be positive that Vining would be the officer to respond to his call, but it was likely to be her. It was Vining's theory that he had patiently stalked her, maybe for months, working out the timing, location, and circumstances until all the elements converged in that one brilliant and catastrophic moment.

Had he pressed the envelope further with Lynde?

She couldn't jump to conclusions. That sort of thinking made for a shoddy investigation. She had to keep her mind open. Otherwise, Kissick and Early would spot it and she would be working on residential burglaries.

During her long months of recuperation, Vining had researched female law enforcement officers in the United States who had been killed on duty. There had been twenty-six over the past ten years. Most deaths had occurred in major metropolitan areas. Made sense. Big-city police forces tended to have female officers.

A guy on parole for murder shot one, a New York City cop, with her own gun while she was at the scene of a domestic violence incident. Another was shot during a bank robbery in Washington, D.C. One was stabbed in a drug sting gone bad outside Austin, Texas. Two were killed responding to calls regarding suspicious circumstances. Four were killed while arresting a suspect. Three were killed during routine traffic stops. Two were murdered when their home problems followed them to work, one in Atlanta by a husband and one outside San Diego by a boyfriend. Vining couldn't see how women who could kick butt in their work lives had let that happen. Love. Killed because of love.

Eleven died in vehicular accidents, the number one killer of police officers.

Then there was Johnna Alwin of the Tucson Police Department. The memorial page on the TPD Web site said she had been ambushed and murdered and little else. Vining called the TPD and asked to speak to the lead investigator. She was put through to Lieutenant Owen Donahue. She told a half-truth, saying she was investigating an ambush of a Pasadena, California, police officer who was brutally attacked but survived. She was searching for similar crimes, trying to determine if the assault was isolated or if they were looking at a serial killer.

Donahue was grudgingly accommodating. Alwin was a detective working undercover to bust a doctor, an internist, who was selling restricted prescription drugs out of his office. Three years ago on a Sunday afternoon in January, Alwin received a call from her informant, Jesse Cuba, a janitor in the doctor's building, saying he had information. It was Alwin's day off, but she called the watch commander and reported that Cuba wanted to meet her in the medical building where he worked. Cuba was a heroin addict on parole for possession. Alwin had met him on the fly and alone before and considered him harmless.

When Alwin didn't return, a patrol car was sent out. The officers found her in a storage closet in the basement. She'd been stabbed seventeen times.

Donahue told Vining that he wouldn't be much help to her because they'd solved Alwin's murder. Jesse Cuba was found dead of a heroin overdose in the seedy motel room he rented by the week. In his room, police found Alwin's purse and jewelry. The purse had Alwin's blood on it. Other suspects didn't pan out. Case closed. Donahue wished her well with her investigation.

Vining hung up. There was no reason for her to second-guess Tucson's investigation, but something about the case bothered her.

Two years later, Vining was stabbed responding to a suspicious circumstances call reported by a man who identified himself as a realtor watching over 835 El Alisal Road while the owner was away.

A year after that, Officer Frankie Lynde was murdered.

And Vining had a panic attack at the scene.

She stood by the coffeemaker, sipping the burnt brew that powdered creamer and sugar did nothing to improve. She saw Lieutenant George Beltran in Early's office. He glanced at her and she felt certain they were talking about her. Then Kissick joined them.

She downed the rest of the coffee, tossed the cup, and

was returning to her desk when Beltran caught up with her on his way out.

He shook her hand. "Hey, Nan. How are you? Good to have you back." Beltran had wavy dark hair and a thick mustache that were starting to show gray. He was medium height and naturally slender in a way that made him look taller than he was. He had a broad smile and an easy manner. He handled the media well and consequently served as the PPD's liaison. He enjoyed the spotlight.

"I'm good, Lieutenant. Nice to be back. Thanks."

It was a pleasant interchange but it put her on edge. Before she reached her desk, Kissick stuck his head out the door of Early's office and asked her to come in.

"Have a seat," Early said.

Kissick was leaning against the wall beside the windows.

Detective Sergeants Cho and Taylor weren't there. Vining pulled a chair from in front of Taylor's desk and sat.

"Coroner's office called," Early began. "It's Frankie Lynde. Preliminary cause of death was the slit throat. She bled out someplace else before he dumped her in the arroyo."

Vining took in the news and said nothing.

"Ruiz is on his way in," Kissick said. "He told Frank Lynde the news. They'd gone for a drink and Ruiz had just brought him home when I called."

As if on cue, Ruiz arrived. His jacket was off, his tie was loosened, and his shirtsleeves were rolled up. He plopped into a chair, set his elbows against his knees, and rubbed his face with both hands. After a second, he sat up and laced his palms over his bald head.

"That was tough. I never want to do that again."

"How'd he take it?" Kissick asked.

"How would you take it?" Ruiz gazed out the window at the bright glare reflecting off the haze. "I told him how you'll never lose the one you love if you love the one you've lost. The usual shtick. I had always believed that was true, each time I made a notification call to a grieving next of kin. I thought I was giving them comfort. Today I realized it's total bullshit. Empty words to fill the silence. There's nothing but silence left. A big, gaping hole where a life used to be."

Vining reflected that Ruiz was ever pompous. He had been working Homicide for barely a year and had worked just three cases on which Kissick had been the lead investigator. Still, his distress was real and touched her heart. She reached out and put her hand on his shoulder. He patted her fingertips and gave her a nod.

Early's phone rang. "I'll send someone down." She looked at Kissick. "Detective Schuyler from LAPD is here. A lieutenant from their homicide desk is here, too."

"You called Schuyler before you had a positive I.D.?" Ruiz's moment had passed and his hard edges returned.

"We had a high degree of confidence it was Frankie Lynde," Early said. "The clock's ticking, Ruiz."

"They sent a lieutenant from Homicide? They think the little-city cops need help from the big-city cops?" Kissick stood. "I'll get them."

Ruiz and Vining stood as well.

Early said, "Vining. Hold up a second. Shut the door. Sit down."

SEVEN

Vining sat in the chair she'd just vacated.

Early got right to the point. "This case may be too close to home for you."

"I disagree." She knew her comeback was too fast. Kissick must have told Early about her episode at the arroyo. Now Lieutenant Beltran knew, too. She wondered what Kissick had seen. At worst, he saw her struggling to breathe. He might have deduced anxiety, even panic. Okay. But she'd overcome it.

"Here's my dilemma." Early folded her hands on the desk. "I'm seeing you on the witness stand, undergoing cross-examination, and I'm seeing the million ways a defense attorney could discredit your testimony."

"Is this a preview of the rest of my career here, my colleagues treating me like damaged goods?"

"My number one concern is managing this case. A lot of attention will be focused on us. I have to look at the whole enchilada, from start to finish."

"Sarge, you know I'm one of the best you have. I'm a better interviewer, I work longer hours, and I'm more thorough than anyone else I've seen on the second floor other than Kissick. And I never complain."

"What about when the media finds out you're working the Lynde case? You're a minor celebrity. Your fifteen minutes haven't ended yet. They'll land on it like a bad smell. We're already going to have our hands full."

This is what it's come down to, Vining thought.

She flashed back to that June afternoon nearly a year ago.

She had been on patrol in uniform, working the Sunday overtime gig she'd been lucky enough to land for the past few weeks. It worked out especially well on the weekends that Emily was with her dad. Vining was the only officer patrolling Section One, the lowest crime area of the city. The service calls usually involved dogs barking too long, stereos that were too loud, or burglar alarms accidentally set off by the household help. The residents there had no clue about what real crime was except for the often-told tale of the home invasion robbery some years ago that had degenerated into rape and murder.

Vining had spent an hour parked in the shade of a camphor tree near a four-way stop, handing out moving violations to drivers doing the California roll through the intersection. She was sweating beneath the Kevlar vest and regulation white, crew neck T-shirt she was wearing under her short-sleeved summer uniform shirt.

At five o'clock, a suspicious circumstances call came in. A realtor was checking on a house for the absent owner and found a window open that he was certain he'd left closed. The house was three blocks from Vining. The call would be her last for the day. Her shift ended in half an hour and then she had a couple of days off.

Vining broadcast, "One Lincoln twenty-one. I can respond from Fillmore and Los Robles."

Residents in the city's affluent neighborhoods were often looking out windows and finding suspicious goings-on. She didn't fault them. But she'd responded to calls where the person who'd made them nervous was a caterer checking on a delivery for a backyard wedding or a couple of nonwhite, non-Asian kids sitting on a retaining wall, taking a break while walking from their public school to the bus stop.

The house at 835 El Alisal was a two-story colonial like many in the area, built early last century. It was an upscale, middle-American neighborhood where happy sitcom families lived. In the neighborhood was the house that Beaver Cleaver entered during the opening credits of *Leave It to Beaver.*

The "For Sale" sign of Dale David, a busy realtor in town, was stuck into the sprawling front lawn at 835. A second placard that said "In Escrow" was perched on top. Not surprising. These homes never stayed on the market for long.

Vining radioed that she was on-scene and didn't need further assistance. She got out of the car.

The front door was open. She rapped hard and noted the solid wood with a pang of envy. The doors in her house were hollow-core and she had always hated the flimsy sound and feel of them.

Standing on the threshold, she announced, "Police." She knocked again and spoke louder. *"Police."*

Not stepping inside and with her hand on her sidearm, she looked around. The floor of narrow oak planks was polished to a high sheen and carpeted with an Oriental runner. Ornate crown and base moldings were throughout. An antique parlor bench was beside a staircase that curved to the right. An elaborate chest of drawers faced it across the entry hallway. To the left was a study or den. A large opening farther down may have led to a living room. At the end of the hall, French doors revealed a patio, a giant magnolia tree, and a pool with blue water. A door was to her immediate right.

Vining had always loved those old houses. They felt solid and dense with history. But that was before such history would torment her and threaten her downfall. That was before her world was turned inside out.

This was odd. Citizens who called the police were usually by the door, counting the minutes. She'd heard of female realtors raped and murdered in houses they were showing, but she'd never heard of a realtor luring a victim to an empty house.

At the sound of rapid footsteps, she pulled her Glock .40 free from its holster and was holding it in front of her when a man walked into the hallway from the dining room.

"Holy moly!" He reared back with his palms facing her.

"Who are you?"

"I called you. I'm . . . I'm Dale David. The realtor." He chuckled amiably as he looked at her gun. "Is that necessary?"

She dropped her gun to her side but didn't holster it, neither did she explain.

He had a pleasant, unremarkable face, with dark eyes and pale skin. It would later confirm for her that the worst monsters came in the most benign packages. His thick hair was raven black and looked dyed. He was tall. Vining estimated six feet. He was dressed in what passed for business casual—a pale yellow polo shirt belted into light green chinos. She would later learn the embroidered design on his shirt of a lamb dangling by a ribbon tied around its middle was the logo of Brooks Brothers.

She'd seen Dale David's placards around town, but had never seen the man. The real Dale David later sent a large basket of indoor plants to Vining's hospital room. He had been a suspect for less than five minutes, having quickly proved he'd spent the entire day showing properties to a couple who were relocating to the area from Michigan.

When Vining later reflected on that incident, as she would do a million times until she felt she had wrung from it all the substance she could, she realized it was all there in his body language. Most people would be terrified to have a gun aimed at them. This man seemed nervous, but he was acting. Instead of fear at the sight of her weapon, his eyes flashed with excitement. In her probably enhanced memory, Vining saw his pupils dilate.

"Here's my card." He indicated that he was going to put his hand into his pocket.

"Hold it right there. I'll get it. Turn around please." She began patting him down.

"You're searching me?"

"The front door was wide open and you weren't waiting."

"I was in the bathroom."

In his front pocket, she found several business cards from Dale David Realty, but nothing else. No wallet. No I.D. She didn't make much of that. Her ex-husband didn't always carry his wallet, depending upon the pants he was wearing.

She pocketed a card.

"I only called because I found a window open in the kitchen. It's this way." He turned and started quickly walking.

"Hold up. What's behind here? Could you open this door, please?"

She pointed to the closed door to her right.

"That's the powder room. In these old houses, they put them right off the front door like that for travelers passing by who might need to use the facilities."

"Open it, please." She stepped back, turning to have a look around the den and the living room next to it. Across the foyer was the dining room, which was also empty. She came up behind him as he opened the closed door. She also had him open the door of a closet that was tucked inside.

She holstered her weapon. She freely admitted she'd earned her other station moniker of Quick Draw. Her rationale was simple. Better to be safe than not go home at the end of watch. This guy struck her as strange, but she felt more annoyed than at risk. She put him in the category of people who were only friendly to the police when they wanted an officer to do something for them. When the tables were turned and an officer was doing his job in pulling one of them over for reckless driving or DUI, forget about it. She'd look at his open kitchen window, call in that the case was closed, and head home to barbecue steaks for her and Emily.

She closed the front door. "How much of the house did you search?"

"All of it. Even the attic and basement. Like I said, I just called the police to CYA in case the house is broken into later."

"Isn't this house alarmed? Why didn't the alarm go off when the window was opened?"

"My assistant was the last one here. The display on the alarm panel indicated a window was open when I got here today. She must have set the alarm anyway when she left. I'm getting on her about that, trust me."

He pointed in the direction of the dining room. "Should you take a look?"

She followed him across the dining room and through a butler's pantry. Glass-fronted cabinets there were loaded with barware and stemware. They entered a large, sunny kitchen. An island with a cooktop and sink was flanked by bar stools. A wood block on the stone counter was crammed with expensive cutlery. A window behind the sink was open.

The realtor spread his arms wide in a mockery of product demonstration. "Here's the updated gourmet kitchen. No expense spared. Granite and stainless steel. Top of the line. Destined to look as out-of-date in ten years as avocado-colored appliances."

His voice became conspiratorial. "Do you know what the buyers are paying for this place?"

Vining again got the feeling that something was amiss.

She moved to the back door, passing on the inside of the island, opposite where he was standing. She looked out the door window at a driveway that led to a detached garage. She flipped open the bolt lock and put her hand on the doorknob.

"I'll take a look around outside."

He had moved to stand in front of the refrigerator.

The refrigerator door was covered with photos, invitations, calendars, and notes held with cute magnets—central command for a busy life. The owners hadn't bothered to clear them away to show the house. Maybe they thought it looked homey. Descending one side were dozens of tiny magnets. Vining recognized them as poetry magnets comprised of words in black type on a white background that one formed into sentences. She and Emily had a set then and used to have fun taking turns being creative. When Vining later threw them out, the reason she'd given Emily was that she was tired of the refrigerator looking cluttered.

The realtor shook his head and smiled at something he saw there, as delighted as if he'd found an Easter egg in December.

This was officially creepy, Vining decided. She keyed her choker mike clipped to the front collar of her shirt and spoke quietly with her head bent close, broadcasting that she was okay, but to send nonemergency backup.

"One Lincoln twenty-one. I'm code four, but send me a back code two."

With his thumb and forefinger, the realtor picked off a magnetized word and turned the printed side toward her. His eyes consumed her.

"Look."

She couldn't make out the word printed there. Her right hand was on the doorknob. She moved it to her sidearm.

"What do you want, sir?"

"Do you see this?" He was panting. Perspiration dotted his forehead and upper lip. "Officer Vining, I want you to see this."

Hearing him say her name sent a chill down her spine. Her nametag was on her shirt. He must have read it, but she didn't recall seeing him do that.

He walked toward her, holding out the magnet.

"Stay where you are." She held her palm toward him and with her right hand pulled her Glock loose from its holster.

He complied.

Easy does it, she thought.

The last time she was alone in a room with a man and had pulled her weapon, she'd shot that man to death. That was five years ago, but it seemed like yesterday. She had started this job wanting to help people. Most cops retire without ever firing their gun in the line of duty. She thought that would be her story. She already had the blood of one man on her hands. This was different, she told herself. He wasn't dirty with weapons and his hands were in full view. Watch the hands. The hands could get you killed.

Easy does it. Everything's fine.

A car that sounded like a PPD cruiser stopped in front of the house. By the slight incline of his head, Vining knew that the realtor had heard it, too.

He was ten feet away. The Police Academy instructors drilled in the twenty-foot rule, testing recruits by walking slightly within and beyond twenty feet of them, requiring salutes if closer than twenty and push-ups if the recruits misjudged. The size of the boundary became innate. It was critical. It could mean an officer's life or death. The theory was that a suspect could run twenty feet and reach an officer by the time the officer could draw and use his weapon.

Without warning, the realtor ran toward her, yanking a six-inch utility knife from the wood block on the island. She pulled her gun. He slashed the back of her hand. She fired and missed. He jammed the knife into her neck. She discharged the gun again but he had his hand on the muzzle, directing it away from him.

Seconds passed. She felt each one. Her hand went to the knife in her neck. The heat of her blood startled her. While she wavered on her feet, he kept his hand on her gun. He looped the other around her waist, holding her up, pressing her against him. His face touched hers. He was breathing through his mouth. She felt his breath. It was fresh, smelling of mint. His eyes were bright, their pupils large. He didn't move his intense gaze from her. He didn't want to miss a thing. It was as if they were making love.

She heard the dispatcher nattering into her earphone. She dropped her hand to the choker mike but he pulled it away before she could key it.

Her earphone blasted three sharp tones. The sergeant had instructed dispatch to try to raise her.

There was knocking at the front door. A male voice yelled "Police!" Sirens approached.

The realtor blinked and sighed. Vining later decided he was wistful, as if taking leave of a lover whom he would never see again. She dropped to her knees, a posture of submission. At the sound of heavy, rapid footsteps across the hardwood floor, the realtor bolted away, tripping on her legs, then ran downstairs to the basement. They'd later learned he'd escaped through a basement door that led into the backyard, and then skirted through a hole he'd cut in the cedar plank fence that was hidden by thick shrubbery.

When the unwelcome image of his last longing look returned to her in nightmares, she felt she knew what he had been thinking. He was sad he wouldn't be there to see her die.

There was shouting and cursing as officers overwhelmed the kitchen. They darted throughout the house and outside, lurching over her body that was facedown on the blood-slick floor. An officer kneeled beside her. She could tell he was trying to keep his panic under control as he gave instructions into his radio. His voice was familiar, but she couldn't place it. Then she barely heard it. Then it didn't matter. On the floor, her hand was near her neck. She opened her fingers to touch the steel blade jutting from her skin that seemed too accommodating of the intrusion. It was the most peculiar thing she'd ever felt.

Sergeant Early's voice jolted her back to the present. "Nan, you're entering this case with your objectivity already shot."

She was right, but Vining wasn't giving up that easily. She spun it.

"Sarge, all of us bring our pasts and attitudes to the job. No one is truly objective. No one is clean. That's reality."

"Okay. Since we're being real, Kissick told me he believes you had a panic attack this morning. What should I know about that?"

She'd wondered when it would come up. "That was a blip. It didn't affect my work."

"What if it does the next time?"

"There won't be a next time." She hoped.

"And if there is?"

All the what ifs, Vining thought. The world was wringing its hands with what ifs. Vining had experienced her what if and it had washed away the hesitation from her life, like the incoming tide eroding a sand castle. Because she hesitated, T. B. Mann was free.

They were distracted by Kissick accompanying two men into the department.

Vining summed up her position. "Sergeant Early, you need me and I need to work this case." Her demeanor dared her to say otherwise.

The sergeant slowly exhaled. "Go ahead into the conference room. I'll be in shortly."

Vining nodded and left.

She didn't breathe a sigh of relief. Early wasn't going to pull her off the case. Vining just had to wait until Early arrived at that conclusion herself. It was a different approach from the old Nan. Before, she would have been quietly but decidedly contentious. Never back down. Never let them see you sweat. It was one of the ways she tried to be as tough as the men. To prove her mettle. Who's the most macho? She was Quick Draw. Poison Ivy, creeping up on everything she touched. Scratch it and make it worse. *Before.* Now she wasn't breaking a sweat. She felt as if she'd slipped into her own skin and found she was just the right size. A perfect fit.

She could give T. B. Mann credit for that. He'd torn her down and rebuilt her. But now he'd have to deal with it.

She flashed back to the kitchen floor at 835 El Alisal Road. While chaos reigned around her, she pulled herself along the floor with her forearms, trailing a slick of blood. The officer assisting her tried to get her to stay still. They later told her she crawled six feet, entering the pantry's open door. Her last thought before she went out was not of her daughter. Her life did not pass before her eyes. Her final memory was of what she saw in front of her in black and white. There on the tile floor was the tiny magnet that had flown from The Bad Man's hand when he'd rushed her. On it was printed a single word: "pearl."

EIGHT

Vining heard Kissick on the phone in his cubicle and saw Early making a call in her office. She took the opportunity to make a quick call herself. Emily had a half day at school and Vining's mom was to take her to the dentist, but another voice answered the phone.

"Hi, Granny," said Vining. "How come you're there? Where's my mom?"

"She went to meet that man she's been seeing. The one who works for Lockheed. One of the ones she met over the Internet."

Vining grimaced. Her mother had been inconsistent help ever since she'd discovered Internet dating. Patsy Brightly had just turned fifty-one and had leaped on the search for husband number five as if she was driving on reserve. Patsy had retained the surname of her fourth husband, which she loved while she despised the man.

"She's gonna get herself killed is what she's gonna do. Taking up with strangers like that."

"Let's hope not." Vining glanced at her watch. "How did the dentist go?"

"Dentist canceled. Your daughter talked me into taking her to Forest Lawn instead. She's in the darkroom, developing pictures she took at a funeral there."

Vining closed her eyes.

"Maybe you should speak to somebody about this hobby of hers. When she asked me did I want to see her photographs, I thought they'd be of her school friends and such. But no. She's got corpses, caskets, graveyards, haunted houses, things she calls swirls and orbs and I don't know what all. Nanette, I tell you. It's not healthy. When I was her age, I was at the soda shop flirting with the boys."

Vining adored her grandmother, who had been her one source of stability when she had been growing up, but the old woman was a wellspring of advice that she freely distributed whether invited or not. "Emily's fine, Granny. She's just working out her fears about what happened to me."

In truth, Vining also didn't care for her daughter's new hobby, but she and Em always presented a united front to the world, especially to other family members. Emily's fascination with the dead, dying, and paranormal began after Vining's attack. It hadn't abated. Vining felt responsible and regretted describing her near-death experience to her daughter. Vining didn't think it was that big a deal, but for Emily, it had profound meaning. She claimed it confirmed the existence of a netherworld that sometimes pierces the veil of our everyday existence. The girl was convinced that if we paid close enough attention and had the right equipment, we could catch glimpses of it. She spent her allowance and the money she earned baby-sitting on materials to assist her in ghost hunting: electromagnetic detectors, black lights, audio equipment, cameras, and other paraphernalia. She belonged to a local ghost-hunting club, but had distanced herself from the group, feeling they patronized her.

Emily was a great kid. She was smart and kind. She

didn't drink, take drugs, or lie to her mother. She liked being one of the brainy students at school and had a small circle of close friends. As she was quick to point out, geeks had never been more fashionable. Other than anxiety about T. B. Mann, which Vining couldn't fault because she shared it, Emily was a happy child and Vining was proud of her.

"Granny, can you stay with her until I get home? I might be late. Real late. I know Em can stay by herself, but . . ."

"You just found a murder victim."

"Yeah. I'd feel better if Emily wasn't alone."

"Happy to do it. We'll get Chinese takeout and I'll watch my shows. When you've gotta work, you've gotta work."

"Thanks."

"Is it that policewoman who was missing? Guess you can't talk about it."

"That's what they're saying on the news?"

"It's all over the news. Someone from the Pasadena Police came out and talked to the reporters on the front steps of the station. Dark hair. Handsome man."

"Lieutenant Beltran. He handles the media. What did he say?"

"Buncha nothing."

"Good."

"Here's our girl."

Emily took the phone. "Hi, Mom. You found Frankie Lynde."

"It's not official."

"After they clear the scene, can I check it out?"

"Emily, it's a crime scene."

"But after they clear it. You can't keep people out of

there forever. It's in the open. Come on, Mom. Please. Before it gets ruined."

Her daughter was as stubborn as Vining. "Em, a woman was murdered."

"I'm not making fun. I'm doing serious work. If T. B. Mann killed her, I might find out something to help you."

"There's no relationship between the crimes."

"You really don't think so?"

Vining lied. "No."

"Is that good or bad?"

"Good, because it means he's not around here."

"Okay. So can I go there? Please."

"I'll take you if I don't get home too late. You can look from the edge. Don't even think about asking your grandmother to take you. You hear me?"

Vining saw Kissick and Early head for the conference room. "Gotta go. Don't know when I'll be home. I've got my cell on."

"How are you, Mom?"

"I'm okay."

"You sound tired."

"I'm fine."

Vining entered the conference room and sat in a chair near the head of a long table. Whiteboards and large maps of Pasadena and its environs were on the walls.

Kissick made the introductions. "Detective Sergeant Kendra Early, Corporal Nan Vining, Corporal Tony Ruiz, this is Detective Steve Schuyler. He's been handling Frankie Lynde's missing person case."

Vining shook his hand. He was slightly overweight with thick blond hair and boyish looks. He didn't give any indication that he remembered Vining's phone call to him while she was on leave. A large cardboard box was on the table in front of him.

"And this is Lieutenant Kendall Moore from the Robbery Homicide Division." Kissick let a hint of sarcasm creep into his voice. LAPD's Robbery Homicide was the department's elite investigative unit. The LAPD had dispatched one of their finest. It suggested that they didn't think the Pasadena Police Department was up to investigating the murder of one of LAPD's own.

Lieutenant Moore was in his forties, tall and lanky. He looked as if he'd played sports in school and still carried a jock's chip on his shoulder, telegraphing to all that he could kick the butt of anyone in the house. He was handsome enough and could probably be charming enough to make it work for him. A spattering of old acne scars on his cheeks and dark circles beneath his eyes gave him a battle-worn, world-weary look that undercut the golden-boy aura. He reached to shake hands across the table.

Early began. "This is a sad day, especially for our family at the PPD."

Moore leaned his forearms on the table and clasped his hands as if preparing to pray. "I stopped at the location by the bridge on the way over." His voice was raspy. He lowered his eyes and exhaled. "Throwing her down the hill like that. Like a bag of garbage."

Vining observed that he was used to being in charge.

"Bad scene," Ruiz said.

Lieutenant George Beltran entered the room and introduced himself. He seemed surprised that Moore was there but didn't comment.

Moore didn't sit after shaking Beltran's hand. "Lieutenant, Frankie Lynde was a fine officer. She deserved better. I'm here to say that LAPD will do everything in our power to help you get this clown."

Beltran also remained standing. He nodded, nonplussed. "Thanks, Lieutenant. You're from Frankie Lynde's precinct in Hollywood?"

"Robbery Homicide. Downtown."

"I see. Who sent you?"

Moore's smile wavered. "I made the decision."

Ruiz noisily changed position in his chair, conveying his disapproval.

Schuyler sat back, his elbow on the chair arm, his fingers against his lips, and looked from Beltran to Moore.

To Vining, Schuyler's body language conveyed that he had information he wasn't telling.

Kissick was reticent, his facial expression indecipherable.

Early turned up a hand to show her confusion but remained silent, deferring to Lieutenant Beltran.

"Of course we're counting on LAPD's cooperation in our investigation. Detective Schuyler's materials will give us a big head start. We'll let you know if we need your help, Lieutenant." Beltran smiled.

Moore smiled, too, but an edge slipped into his voice. "Officer Lynde lived, worked, and was last seen in Los Angeles. She was probably murdered there. I know she's the daughter of one of your own, but an argument could be made that this is LAPD's homicide."

Beltran cut to the chase. "Lieutenant, I know you see us as the little, sleepy Pasadena Police Department. It's true that we don't have ten thousand sworn officers like LAPD. You yourself have probably handled hundreds of homicides. No one here can even come close. But we're more than capable of solving this case and we will."

"I realize this is *your* investigation, Lieutenant, but Lynde was *our* officer."

"Any officer down belongs to all of us, Lieutenant Moore," Beltran said.

Vining whispered, "Amen."

Moore swung his attention to Vining for the first time and openly frowned at her scar. It was rude and she suspected that was what he intended.

"Aren't you the officer who got stabbed on duty?"

Vining felt herself flush.

That tore it for Ruiz. "What does LAPD want with one more homicide? Don't about forty percent of yours go unsolved?"

They might bicker among themselves, but they were family and family stuck together.

Early threw a punch. "LAPD's jurisdiction ends somewhere around Figueroa Street, last time I checked."

Moore's lean cheeks grew deep hollows. A corner of his jaw pulsated. "Officer Lynde's murder is not just another homicide."

"Did you come here to lecture us, Lieutenant?" Early's posture suggested she was coiled to strike.

"I in no way intended to imply that your department's not up to the task or that LAPD should take control. If that's how I came off, I apologize."

The coolness with which he told the lie touched something deep inside Vining. It was an easy lie, told by someone confident the listener would either believe it or be too polite or shy to challenge it. T. B. Mann had told such a lie. The same thread connected all the evil and deception in the world.

Lieutenant Beltran flashed a large, don't-bullshit-abullshitter smile at Moore. "Then why are you here, Lieutenant?"

Moore relaxed his antagonistic posture and assumed an aw-shucks mien. The genie had come too far out of the bottle for it to work. "Here's the deal. Frankie Lynde and I had a relationship that ended about two months before she went missing. You'll find it all in Detective Schuyler's records. You'll also see that I'm clean."

Now that the secret was out, Schuyler dropped his fingers from his lips. His comment was diplomatic. "There's no evidence to indicate that Lieutenant Moore was involved in Frankie Lynde's disappearance."

Moore said nothing but his eyes were smug.

Early hiked her eyebrows. "So what was all that before? Were you just trying to be cute?"

Vining tried not to smile.

Ruiz tipped back his chair. "A relationship . . . That's what you told her, huh? Did you at least take off your wedding ring before screwing her?"

"Pal, it was more than that."

"Hey, Frank Lynde is my pal. You're not my pal. You're what we call a suspect."

Moore reared back his head. "Look. I didn't have to come down here. I wanted to be up front about it. I don't have anything to hide."

"But since you are here, you thought you'd just try and see how big a pushover the PPD is. See if we'd roll over for you." Early punctuated her words with sideways jerks of her head, letting her northwest Pasadena upbringing peek out.

"I cared for Frankie," Moore said. "If I can do anything to help, I'm here. That's all I wanted to say. I thought it best I say it in person."

"We heard you. We'll be in touch." Beltran did not shake Moore's hand.

Kissick was already out of his seat and heading for the door. "Lieutenant Moore, I'll walk you out."

"Let's take ten," Beltran said.

NINE

*V*ining returned to her cubicle, still angry from being caught off guard by Moore. From her purse, she took out a mirror and examined her reflection. She tried fastening the top button of her shirt, pulling the collar as high as it would go. The pink line that marked the path of the surgeon's incision was still visible above the fabric. Grimacing, she undid the top three buttons, spread the collar open, and flicked her hair over her shoulder away from her neck.

Come on. Take a good look.

Watching Moore spin the truth and smile made her feel dirty and rattled. She craved a few minutes alone. She wondered if she had time to go to the AM/PM mini-market near the station that practically served as a cafeteria for the PPD. She decided she didn't. Her grandmother would recommend a cup of herbal tea to calm her nerves. She headed for the break room.

On the way out, she overheard Lieutenant Beltran talking to Sergeant Early. "Let me worry about the budget. I'll handle the people upstairs. You've got Vining. Who else do you want?"

Vining clenched her fists. *She was in.*

Returning with her Styrofoam cup of tea, Vining took the same seat in the conference room. Detectives Doug Sproul and Louis Jones were also there, pulled into the investigation from other desks under Early's control.

Officer Alex Caspers plopped into the chair next to Vining, slapping his yellow notepad onto the table.

"Poison Ivy. Looks like we're going to be working together."

"Caspers, piece of advice. Calling me that name is not a good way to start off."

"Thought that was your moniker. Ruiz calls you that."

"But *you* don't. Understand?"

He raised his hands as if he was backing away from something dangerous. "Whatever you say, *Corporal* Vining."

"Thought you couldn't wait to get back on the street."

"Beltran and Early talked me into this deal. It'll look good on my résumé when I go for my corporal stripes." Caspers gave her a big smile. "Who wouldn't want to catch a cop killer?"

She gave him a searching look then turned away.

He kept talking. "Kissick's leading this thing. I like him. He's very cool."

Vining sensed he was baiting her, trying to fish out a clue about her rumored relationship with Kissick. She just nodded.

Kissick entered the room and sat at the head of the table.

Sergeant Early began. "Jim Kissick is the lead investigator. He'll coordinate your activities. Answer your questions. Listen to your concerns. Any bitching, take it to him, not to me."

That brought a chuckle.

"With that, Jim, it's your show."

"Let me first say welcome to Doug, Louis, and Alex. Thanks for pitching in. Say good-bye to your wives or girlfriends. Cancel your plans for recreational activity. Don't plan on seeing your kids while they're still awake. Your asses belong to me until we find the dirtbag who murdered Frank Lynde's daughter."

Caspers gave him a thumbs-up.

"Lieutenant Beltran is going to handle all contact with the press."

Beltran gave a smile and a jerk of his head that conveyed, "Bring it on."

Kissick continued. "Any reporters stop you on the street, show up in front of your house, get through on your private line, just say you can't talk about an ongoing investigation, and refer them to the L.T."

Beltran added, "They will stake out your house and worse. The press gobbles up a case like this with a spoon. Frankie Lynde had those all-American looks, beautiful smile, and a tragic, mysterious death that the public won't be able to get enough of."

"Laci Peterson," Doug Sproul said. "And that college girl who disappeared in Aruba."

Louis Jones pulled out the name. "Natalee Holloway."

Vining was grateful that no one mentioned her name, but she wasn't an official member of that club, only having flat-lined for two minutes.

Early pointed at herself. "Suffice it to say that if Frankie looked like me, we wouldn't be having this conversation."

They enjoyed the joke at Early's expense, then Kissick took over. "Best we can hope for is a bigger news story to blow us to the back pages. Let me introduce Detective Steve Schuyler from LAPD's Hollywood Division. He was in charge of Frankie's M.P. investigation and was nice enough to save us a bunch of time by coming out to Pasadena.

"Let me fill in a piece of the story for those of you who weren't at our earlier meeting. Frankie had a romantic relationship with a Lieutenant Kendall Moore of LAPD Robbery Homicide. Lieutenant Moore showed up here earlier on his own, ostensibly to help us with the investigation. He was waiting in the lobby when Detective Schuyler arrived."

"He didn't come with you?" Ruiz asked Schuyler.

Schuyler raised his hands. "I walked in and he was sitting on the bench. He outranks me."

"Did he approach you after Frankie went missing?" Early asked.

"No. Frankie's phone records led me to him. He copped to the relationship right away. They were together over a year. He said they'd been doing a long good-bye, fizzling out, starting about two months ago. He said he hadn't spoken with her for about a month before she disappeared. Her phone records substantiate that."

"Did you get his?" Beltran asked.

"He gave them to me," Schuyler responded.

"Isn't he the helpful guy?" Early said.

"It's possible he had a face-to-face with Frankie,"

Schuyler said. "Followed her from her strip club outing. Waited for her at her home. Let me be clear. I didn't eliminate him as a suspect. I had him under surveillance. Other than his job and a little adultery, he leads an ordinary life."

Kissick took notes. "Who ended their relationship?"

"He says they just drifted apart. That the split was amicable."

"Baloney," Vining said. "Someone always ends it."

Kissick raised his eyes from his notepad to look at her, then quickly resumed writing.

Schuyler explained. "I found nothing to corroborate Moore's story because he and Frankie kept the relationship close to their chest. Moore didn't talk about it with his buddies. Her friends knew she was seeing someone, but she wouldn't name names. The only one Frankie talked to about Moore was her best friend, Sharon Hernandez, an officer out of Van Nuys. They went through the Academy together. But after Hernandez was critical of the relationship, Frankie went silent about it."

"How did Moore and Frankie meet?" Kissick asked.

"Backyard barbecue given by mutual cop friends."

Early rubbed her eyes with her fingertips for the umpteenth time that day. "What about Moore's wife? Did she know?"

"She's used to him working long hours." Schuyler said it in a way that suggested Moore's wife had become accustomed to him screwing around with other women. "I reiterate that I found no evidence linking Moore to Lynde's disappearance."

"Did he try to horn in on your investigation?" Kissick asked.

Schuyler thought before responding. "He called once

or twice to ask how it was going. That was it, other than showing up today."

"Her dad told me you'd tracked down a dozen or so guys Frankie was involved with." Ruiz's voice was low as if trying to preserve Frankie's honor. "You like any of them?"

Schuyler shook his head. "No evidence she'd been in contact with them for a long time. Frankie was known for partying hard, but when she took up with Moore, she cut out the rest."

"She was in love," Vining said.

The way she'd been staring at the table would lead one to believe she had been daydreaming.

They all looked at her.

She looked back. "She talked to her friends about the other men in her life, but not about Moore. She even stopped sharing information about him with her best friend. She knew what they would say and she didn't want to hear it."

"She *thought* she was in love." Caspers sneered.

"If she thought she was in love, then she was," countered Vining. "There's no blood test for love. Moore ended it, and her life went spinning out of control."

Ruiz grinned. "I think you watched too much of that Lifetime channel for women while you were gone."

Vining gave him an amiable smile, showing she could take a joke, while thinking, *Just keep pulling the rope, my friend. Eventually, you'll hang yourself.*

Early raised her index finger. "Vining's got a point."

Ruiz's grin stiffened.

"Granted, Moore's got some agenda he's working through, but we're ignoring that little play Frankie and Chauffeur Girl put on at the strip club. Who was the girl? Where was Frankie for the past two weeks? And why the hell was her body dumped in Pasadena?"

"Let's back up and start at the beginning," Kissick said.

Schuyler took the lid off the banker's box. "Frankie Lynde," the date of her disappearance, and the case number were written on the side in black marker. "I have Lynde's paper trail for the past two years at the station. Feel free to come down and run our copy machine. I brought copies of my and my partner's notes, the reports of the interviews we conducted, and the other research we did."

From the box he took out the flyer that was posted all over L.A. County, that had appeared in all the local newspapers and on the local and national news. The flyer showed Lynde's official police portrait, in uniform in front of the U.S. flag, and a second photo of her on a sailboat, tanned, windblown, and smiling.

For the next hour, Schuyler summarized what he'd learned.

Frances Ann Lynde was twenty-eight years old. She had been an LAPD officer for seven years, the last three working undercover vice out of Hollywood. She had a reputation as a solid cop. She and her team were awarded medals for their role in busting a group of Thais running a prostitution ring out of a house in East Hollywood, smuggling in women to work as sex slaves. She'd also done important work in busting porno film producers who were hiring underage actors. By all accounts, she was passionate about her job.

She grew up in Azusa, a small city in the San Gabriel Valley about fifteen miles east of Pasadena. She was an only child. Frank and Debby Lynde decided to name their firstborn after Frank whether a boy or a girl. Frankie grew up to be a tomboy who loved hanging around with her father. Her childhood turned tragic. When she was eleven, her mother was murdered in a convenience store robbery, in the wrong place at the wrong time. Debby had gone out to get milk. Frank was watching the game and asked her to pick up cigarettes for him. The store's security camera showed Debby at the counter waiting for the clerk to get the cigarettes from the locked cabinet when the gunmen entered. If she hadn't stopped for Frank's cigarettes, she would have already left.

Frank never recovered. He worked all the hours he could, then spent his time off playing pool and drinking at a local bar. His sister and mom took care of Frankie, but her aunt had her own family and her grandmother was in poor health. Frankie was often in trouble. After graduating from high school, she worked in a veterinary clinic. She liked animals but grew bored. She started a degree in criminal justice part-time at Cal State Los Angeles. She dropped it after a year, applied to the LAPD and was accepted.

Frank Lynde was doubly proud that Frankie had pulled her life together and had followed in his footsteps. She was more ambitious than he and earned prime assignments early on. He envisioned good things for her. He'd remarried when Frankie was in high school, to a woman with four young children. He'd recently divorced but still lived in the same tract home in Azusa at the base of the foothills.

Frankie was last seen Friday, May 20, just before midnight at XXX Marks the Spot near the Los Angeles airport. Her body was found Monday, June 6, in Pasadena.

She was not reported missing until Wednesday, May 25, when she didn't show up for work. With the LAPD's 3/12 workweek, she worked three twelve-hour days and was off Saturday through Tuesday. Her friends said that lately it was not unusual for her to disappear on her days off.

An artist's rendering of the female in the chauffeur's outfit who met Frankie at the club had been widely distributed and LAPD cataloged and tracked down thousands of leads, none good.

Witnesses in the parking lot saw Frankie and the chauffeur running from the club into a black limousine that one witness identified as a late-model Lincoln Town Car. The chauffeur climbed into the driver's seat and pulled onto Century Boulevard heading south. No one noted the license plate.

"They were too busy checking out the females," Kissick said.

"Women wearing men's suits . . ." Caspers let the comment hang.

Early challenged him. "Women wearing men's suits what? You find that hot, huh?"

Caspers raised a shoulder. "I'm just saying . . . Chicks don't play dress-up for each other. Where was the guy? In the back of the limo or someplace else?"

Kissick pulled over the photograph of a Lincoln Town Car. "He sends her out while he stays in the shadows."

Schuyler had done a perfunctory search of limo rental companies who employed female drivers and had turned up nothing. In Southern California on a warm Friday night, hundreds of limos are likely on the streets.

A search of Lynde's condominium in Studio City turned up $10,000 in hundreds hidden in the wall behind her bedroom dresser. Also hidden there was a pair of diamond-and-aquamarine earrings that retailed for about $7,000. What wasn't there was her laptop computer or datebook.

Frank Lynde didn't recognize the earrings or know where Frankie might have obtained the money. Prior to the past two months, her financial records showed she had trouble meeting her monthly bills.

Schuyler told about Frankie's neighbor Mrs. Bodek encountering a woman leaving Frankie's condominium the Sunday before Frankie was reported missing. Mrs. Bodek found a resemblance between the woman and the drawing of Chauffeur Girl. The woman Mrs. Bodek had seen with Frankie's keys was similarly disguised, wearing a wig and oversized sunglasses.

Frankie's car was stolen from the XXX Marks the Spot parking lot sometime Monday, May 23, or Tuesday, May 24. The manager noticed the black Honda Accord parked there Sunday. When he returned to the club the following Tuesday afternoon, it was gone. The car body was found, completely stripped, on a street in the Pico/Union district west of downtown Los Angeles.

"He knew he was going to kill her." Early dumped the earrings from the evidence bag into her palm. "Kept her for sixteen days, knowing all the time he was going to kill her. He took care of the evidence before she was on the radar. Got everything except what Frankie hid."

"Guess he ensured Chauffeur Girl's cooperation by threatening to kill her." Caspers rocked back in his chair, pleased with his insight.

Kissick shook his head, disagreeing. "There's a line that people will not cross regardless, with two exceptions. One, she's psycho. Given that Frankie's neighbor saw her crying, I don't think so. Shows she has a conscience."

Caspers's bluster faded and he righted his chair.

Kissick continued. "Or two, she's a drug addict and will do anything for drugs."

Early held up one of the pricey earrings. "I doubt Frankie was on drugs though, given she had this and ten large hidden in her wall."

"She did blow through twenty-five grand over several weeks," Schuyler said. "But she spent it on clothes, shoes, cosmetics—you name it—at the best shops in Beverly Hills."

"All an addict wants is more drugs, not pretty clothes," Kissick said.

"Twenty-five grand is a lot for someone making maybe fifty a year to go through in a short time," Vining said. "She was trying to fill the hole in her life with stuff. The deeper in she got, the more she spent."

Schuyler added, "Frankie spent, but she saved some, too. Every Monday during the two months prior to her disappearance, she made thousand-dollar cash deposits into her checking account. The sums were too small to attract the bank's attention. She also started paying her bills with money orders purchased with cash."

"Someone had the dough to keep Frankie in cash and jewelry and Chauffeur Girl in drugs." Ruiz tipped his head at the sketch of the chauffeur. "Maybe this one is a prostitute. Frankie could have met her working undercover. Did you check that angle?"

Schuyler said, "Frankie could have met her on the street, but she looks high-end for that kind of action. You can throw a stone and hit twenty girls who look like her in L.A. Here's a sample of local porn movie and escort agency talent."

He tossed a stack of professional photos of nude and nearly nude women onto the table. They all had long, blond, rumpled hair; button noses; too-full lips; and overdone breasts.

Vining took a cursory glance. For the men, this was the best part of the afternoon so far.

The banker's box was empty, the contents strewn from one end of the conference table to the other. Schuyler finished his summary. He shook hands and left the station, his missing person investigation closed.

Kissick began. "I shouldn't have to say this, but I will. Everything about this case stays here. Even if the chief asks you a specific question, tell him to talk to me, Sergeant Early, or Lieutenant Beltran. I want to keep tabs on who knows what. No chitchat in the gym. No having too many beers with your buddies and next I'm hearing about ten grand found in Lynde's apartment. This goes double for conversations with Frank Lynde. Emotions about this case are running high all through the department. I don't want any freelancers working this. Got it?"

The speech wasn't directed to the seasoned detectives but the wake-up call didn't hurt.

Kissick continued. "The knock-and-talks haven't turned up anyone who saw anything around the arroyo last night. Disappointing but not surprising. Hopefully, after we get some publicity out there, the tips will come in. So, thoughts anyone?"

Ruiz picked up the diamond-and-aquamarine earrings. "Frank has no clue that his daughter was into something like this. Finding out she crossed over to the dark side will destroy him as much as finding out she was dead."

"Three years is a long time to work vice prostitution," Early said. "For a man or woman. It's a shitty job. You do your year and rotate out."

"Vice prostitution is harder for females," Vining said. "A male cop gets a massage and hopes the girl offers him a happy ending so he can arrest her. The female struts her stuff on the street. You have to dress like a whore. Act like a whore. Talk like a whore. Describe the sexual favors you'll do. A lot of the johns are well-dressed guys with good jobs. Somebody's husband. Somebody's father. It's tough to see their depraved side. Sometimes the johns want the females to show them their breasts before they'll offer money. It's degrading. We all compartmentalize in this job, but working undercover prostitution can get real personal."

Caspers chewed a sliver from the tip of a bitten-down fingernail and spit it out. "Looks like she only got really into the life about two months ago."

"About the same time she and Moore hit the skids." Early picked up the drawing of the chauffeur. "That act at the strip club was not a one-night fantasy. Chauffeur Girl and Frankie had been having play dates for a while. When and where did Frankie meet Chauffeur Girl and her partner?"

"Lolita," Kissick said.

Early gave him a sideways glance. "Excuse me?"

"Lolita," he repeated. "You know. Like the old movie. A sexy young girl who wore heart-shaped glasses. An old man who lusted after her."

Early turned the drawing of the chauffeur to face the group. "Find her and we'll get to him. Find our Lolita."

Ruiz set down the earrings and Vining picked them up. Holding one by the stem, she rolled it between her fingers. The large, square aquamarine was the same impossibly blue hue of the waters off a Caribbean island. As she rolled the stone back and forth, the color drew her in. So blue. So beautiful. Refreshing, like looking at a swimming pool on a hot day and imagining the coolness of the water. She saw something at the bottom of the gem. Something dark. Was it an occlusion or something else? She turned the earring, trying to catch another glimpse. She saw it. It looked like a man's face, rising up from the bottom of the pool, the sun and water casting him in a jacquard patchwork.

She turned the earring a different way and the image disappeared.

You're losing it, Nan, she chided herself.

She returned the earrings to the evidence bag.

TEN

What's new, Pussycat? Whoa—oh-oh-oh-oh-oh . . ." John Lesley sang the old Tom Jones song to his wife, trying to make her smile. It usually worked. Not tonight.

A bass downbeat pounded through the glass wall of the nightclub's private suite. In an aquarium that lined a wall of the club, women wearing air tanks, scuba masks, and nearly transparent swimsuits frolicked with one another underwater. It was early for scenesters, but there was already a crowd. A popular D.J. held court on Monday nights. The dance floor pulsated, a sea of bodies in frantic motion, like an anthill disturbed by a stick.

"It's good to be king, Pussycat. And you're my queen. Isn't it good to be queen? Say it. Say, 'It's good to be queen.' "

"It's good to be queen."

"Say it like you mean it. It's *good* to be queen."

"It's *good* to be queen."

"Poor itty-bitty Puddycat with the sad little face."

She turned away from his gaze.

"Not even a twenty-five-thousand-dollar watch can cheer you up." He fussed with the gold-and-diamond Patek Philippe watch on her wrist.

"You took it off Frankie. Took off her earrings, too."

"I bought all that jewelry for you. Frankie was just borrowing it. You'd have those aquamarine earrings, too, if you'd found them in her condo. Wonder what she did with them. I thought they were very attractive. Nice, but not too flashy. F-ing police probably have them now."

Pussycat stared straight ahead and shook her head.

"Hey, baby, if you don't want this jewelry, there are plenty of poor deprived women out there going to bed without Patek Philippe watches in their jewelry boxes. Just hardly able to sleep night after night."

A tear dropped down her cheek.

He put his arms around her and playfully jostled her. "Baby, I know you're upset over Frankie, but you've got to put it behind you. It was one of those things."

"It wasn't supposed to end like that. You promised."

"You gotta go with the flow. Expect the unexpected."

"I meet my sister for lunch and come home and see what you did to Frankie . . ." She brushed tears away.

"That's right. Listen to what you just said."

"I had to see my sister. She was wondering what was up with me."

"Baby, you don't think. You're not practical. I needed you there. Frankie went crazy and I didn't have any choice. I told you not to go, didn't I? If you'd been there for me, things might have been different."

"What are you saying? It's my fault?"

She scrunched her face and the tears flowed.

"Knock it off," he said meanly. "I hate you moping around."

"It's bullshit. You were going to do what you did to Frankie anyway. She kept asking me and I kept telling her no, but I knew in my heart. I knew when you sent me to take the stuff from her place. I knew. You lied to me."

"I didn't lie. It happened like I told you. You weren't there, were you? So you can't say."

He pulled the bottle of Cristal from the ice bucket and topped off their champagne flutes. He pressed a flute into her trembling hand. He held her hand to steady it and clicked her glass with his.

"Besides, sweetmeat, why do you want to spend time with anyone but me? It hurts my feelings." He pressed out his lower lip.

She set down the glass after taking a tiny sip. "I can't live this way."

He fished his hand inside his pocket and took out a tiny Baggie containing high-grade methamphetamine. It looked like shards of glass.

"You're crashing, that's why you're depressed." He tried to push the bag into her hand. "Do a bump."

"No." She shoved his hand away. "I don't want to do it anymore. It's gotten out of control."

He set the Baggie on the table in front of her. "Baby, who are you kidding? Just wait until you come crying to me because you need your Miss Tina."

"You turned me into an addict."

"Yeah, right."

"When I met you, I only took it when I had to lose weight or work a long shift."

"Now you're on the Jenny Crank diet." He started laughing.

"That's not funny." She dabbed her eyes with a cocktail napkin. "I hate my life."

"Hate it later. Do a bump now." He nudged the Baggie closer to her.

She sobbed, "Stop making fun of me. I'm a human being, you know. I have feelings, too."

He again put his arms around her. "I'm just playin' with ya. Come on."

She wasn't consoled.

He slugged down his Champagne and threw himself against the couch, his arms draped across the back. "Baby, enough of this crap, okay? We're here to have fun."

"But why did you do that to Frankie? *Why?*"

"Poor, sweet Pussycat. You've gotta understand. A woman like Frankie is a wild animal. If we turned our backs on her for a second, if we made one mistake, she'd have killed us or gotten away and put the cops onto us. The three of us went too far. And she went willingly, believe me. She knew what she was doing. She marched right down to that place called the point of no return."

"Never again. No more."

He shrugged. "I can't see the future."

"What are you saying? There's going to be more? Have there been others?"

"Baby, don't ask questions that you don't want to know the answers to. And knock off the woe-is-me bit. Playing Little Miss Innocent. You got your jollies with Frankie."

He slid his hand up her skirt and laughed when she pushed it away.

He leaned to look through the window at the action on the club floor beneath them. "Look at that redhead standing by the bar, acting like she's bulletproof. I'd like to put a hurt on her."

"No way. They just found Frankie today."

"Don't worry." He smoothed the furrows from her forehead with his thumb. "We're not going to get caught. I know all about the police. How they think. How they work. They're not that smart. We'll stay a step ahead of them. I always have."

"It's not right."

"Who are you to talk to me about what's right, huh? You think you're better than me?"

She hugged herself.

"Well, do you?"

She whispered, "No."

"Who the hell were you before I took you off the street? Nobody. I made you. I took you from dirt and put you on a golden pedestal. I can take you down off that pedestal and put you back in the dirt, too, and I mean underground. I'll do it. I don't want to, but I will."

She blinked back tears and said nothing.

"What are you thinking?"

"I'm not thinking."

"Good. Don't think. You especially shouldn't think about going behind my back and talking about our life to anyone, especially that sister of yours, or I'll fix it so you won't be talking to her or anyone again."

"I'm not. I wouldn't."

"Yeah, right. Baby, one thing I know is women, better than they know themselves." He looked at the gyrating bodies on the dance floor. "Last night was a long one, but I feel energetic." He gave her a look that suggested she should be impressed.

"Don't worry, Pussycat. We'll just catch and release tonight. I'll be the perfect gentleman."

ELEVEN

After the team meeting broke late that afternoon, Kissick sent Caspers to Hollywood to photocopy the rest of Schuyler's records. Lieutenant Beltran held a news conference on the police station steps and released a tip-line number. Sproul and Jones began logging and evaluating tips that started coming in as soon as the phone number was announced. Vining, Ruiz, and Kissick poured over Frankie's paper trail and built upon Schuyler's timeline of Frankie's activities for the past year. When

Caspers returned, Kissick started him on scrutinizing the arrests both Frank Lynde and Frankie had made over the past several years, running suspects through NCIC and other databases, researching criminal histories to see if anyone was worth a closer look. Kissick contacted Frankie's Internet service provider to gain access to her e-mail messages. He and Ruiz then drove out to Frank Lynde's house for a dreaded face-to-face interview.

At 9:00 p.m., Vining was still working at her desk and Caspers was at his in the adjoining cubicle. The comments he shot to her through the fabric wall grew further apart and less energetic. He clearly wanted to leave, but wasn't going to be the first to say it. Vining was ready, too. She was drained. But there was a lot of work to do and she enjoyed giving Caspers a hint of what it meant to run with the big dogs. Someone needed to give this guy a lesson in humility.

His cell phone rang relentlessly. His hopped-up chatter laced with street jargon was to her like nails on a blackboard. Her cell rang once.

"Hi, Mom," said Emily. "Still there, huh? I'm ready. Are you coming home?"

Vining remembered her foolish promise to take Emily to the crime scene, enabling her daughter's dark hobby.

"Em, it's nine o'clock. You have school tomorrow. Don't you have homework?"

Vining answered her own question aloud, in harmony with her daughter, "I finished it hours ago."

Emily was a more serious student than Vining had ever been. Sitting down and attacking homework right after arriving home from school was still beyond Vining's comprehension, but it was second nature to Em.

"I don't go to bed until eleven, Mom. We'll be home by then."

Vining told Emily she would wait at the bridge for Granny to drop her off there. Vining was ready to leave but didn't actually mind not going straight home. She was feeling restless. The bridge was a good place to go. She'd seen it a million times, at all hours of the day and night, but was drawn to see it again, to see it as it was now. The energies of Frankie Lynde, Lolita, and her partner were now fused to the place where so many desperate souls had said a prayer—or not—and taken a free fall into the arroyo. The plunge from the top had lured them. Vining felt its allure, too.

The PPD had opened the bridge to traffic late that afternoon, but crime scene tape still surrounded the area off the west end where Frankie's body had been found. Vining rounded the curve of the bridge and her anger flared when she saw cars parked everywhere and people standing around, some past the yellow tape. She did a tight U-turn in her old Jeep Cherokee—tomorrow she'd take home one of the Crown Vics—parked haphazardly, and punched on her hazard lights. With her shield in one hand and a lit flashlight in the other, she confronted the ghoulish sightseers.

"Folks, you've got to clear out of here. This is an active crime scene."

They were young and old, male and female, some with children in tow. A young man climbed up and over the steep slope, a camera dangling from his neck. Crime makes the most mundane locales fascinating.

"Come on, people. Time to go home."

They gave her that disoriented look that annoyed her;

they were not processing the sight of this lanky female with a badge interrupting their fun. Vining was tired enough to be tempted to go off on them. Instead, she was taciturn as they muttered half-hearted apologies and a few sarcasms while taking their time walking to their illegally parked cars. She let the parking violations go, although she could have wreaked havoc. She just wanted the people gone.

The street grew quiet. Few cars passed. The 210 to the north hummed with traffic, but it blurred into white noise. The songs of crickets enriched it.

Vining took it in. She loved this time of year. The longer days, warm nights, and crickets brought back the simple pleasures of her troubled youth and the occasional happiness she'd found then. She'd been so focused on getting back to work, anxious about what it would be like, she hadn't noticed that the endless, rainy winter and spring had passed and it was almost summer. She and the world had somehow made it to another season. The crickets' sawing sounded like the air was breathing. It made her feel alive. She was alive. In this place that resonated with death, decades old and brand-new, Nan Vining felt alive.

She stepped over the yellow tape, turning the flashlight beam on weeds mashed down by tires. The slick straw held no distinctive marks, protecting the tires' identity. No evidence had been found in the area other than small blood drops that probably came from Frankie.

She looked across the Arroyo Seco. Few lights shone from the federal courthouse on the other side, a quarter mile away, or the grand mansions flanking it. A crescent moon was high. It was a waxing moon, open toward the east—a good time to plant vegetables, according to her grandmother's folklore.

She heard rustling in nearby bushes. Her flashlight beam reflected off two shiny coins that were the eyes of a raccoon. They stared at each other for a second, both motionless. She turned off the flashlight and heard the animal continue on its way.

"Lolita," Vining whispered, her voice as soft as the other night sounds. "Talk to us. You'll never find peace until you talk to us."

She shone her flashlight down the slope where Frankie Lynde's body had lain. For the moment, it still belonged to them, to the PPD. Soon they'd release it and it would be as if nothing had happened there.

"We'll find you, Lolita. And when we do, you'll rat him out faster than you can say 'plea bargain.' "

A car crossed the bridge and stopped in the street near Vining.

"Hey." Kissick leaned out the window. "Thought you were going home."

"I am. What are you doing?"

"Going over to Stoney Point. Meet Ruiz and Sproul for a drink. Care to join us?"

Stoney Point was a locals' place just beyond the bridge with a lively bar and a piano player who knew the words and music to every request. It was tempting, but she was waiting for Emily. She was glad she had a reason to turn down his invitation. She needed to keep her distance from him. She was feeling vulnerable. She had not forgotten what it felt like to be in his arms. Mostly, she didn't think about it. It was a diet of the mind, tough at first, but easier as time passed. And lots of time had passed.

"That sounds great, but I'm waiting for my grandmother to drop off Emily. I promised to take her for an ice cream. But another time, huh?"

"Sure." His tone suggested that he didn't believe her.

She didn't mind his company, though. "Why don't you stay and say hi to Emily."

"I'd like that." He pulled his car onto the curb, out of traffic, and came over to her.

They naturally turned to face the bridge and the moon.

"Beautiful night," he said.

"Hmm."

"Strange."

"What's that?"

"Looking at that bridge. Why are people drawn to jump off a bridge? A gun is plenty effective."

"If you aim it right," she said.

"Messy business any way you look at it, taking a human life."

She blew out air in a half laugh. "Yeah. They should do a study."

"I'm sure they have. That's how the term 'lethal injection' entered our vernacular."

Kissick occasionally used words that Vining didn't understand. It reminded her that he was a college graduate and spent much of his free time reading. She had barely made it out of high school and had never been much for reading. Her lack of formal education bothered her, especially around people who talked about their blah blah degree from blah blah school. She had street smarts, she told herself. That would always get you further in life than a degree any day. She didn't mind Kissick being more educated than she. She liked it. Made him bigger in her mind. And he never threw it up to her that she was just a high school graduate.

He said, "Coming up to a year since you were attacked."

"Hard to believe."

"Were you thinking that maybe the same guy murdered Frankie Lynde?"

She thought of Frankie Lynde's message: *I am you. I am not you.*

Hallucination maybe, but it was right on. She understood and accepted it, but not without a pang of loss. It was her hopeful wish that T. B. Mann had abducted and murdered Lynde. It kept him close to her. Continued their macabre dance. Her business with him was not over. He was still out there. Their next dance was yet to come.

"For about five minutes. The M.O.'s too different. Plus my guy worked alone."

"I agree. Hopefully your guy's dead or in jail."

She nodded even though she doubted it. T. B. Mann knew how to get away. He had gotten away.

"Are you still concerned he'll come back?"

She shrugged. After she'd returned home from the hospital, it had been her obsession. With her ex-husband's help, she had just about turned her hillside home into a fortress.

"Odds are he wasn't out to get you in particular."

"Is that what you tell yourself in the middle of the night?"

His face was in shadows. Still, she saw that her dart hit its mark.

"Yes," he admitted. "When I feel like being in denial."

"What do you think? We've never discussed my case. You were the lead investigator."

"I *am* the lead investigator. The case is still open. In my heart, I feel he did come after you. If he was out to kill a cop, any cop, he could have shot one on the street, escaped to Mexico, and be living in the open, knowing the government there will never let us extradite him. But he didn't do that. Our guy planned every move. Start to finish. He wanted you. But why?"

"I've been asking myself that for a year. Do you think he's done it before?"

He exhaled slowly, not wanting to answer in haste. "I believe he has. It was no amateur gore-fest. This is an assured, methodical killer."

"I want to see my case file. I'm ready."

"I'll give it to you tomorrow. Looking at it with fresh eyes might reveal a new angle." He paused before continuing. "Have you gone back to the El Alisal house?"

"No." That wasn't completely true. She'd tried without success.

On her first attempt, her grandmother had driven, parking her Oldsmobile Delta 88 in the shade of one of the giant camphor trees that lined the street.

Vining looked out the car window and recalled that day she'd responded to the suspicious circumstances call placed by her attacker. She had walked up the brick path lined with mounds of white petunias, passing the "Offered by Dale David Realty" sign. She remembered looking forward to going home, taking a shower, and firing up the barbecue to grill steaks for her and Emily.

She relived approaching the open front door and knocking. Suddenly, in Granny's car, she began gasping for breath and seeing spots. She awakened with her grandmother patting her face and hands.

"Let's go," she told Granny, and couldn't get away quickly enough.

A few weeks ago, she tried again, alone. She took three steps down the path before she began hyperventilating and turned back, feeling a failure.

She said, "I heard the people who bought that house had the kitchen completely gutted and redone."

"Like the people who bought the Barrington Avenue condo where Nicole Brown Simpson and Ron Goldman were slaughtered. They remade that notorious entryway. You'd have to, I guess. Maybe you'd be able to destroy some of the bad karma."

His choice of words made Vining shoot a glance at him. She privately disagreed. A new kitchen at 835 El Alisal Road would do nothing to change the karma of that house.

"When I try to visualize his face, it gets confused in my mind with the pictures of Dale David I see all over town, hawking his real estate business. My guy wore a black hairpiece to look like Dale David. He knew the neighbors wouldn't question the realtor being around that house."

"My guess is he's long gone. I'm not saying that to give you a false sense of security. He may be insane, but he's not stupid. Therein lies the problem."

"He has a name."

Kissick gave her a surprised look.

"T. B. Mann. That's what Emily and I call him. It means The Bad Man."

Kissick's face showed he liked it.

They turned to look as a car crossed the bridge traveling well below the speed limit. The widely spaced headlights indicated it was a monolithic older car. In the dim light cast by the antique globe lampposts lining the bridge, Vining identified her grandmother's baby blue Oldsmobile Delta 88.

She saw her grandmother peering at Kissick as she passed. Granny stopped the car in the street and rolled down the driver's window as Vining and Kissick approached.

"Hi, Mom. Hi, Jim." Emily bounded from the car and ran toward them, stopping just before she ran into the path of a car that darted around Granny's.

"Em!" Vining scolded. "Watch where you're going."

"Hey, Emily. Can I get a hug?"

She and Kissick embraced. Emily didn't know about Vining's romantic relationship with Kissick. She knew him only as a trusted friend.

"Seems like I just saw you, but you've grown so much. You're almost as tall as your mom."

Emily was at that horrible age for a tall girl in which she towered over nearly all her classmates. She claimed it didn't bother her, but Vining lately had to remind Em to stand up straight. Vining remembered slouching to compensate for her height when she was her daughter's age. Emily was more grounded than Vining had been, and Vining took her share of credit for that, but adolescence was tough any way you cut it.

Vining ran her hand down Emily's long, straight hair. The girl's eyes were green-gray, like Vining's, but shone with the brightness of youth. That spark had left Vining's eyes when she was too young. Emily's enthusiasm buoyed Vining's spirits. It made her proud yet sad that her little girl was almost grown.

"Jim, come meet my grandmother."

Granny rolled down the driver's window as they approached. She gave Kissick an appraising look and it wasn't hard for Vining to read her thoughts.

"Corporal Jim Kissick, I'd like you to meet my grandmother Nanette Brown."

"Pleased to meetcha." She extended a hand and arm festooned with diamond rings and heavy, gold bangle bracelets.

Kissick shook her hand through the window. "Very nice to meet you, Mrs. Brown. I've heard a lot about you."

Granny made a dismissive wave. "You can't believe anything she says." She had probably been dead asleep in the easy chair at Vining's house when roused by Emily, but nothing short of nuclear war seemed capable of mussing her stiff, set-and-comb-out that she had done once a week.

"So Nan's your namesake. I never knew that."

Granny's toothy smile showed Kissick's charm was working. She'd had the same set of dentures for years and as her body shrunk, the teeth appeared ever larger in her mouth. "She wears it well. She's a good gal." She extended her hand toward Vining.

Vining took it, always surprised by how frail it felt. "I told Jim that I'm taking Em for ice cream."

Emily immediately took stock of the situation and didn't reveal her true motive for being there. "Do you want to come with us?"

"Thanks, sweetheart, but a couple of guys are waiting for me. I'd better get going. Hope to see you soon. See you bright and early tomorrow, Nan."

"You got it."

He climbed into his car and took off.

Vining knew what was coming.

"Nanette, he seems nice. He married?"

"Divorced. Yes, he is nice."

"He likes you. Anyone could see that."

"We work together, Granny."

"So work someplace else."

"You're funny."

"You're not getting any younger, Nanette."

"I feel like I'm on fast forward lately." She turned to her daughter. "Okay, Miss Ghost Hunter. Get your gear. You have half an hour."

Emily took her equipment from the Olds's trunk as Vining kissed her grandmother good-bye. She gave Granny directions to the freeway on-ramp and she took off.

"Emily, stay up here. I don't want you going down the hill."

"But Mom, that's where she was."

"We might still find evidence there. Plus it's steep and we saw a snake this morning. And I just don't want you down there."

Emily set up her tripod and camera at the edge of the slope. She stretched as far as she could to position her audio equipment and microphone down the hillside on the trail of smashed brush where the body had rolled. The girl began taking photographs with both a film and digital camera.

Vining sat in her car and turned on the radio. She tuned in the nightly love songs broadcast with the songs introduced by a woman who read sappy dedications in a dulcet voice. Vining listened to the lovers' tributes and laments with an almost clinical detachment. It had been a long time since hearing a song on the radio had made her wistful. Even her sentiments about the songs she'd shared with her ex-husband had faded until they now seemed a curiosity. Still, as much as she told herself the love songs show was stupid, she often listened to it, claiming there was nothing else on at that hour that was any good.

The Eric Clapton song "Wonderful Tonight" came on. It reminded her of the last night she'd spent with Kissick during their short romance. Emily's and Kissick's two boys were spending the weekend with their respective ex-spouses. Vining had come over to Kissick's Craftsman bungalow in Altadena and they had made dinner. It had been a small and cozy evening. They had eased toward such a routine and it was starting to feel like domestic bliss. They had just finished making love on the floor in front of a crackling fire. A CD began playing the Clapton song.

Kissick stood, pulling her up with him. They danced nude by the firelight. He told her he loved her. It was the first time. She could have told him she loved him back. It would have been an honest response. She felt she loved him. If she felt it, she did love him. No blood test for love, like she said. But she couldn't say the words. She was bold as a police officer, unafraid to kick butt, but she couldn't tell Kissick she loved him. Guns and knives could inflict pain, but the damage was finite. Measurable. The joy and pain of love had no restrictions. She'd been on the losing end once and that was enough.

The next week, she told him it was best if they cooled things off. As discreet as they tried to be, they were attracting attention around the station. Didn't look good for either of their careers, especially hers. It always looked worse for the woman. Plus it was potentially confusing for their kids. Set a bad example. Her life was too complicated to include a man. It was best to end it now, before they got in too deep. Best for both of them.

He didn't squabble or squirm or say a thing other than, "If that's what you want." That was Kissick. Her Gary Cooper. Her old-school hero.

That was over two years ago. She'd had few dates before and hadn't been with anybody since. Joked to herself that celibacy was fun. As for him, she didn't know.

He was the soul of discretion. She wished he did have someone. Someone who treated him better than she had. Who was more available. He deserved that. Still, she sensed his presence always, watching over her.

Sitting in her car, keeping an eye on Emily, Vining made up a love song dedication.

"I'd like to dedicate this song to Jim, the good man I threw away."

Exhausted, Vining welcomed going to bed only to find herself alert as soon as her head hit the pillow. After using every relaxation technique she knew and not finding sleep, she went into the family room, pulled up a chenille throw, and watched an old black-and-white Hitchcock movie, *Shadow of a Doubt,* on a station that had lots of commercials. The actors' voices eventually drowned out the chatter in her head and she fell asleep on the couch.

TWELVE

Vining played car-pool mom in the morning, dropping off Emily and her friend Aubrey at school early to work on their project for a science fair. Emily insisted that Vining come inside and say hello to her favorite teacher, Mr. Walthers, who taught math. Vining sensed her daughter had pulled herself taller as they walked side by side to the classroom. She and Em made quite a pair, both of them tall drinks of water with straight, nearly black hair. She walked a little taller herself.

Tom Walthers rose from his desk when they entered his room. He, too, was tall, a lean redhead with piercing blue eyes and a full beard that was mostly brown. Vining had met him at a parents' open house but didn't recall if she had detected then the spark in his eye that went beyond mere interest in the parent of his star pupil.

When Emily walked her out, she let slip that Mr. Walthers had lost his wife to breast cancer awhile back and had a daughter in grammar school.

"Are you trying to set me up?" Vining couldn't hide the amusement in her voice.

"I'm just giving you information. You like information." Emily was prepared for her mother's reaction. "He's nice and smart. I think he's cute, you know, for someone as old as him."

Vining reined in her attitude. "Yes, he is."

"Anyway, I told him I'd sit with his daughter, if that's okay."

"Sure."

Back inside her car, Vining thought of the warmth from just being with Kissick last night and the undeniable look in Tom Walther's eyes. There were men in the world. She *knew* there were men in the world, but for years now she had tried to give them as little of her time or interest as possible. She co-existed with them. She had gone so long without sex that passion with her ex and Kissick had become a dim memory.

She hadn't always felt that way. During those first, tough years as a single mom, she'd plunged into dating as distraction and revenge. Men were a necessary evil. One evening, her date came to pick her up and she saw the bewildered look in Emily's eyes as she blew her a kiss good night and stepped out the door. That look had probably always been there, but Vining had been too caught up in her own drama to see it. Once she had, she couldn't shake it. She became Emily's age again, observing with her sister, Stephanie, the revolving door of their mother's men. Some were cloying, as if to demonstrate how good they were with children. Others fixed them with gazes that would have vaporized them if possible. She stopped dating. Her armor cracked just enough to let in Jim Kissick.

He turned her beliefs upside down. He was proof that men weren't all wife-and-child-abandoning scumbags. He adhered to her rigid rules about never coming to the house when Emily was there. It was working and it was wonderful, until he blew it by saying he loved her. Her reasons for ending it were valid but not honest. It was about love. She couldn't do it. Had to run.

She remembered her mother chanting the dismissive slogan "A woman needs a man like a fish needs a bicycle" whenever she was on the outs with her current flame. Vining embraced it and lived it. Just like that, she turned off the spigot on that part of her existence.

But lately she'd felt familiar and not unwelcome stirrings. Her near-death experience seemed to have re-awakened her primal instincts. She hadn't yet decided what to do about it, and until she did, she would do nothing.

She had to smile at the thought of herself with a high school math teacher. How would he handle her being called out of bed in the middle of the night to go to a homicide scene or tales of wrestling cuffs onto a gang member? The Job eventually wore down the good intentions of dedicated couples. It was stronger than they were. Few professions could co-exist with that of a police officer. The wives of officers were often homemakers who socialized with an insular circle of friends. Many officers dated nurses because they shared crazy work schedules and the atmosphere of never knowing what was going to come down the pike.

What chances did that leave the female officers?

Slim and none.

She thought of Frankie Lynde and wondered if her fatigue with chasing a normal life had led her to accept cash and jewelry. It couldn't have been about the money or the jewelry. It never is. There was no pretense of love. Lolita being in the picture took care of speculation about that. The three of them knew the score.

Frankie couldn't have always been so jaded. Vining hadn't been born jaded. Was there hope for love among the jaded?

She went by Starbucks on Lake and California for a grande low-fat latte. It was an extravagance. Here she was, a person who washed her car at home because she couldn't see giving someone ten bucks to do it, paying four bucks for a cup of coffee. She cut herself some slack.

She left Starbucks and headed for the Winchell's doughnut shop next door. She took a short detour around the bus bench on the street corner where she'd seen Dale David in an ad. She wondered if T. B. Mann had found his inspiration from looking at the same ad. Dale David's smiling face adorned with graffiti was still on the bench back. Someone had drawn a penis near his mouth with a felt marker. Vining had to laugh.

On impulse, she cruised by the bridge, stopping at a small park where South Grand Avenue dead-ended on the east side, across the arroyo from where they'd found Lynde's body. Magnolia trees there were beginning to bloom as the jacarandas were shedding the last of their blossoms, decorating the ground with lilac-hued confetti.

She carried her coffee from the car. A handful of people in the park were working at easels doing renderings of the bridge, a favorite artists' subject. A woman observed and commented. It was an early-morning plein air painting lesson. The people looked like retirees. Vining wondered about her sunset years. She couldn't wrap her mind around it. People her age talked about grandchildren and golf lessons as if they were done deals. Getting through each day was a sufficient challenge for Vining. She wondered if life would ever get easier.

Her conscience, like a Magic 8-Ball in her head, answered: *Don't count on it.*

Across the arroyo near the opposite side of the bridge, she spotted someone standing above where Frankie's body had been found. Another person who wanted to rub elbows with murder, she figured. She opened the Jeep's hatchback and unzipped the black, nylon duffel bag that she'd transfer to the Crown Victoria she'd be assigned today. It held a box of latex gloves, waterless antibacterial gel to clean her hands after touching questionable people or objects, sunblock, and other personal equipment she might need in the course of her work. She took out binoculars and brought the individual into focus.

He put down the binoculars through which he'd been watching her so she could see his face.

It was Lieutenant Kendall Moore of the LAPD.

It would have taken Vining ten minutes to loop around to where she could drive across the bridge. She dashed across it in three. Moore had pulled his car off the street, onto the curb where it still impeded morning traffic. Cars swerved around it. Unfazed, he leaned against the hood, smoking a cigarette.

"Morning." It was already hot and she was perspiring from the brisk walk.

"Morning." His dress slacks, tie, and shirt looked as if he'd worn them through the night. The smoke he exhaled melted into the morning haze. She could smell alcohol within three feet of him.

She waited for him to begin. He didn't.

"What brings you here?"

He made a "don't know" face as if he'd simply awakened with a notion to drive crosstown to stand there after an all-night bender.

"Moore, I don't have time for cop games. What is it? Love? Guilt? Trying to get close to her in death because you screwed her over in life? All of the above?"

She pointedly looked at his plain gold wedding band. "I suspect your wife knows." She was playing the female intuition card, though she knew firsthand that even with the clues splayed out, the wife could be so caught up in her own la-la land that she'd miss them all. She had with Wes.

"Why ask me? You already know everything."

"I don't know what went on between you and Frankie. You could help us out."

"I showed up at your office yesterday trying to do that as a favor to the PPD."

"Right. We're just a little backwoods police department out here in Pasadena. We'll roll over for the important lieutenant from the big-city police."

"Seems to be a sensitive issue for the PPD. Lack of training seems to be an issue, too." He tipped his chin in the direction of her scar.

She felt herself blush, as she'd responded yesterday. He relished it. He was cruel. And Frankie loved him even though he was cruel to her, too. Frankie couldn't stop punishing herself for her mother's murder and her father's alienation. She had nothing to do with any of it, but kids always blame themselves.

"What exactly happened when you got stabbed?" he asked. "I never heard the whole story."

He looked at her and she looked back, both with a practiced, cool detachment that both knew was phony.

"Were you as nice to Frankie? What did you do to her that sent her spinning out of control?"

He dragged on his cigarette. "She made her own decisions. What happened between me and Frankie has nothing to do with why she ended up here."

"Sure. That's why you're here and not home with your wife and kids."

"Leave them out of it."

"I bet you used them in your talks with Frankie. First it's the old 'My wife doesn't understand me' bit. Then, when she wanted to get serious, it's 'I could never abandon my wife and kids.' She was useful to you as long as she played by your rules."

He was looking at her mouth as she spoke. Men often did. She was lucky to have naturally white teeth, but she had a slight overbite that pushed out her top lip and there was a small gap between her two front teeth. Men had told her that her teeth were sexy. She'd always hated her teeth and hated when people looked at them. If she had the money to have them straightened, she would. That was one good thing about the scar. People didn't notice her teeth as much.

"You think you're something, don't you?" he said. "You get your picture in the paper enough. Seems like you're always finding trouble."

"Trouble is my business." She smiled crookedly.

He threw his cigarette butt on the ground and mashed it out. "You gonna cite me for littering?"

"I'd like to cite you for being an asshole, but unfortunately they haven't passed that law yet."

He got into his car. "Stay out of trouble, Officer Vining."

He pulled a U-turn with a screech of tires and drove off.

The way he'd said her name stayed with her, like an ice cube melting in her belly.

THIRTEEN

Vining carried the box of her personal items with a box of Winchell's doughnuts on top into the Detectives Section.

The doughnuts immediately caught the attention of a detective who was passing by.

"Take it," she told him. "Breakfast of champions."

He slid off the Winchell's box and opened it. "Doughnuts for the cops. Isn't that a cliché?"

"I am a cliché."

He dove for a jelly-filled. "This is for you, Quick Draw. I know you won't eat one."

"You can have the indigestion they give me, too."

"That's more information than I need."

"Would you put them over by the coffeemaker, please? Thanks." She carried the other box to her cubicle. On her desk were several accordion folders all labeled with her name, the date of her assault, and a case number: her case files. There was also a three-ring binder, inches thick with paper, the spine similarly labeled. It was Kissick's personal file of salient details from her case. His take-home file.

She set the box on the desk, shoving everything over. Without touching the case files, she opened the box from home and set the mug that Emily had given her one Mother's Day on the desk. It was decorated with a photo of her and Emily and said "I love you, Mom." She set out framed snapshots of Emily as an infant and toddler, her current school portrait, and photographs of her sister and her family, her mother and grandmother. On the other corner went the pottery pencil holder and business card display that Emily had decorated in one of those paint-it-yourself shops.

Onto the carpeted wall she tacked artwork done by her nephews and an eerie photograph that Emily had taken of rows of gravestones at night in an old section of Evergreen Cemetery in East Los Angeles. A couple of the gravestones were tilted and some had fallen over. Vining thought the shot was first-rate. Each gravestone had a story. It reminded her of the importance of her work. Beside it, she hung a calendar with photos of kittens and puppies that her grandmother had given her for Christmas. It was sentimental, even for Granny, but it had been an emotional holiday season for the entire family. She took out an inexpensive, crystal bud vase and a yellow rose she'd clipped from bushes along the driveway of her house that persisted in blooming in spite of years of neglect. She gave the rose a drink from a bottle of water she'd brought from home.

She picked up the accordion files, set them inside the box, and put the box on the floor in the corner. The notebook was still on her desk. Kissick's personal file of her case. She grabbed the edge as if to open it. Didn't. She drummed her fingertips on its cover, then left her cubicle.

Kissick was in the conference room–turned–war room, surrounded by piles of documents relating to Lynde's case. Two whiteboards were covered with time and events schedules of the final months of Lynde's life sketched out in red and black marker. Another whiteboard listed the leads to be followed: Lincoln Continental limo, the money trail, aquamarine earrings, Lolita, strip club witnesses, Frank and Frankie arrests. On the table were copies of that morning's *Los Angeles Times* and *Pasadena Star News*, the pages turned to articles about the case.

"Morning." Kissick barely looked up from scribbling on a yellow pad.

"Hi. I brought doughnuts."

He patted his middle. "Afraid they're not on my diet for a while. Maybe never."

"Mine either." Vining sat in the chair she'd occupied most of the previous day. The pile of phone bills she'd been reviewing was still there.

"What a sport, buying treats for the others."

"A sport. That's me all over. Did you spend the night here?"

"Came in early. Couldn't sleep anyway."

"I know the feeling."

Vining looked up as Ruiz and Caspers filed into the conference room. Ruiz was holding a half-eaten glazed doughnut and Caspers had a patch of powdered sugar on his face. She didn't draw his attention to it.

Ruiz made a small noise when he sat.

"Good morning." Kissick grabbed a manila file folder crammed with papers. "Jones and Sproul logged fifty-seven telephone leads yesterday. Another thirty-one were e-mailed in and twelve were left on voice mail overnight."

"We're superstars," Caspers said.

"They didn't get hot over anything from the phone calls they took. Mostly crackpots who want to rub elbows with the big case. Let's hope there's a pony in there someplace." Kissick placed the file on the table in front of Ruiz. "I'd like you and Caspers to work the leads, rank them, follow up on the best ones, take note of trends. . . . You know what to do."

Ruiz looked at the folder as if Kissick had presented him with his dirty laundry. "Me and Caspers?"

"You and Caspers. Show him how it's done."

"Ohh-kay. Where are Jones and Sproul?"

"Already on the road. Working through Frankie's recent arrests. A couple of guys spent time in jail for rape and sexual assault. Jones used to work sex crimes. He knows how to play these jerks. Personally, my money's on someone on that list."

"I hope he's on one of our lists," Caspers said.

Kissick picked up another sheaf of papers. "Earthlink gave me access to Frankie's e-mail account. She last downloaded messages Thursday night, May nineteenth, the day before she was seen at the strip club. Earthlink doesn't store e-mails after they're downloaded, so those are gone unless we can locate her computer. The more than two weeks of messages we did get, from May twentieth on, are mostly spam and e-mails from her friends wondering where she is. Couple of jerks got her e-mail address. One of them sent a love note. 'Hope you got what you deserve, bitch.' "

It reminded Vining of the cheery get-well Hallmark card she'd been sent with the note "You should have died, bitch," scrawled inside. The b-word. They loved the b-word.

Kissick continued. "Last night Josh down in Community Services, my computer guy, tracked the e-mail address through the sender's ISP. It belongs to a guy Frankie arrested earlier this year for solicitation."

He handed a sheet of paper to Ruiz. "Add that to your list of leads to work."

From his breast pocket, Ruiz took out a pair of cheaters and set them on his nose before beginning to read. He looked up at the other three who had started snickering, their laughter growing louder at the sight of him full-face.

"Ruiz, it takes a real man to wear something like that," Caspers said.

The reading glasses were pink and speckled with multicolors.

"My wife got them at a two-for-one sale at the drugstore."

"Hey, can't beat a twofer," Vining said.

Irritated, Ruiz resumed reading the document, leaving the cheaters in place.

Trying not to smile too much, Kissick went on. "The

only other e-mail of interest was one sent from Lieutenant Kendall Moore on Friday, May twenty. He wrote: 'That was your decision. Don't try to hang that one on me.' No salutation. No sincerely or kiss my ass. Just the message."

"Hostile," Vining commented.

"What decision?" Caspers asked.

"Good question," Kissick said. "Clearly a response to a message from Frankie. His computer wasn't set to quote the original message."

"Could still be on his computer," Caspers said. "Did he send it from home or his office?"

Kissick said, "Can't tell. He used Hotmail, a Web-based service. Shows he didn't want it going through his LAPD e-mail."

Vining stayed in the background during this conversation. She had no love for computers and barely managed the basics.

"If Moore didn't delete her message at the time, I'm sure he got rid of it since," Ruiz said.

"I know Hotmail," Caspers said. "It automatically purges the trash file every few days. Depending on his computer setup, it could still be in his recycle bin. It's possible Frankie sent her e-mail to his LAPD or home address and he used Hotmail to respond. Maybe that's not a response to an e-mail from her. He sent it fresh."

"Try to get a search warrant for his computer?" Kissick suggested.

"Good luck," Ruiz said. "He admitted having a relationship with Frankie. That isn't enough for a search warrant."

"Could be enough," Kissick said. "Depending on the judge."

"That message proves their relationship got ugly at the end," said Vining. "Moore was never off my radar and I'll tell you why."

She described her encounter with Moore by the bridge.

She had barely finished when Ruiz cut in. "Because you happened to see him by the bridge, mourning his murdered girlfriend, he's a suspect."

Vining kept her composure. "I'm saying we haven't eliminated him as a suspect. At minimum, he has information he hasn't revealed."

"What about the cash and earrings Frankie hid in the wall?" Ruiz wagged his index finger as he talked. "What about Lolita locking up Frankie's condo with Frankie's keys? Where did he keep Frankie the sixteen days she was missing? Don't get me wrong. I think Moore's a jerk. I'm old-fashioned. I don't have any respect for a guy who cheats on his wife, especially with the daughter of a good friend of mine. I realize we've gotta keep an open mind, but Moore's not our guy. Think about it. He's a homicide cop. On LAPD's elite team. If he wanted to eliminate a troublesome girlfriend, wouldn't he know the best way to do it?"

"He does know the best way," Vining said. "A kills B and C gets blamed for it. Maybe he knew Frankie was into something rotten with Lolita and her partner and took advantage of it."

"To do it right, you don't leave a body." Ruiz was worked up, gesturing with his hands. "Frankie had already disappeared. She could have stayed disappeared. Why dump her on our doorstep in the same city where her dad works? But hey, you should know. You're the seasoned homicide detective. I've only been at the desk a year, even though I've got nineteen years on."

"We get the point, Ruiz," Kissick said.

He wouldn't back down. "You want to know what I think?"

Vining sat stone-faced. *Tell us what you really think, Ruiz.*

"I think Vining's after the guy because he embarrassed her in front of everyone."

Keep pulling out the rope, Ruiz.

The outburst caught Caspers off guard. He watched wide-eyed.

"Anthony, ease up." Kissick held out his hands as if to arrest the flow of venom.

"Am I right?" Ruiz asked.

"Nobody's right or wrong at this point," Kissick said. "We're throwing ideas against a wall and seeing what sticks. We've had a late night and an early morning and we're all feeling ragged."

Vining hadn't moved her eyes from Ruiz nor had her expression changed.

Caspers wasn't about to say a thing.

Detective Sergeant Early knocked on the doorjamb and stuck her head inside the room. "Morning, gang. Good news." One look at their faces and she stopped smiling. "What's going on?"

Kissick was tactful. "Just having a spirited exchange of ideas."

"I see. If you start throwing punches, I'm calling the cops. Hey, we're offering a ten-thousand-dollar reward for bona fide information that leads to an arrest."

The news broke the tension in the room.

"LAPD's kicking in bucks. We are, too, as is Frankie's family," Early said. "Hopefully it will flush out someone who knows something."

"Or encourage another million goofballs out there to call in," Ruiz said.

"That comes with the territory," Early said. "Kissick, can I talk to you for five minutes?"

Ruiz stood at the same time, picking up the file of leads. "C'mon, Caspers. Let's try to make chicken salad out of chicken shit."

Alone in the war room, Vining tried to shake off Ruiz's verbal assault. Bastard thought Kissick was favoring her in handing out assignments. She had been Kissick's partner for two years. It felt natural for him to work with her. Ruiz had never been one for subtlety, which was part of the reason he'd not advanced through the ranks as quickly as she had.

She again focused on the case and reread Moore's e-mail to Frankie. "That was your decision. Don't try to hang that one on me."

She riffled through Frankie's cell and landline phone bills and her bank statements. She arranged the documents on the table by month, picked up a yellow marker and started going through them again.

Her back was to the door as she annotated the whiteboard. Kissick startled her when, out of the corner of her eye, she saw him watching her. Her hand flew instinctively to her neck.

"Sorry. What are you working on?"

"I think Frankie had an abortion. It was Moore's baby. Could have been an accident on her part, but I'm leaning toward an act of desperation to force him into a decision. He convinced her to get rid of it. After she did, he dumped her. That's when her life went haywire. Something happened to make her start having sex for money. She could have got that money selling drugs, but I don't think so. She got into kinky sex games with high rollers and came across someone bad. It's possible this Lolita is dead, too. She could be a runaway teenager or a junkie streetwalker and no one's noticed she's missing yet."

He frowned, processing what she'd said.

She pointed to a column on the whiteboard. "I think she had the abortion the first week of April. Wednesday, April sixth, she withdrew six hundred dollars from her savings account, taking the balance down to fifty-one dollars. She also wrote a check to herself for cash for four hundred dollars. She needed a grand in cash for something.

"You can track her and Moore's relationship through her phone bills. She always called his cell phone, never his home or office number. Appears they first got together a year ago March. Her phone bills show these long, bonding, spilling your guts, getting to know you conversations with him. Some a couple of hours long, late at night, after her free cell phone minutes kicked in. After a month or so of that, they'd settled into a routine. Her calls lasted a minute or two, like she was leaving a message, or fifteen minutes to half an hour for chitchat. They talked maybe three or four times a week and sent an occasional text message.

"Then late March, early April this year, we return to hour-long phone conversations. Something's changed in their relationship. Lots of calls from her to him. Text

messages. He's not returning them. After April fourteenth, she gives it up. No telephone contact."

"She met somebody new."

"That's when we start seeing calls to her cell phone
made by someone using a calling card—someone who
didn't want to leave any traces. She also covered her
tracks to him. Maybe she didn't know how to contact
him or she didn't want anyone following the money trail,
which starts right away. She made her first thousand-
dollar-cash bank deposit on Monday, April eighteen."

On the whiteboard, Vining circled Thursday, April 14.
"Here, there's a flurry of text messages between Frankie
and Moore. She sent one at eleven-forty. He responded
at eleven forty-three. She shot back at twelve-twenty.
He responded at twelve thirty-seven. That's the last record of any communication between them until Moore's
e-mail on May twenty."

Vining chewed her lip as they looked at the timeline.
"Had to be some reason they didn't just call each other
on April fourteen. Maybe one of them was in a meeting.
Wonder what was so darn important?"

Kissick joined Vining in looking at the whiteboards.
"Could have been the day they broke up. As you said before, somebody always ends it."

She shot him a glance, her face dark. "That's what I
said. Guess I should know."

He seemed to regret the comment as he changed the
subject. "Personally, I can't deal with text messaging.
Typing on that tiny keypad. My sons live for it. They do
it when they're sitting next to each other."

Vining let the prickly moment pass. "Wish we had
Frankie's datebook." She walked to the conference room
door and called, "Hey, Caspers."

His head popped over the top of the cubicle. "Yo."

"Didn't you say that you saw Frankie at the service awards luncheon at the Huntington Hotel?"

"Yeah. She was there with her dad. He got an award for twenty-five years on the force."

"When was that?"

"Month or more ago. Sometime in April, I think."

Kissick was already on the phone in the conference room. He hung up. "Community Services says the banquet was on April fourteenth. Someone's bringing up the guest list. Frank Lynde said that was the last time he saw Frankie."

"Frankie had a text message fight with Moore, flirted with someone at the banquet and left with him."

Kissick arched dubiously an eyebrow. "Maybe she did flirt with somebody, but you can't mean that she met *the* guy and maybe Lolita, too, at an event that was rotten with cops."

"Why not? She met him or them somewhere. Her life took a turn around then."

He considered her comment. "The assholes who got Frankie could be cop groupies."

"It is a Pasadena connection."

"That's the part that doesn't gel for me. They didn't like the rubber chicken lunch, so they found a way to get back at the city?"

An officer from Community Services found them in the conference room. She handed Kissick the banquet guest list arranged by table and a layout of the room with a numbered grid of the table rounds. Table seating had been assigned to those receiving awards, their guests, and other luminaries. It was open seating for everyone else.

Kissick looked over the materials. "Here's Frank Lynde's table. Number five. Frankie likely sat beside him. I know all these people who were at their table. Find out if they remember anything. Wish we had more to go on than just a hunch. It's all yours."

He gave the materials to Vining and went to Ruiz's desk. "Tony, see what Frank Lynde remembers from this luncheon. Then talk up this buddy of Frankie's. Sharon Hernandez. If Frankie had an abortion, I find it hard to believe that she didn't talk about it with her best friend."

"I agree." Ruiz grabbed his jacket. "Schuyler didn't get the juice from her."

Unless it was too big and too bad a secret to tell. Vining picked up the banquet lists. *I know that place.*

"The autopsy's in an hour, right?" Vining asked.

"Why? You want to come?" Kissick was kidding, already knowing she did.

"If Frankie did have an abortion two months ago, wonder if the autopsy will detect it," Vining said.

Caspers was sticking out his tongue with disgust.

Kissick looked at him. "Alex, you've never been to an autopsy."

He cringed. "Nope."

Grinning, Kissick said to Vining, "Caspers is starting to think he's not cut out for Homicide."

Caspers exhaled noisily. "This is crazy-making, what you guys do. I'd rather take my chances on the street."

FOURTEEN

*O*n *the* drive to the county morgue, Vining and Kissick kept the conversation light, talking about small family dramas and current events. He didn't ask her if she was nervous about the autopsy. She'd attended several before her attack and it was tough getting through them, but she wasn't nervous about this one. Truth be told, she couldn't wait. They had little evidence. Frankie Lynde's body could hold the key to identifying her murderer.

Kissick did not bring up their truncated romance and she was grateful.

They arrived at the morgue to see Frankie's corpse on her back with her legs spread open. Medical Examiner Ron Takeda was sitting on a stool at the end of the table, examining her genitalia. X-rays of Lynde were hanging on a light box.

"Good morning, Detective Kissick and Detective Vining, is it?" Takeda raised his gloved right hand that held a swab. He was in his mid-fifties. He smiled and amiably raised his eyebrows, deepening the lines in his face. He looked like the pastor of a neighborhood church greeting his congregation.

"It's been awhile since we've seen each other, Detective

Kissick, but in our circumstances, that's a happy absence."

"Yes, it is, Doctor." Kissick looked over the body, not spending a second more than necessary.

Vining had acted tough about not being bothered by the autopsy, but she couldn't be certain she could handle it until she was actually there. Before the arroyo incident, she'd also thought she'd mastered her panic attacks.

Lynde's eyes were half-open, milky and unfocused as they had been on the hillside. Vining remained calm. What had happened the day before would not be repeated here. Lynde was somewhere, but this flesh was no longer her home.

The blood, dirt, and weeds that had covered Lynde had been washed off. The slash in her neck gaped open like a jack-o'-lantern's grin. It was a clean cut from ear to ear, without hesitation marks. The bruises on her face and torso were garish under the unforgiving lights.

Takeda handed the swabs he'd taken of Lynde's vagina to his young assistant, Jason, who took them to a microscope and began examining them.

"There are several vaginal tears." Takeda pulled a light closer and probed with gloved fingers. "First and second degree with bleeding. Bruising also."

Kissick didn't move to look, but Vining did. She stood behind Takeda and bent over his shoulder. He obliged by pointing out the damage.

"Brutal rape," she said.

"Could possibly involve the insertion of foreign objects. The anus shows evidence of trauma also." He rolled back the stool and stood. "We'll gather as much as we can for a rape kit."

Kissick hadn't moved from his spot three feet from the table. "What do you mean, as much as you can?"

"We have vaginal and anal swabs and blood and hair samples, but you may have noticed that Officer Lynde has no pubic hair."

Part of the rape protocol was combing the victim's pubic hair to search for possible transfer of the assailant's hair.

Vining frowned as she looked at Lynde's pelvis. "She came in that way?"

"Smooth as a baby's bottom. This wasn't a so-called bikini wax. This hair was shaved, not pulled out." Takeda drew his glove across Lynde's mons pubis.

"There's another situation that robbed us of potential evidence." Takeda picked up Lynde's hand. "Her fingernails are short and clean. We swabbed what we could from underneath and found nothing but soap residue."

"She knew about evidence," Kissick said. "You would think she would have wanted to be as filthy as possible whether she was found dead or alive."

Takeda added, "Everything points to a thorough scrubdown before her body was disposed of. The deputy coroner at the crime scene reported finding the hair on Lynde's head damp. Combing turned up weeds and dirt consistent with the hillside. Her hair felt sticky to me. I washed a sample under water and a bubbly substance came off."

"Cream rinse," Vining said.

Takeda pulled locks of Lynde's hair through his fingers. "Someone went to the trouble of combing it after washing it. It's tangled and full of weeds but it's not matted."

Kissick paced, too frustrated to remain still. "He brutalizes her for over two weeks, treats her like a piece of meat, then washes her hair and puts in cream rinse so it won't hurt when it's combed out. Doesn't jibe."

"Lolita?" Vining suggested. "He could have forced Frankie to do it, but if I were her I would have done a half-assed job, figuring he was trying to destroy evidence, so maybe she was already dead."

"What about semen?" When Kissick asked the question, all three turned toward Jason, who was peering into the microscope.

Takeda called him by name.

Jason looked up, surprised he was the object of attention. "We'll need a closer look, but I'm not finding semen. I do see a foreign substance. We'll have it analyzed, but if it's what I think it is, it's condom lubricant."

Kissick's clenched teeth made depressions in his cheeks.

Vining moved closer to Lynde's wrists, then to her ankles. "Impressions on her skin. Likely ligature marks. Not consistent with rope or twine. Perhaps handcuffs."

Takeda probed the slash wound in Lynde's neck, directing a lamp beam on it. "This cut was made by a good, sharp blade in an unhesitating hand. A straight edge at least six inches long. Whoever inflicted this injury was strong. The blade nicked her spinal cord."

He circled the table until he was behind Lynde's head and tipped her chin, revealing bruises beneath her jawbone.

"I suspect he held her from behind with his left hand like this. She struggled, thus the bruising. He inserted the knife here and pulled across to the right."

"Right-handed," Kissick said.

Takeda drew his hand across Lynde's hair, smoothing

strands of it from her face. He took his time, seeming to drift into private reflection.

After a while, he said, "That concludes my external examination."

He moved to the next task, his hand hovering over a tray of instruments before selecting a scalpel. "Jason, I'm ready." He began his Y incision.

The autopsy proceeded efficiently. Lynde's organs and arteries confirmed what seemed obvious from her appearance—she had been healthy and fit.

Takeda dissected the uterus, probing the interior with his gloved hand. "You suspected she had an abortion two months ago? I find no evidence of abortion."

"You can't tell whether she's been pregnant?" Kissick asked.

"I can determine that she's never given birth and hasn't been pregnant very recently. That doesn't rule out the possibility that she had an early-term abortion without complications at some point. Two months is ample time for the endometrium to return to normal."

Vining sighed. "Crap."

Takeda looked at her. "Evidence of abortion is important to your case?"

"Would have made the motives of some of the players clearer," she said.

"Sorry. Hopefully her stomach contents will hold secrets to help you." Using a ladle, Takeda spooned the contents into a plastic tub, examining as he slowly poured. It looked like thick, lumpy soup.

"She ate within three hours of her murder. Food usually moves through the stomach within three hours. She had a substantial meal, which would take longer to process. It's been fairly well digested by the stomach and was moving into the small intestine. I see small bits of meat, likely beef, and something green and leafy. I detect alcohol."

"Steak, salad, and a cabernet." Vining glowered. "Wonder if she was that well fed all along or if that was a special last meal."

"The X-ray showed a foreign body in her stomach."

"Meaning?" Kissick asked.

Takeda peered into the plastic tub as he moved the ladle through the stomach contents. Setting the tub down, he pulled open her stomach. He grabbed forceps.

"Jason, a small tray, please.

"Voilà." The object Takeda dropped onto the tray made a metallic clatter when it hit the steel. He tilted the tray for the others.

Kissick couldn't believe what he was seeing. "Is that a crown off a tooth?"

"That's what it appears to be, folks." Takeda held it up with the forceps. "A porcelain veneer crown off a molar." He dropped it back onto the tray. "It must have fallen off one of Officer Lynde's teeth and she swallowed it. Jason, would you please put up the shots of Miss Lynde's skull?"

Jason took a stack of X-rays from an envelope and shuffled through them. He pulled down films from clips on the light box, shoved in the new ones side by side and switched on the power.

"She has five fillings." Takeda pointed them out. "No crowns. Nothing's missing."

He returned to the autopsy table and jammed his index finger inside Lynde's slightly open mouth. "There are no jagged teeth, nothing suggesting a missing crown."

"Dr. Takeda, a crown must be very individual," Vining said.

"I'm not a forensic dentist, and I will call one in, but I would say it's about as unique as a fingerprint. It's cast to fit the structure of both the tooth it sits on and that of the opposing tooth. It's something that can be individualized to the exclusion of all others."

Kissick was incredulous. "How can you get a crown out of somebody else's mouth?"

"A possible scenario," Takeda began. "It came loose from the tooth of the person who owned it, who set it aside. Miss Lynde picked it up and swallowed it. It's small enough, it's likely it would have passed through her G.I. system. Since it's not broken down by the stomach acids, hard to pinpoint exactly when she ingested it."

"She was alive when she was scrubbed down," Vining said. "He knew it would be a signal that her time was nearly up. He may have forced her to do it herself to torture her, to tell her they'll never link your murder to me. She complied because she had a card up her sleeve."

Vining smiled as she walked to the body. She put her hand on Lynde's hair and spoke to her, ignoring the gore of her mutilated body. "You clever girl."

FIFTEEN

B ack at her desk, Vining reviewed the attendees of the thirty-fourth annual Police-Citizens Awards Luncheon. The event had not been open to the public. Formal printed invitations were sent out by Community Services.

There were over two hundred guests, but more than half were PPD officers and employees. Another dozen or so were city officials. There were three judges from the local superior court and a couple of deputy district attorneys from the Pasadena office. Nine PPD officers and employees received awards for length of service. Twenty-one officers, volunteers, and others associated with the PPD received awards for dedication to duty. A PPD officer and a sheriff's deputy were awarded the Silver Medal of Courage for rescuing a man from a burning house. Seven citizens were honored for heroism. Many of the award recipients brought spouses, parents, and children.

A local news personality served as mistress of ceremonies. A three-piece jazz combo provided entertainment. There was a photographer. A writer from the local newspaper covered the event. PPD's chief was there as was the deputy chief and four commanders.

The remaining attendees were generally citizens with ties to the community—local business owners, graduates of the PPD's Citizen's Police Academy, doctors, lawyers, and Indian chiefs—people from all walks of life who had an interest in supporting the police and hobnobbing with real-life heroes. The event was held at the Ritz Carlton in Pasadena, a stately space that the locals still called the Huntington Hotel.

Vining blinked at the long list of names. There would be hotel employees to check out as well. This was going to take lots of hours and would likely lead nowhere. Such was much of the work they did—following dead ends. And it had been her idea. She had to follow through.

She started making marks beside names to check out. She skipped employees of the PPD, city officials, and others whom she knew. She excluded the women. Even though Frankie appeared to be partying with Lolita, Vining sensed a man pulling the strings. Frankie went for attractive, dangerous men, like Moore, enjoying the threat of a lit fuse burning closer. Lolita in the picture at the strip club was part of his game, not Frankie's.

She heard Caspers on the phone in the adjoining cubicle, trying to make sense out of the leads, questioning the people who had called in, pressing for specifics, probing their motives. He was doing his best with a job as thankless as hers.

She pared the list down to forty-seven men. Each would have to be run through the criminal databases that would report warrants, wants, felony arrests, and certain misdemeanors. She didn't have birth dates, but it was likely safe to exclude anyone without a local address. NCIC would bring up phonetic matches with the names entered. This was an advantage as there was no telling if the names on her list were accurate or complete. The names also needed to be run through the DMV.

She wasn't in a position to be a diva, but someone else could do this job. She wanted to get to the bottom of what went on between Moore and Frankie. He was hiding something. If it was important enough for him to hide it, it was worth her time trying to uncover it.

She thought of a way to shortcut the luncheon angle. She called the manager at the Pasadena Ritz Carlton who told her they kept security tapes for a month before copying over them. He would check. It was possible somebody screwed up and didn't properly rotate the tapes. He'd also obtain a list of employees who worked the luncheon.

She said she'd be right down. She took her purse from her desk drawer and picked up her list of forty-seven luncheon guests to investigate. From the war room, she took a copy of Frankie's missing person poster and the artist drawing of Lolita as seen at the strip club. She went to Sergeant Early's office and rapped on the doorjamb.

Early waved her inside.

Seated at his desk, Sergeant Cho muttered, "How are ya, Vining? First one here this morning. Last one out. Sorry now you didn't stick with me?"

"Cho, stop harassing my investigators," Early said.

Sergeant Taylor piped up from his desk. "His mother didn't breast-feed him. Ruined him for life."

"Leave my mother outta this."

Early called Vining over. "I got a call from a woman over on San Rafael. Her house overlooks the bridge. Says she's got something on her security camera the night Frankie's body was dumped."

"Okay, I'll go there before I head to the Huntington Hotel. Kissick fill you in about the luncheon?"

"Yeah." Early did not sound enthusiastic. "Hope the reward brings in better information. We could use it."

Vining could see the strain taking its toll on her. Frankie's body had been found thirty-six hours ago. The clock was quickly ticking toward the forty-eight-hour mark. If they had no solid persons of interest by then, cases went cold fast.

"Take Caspers and go over there."

"Caspers? Sarge, all due respect, but I think I can handle talking to some trophy wife in San Rafael and the Huntington Hotel's manager on my own. Caspers is busy following up leads. If I may suggest, it's a better use of manpower."

Cho was amused by her backpedaling.

"Okay. Fine." Early took a two-way radio from a charger and handed it to Vining. "We were giving you a car today."

"I'll get it tomorrow. I'll take my own car."

"We'll do it right now."

"Really. It's fine. I'll get it tomorrow."

"You just want to get the hell out of here."

"I haven't been outside all day. I'm getting cabin fever."

"Go. Don't forget to let us know where you are."

"Sure. Sarge, by the way, is there someone who can run the names of these luncheon guests?"

"But of course. Sergeant Cho, you have anyone I can use?"

"Unfunny, Early."

On her way out, Vining swung by her desk and picked up the notebook labeled with her name.

It was midafternoon and hot. The sky was blue-white, blanched by the heat. It was still good to see it.

Vining again headed for the bridge, crossed it, and turned left on San Rafael Avenue. It was a neighborhood of large, architecturally significant homes at the end of long drives sequestered behind security gates. The hilly streets meandered. The landscaping was lush. It was a neighborhood where it looked as if nothing bad could happen. Vining knew there was some truth to that. Other than the occasional car or home burglary, goings-on here rarely attracted the attention of the police. Family dramas, however, were played out even in the best homes.

Vining wasn't thrilled about interacting with the San Rafael wife. Her prejudice was firmly in place. She saw the neighborhood as twisted traditional. Soon, the men would be home from the office for cocktails with their wives, who would lament about having too few hours in the day.

The twist, in Vining's view, was that these women never did anything resembling real work. They spent their days exercising at the gym, shopping, gossiping, planning vacations at high-end resorts, and consuming the services of exotic personal care professionals: aestheticians, herbalists, acupuncturists, and Pilates instructors. They arrived home to say good-bye to the nannies who watched their kids and housekeepers who kept their homes shipshape. It was a perversion of women's lib. These women were free to self-indulge.

She knew about their lives. She eavesdropped on them at Starbucks, the town square of the new millennium, while they stood in line with yoga mats slung over their shoulders, splurging on shared crumble cake and chatting about the events of their lives with the gravity of a U.N. Security Council meeting.

Sure, she had a well-developed attitude. She blamed her ex-husband Wes's wife of seven years for it. It had taken Kaitlyn just over twenty-four months to evolve from stylist at Supercuts, where she'd started her affair with still-married Wes, to über–soccer mom. Kaitlyn's upbringing had been as blue-collar as Vining's, but she now affected that snobbery unique to those whose lives had transcended from hardscrabble to highbrow by the power vested in a wedding ring.

Vining had struggled most of her life to get by. The exception was the two years after Emily was born. Then

Wes's business was finally doing well and Vining had experienced what it was like not to go to an outside job every day. Not to struggle to make ends meet. Not to fret about how she should have paid the telephone bill instead of having dinner out. She had been taken care of and it had been nice.

Vining refused to put her daughter through the childhood she had endured. She and her younger sister, Stephanie, had never known their fathers, who had both left when they were toddlers. All their mother would say about her first two husbands was that they were bums and it was good that they weren't in their lives. After school, the two girls would hang out at their grandmother's home beauty salon while their mother was at work or on a date. Patsy married twice more. By the time husband number four, Mr. Brightly, had come around, Vining was married herself to her high school sweetheart, right after graduation. It was her ticket out of Dodge. A year later, she was pregnant and never happier.

She and Wes decided she would quit her job in the billing office of a dermatology group and stay home with Emily. Vining worked part-time managing Wes's property development business. Through Wes's hard work, he had become an in-demand general contractor and was initiating his own projects. He'd done well on the fixeruppers he'd turned around and was building houses on spec. They'd just bought their first house, an early-sixties tract home suspended from a cliff on cantilevers, in the then-unfashionable L.A. neighborhood of Mt. Washington. Wes was rehabbing it himself on weekends. Vining considered getting her real estate license and capitalizing on the rebound of the California real estate market. They were living the American dream.

Vining loved those first years after Emily was born. She was finally in control of her life. She had a family and a good man who loved her. Wes was so easygoing. They never fought. Their lives were free of the relentless tension and energetic arguments that characterized her mother's marriages. Life was great for the first time in Vining's memory, until the day shortly after Emily turned two. Wes had come home and said he didn't want to be married anymore. He piled clothes into his pickup truck and left.

Vining found a job as a civilian jailer at the PPD. Emily stayed with her mother or grandmother while Vining eked out a living. Wes paid child support, but Vining still struggled to make ends meet. She applied for a better-paying job as a police officer and surprised herself by making it through the Academy. Five years after Wes walked out on Vining, they finally divorced and he married Kaitlyn, eight years his junior. They bought a five-thousand-square-foot house in a spanking new development thirty miles away in the quiet and safe city of Calabasas, snuggled among the rugged hills east of Malibu. There, Kaitlyn was a stay-at-home mom with her two boys: Kyle, five, and Kelsey, three.

Kaitlyn had not been shy about expressing her opinion that Vining's career was a negative influence on Emily. Five years ago, when Vining shot and killed a man while on duty, Wes began a fight for full custody of Emily. Emily was nine then and pitched a fit that had no effect on her father. Vining met with Wes privately.

"If you care as much about Emily as you say you do, you wouldn't have abandoned her in the first place. I know Kaitlyn is putting you up to this. Understand one thing. Don't even think about taking my daughter. I will make your life a living hell. And you know I know how to do it."

Wes dropped the issue. As for Emily, she never forgave Kaitlyn. She extracted revenge by jerking Kaitlyn's chain. Vining had to swear to Wes that she didn't put their daughter up to it. On a girly shopping trip, Emily regaled Kaitlyn with tales about mother-daughter time at the gun range putting the family arsenal through a workout. Emily's gun tale had a happy consequence for Vining. Kaitlyn stopped allowing Wes to bring their children into Vining's home, in spite of Vining's assurances that she secured her weapons at all times.

Vining was glad she didn't have to put up with her ex's spawn, although it seemed appropriate for Emily to have a relationship with her half-siblings. Still, at this stage of her life, Emily couldn't care less about her half brothers and Vining knew she couldn't force-feed relationships to her daughter.

Kaitlyn wasn't the only reason Vining had developed an aversion to that type of woman. During her police career, Vining learned that the moneyed of the city, regardless of age, and especially the women, were often as ruthless as gangbangers in laying on attitude.

Pasadena had attracted the wealthy for generations. At the turn of the century, titans of industry built winter homes there and eventually relocated permanently, the balmy climate overwhelming all objections. Lesser neighborhoods sprouted like moons around the vast estates.

Many PPD officers who had arrested or written a traffic citation to one of the city's affluent had heard, "I pay your salary. You work for me. I know your boss. I'll have your job." When Vining was a rookie, the tales of class distinction surprised her. It seemed something old-world and un-American. Before she'd personally experienced it, she'd thought of herself first and foremost as a cop, a member of the thin line that divides civilization from anarchy. Until she'd busted a judge's son, she'd never thought of herself as a civil servant, a mere city employee.

She'd watched the teenager, wearing his private school uniform, give money to a guy outside a motel on the east side of town that was a known drug trade site. Minutes later, someone threw an eight ball of crack down to the kid from a second-story window. When Vining collared the boy, he went off on her. Something inside her snapped and she yanked and shoved him more than necessary while he threatened lawsuits and demanded to know if she knew who his father was.

"Yeah, he's the father of a criminal," she'd shot back.

Vining had to admit she'd developed attitudes of her own during her years on the Job. She was embarrassed to lay claim to some of them. She'd always wondered if she hadn't mouthed off to that man she'd shot, whether things might have turned out differently. She resisted being a jaded cop, but feared she was on a one-way street and powerless to turn around. The Job got under one's skin that way, like a slow-moving virus. T. B. Mann had hastened the journey.

She found the address on San Rafael Avenue. It wasn't far from Frankie Lynde's dump site. None of the investigators considered there might be a suspect among the affluent residents. Perhaps that reflected prejudice as well, but the police would say it was a judgment call. Outsiders called it profiling. In the grand scheme of things, it was unfair but practical.

The sun had dropped behind the hills along the arroyo's west side, casting everything in a violet haze. Drivers traveling westbound on the 210 freeway, which ran north of the bridge and swooped around the foothills, had a tremendous view of the sunset and the silhouette of downtown L.A. At dusk or in the early-morning hours, if the smog wasn't heavy, the way the light hit downtown L.A. miniaturized the buildings, putting Vining in mind of storybook cities in the books she'd read to Em, like the view Peter Pan and Wendy had when they'd soared above London. Or some of the old Fantasyland rides in Disneyland.

L.A. was some Fantasyland, all right.

She turned into the driveway and stopped at imposing iron gates shaded by a pair of olive trees. All she could see beyond the gates were poplar trees lining a curved cobblestone lane. An engraved brass plaque on the stone gate post said "Casa Feliz" with "Hughes" beneath it. There was a security camera above the gate keypad. The camera's red light told Vining she was being recorded.

She looked at the camera's make and model. She wanted such a motion-activated device for her home. After the attack, Wes had used his connections and helped Vining buy and install a security system, but cameras were the next step. Vining had not slept with a weapon in her bedroom until T. B. Mann. She knew lots of cops who did, but she had refused to live in paranoia. *Before.*

Emily had asked if T. B. Mann would come to their home. Given Vining's increased interest in home security, it would have been disingenuous to rule it out. Vining told her daughter a half-truth. T. B. Mann's return was a possibility. There was no need to be afraid, but it was smart to be prepared, just as they had set in supplies for the big earthquake that might or might not occur in their lifetimes. Emily had seemed satisfied with that answer.

But Vining knew she would meet T. B. Mann again. It was her destiny.

Vining called out her location on the portable. As she signed off, the gate rolled open. She heard the approach of a car, the sonorous rumble of an older model, and saw a red streak between the spaces in a stand of bamboo planted for privacy along the iron fence. With a screech of tires, a sports car, low to the ground and fire engine red, rounded a curve in the driveway and sped into view. The convertible top was down and the driver, wearing huge Jackie O sunglasses, the tails of the long scarf tied over her head flapping in the wind, looked as if she had no intention of stopping at the now-open gate.

Vining froze, wondering if the woman was going to ram her Jeep head-on.

The woman awakened from her driving-daze and slammed on the brakes, sending the car fishtailing and skidding sideways, coming to a stop inches from Vining.

The sports car's door dropped open and the woman extracted herself from the small vehicle, shooting out long legs clad in tight jeans and expensive boots with dangerously high heels. She stomped over to Vining, tearing off her sunglasses with one hand and planting the other on her hip. Her ring finger was weighted with a huge diamond wedding set. She looked to be around forty.

"Jesus, Mary, and Joseph. What the hell are you doing there?"

Vining fumbled to find her shield that was hanging from a chain around her neck. Her rattled state was due to the accident that had nearly happened, but the woman's ice blue eyes and gimlet stare weren't helping.

She regained her composure, got out of the car, and fired back her own take-no-B.S. gaze. "I'm Detective Nan Vining with the Pasadena Police Department."

"Oh, oh, oh . . ." Each exclamation ascended the tonal scale. The woman gaped as she crept forward for a closer look at the shield. "So you are. I've been waiting an hour. Have to leave. Cocktails on the west side. Traffic. Last thing I want to do, but . . . I didn't even think about checking it out until I turned on the news. I went out to get it and there it was."

She couldn't follow the woman's elliptical story. "There what was?"

Vining's cell phone rang. The display said it was Sergeant Early. The fact she was using her cell phone said she was avoiding the police dispatch frequency that was often monitored by reporters and cop geeks.

"Hi, Sarge. I'm talking to her. Thanks." Vining ended the call and looked again at the brass plate that was engraved "Hughes." "Are you Iris Thorne?"

"Yes, I am. My poor husband . . . I try, but I can't get the hang of a new name. I had the old one for so long. So I'm sticking with Thorne. Just call me Iris."

"You have a video—"

"That's what I was trying to tell you." Thorne grimaced as she looked at a big wristwatch. She swatted the air. "Jam cocktails. Come up to the house."

Before Vining could protest, Thorne put on her sunglasses and climbed back into the sports car. She gunned the engine, sending a puff of exhaust out the tailpipe, and headed up the lane.

Vining caught the TR6 decal with the British flag affixed to the rear fender.

SIXTEEN

Thorne drove fast and Vining kept pace. The sight of her scarf tails flapping and the older car speeding past formal landscaping of trimmed boxwood, white roses, and citrus trees made Vining feel as if she were in another country. She had never traveled, but Italy, Spain, or maybe Greece seemed about right.

Around a bend, a house came into view. A manse was more accurate.

Thorne rounded a tiered fountain framed by a hedge in the center of a circular driveway, scattering several cats lounging on the warm cobblestones.

She cut the engine. Again, the car door dropped open and out flew the legs. From a tiny purse, she fished out a cell phone. With an annoyed jerk of her hand, she freed the earpiece from the purse, disgorging tubes of lipstick that went clattering across the stones.

"Son of a bitch."

Vining parked and got out, picking up an errant lipstick tube. She noted the interlocked Cs on the label. Chanel, pricier than anything Vining could afford.

She handed it back. "Ma'am, I'll take the video—"

Thorne mouthed "Thank you" as she put on the earpiece and began pressing speed-dial numbers on the face of the cell phone. "It's a DVD. I'll play it for you. Come in." She jogged up worn marble steps to the massive front door.

The house was impressive. Surrounding the front door and extending to the second story was an elaborate façade of gray stone that seemed lifted from a medieval church. The plaster walls were terra-cotta red, shades lighter than the tiled roof. Mullioned windows lined the lower and upper floors. An incongruous touch diluted the formality. In the flower beds on either side of the porch were dozens of plastic pink flamingos.

Vining took a step toward the house then remained in the driveway. There was no need for her to go farther.

"Gar, sweetheart, I don't think I can get there before Wink has to leave," Thorne said into the cell phone as she opened the door. A prealarm sounded. She disappeared inside, the alarm quieted, and she reappeared to stand on the threshold, looking at Vining.

"A police detective is here. You know the homicide victim they found by the bridge yesterday? Our security camera off the back wall picked something up. Wild, huh? With traffic, I'll just be showing up when Wink has to leave for the airport." She waved for Vining to come up before again going inside, heels clacking against the marble floor.

Vining looked at the stairs and the darkness beyond the open front door. She didn't move. She found this pushy woman tiresome. She had to go to the Huntington Hotel yet. Who knows how long that would take? Emily was waiting at home. And Vining was feeling drained.

Go inside the house.

Her conscience was pitiless.

She wasn't doing it. Especially an older home like this. It looked heavy with memories. Hidden behind gates on a hilltop, anything could have happened. Just thinking of it made her palms perspire.

This is your job. Do it.

She'd demand the DVD and leave. She could avoid it this time, but the day would come when she would have to enter a house that felt wrong. On that day, she might not have the luxury of no other PPD officers around to witness her meltdown.

She heard the click, click of high heels returning. Thorne stood on the threshold, holding the cell phone by her side and talking into a twig of a microphone that extended from the earpiece. Her free hand was again on her hip. She'd taken off the scarf. Straight blond hair fell to her shoulders.

"Oh, hell. Wink won't care. He never liked me anyway."

She looked at Vining as she spoke, her eyes asking what was going on.

"He called me a trophy wife to my face."

Vining flushed, recalling her use of the same epithet.

"Nobody puts Baby in a corner. Garland, I've told you what that means a million times. It's from *Dirty Dancing*. Forget it. I'll see you later. Give Wink a big kiss for me. Love you." She chuckled before snapping closed the clamshell phone.

"Detective, your timing is perfect. You saved me from having to see this business associate of my husband's. A Neanderthal in Armani. Going to the Westside after two o'clock on a weekday? Puh-leese. Won't you come in? Don't you want to see the recording?"

"I'd rather you bring it out. I don't have much time. We'll need to watch it at the station anyway."

She gave Vining a puckish look. "Are you afraid of me?"

"Of course not."

"I mean, you're the one with the gun." Thorne entered the house while saying, "Suit yourself."

Vining felt foolish. She climbed the steps, counting each one, attempting to distract herself. There were six. Six marble stairs with hollows worn into them from the innumerable footsteps of people, each with their own story that had unfolded inside that house. She stepped over the threshold and entered the foyer where Thorne was standing beneath an alabaster and brass chandelier. Staircases with wrought-iron banisters circled to the right and left. Suddenly, the foyer began to expand and telescope, making Vining's stomach churn. She blinked to shake the illusion, only to dizzily see Thorne looking at her scar. Damn the blasted thing. Maybe she would invest in that heavy-duty makeup they used in mortuaries after all.

Thorne shifted her gaze, embarrassed at being caught. "Are you all right? Would you like a glass of water or something?"

Vining started when a cat darted across the hallway. She felt nauseous.

The hell with it. If I faint, I faint.

"Thank you. I would."

"This way."

They circled a marble-topped table that held a crystal vase of white gladiolas. Arched doorways opened onto rooms carpeted with Oriental rugs but scant furnishings.

Vining's breathing grew labored. She wanted to turn back, but kept on. She couldn't give in. She had been pumped-up arrogance the week before her return. Simply seeing a corpse and entering a strange house had cut her down to size. Her career was dust. She'd get it over with and tomorrow would ask for a transfer to a desk job in Community Services.

The soul of this house cannot harm you.

Her conscience was trying to set her straight. She tried to pay attention.

Thorne walked surprisingly fast on stiletto heels. She flicked her hand toward a room that contained only a shabby recliner, an end table overflowing with reading material, and a floor lamp in front of a fireplace with a massive stone surround.

"We haven't furnished most of the rooms yet. I'd like to tell you we've just moved in, but it's been over a year. I should hire a decorator, but the first thing they all want to do is junk my pink flamingos. Too trashy for the grand manse, you know."

Vining slumped onto a parlor bench. "Ms. Thorne . . ."

"Iris, please. Whoa . . . Should I call somebody?"

Vining drew fingers across the perspiration on her forehead. "No. Just . . . " she panted. "If you wouldn't mind, would you please bring me the DVD outside?"

She stood, steadying herself against the bench and then began walking, working on placing one foot in front of the other. She felt Thorne's eyes on her back and was relieved when she heard her footsteps receding. She reached the front door and pulled it open. The air was warm and smoggy but it felt like a balm. Dropping to sit on the top step, she rested her head in her hands and gasped.

She shook her head, recognizing the ridiculousness of her situation. How she had thought she could beat this thing by lifting weights and going into strangers' homes.

She saw now that she had tried to stop a hemorrhage with a Band-Aid.

She straightened when she heard Thorne come onto the porch.

Thorne sat beside her. She carried a DVD in a plastic box, a portable player, and a bottle of water. "How are you?"

"Fine. I'm fine. Thank you." Vining opened the water and guzzled it. She twisted the cap back on and slowly inhaled and exhaled. Her physical symptoms faded, but she felt defeated.

"Iris, I apologize. I'm overly tired. It's my second day back at work after a long leave."

"You're the officer in the El Alisal Road—"

"Yes."

Thorne opened her mouth as if to say more, but did not. She turned her attention to the DVD, pressing the top of the player. The screen popped open. She slid in the disk.

Vining was grateful for the unasked questions.

"I had a guy from the security company out. I couldn't figure out their software. He copied the section I wanted onto DVD."

The small screen filled with an image in that extreme black and white created by night-vision cameras. A digital clock on the recording reported the time as 3:12 a.m. and kept a running count of the seconds. The view was from up high looking down onto scrub brush and trees. Something was moving in the brush. After a few seconds, a coyote came into view, sniffing the ground.

Thorne said, "The camera's on the back wall. The coyote triggered the motion detector. We installed cameras around the perimeter of the property after a couple of people camped out in our backyard one weekend while we were gone. They used the pool and the barbecue. Hey, I would have, too. We've got barbed wire on top of the wall now. But look what's going on in the background."

Tiny in the distance was the western edge of the Colorado Street Bridge, the globe lights lining it glowing. Barely visible was an SUV parked on the packed dirt off the end of the bridge. A person was standing at the edge. Something large flew out and dropped over the slope. A second person of smaller stature who had been hidden by the first started running. They appeared to be a man and a woman. She ran away from the bridge and the street, past the car, and started heading down into the brush and trees. The man chased and tackled her. They disappeared over the slope only to reappear a minute later as he dragged her up onto the asphalt. She shook him off and ran toward the car. The recording ended.

"The coyote went back into the brush," Thorne said. "So the camera shut off."

Vining blinked at the dark screen, her mouth gaping.

"It's the people who threw that policewoman into the arroyo. Don't you think?"

"Could be," Vining said.

"Too bad it's so far away. Maybe you could have it enhanced."

"Let's hope so."

Thorne removed the DVD and returned it to the case. "I hate coyotes. One of my cats disappeared and I'm sure a coyote got it, but this mangy beast here is my hero."

"No kidding."

"I wonder why they picked that spot to dump a body. They're almost underneath a streetlight. It was after three in the morning, but someone could have come by. They took a huge risk to do that."

Vining agreed. She climbed to her feet, using the railing for assistance. She felt as haggard as she was sure she looked. She brushed off the back of her slacks and held out her hand for the DVD.

"Thank you, Iris."

Thorne stood as well. "You're welcome."

Vining remembered to fish a card from her jacket pocket. "I'll find this camera around the back?"

"Yes. There are two cameras, one on each corner. The one responsible for this is on the left as you face the arroyo. I can show you the backyard."

Thorne turned and again started up the marble staircase.

Vining spotted a side yard lined with stepping-stones and creeping rosemary. "Can we go through here?"

"Sure."

After passing through the side yard, they entered a pergola-covered patio set up for outdoor cooking and dining. The property was deep and terraced down the hillside. Steps took them to another level and a large pool. The bottom was painted off-black, making the water look like a pond. Pricey outdoor furniture and desert-hued, drought-resistant landscaping surrounded it. Vining felt as if she was at a luxury resort. She'd been with the PPD for twelve years and this was the first time she'd been inside one of these homes.

Surrounding the property was a six-foot-high wall of cement painted with a straw-hued wash that complemented the house. A spiral of concertina wire was on top.

"It's that camera on the corner. Here . . ."

Thorne began dragging a teak bench and Vining helped. They both stood on it to see over the wall. On the other side, the hillside dropped steeply. The brush had been cleared fifty feet from the wall as a baffle to protect the house in case of fire. Looking right and left, Vining observed that not all of Thorne's neighbors were as conscientious. There was an unobstructed view of the bridge. Vining looked back at Thorne's house and saw that windows and terraces were well-positioned to take in the view.

She replayed in her mind the couple throwing Frankie's body down the slope. There were many remote, isolated areas not far from here, but they had chosen that place. It was not random. She climbed off the bench.

Thorne yelped and windmilled her arms when she stepped wrong and one of her high heels hit an opening in the bench slats.

Vining steadied her as she made her way to the ground. They moved the bench back in place and returned to the driveway.

Vining took the hand that Thorne offered.

"Thank you very much. I'll call you if we need anything else."

"My pleasure." Thorne looked at her watch. "I have newly found time. I can go back to my office and catch up. Hooray. Thank you, Detective." She ran back inside the house.

Vining got in her car. She was elated by the confirmation that Lolita had been working with someone. Lolita was alive. At least she had been early Monday morning.

She called Kissick on his cell phone. He and Ruiz had met with Frank Lynde, who recalled a couple of details about the luncheon. Ruiz could seek out Sharon Hernandez alone. Kissick wanted to see the DVD right away. He would meet her by the bridge.

Vining ended the call and the afterglow of her win sputtered out. She grabbed the steering wheel with both hands.

"What's wrong with me?"

Her voice was low and guttural, like a growl.

"What's happening? Why can't I fix it? Damn it, damn it, damn it. Damn him! Damn him for screwing up my life."

She pounded the steering wheel.

"I'm not gonna let you do it, you bastard. I'm not giving you power over me like this."

She covered her face with her hands. T. B. Mann already had the power. He'd taken her life and tossed it. She felt powerless to fix it. Powerless. Until last year, she'd never thought that word would apply to her. Who was she kidding? She couldn't do her job.

She abruptly sat up, realizing Thorne had come out of the house and was locking the door. Too late, as the other woman had seen Vining's meltdown.

Thorne came over, reached through the open car window, and rested her hand on Vining's shoulder.

Vining smiled thinly. "Personal problems, you know?"

"Sure. I know. You won't always feel this way. You'll be all right."

Vining nodded. "Thanks." She started her car engine.

"And in case you're worried, this won't go any further. It stays here."

Vining believed that Thorne would keep her word, but was not certain she'd ever be all right.

SEVENTEEN

Vining returned to the flat outcropping off the west edge of the bridge above where Frankie's body had been found. It was the fourth time she'd stood on that patch of packed dirt and dried brush within the past thirty-six hours, but this time the space seemed to tremor with the vibrations of Lolita and her partner. The images on Thorne's DVD played repeatedly in Vining's mind. She had imagined such a scene, but actually witnessing what happened made it come alive.

Most of the crime scene tape that had encircled the area was gone. It was probably decorating some teenager's bedroom now. Vining retraced Lolita's and her partner's movements, narrating the action that night as she embellished what she'd seen on the DVD.

"He came over the curb. His headlights were off. The streetlight and moon were enough to show him where the cliff began. He got out and opened the trunk. Made her get out. He said, 'Grab her legs.' You did what he wanted, Lolita. You helped him hoist Frankie, swinging her to get her rolling downhill. You couldn't bear it. You tried to run, but he wouldn't let you. How do you live with it, Lolita? How do you face each day, knowing what you did?"

They had searched this area before. It was a good ten

yards from where the couple had rolled Frankie's body, but the PPD team had cast a wide net. Vining needed to see the DVD again to be sure, but she thought Lolita had headed for a clump of low trees, maybe thinking she could hide inside them. Probably not thinking at all. Just running.

Vining headed toward the trees. The earth was bone dry, but softer here. The thick bushes, trees, and fallen leaves sheltered the ground from the relentless sun. The grasses weren't forced to cling as tightly. It was more gently sloping and easier to traverse. Lolita was trying to escape, not kill herself by plunging headlong into the arroyo.

A small animal rustled through the undergrowth. Vining was mindful of snakes. Birds hidden by the tree branches sang.

Vining saw evidence of a struggle in the beam of her flashlight. Twigs on a bush were broken. Weeds were mashed and churned. The branch of a tree had been partially torn free, the wound fresh. Beneath the thatch of trees was a cache of empty beer cans. Bud Light. Crushed and tossed. The canopy of leaves insulated an aroma of dried sage, stale beer, and urine. The beer drinkers had likely sat with their case at the top of the slope, enjoying the view, and tossed their empties beneath the trees. It was a good spot as the trees would provide quick shelter should the cops cruise by.

This was where he had grabbed Lolita and dragged her back to the street. Fibers from their clothing had possibly become caught in the bushes and trees. She called Forensic Services. Tara Khorsandi said she'd head out right away.

Vining turned to head back and in doing so, saw a different view of the ground beneath the trees. She squinted and leaned forward. Her heart skipped a beat. She crept in to make sure her eyes weren't playing tricks on her. There was a footprint in the dirt. It was a good, clear print, the sole markings consistent with an athletic shoe. It was small enough to have been made by a woman. The earth was dry but it looked as if it was likely moist when stepped on as the markings were well-defined. The beer drinkers had either spilled their brew or filtered it out through their kidneys. Someone had stepped in it.

She heard a vehicle approach and park. Car doors slammed. She stepped from beneath the trees and saw Tara Khorsandi and another field I.D. tech looking around for her.

Kissick pulled up behind them.

When Khorsandi approached, she said, "You look happy."

"This is a good day."

Vining recalled something her mentor Bill Gavigan always said: Count your wins.

She gave Kissick the DVD, telling him, "This will give you chills."

"Be great if we can see faces."

"I don't know what magic they can do these days, but it is from a distance and was taken by a security camera."

"I'm taking it to Sami. He's done work for us before. Says he can lighten it, sharpen it. All that. He's waiting for me. Where are you headed?"

"Huntington Hotel. Meeting with the manager about that luncheon. How was Frank Lynde? Have anything to add?"

Kissick's expression darkened. "He's suffering. A lot of regrets."

"That's tough."

"He doesn't know whether Frankie was dating someone. Didn't know much about her personal life. They weren't close. He blames himself for that. He withdrew after her mom's murder. When he remarried, he focused on his new wife and her kids. Frankie was a difficult child. Not easy to love."

Vining made a face. She had no tolerance for people who made excuses for not parenting their kids. She'd heard every excuse from the lips of her mother.

Kissick expressed her view. "That doesn't make his behavior okay. I've got kids of my own. But Frank was proud when Frankie joined the LAPD. Felt as if he'd had a small positive influence on her. She started coming around more. They had the Job in common. Now he feels bad that she got into police work. Thinks she wasn't mentally strong enough. It opened doors that should have stayed closed to her.

"He confirmed the text messaging she was doing at the luncheon. As he put it, she was fooling around, typing things into her cell phone. She seemed troubled that day. Barely touched her food. He asked what was wrong. She shrugged and said, 'Man problems.' At one point, when everyone was eating, she bolted from the table. Said she was going outside for a smoke. She was gone fifteen, twenty minutes. Got up again later. After the luncheon was over, she said a quick good-bye. Slipped away. It was the last time Frank saw her."

"Does he know about Moore?"

"Doesn't know his name. Asked us, but there's no benefit to the investigation to reveal that."

"Sounds like he's primed for a breakdown. Ruiz said he was divorced recently. Think Lynde's capable of hurting himself?"

"Who knows?" Kissick closed his eyes, not wanting to speak of it anymore. "I hope not."

"Yeah."

"You want to nine-eleven at the hotel bar later?"

He was asking her in police jargon if she wanted to meet. She didn't answer right away.

"We had a good day, Nan. Let's celebrate."

"I need to get home. Emily's by herself."

"I'm sure she's set the alarm on your fortress on the hill. We won't be late." He gave her a playful shove. "I'm not asking again, you hard-ass. Relax. Live a little. I don't bite." He added under his breath. "Much."

"Excuse me?"

He had a big grin on his face. "What?"

She narrowed her eyes at him and jabbed his ribs. He laughed.

She said, "Call me when you're heading over."

Vining called Emily on her way to the hotel. She was fine, working on her computer with the photographs and audio recording she'd made the previous night by the bridge. Her homework was finished, of course, and she'd secured the house.

Vining took a detour by the house on El Alisal Road, pausing in the street in front. The lawn was dug up. People in that neighborhood were always doing something to their homes. She'd heard a young family lived there now. The neighborhood was turning over as the older residents, children gone, sold to downsize.

Today, in the kitchen at 835 El Alisal Road, a young

family had cereal and orange juice. Later would be cold cuts and soft drinks. Tonight, cheese and wine with friends who preferred to congregate there rather than in the formal rooms. Close friends always hung out in the kitchen. There would be the shrieking of children and laughter at the buddy who always had an off-color joke. Smells of cooking. Everyone oblivious to the ghost of Vining's former self that she'd left there. Vining's well-being had seeped onto that floor along with her blood. The doctors had replaced her blood.

Did the new owners ever think of her? Was there time in their whirl of social and school events to devote a moment to the police officer who had nearly died there?

The panic attack she'd had at Iris Thorne's house was a rude wake-up call. This thing had shown its mettle. It was bigger than her. The time had come for her to accept that and make a decision about what to do.

EIGHTEEN

*S*he drove down Oak Knoll Avenue, past large mansions set back on sprawling lawns and turned onto the Huntington Hotel's long drive. The median was planted with colorful flowers that changed with the seasons. At the drive's end, valets attended to expensive foreign cars at the entrance of the sprawling, Mission Revival–style building.

Most of the hotel had been reconstructed in the 1990s. The original 1906 structure, one of several grand Pasadena hotels popular with wealthy Easterners, was shuttered in the 1980s because of earthquake damage. It fell into disrepair and part of it had been set ablaze by transients. Two of the original grand ballrooms and a wooden bridge painted with murals of California scenes were all that had been saved and restored.

The only time Vining had been there off-duty was when she'd attended a wedding in the Japanese garden. It was too pricey for her. She found it cloying when the staff responded to every thank you with "My pleasure." Still it was far superior to the flippant "No problem" she had pounded out of Emily's speech.

A young man dressed in pressed chinos and a polo shirt approached her car. Vining showed him her badge and he directed her where to park.

The hotel manager gave Vining the unfortunate news that the security tapes from the luncheon had been reused. He had put together a list of employees who worked the banquet. There were a dozen waiters, a dozen busboys, and an assistant banquet manager, Tricia Durwin.

Some of the staff who had worked the banquet was available for Vining to interview now. The hotel manager would arrange for her to speak to the rest tomorrow. A waiter she was able to speak with had worked the table where Frankie Lynde sat with her father. He didn't recall anything unusual, but he'd worked thirty luncheon banquets since and barely remembered the police service awards, other than the mistress of ceremonies, the local news anchor, who'd autographed his program.

Vining walked through the ballroom and located

Frankie's table and the guests with assigned seating nearby. She imagined Frankie going outside for a smoke—that surprised her as she hadn't thought of physically fit Frankie as a smoker—and found a likely path outside. The closest route would have taken her to a café overlooking the pool. It had been lunchtime on an April afternoon. She'd have to check the weather that day. She'd ask the manager about speaking with the waiters at the poolside café.

This was all hunches and circumstance. She was starting to believe that maybe Kissick was right about this luncheon issue being a wild-goose chase. Still it nagged her. Something had happened around the time Frankie was here that sent her life veering sideways.

A waiter passed, carrying a tray weighted with platters of hamburgers and French fries and a large salad, heading for a table of teenagers supervised by one mom. The aroma made Vining realize how hungry she was. However, she refused to pay the fifteen dollars for a hamburger they probably charged here.

She walked to a short wall that separated the café from the pool area. A man was swimming laps. As the swimmer churned the water, the ripples shimmered in the pool lights. The body cutting through the water made her recall the man's face she'd seen in the blue gemstone. The face was distorted as if underwater, but it was becoming clearer. Just coming here had made it clearer.

He was here.

Her phone rang. It was Kissick.

"Meet me in the bar."

She spent several minutes wandering a thickly carpeted corridor lined with arched windows overlooking a garden. She was asking an employee where she could find the bar when she felt a hand on her upper arm turning her in a different direction.

"Mrs. Vining," Kissick said. "Cocktails will be in the library tonight."

"Divine," she deadpanned. She said "Thank you" over her shoulder to the man who'd given her directions. He responded with a cheery, "My pleasure."

"That 'my pleasure' thing. Whatever happened to 'You're welcome'?"

"It's their style. Obsequious, but I like it. This is a great hotel. Have you ever stayed here?"

"No. I guess you have."

"I take all my women here."

"I see."

He laughed. "Nan, we've got to inject some humor into you. You're turning into stone right before my eyes."

She laughed, but his comment hurt. Her life was awry and everybody saw it.

She heard a piano tinkling and exaggerated party voices well before they walked through the bar entrance. It was a dimly lit, dark wood, plush couches, oil paintings, lit-fireplace-in-June sort of place.

Kissick guided her to a small table and chairs for two in a quiet corner.

She was glad he hadn't opted for one of the couches. She wasn't sure where this chummy "Let's have a drink" invitation might be headed. But he was right. She needed to lighten up. They had been lovers once, but he'd remained her friend. And she needed a friend.

She pulled out the chair but didn't sit. "I must look a sight. Tromping around in the arroyo. Let me . . . fix myself."

"I think you look great. But go ahead. What would you like to drink?"

She didn't know. She rarely went anyplace where she ordered alcohol, other than an occasional dinner with her extended family at a local Mexican restaurant where her mother always ordered pitchers of margaritas for the table.

"A piña colada. Not too strong."

In the restroom, she combed her hair and freshened her lip gloss. She enjoyed the extravagance of the cloth hand towel that she flung into a basket when she'd finished. She didn't enjoy the way the fluorescent lights turned her scar a garish purple. She thought the woman fixing her lipstick beside her was staring at it, but realized she was looking at her shoulder holster visible as her jacket gapped open.

Women and guns. The public still couldn't wrap their minds around it.

Kissick embarrassed her by standing when she approached. He was smiling.

"Now what?"

"You look good," he said. "Nice to be with you."

She picked up her drink and tapped it against the glass of red wine he raised. "Nice to be here." She took a sip and snatched mixed nuts from a bowl on the table.

He picked up a little sandwich board that listed the bar menu offerings. "Let's get some munchies. What looks good?"

She started in on the shelled pistachios and peered at the prices. "Jeesh . . . They sure gouge you here."

"That's Nan. Still so tight she squeaks."

"I'm a single mother."

"I'm treating. We're celebrating."

"I don't want you to treat."

"Well I do." He raised his glass. "Drink up."

"Trying to loosen me up, huh?"

"Who, me?" He looked again at the menu. "I know what you like. Sliders with banjo fries."

She let out a little moan.

He placed an order for two platters and more drinks.

"I've hardly started this one."

"You'd better get busy."

"I have to drive home."

"I'll drive you home. You can leave your car here."

The tiny amount of booze she'd consumed was already hitting her. She felt the tension loosening its grip. It felt good to take a time out.

"You saw the DVD."

He grew serious. "Looking at that will sober anyone up. Sami will do what he can to enhance it, but it was filmed from far away. He didn't think he'd get close enough to see faces, but we'll see."

"What else happened on your end today?"

"Touched base with Jones and Sproul. They're working through Frankie's arrests. Everyone they've talked to so far conveniently has an alibi for Frankie's Friday night at the strip club."

"Of course. Good alibis?"

"Not unshakable."

"Ruiz talk to Frankie's friend Sharon?"

Kissick nodded. "Sharon holds to her story that she didn't know what Frankie was up to. She said Frankie was not one to spill her guts about her life anyway. She was taciturn. Bit of a hard-ass." He winked at her.

She smiled and looked away.

"Has Ruiz calmed down since this morning?"

"He calmed down."

When Kissick didn't elaborate, she let the topic drop.

"Enough law and order. How are your boys spending the summer?"

He grinned, relieved to move on to a new subject. "How *aren't* they spending the summer? Cal wants to go river rafting with his buddies for his thirteenth birthday. And Jimmy . . . Oops, I forgot. He prefers to be called *Jim* now. Is driving. A mixed blessing. Hounding me and his mom to buy him a car. Maybe for his birthday, if he keeps his grades up."

"Onward."

"Yep. As for me, I've decided to pursue a bump up to sergeant. I was supposed to take the test next week, but with the Lynde case, had to reschedule."

"That's great, Jim. You'll have no problem. The brass loves you."

"You never know what tiny infraction you committed years ago that will come back to haunt you. Some toe you stepped on."

"I hate the politics. I just want to do my job."

"I heard that." He turned his wineglass by the stem against the table. "So howya doin', ol' gal?"

She smiled. "Good." She maintained eye contact even though she was not being truthful.

"Got anything going on in your personal life?"

"Yeah. Trying to pull it back together."

He raised his glass to that. "You stickin' to your plan not to date again until Emily is out of the house?"

"Yep. Although lately she's been pushing me into it. Trying to hook me up with her math teacher." She raised her eyebrows, conveying she found the idea ridiculous.

He gave a knowing nod. "Well-meaning friends and relatives."

The waitress brought fresh drinks. He tipped the rest of his wine into the new glass. She let the waitress take her half-finished piña colada.

She grabbed the stem of the maraschino cherry and stirred the foamy cocktail with it. "What about you?"

"I dated somebody for a while. Broke up a couple of months ago."

"What's a while?"

"Over a year."

She picked cashews from the nut bowl and wondered where the sliders were. "She didn't get you to the altar."

"Like my father used to say: Why buy the cow when you can get the milk for free?" He leered, baiting her.

"Ow. My mother has a saying: Men are dogs."

"Woof."

"See? Mom was right." She sipped her drink. "What does she do?"

"Works for Kaiser here in Pasadena. Business planning. Finance. Brainy stuff."

Vining felt that pang of not measuring up. "A real live citizen. Who ended it?"

"I could claim it was mutual, but you're right. Someone always ends it. She did. She wanted more. Marriage. Kids. The white picket fence. I *was* married. I *have* kids. I think marriage is great. I wouldn't mind being married again, but I don't want to start a new family. I know so many guys who have gone that route. First kids in college. Little babies at home. I want to stop paying my dues at some point."

"I hear ya."

"I was up front with her from the beginning. She was cool with it then, said she was focused on her career. Didn't need to be married to feel complete. What's a wedding ring anyway? Half of her friends are divorced, yada, yada . . ."

"Then the baby bell started clanging."

"You got it. Hey, she deserves more than a battle-scarred, broken-down cop."

Vining pointed at her scar. "Me and a math teacher."

"My point exactly. So . . ."

He looked at her and she looked back. It was nice seeing him by candlelight. He'd visited her often in the hospital and checked in on her at home. Those times were tense and heavy. Her situation had been touch and go for longer than she admitted. Her visitors worked on keeping up her spirits. She did the same for them. He'd taken Emily along on outings with his boys: movies, bowling, ball games, miniature golf. Vining was grateful for that.

She repeated what he'd said. "So . . ."

He hesitated.

She felt ready for whatever he was going to say. She was firmly planted in her chair. She wasn't going to run away, no matter what.

"So . . . I've missed you, Nan. I've always missed you." He crept his fingers across the table and touched hers.

She did not pull away. He moved his fingers until he grasped her palm. His hand was warm and dry. A big, strong hand. She felt his pulse beating beneath his skin. It had been a long time since she'd shared even this small intimacy. She wanted more. Craved more. She wanted him. She laced her fingers in his. He looked into her eyes. He didn't stop looking. Her lips parted and she breathed shallowly through her mouth. He pulled himself closer. She met him halfway. They kissed. Her heart pounded while the rest of her melted. His other hand caressed her chin. After what seemed like a deliciously long time, she turned her head, breaking the kiss. His lips landed near her ear.

He whispered, "We could get a room."

She playfully swatted him. "You *are* a dog."

"I didn't plan this. I swear. But, what the hell, Nan?"

What the hell? A lovely room in the lovely hotel. A lovely night. After being so tightly wound, grappling to hold herself together, the mere thought of letting go was like a lifeboat and a cool drink of water after being stranded on a rooftop. He was the last man she'd had sex with over two years ago. She had shut away that part of her life. Never allowing herself a visit. Her struggles now were different. For the first time, Kissick didn't feel like another complication. One more thing to handle. He felt like a solid oak in a forest of saplings. Here she could lean. Let down her guard. Here she could find comfort and rest.

While his lips brushed her ear, sending electricity to her toes, she raised her eyes and learned they were entertainment for a group of women sprawled across couches. It was an awakening. She anticipated Emily's bewildered look upon seeing her dragging home in the wee hours. She saw the crass gaze of their coworkers when they detected the heightened tension between her and Kissick *again*. What message did it send her daughter? How could she and Kissick work the same case? She'd just returned and was lucky to have a desk in Detectives. This couldn't happen.

She sat back and nervously touched her hair, but managed a withering gaze at the snoopy women.

His demeanor showed he knew it was a no-go.

"It's not you, Jim. It's too sudden. So much has happened . . ."

"You're right. I'm not thinking with the head on top of my neck. I'm sorry."

"Don't be sorry. It was wonderful. It brought back nice memories."

"Really?"

She gave him a sly smile. "I used to like it when you stopped being so . . . you know, in control. When you let yourself go."

He gave her a sly smile back. "Mrs. Robinson, you're trying to seduce me."

She snickered.

"Aren't you?"

She laughed harder and was grateful when the food arrived. They devoured it. Vining drank water, leaving the second drink untouched. The alcohol she'd already consumed had quickly gone to her head, scattering the few wits she had left.

He waited for her to get inside her car and drive off. He said he was heading home, but she knew he would go back to the station.

NINETEEN

The place was a run-down nightclub on Pier Avenue in Hermosa Beach called The Lighthouse, and Pussycat knew she had been there too long. A rock-and-roll band had taken the stage at 10:30 p.m. and they were grinding out Metallica covers, their amps at full volume. The music reverberated through Pussycat's bones and shook the thoughts from her head, which was fine with her. The dance floor was crowded with guys in tank tops and girls in spaghetti strap camisoles and shorts or skirts that fell well below their belly buttons. The footwear of choice was flip-flops.

A sign on the door said "No shirt, no shoes, no service" and the clientele barely met those minimal requirements.

Pussycat sat on a stool at the wooden bar, marred with generations of graffiti etched with knives or ballpoint pens if nothing more lethal was at hand. The club's décor was near-Hawaiian with a sprinkling of yard sale. Thatched roofs over the bar and the conversation nooks were studded with tiki heads, plastic bananas, monkeys carved from coconuts, rubber chickens, and pieces of surfboards. On the brightly painted walls were photographs of surfers with inscriptions to the owner. "To Sharkee, keep shredding!" A life-size plastic shark hung behind the bar. A roll of paper towels on a dowel was attached to each table. Televisions of all shapes and sizes were bolted to any remaining wall space.

Hundreds of dollar bills with names, dates, and sometimes phone numbers written in black marker were thumbtacked to the ceiling, completely covering the acoustic tile. Here and there among the curled bills were brassieres and thong panties like exclamation points, flares sent up by female patrons, sky writing that announced that their night had gone on a shade too long.

"Pace yourself, Pollywog." The bartender cautioned a customer, apparently a regular, at the same time he refilled his shot glass with tequila. The admonition had come too late or was pointless anyway as the bleary-eyed guy raised the glass, reverently held it for a moment in the direction of the bartender, and knocked it back. He fumbled to take a lime wedge from a saucer, bit it between his teeth and dropped the rind on the bar.

Pussycat signaled the bartender to serve one of the same for herself. She *had* been pacing herself, nursing a Sierra Nevada, then a second, but itched to cut loose. Things were not going well. She was down in spite of the meth she'd done. She'd do more if she had it, but he'd rationed her dose. Bastard. He wanted to make sure she came back with what he wanted. She hated craving more meth, hated herself, but craved more Tina just the same. How did her life get so screwed up? She had always prided herself on being the kind of woman who made choices and decisions that would bring her the greatest freedom in life. Her axiom was simple: money bought freedom.

Now she had lots of money. All she wanted. More than she'd ever aspired to. More than she could ever spend. She had beautiful things. Her every shopping whim was fulfilled. She had the house of her dreams. When she was in high school, she used to drive around neighborhoods like where she now lived and look at the beautiful homes. She especially loved wandering at night when the landscaping was skillfully illuminated and lamps shone brightly through spotlessly clean windows, setting off the houses and gardens like they were in a storybook or a Thomas Kinkade painting. No one had drapes or blinds over their first-floor windows. The homes were as openly on display as Fifth Avenue department stores at Christmas.

Christmas was the best. The professional trim-the-home crews strove to outdo each other with garlands, wreaths, and twinkling lights. Huge Christmas trees went up in the expansive sitting rooms.

Sometimes when cruising the neighborhood at night, she'd spot people through the windows chatting with friends, raising a glass or a coffee cup. Or she'd catch guests leaving in a shower of good-bye hugs and kisses and laughter, children chasing each other across spacious lawns.

Then she'd drive on and feel a stab in her heart as she returned to the small house her parents rented in Pomona on a faceless street in a hopeless neighborhood. Her two brothers and sister lived there, too, all of them crammed into a three-bedroom, one-bath stucco tract home. Closing the door was like a jail lockdown. During summer, she'd roll a sleeping bag out in the backyard and spend the night under the stars. Often her sister, who was only a year younger, would join her. Pussycat told her parents it was too hot inside the house, which it was. But mostly she liked looking at the stars and the open sky. It reminded her that there was a big world beyond Pomona. It made her feel free.

She'd learned early that a lack of money imprisoned one. Needing money, you went to a job you didn't like, were nice to a boss you hated, lived someplace you barely tolerated, and were grateful for that crummy roof over your head. Money even dictated whom you married. People rarely married above their class. That was so rare they wrote books and made movies about it.

She'd bought a plaque that said "If you think money won't buy happiness, you don't know where to shop." She vowed that if she ever had money, she would support her family, give generously to charity, and she'd never forget where she came from.

People never gave her credit for brains. Maybe she wasn't the smartest cookie in the jar, but she knew how the world worked. She knew she'd never earn the kind of money she wanted on her own. But she could marry it. The social climbing heroines in those books and movies told her how. She took a seminar about meeting rich men. Guys with that kind of dough weren't looking for girls like her. She had to transform herself. She needed to look money to meet money. She needed to go where the money was.

She got herself the highest-paying job she could find—a stripper at a classy gentlemen's club. She brought down $2,000 on a good night. Private parties paid even more. It wasn't the most respectable job. It was a long time before she told her parents. They didn't like it at first until she told them how much she earned. And she never went home with the men. Ever.

The club manager said she needed a stage name. Pamela, her paternal grandmother's name, didn't cut it. The manager christened her Pussycat, and it stuck, even off the job. She wasn't crazy about that, but this was just phase one of her plan. Plenty of time to reinvent herself again.

In her spare time, she attended trade school where she studied for a certificate in fashion design. She planned to become a top clothes designer and build her own fortune. Then she would marry a man equally wealthy, from her new social class. Prenups would be mandatory.

Then one of those shining moments occurred when all her hard work and luck intersected and fate was born. She met her future husband. She'd been invited with some of the other girls at the club to work a weekend stag party given in a huge, rustic cabin on Lake Arrowhead. The host was a club regular.

Pussycat made it clear that she was not a prostitute.

She was there just to dance. As the first night wore on, most of the girls went off to the bedrooms with the men. Pussycat stuck to her guns and kept dancing. Eventually, she danced just for one man—John Lesley. When she declared the show over, he gave her a $1,000 tip and a kiss on the cheek. He uncorked a bottle of Champagne and asked if she'd have a drink with him. She suspected he had more in mind, but they ended up talking for hours. She told him her whole life story. He listened attentively and was the perfect gentleman.

He was handsome and well-groomed. She liked impeccable grooming. She knew he was rich, a self-made man who owned a trendy nightclub in West Hollywood. He used to play in a band that had a couple of hits in the eighties. He found greater success as an entrepreneur. She also knew he was married to a well-known fashion model.

Pussycat had seen them in *Angelino*, a glossy magazine that consisted of photos of Los Angeles society on the town, ads for expensive jewelry and clothing, and a handful of articles squeezed between the ads that told about the latest and greatest trends. Pussycat studied *Angelino* and other magazines for wardrobe cues, behavior tips, and to evaluate the charities with which she'd eventually affiliate herself. Scanning those slick pages, she felt that familiar pain of being on the outside looking in.

Sipping Champagne and talking to John Lesley that night in Lake Arrowhead, she didn't for one minute believe he was interested in her beyond a weekend's entertainment. She clearly wasn't his type. His wife was willowy and elegant. Pussycat was shorter and had a figure best described as voluptuous. And she was a stripper. She wasn't proud of her job, even though strippers and porn stars were the latest in celebrity arm candy. After she became a successful fashion designer, she would never mention her previous career or the name that went with it.

"I'm getting a divorce."

His statement made her sit up from the sofa cushions where she'd been reclining.

"I'm ready for children and my wife is not. I know she has her career to consider, but a few months ago she threw a bombshell and told me she doesn't ever want children. If I'd known that, I wouldn't have married her." He inched his fingers across the leather upholstery to touch hers. "How do you feel about children?"

She would later come to think of that first night as a job interview. He was looking for somebody vulnerable. Naïve. Insecure. Someone he could mold and control. He'd pressed her about her relationship with her family. What were her parents like? She'd told him her father was remote and hard on her. Nothing she did pleased him. Her mother was passive.

"Poor baby. That must have been tough."

His eyes were kind. They always were. She believed the eyes were windows to the soul. She would learn his eyes couldn't betray his soul because he didn't have one.

A couple of years later, Pussycat had a chance meeting with his ex-wife at a charity fashion show where the ex was one of the models. Pussycat saw her catching a smoke on the terrace and introduced herself.

"I know who you are." The ex angled her head back to blow a stream of smoke over her shoulder. She leveled chartreuse eyes at Pussycat. "So how do you like being married to the freak?" She darted her cigarette at a potted palm, dropping ash. "Don't answer that. If anyone asks, the subject never came up. I'm forbidden to talk about him and I don't want him suing my ass."

By that time, Pussycat knew what the ex meant. Pussycat had been married to John Lesley for three years after a brief courtship. Their sex life had been active and anything but homespun. He'd started out slowly, easing her in, revealing both his true self and the depth of his perversions. There was a word for what he was doing: grooming. It was how child molesters lured their prey.

She'd never been a prude but he'd involved her in situations that she'd only seen in triple X porno movies. When scenarios exceeded her personal boundaries of both propriety and pain, he hired call girls for the dirty work. That was the power of money. Some women would debase themselves to get it.

By then, Pussycat was in too deep. If she left him, the prenup she'd signed would provide her a small income, but nothing near what she'd known. She could get by on it if she absolutely had to, but she didn't have just herself to consider. He'd bought her parents and younger siblings a house in Claremont in a good neighborhood with excellent public schools. The house remained in his name. If she left him, her family would be on the street. Her two brothers were still in high school. Her father was on disability and her mother made little as a homecare provider.

It would be the end of her charitable work. She could still volunteer, but the perks of being a deep-pockets donor would evaporate.

And then there was Miss Tina. He'd lured her into that, too. Taken what had been a recreational drug for her and nurtured it into a full-blown addiction.

When Pussycat had gone to the charity fashion show

the day she'd met his ex, he hadn't yet tired of professional sex partners. Their games with them were rough, but Pussycat reconciled her ill feelings with the knowledge that the women were well paid. Some of them were regulars and knew full well what they were getting into. When she'd had her too-brief exchange with the ex, Pussycat thought the other woman was referring to that already explored dark world. Pussycat by then had gotten used to it. Thought she understood its boundaries. That was before they'd met Officer Frankie Lynde.

Pussycat downed the tequila shot, slamming the glass on the bar with a bang that went unheard over the band's noise. She followed up with a lime wedge, holding it between her front teeth as she turned to watch the dance floor. People weren't really dancing but were swaying to the music, many dangling beer bottles by the necks between their fingers. The girls were cute and acted loose and tough. Pussycat knew that act and knew better. They shook their loose hair and waved their arms. None of them was a great beauty, but they had that California beach girl aura or were doing good imitations. Pussycat tried to pinpoint one she could peel away from her friends, like a lioness searching for the weaker members of the zebra herd. Better yet, she'd find someone who had come alone. He'd taught her how to hunt.

Hermosa Beach was a locals' town. It wasn't close to a freeway. The pier had no shops, restaurants, or carnival rides; it was simply a fishing pier. Other beach cities offered more to attract families and tourists. The beachfront businesses drew local teenagers and young singles, some of whom prided themselves on having never ventured east of the 405 freeway or worn long pants. The police department patrolled the beach on bicycles and wore shorts. Surfing was decent. There were no hot restaurants or clubs to entice L.A. scenesters to make the twenty-mile trek south. It was a real So Cal beach town.

Pussycat's husband had suggested going to Orange County, but she had an L.A. County native's natural aversion to the O.C. She didn't know the layout of the freeways there. Everything looked too new, too shiny, and too Caucasian. It felt peculiar. She always felt lost there.

Her husband became angry. "We have to look outside L.A. Someplace where no one knows us."

"Why do we have to look at all?"

"Don't get cute with me, baby. You don't even know how to begin to play that game."

"How about Hermosa? I used to fish off the pier there with my dad when I was little. It fits, huh? We're still catching and releasing, right?"

Since he'd made that promise to her, they'd done just that, he'd had raucous fun, she'd pretended to, and they'd sent the girl on her way. But she sensed a change brewing. She was used to that rising tension in him, underneath the surface, like a piano wire twisting tighter. The sexcapades used to calm that beast. Lull it to sleep. The girl last night had only taken the edge off. Something else was at work. Something new, awakened from the depths of his being. That soulless being. She feared the thing with Frankie had permanently changed him. There was no going back.

She ordered another shot, downing it as soon as the bartender set it in front of her. Guys around the bar hooted and clapped. She gave them one of her stage smiles and a slow pirouette before turning back to watch the dancers.

She used to tell herself she knew everything about her husband. But whenever she dared to be honest, she had to admit there were depths she could not penetrate. The many layers were revealing themselves now. Maybe he'd kept them hidden until he found and trained the perfect coconspirator and turned her into a drug addict. She'd not only walked right into his scheme, she'd grabbed hold with both hands.

She thought of what he had told her when he'd dropped her off tonight.

"Baby, haven't I been the perfect gentleman, like I promised?" He smiled his charmer's smile. That boyish man smile that made the VIP visitors to his club, the celebrities and socialites, feel like royalty. What a great guy. Isn't he the best? Don't you just love him?

Pussycat would like to say she could see through it, but she couldn't. It was only through experience that she learned it was false. It was only because of Frankie Lynde's blood and tears that she'd discovered the lie.

Thinking of Frankie made her eyes fill. She thought of something else.

"Hey, Red, buy you a drink?"

It took Pussycat a second to realize he was talking to her. When she turned in his direction, she caught her reflection in a wall covered in mirrored panes with gold vines. A happening relic from the 1970s. Pussycat nearly didn't recognize herself. She was wearing an auburn wig with locks that brushed her shoulders. She'd disguised her blue eyes with contact lenses that had hypnotic spirals in them. Her attire matched that of the other women in the joint, but her scanty blouse revealed press-on tattoos of barbed wire encircling her arm and a rose atop the curve of her ample breast.

That was where he was now looking.

"I'm okay, thanks."

He was one of the guys who had cheered her on earlier. "Come on. Don't you like me? No pressure. Just friendly."

He was kind of cute and she was already more than a little drunk and amped on meth.

"Wow. Crazy eyes."

She batted her lids at him. "You are getting sleepy."

"No shit. Tequila shooter?"

"Yeah. But I'm paying."

"No can do."

"I bet you can." She peeled a twenty from the roll of bills stashed in the pocket of her low-rise jeans skirt and set it on the bar.

The bartender lined them up. The guy licked his wrist and sprinkled salt onto it from a shaker. Pussycat did the same. They clinked glasses, licked off the salt, and knocked them back. He gave a violent shake to his head before cramming a lime wedge in his mouth. She didn't even blink. He smiled loosely at her. He was definitely a cutie, even with the veneer of beach grime.

"You got any women tied up in your basement?"

"Wha . . . ?"

"Kidding." She slapped the bar. " 'Nother round."

Boy was she in trouble. Big time. Her husband could kill her. She had no doubt he was capable of doing just that.

"You're kind of crazy, you know that?"

She hissed air through her teeth. "You have no idea."

"You're cute." He tickled her bare belly.

She didn't stop him. He used to be her type, lanky and muscular with a nice, strong jaw and pretty eyes. She used to have a type before the first thing she started to look at in a man was his portfolio.

"You're drunk."

"Doesn't matter. I know cute, drunk or sober." He kept tickling her. "Woman with ink. She's tatted up. I love it. Where does the rose go?" He drew his index finger down the fake rose tattoo until he reached the opening of her top. He pulled the fabric away, then bent his head to kiss the rise of her breast.

She ran her fingers through his hair that could use a wash. Grabbing his hair, she pulled up his head and planted her lips on his. It was an honest kiss. The first honest kiss she'd had since she'd met John Lesley. She and the beach guy had one agenda that neither one was hiding. She was hot for him and messed up enough and weary enough not to care about the consequences.

He smelled like booze, perspiration, and sea spray. His clothes were paint-splattered. He looked like he'd knocked off work and had come straight to the bar. He looked like he'd forgotten to shave that morning. In spite of all that, he seemed clean to her. Uncontaminated. Uncomplicated. She craved his simplicity. She needed it.

"Want to get out of here? My apartment is around the corner."

She turned, too quickly. Her head spun. She held on to the bar to steady herself and noticed one of the televisions bolted to the ceiling. It was tuned to the eleven o'clock news. Another tube a few feet away was broadcasting the same thing. They were again showing that dumb artist's rendering of her wearing the chauffeur's outfit. It didn't even look like her.

"Wait a second." She held her hand up to her companion. The TV was broadcasting something else. Something new. It was shadowy and dark, filmed from far away and at night but she recognized that place. It was the bridge where they'd dumped Frankie's body. That was her and John, tossing Frankie's body down the hill. That was her running away.

She put her hands over her mouth. She ran from the bar.

Pollywog ran after her. "Hey! Where ya going?"

She stumbled and bounced off a wall, rounding a corner onto a side street. She heard Pollywog running after her. He caught up.

"Leave me 'lone."

She stumbled again and fell. She tried to stand and he grabbed her, trying to steady her.

Nearby, she heard sounds of a party on a rooftop. People were talking and laughing.

She wrenched herself from his grasp and staggered forward. She reeled around. Walls seemed to soar crazily on either side. She was in an alley.

"Where you gonna go like this? You can barely walk. I live around the corner."

She pushed him. "I tol' you t'leave me 'lone. Go!"

He grabbed her arm. "Baby—Yo!"

He jumped back as she vomited.

A woman passing on the street stopped and poked him in the arm. "You heard her. She doesn't want you here."

"I'm gone. You don't need to tell me twice." He turned the corner and disappeared.

The woman grabbed Pussycat's hair and held it away from her face. "That's okay. Get it all out." She rubbed her back. "That's good, sweetheart. Don't be ashamed."

Pussycat finished and leaned against the wall. She

pressed the heel of her hand against her forehead. "Thanks," she slurred.

The woman was younger than she sounded. Maybe in her twenties. She was petite and slender with blond-streaked hair cut in a fringe down her face. She was tanned, like everyone who lived at the beach.

"No problem. Been there, done that. More times than I want to think about."

Pussycat started tottering from the alley.

"Where are you going?" The woman followed her.

"Home."

"You can't drive, sweetheart."

"Don' worry 'bout me."

"You know, I used to drink like that. I just came from an A.A. meeting. It's still going on over there on the roof of the Elk's Lodge. Let's go over and we'll get a cup of coffee."

"You're nice. I'm gon' be okay. Th's m' ride."

A black Hummer with broad tires barreled toward them, turning to block the street. The passenger window rolled down. John Lesley leaned toward it and said, "Get in."

Pussycat opened the back door and clambered inside.

"Wait a minute," the woman told Lesley. "Does she know you?"

"It's 'kay," Pussycat mumbled.

"This is my wife. We had a little tiff tonight. I've been driving all over looking for her."

"Thanks. G'bye." Pussycat almost fell out when she leaned to pull the door closed. "Bye now. G'bye."

The woman leaned against the open passenger door window. "This is none of my business, but there's an A.A. meeting going on right up the street. It's a great group of people. I don't need to know your wife to see that she has a problem. I've only been sober for a month, so I'm sort of fired up about sobriety."

"Sober for a month? Congratulations."

From the backseat, Pussycat saw him smiling his snake smile. So warm. Friendly, as if he wouldn't hurt a flea.

Her stomach roiled, but she held it down. At least everything had stopped spinning. She reached to stroke his neck and shoulders. "Baby, I'm tired. I jus' wanna go home. Thank you, lady, but I don' drink like that. I really don't. Tell her, baby. I don't have a drinkin' problem. I was jus' upset."

He glanced at Pussycat then met the woman's eyes. He winked at her. They were conspirators now.

"No, baby," Pussycat pleaded. "Le's go home. Please. Le's go home."

"Where did you say this meeting was?"

"I can show you."

"I couldn't trouble you like that."

Pussycat started screaming. "No! Take me home!"

"It's no trouble at all. It would be my pleasure."

"If you're sure it's no problem. Okay. Climb in." He flipped open the door and he offered his hand. "I'm Bill Binderman."

"I'm Lisa Shipp."

"Nooo!" Pussycat cried. "Lisa, get out! *Please.* He'll kill you! I beg you! I beg you . . ."

Pussycat couldn't open the door. He'd activated the childproof locks. The Hummer wrenched into the street, tossing her back.

He grimaced as he glanced into the backseat. "Sorry about that."

"Hey, I'm the last one to pass judgment on the people struggling with booze."

"It's a miracle my wife ran into you tonight," Lesley said. "I've wanted to get her to a meeting for months."

"Sometimes it takes something like this. You've gotta hit bottom, you know?"

"Lisa, you're an angel. It's like an angel reached out and touched us."

Pussycat curled into a fetal position and sobbed.

TWENTY

Vining headed home on the narrow and twisting Pasadena Freeway—the first modern freeway in the United States. Leaving affluent Pasadena and South Pasadena, Vining's route took her through solidly working-class and poor neighborhoods northeast of downtown L.A. She exited at Avenue 43. Turning north at the Taco Fiesta stand, she headed into Mt. Washington.

Known as "the poor man's Bel Air," the hilly, artsy neighborhood of winding streets and woodsy cottages had been among the few where Vining and Wes could afford a spacious house with a view and good public schools. The view wasn't remotely as grand as the legendary "city to ocean" sights from the Hollywood Hills. From Vining's house, the lights of downtown L.A. were partially hidden behind a hill, but she had a direct shot of the County USC Medical Center and the Alameda Corridor—railroad tracks that went all the way to the Port of Los Angeles in San Pedro. Unglamorous during the day. At night, the lights twinkled as brightly as those seen from Mulholland Drive.

Wes had correctly predicted that Mt. Washington, with its neighborhood feel and quick commute to L.A.'s civic center, would be discovered. Of course, he had long ago abandoned it for the ultra-trendy Calabasas, where television executives built McMansions with horse stables. Vining had held on to the 1960s cliff-clinging house on a quiet cul-de-sac. It hadn't been easy to keep up with the maintenance and taxes, but she wanted Emily to have the stability of growing up in the same house and keeping the same friends through the same schools. Something Vining and her younger sister, Stephanie, had not had with their much-married mother.

Vining turned onto Stella Place, not activating the garage door opener until her house was in sight. She used to click it when she entered the street so the garage would be open by the time she reached it, but that gave an intruder ample time to slip inside. One of her many concessions to T. B. Mann.

The houses on her street were not bunched together. Patches of chaparral-covered land separated the homes on either side. There were no houses on the steep hillside directly below. She'd always liked the privacy and quiet. Now she appreciated the lack of places for someone to hide and the clear view of anyone approaching from any side.

Like just about every neighborhood in California, Vining's was in transition because of the booming real estate market. A year ago, the elderly couple who lived in the house on the corner had cashed out. The house was part of the same 1960s development as Vining's. New owners from the San Fernando Valley had razed it and were building a big, modernist structure of curves, angles, and steel.

At the end of the cul-de-sac, a couple from out of state had razed one of the other original homes and bought a neighboring vacant lot. From the terrace off Vining's house, she could see the large Tuscan-inspired home they'd set into the hillside and the pool and patio beneath. All that was visible from the street was painted cement walls inlaid with tile, sand-hued pavers, and massive iron gates—the first to sprout up in the neighborhood.

Vining had formally met the couple once. Since then, they waved and said hello in the manner that nowadays stood in for neighborliness. When they told Vining what their occupations were, she said "That sounds interesting," having no clue what they were talking about. Something to do with new ventures, technology . . . Whatever they did, it appeared to pay them lots of money. Vining and Emily were the only native Californians they'd met, which Vining found curious. Just about everyone Vining knew was born in or near the San Gabriel Valley. Vining was the only police officer they'd known personally. Somehow they made *her* feel like the outsider. They did not invite her to their large parties. She repaid the favor by not calling the police when the racket went on too long. The cops usually broke up the gatherings, but the call out wasn't on her account.

Wes had been prescient. The neighborhood had been discovered. Realtors now pestered Vining to sell. She and her remaining longtime neighbors joked about it. She'd learned her boxy, low-ceilinged, stucco house was a "midcentury gem" in "highly desirable, historic Mt. Washington." The value of her home had skyrocketed. For her, it was funny money. She'd never tapped into the equity. Short of paying for Emily's college education or a catastrophic event, she never would.

Carrying a sack of groceries in one arm and Kissick's notebook in the other, Vining entered the house from the garage into the laundry room, setting off the prealarm. She punched the codes to deactivate then realarm the house. She set the groceries on the kitchen sink but held on to the notebook. The small lights that switched on automatically at dusk lit the family room, small dining area, and living room. The house was quiet.

The television in the family room was not on as her grandmother was not there, as she normally was, dozing in the La-Z-Boy. Vining knew as much, not seeing the baby blue Olds in the driveway. She thought Granny was going to stay until she got home and found her absence disconcerting.

Next to the pile of mail on the kitchen table was a small plant. It looked like a tomato seedling with strands of raffia tied into a bow around its terra-cotta pot.

"Em?"

A plastic florist fork stuck into the plant soil held a three-by-five card. On it was a photograph of a husband and wife realtor team and a cheery note.

"Emily . . ."

Vining walked through the family room and living room. The drapes over the sliding glass doors were open. Vining caught her reflection against the darkness outside. She clicked off the lamp on an end table. Her image disappeared and the city lights came into view.

Emily was probably in her room downstairs, but the quiet emptiness of the house rattled her. She quickly went into her bedroom and stashed the notebook under the bed, not wanting Emily to happen upon the crime scene photos. She turned and headed for Em's room.

Her cell phone rang. The display said the call was from Emily.

"I'm in the darkroom. I heard you turn off the alarm and now you're stomping all over the house."

Vining exhaled. "Hi, sweet pea. Where's Granny?"

"Her doctor called and said she had an opening. Granny asked if I minded and I said I'd get a ride home with Aubrey's mom. She went by Trader Joe's and I bought a California roll that I ate for dinner. I've been in the darkroom ever since. I know where the guns and ammo are and how to use them. This place is alarmed like I don't know what. I'm fine."

"That's all you had for dinner? One California roll?"

"Mom, why are you stressing? You didn't even sleep in your bed last night. Is working on the Frankie Lynde murder doing a number on you or is it something else?"

"I expected Granny to be here, that's all."

"Like Granny's going to protect me."

"She's another person in the house. It matters." Vining realized her voice was strident.

He's moved on.

Vining took a deep breath.

You'll draw him out, but not now.

"Mom, I babysit for people. I'm capable of staying by myself. I'm fourteen."

"Yes, you are. You're a young lady now. I'll come down." She ended the call.

Walking back through the living room, the windows'

black eyes made her feel exposed. She yanked the cord to close the drapes and made busywork straightening the folds. The Lynde investigation wasn't doing a number on her. Working it energized her. But it was the messenger. Through it she'd learned how deeply T. B. Mann had seeped into her life, how indelibly he had stained it. It could not stand. She refused to live this way.

Returning to her bedroom, she took off her ankle holster and put the Walther under her pillow. It had been her sole companion in bed from the day she was able to get up and load it, out of sight of her caregivers, after she'd returned from the hospital.

In the kitchen, she took off her shoulder holster, removed her Glock .40, and ejected the clip. She hung the empty holster on a hook beside the back door. The gun she put into a cabinet inside an empty box of Count Chocula cereal that resided between Emily's box of Cheerios and Vining's full box of Count Chocula. The clip she stashed in a drawer behind tea towels. The other firearms in the house were formally secured. The Walther and the Glock were her working weapons. They had to be nearby in case she needed them.

She went down the stairs off the kitchen to Emily's floor, which was the former rumpus room. After she and Wes had bought the house, they'd made full use of it, installing a pool table, Wurlitzer jukebox, and wet bar and having friends over most weekends. Sliding glass doors opened onto a concrete slab patio that was perfect for barbecuing. Fun times. Wes wanted the toys when they'd split and she hadn't objected.

When Emily turned thirteen she laid claim to the space. Wes did a great job of transforming it into a bedroom and workroom for her.

Vining saw that Emily had closed the plantation shutters and was glad. Beyond the patio, the backyard was ragged hillside, surrounded with a chain-link fence marking the property line. The yard was not as secure as Vining would like. The neighbor's cat often triggered the motion lights. Emily argued for a black Lab, but Vining resisted this new responsibility and expense. Plus pet dogs were unreliable for security as they were easily placated or eliminated. What Vining coveted was the surveillance cameras she saw at Iris Thorne's house.

Enough, she told herself. T. B. Mann was not coming here for her or Emily. Even if he did, the house was secure.

She recalled Kissick's words. He may be insane but he's not stupid.

T. B. Mann's time would come. She would find him. She would follow the threads that drew him to her, the slender skeins that had transformed into links of a chain, binding her and him forever.

For the moment, her obligation was to Frankie Lynde. Vining owed her nothing less than her best effort.

The light outside the darkroom door was off, meaning it was safe to enter. Vining knocked. A strange, unfamiliar noise came from inside. She drew her ear close to the door to listen.

"*Avanti,*" Em yelled.

Vining did as instructed.

The small room was illuminated by a red light. Emily was taking wet photographs from the fixing bath and hanging them on a clothesline with plastic clips. She loved her digital camera, but she also loved the craft of working with film and experimenting with different techniques. On her wish list was equipment to develop color photographs, but that was beyond Vining's budget for the moment. There was always Dad she could lean on. He had proven to be "leanable" in the past. Em knew how to tweak the guilt factor and was not above judiciously doing just that.

"Hey." Emily did not stop her work.

"Hey back atcha."

A CD spinning in a player was the source of the strange noise.

"What is that?"

"The recording I made from Frankie Lynde's hillside. Disappointing. All I've heard so far is traffic and crickets. Nothing's turned up in the photographs either. There's something that could be orbs in a couple of them, but I think they're reflections from the streetlights or dust on the lens. They're hard to verify without an infrared lens or night goggles. Night goggles would be great, but they're expensive."

To Vining, the wet photographs showed a vacant hillside at night. "Are these what you call swirls?"

"Orbs," Emily corrected her. "Swirls are long and squiggly. Orbs are like balls of light. Then there are vortexes that look like funnels, and mists that look like . . . well, mist. They all suggest the presence of ghosts. And if you're lucky enough, you'll see an actual ghost that appears in the form of a human being."

She took a stack of photographs from a shelf and sorted through them. The edges were wavy from the home developing process. She pulled out images of a cemetery at night. The darkness was marked with crooked trails of white light, like that left from writing in the night sky with a lit sparkler on the Fourth of July.

"These are swirls."

"I see."

Emily found shots of an abandoned house where she'd prodded her father to take her one night. It hadn't been Wes's idea of family time, but Emily had loved it.

"These are orbs." She returned the photographs to the shelf. "I'll scan the shots of Frankie's hillside and e-mail them to the San Gabriel Valley Ghost Hunters Club for an opinion."

"Thought you weren't involved with them anymore."

"They have their uses." Emily caught the slight upturn at the corners of her mother's mouth. "This is not a joke, Mom. I wish you'd take it more seriously."

"You're right, sweetheart. I shouldn't make fun of things I don't understand."

"You of all people."

Vining accepted the dig without comment.

Also drying on the clothesline were self-portraits of Emily.

"These are cute."

Emily raised her upper lip. "Uh, not. I just took them to finish the roll."

"They're adorable. Look at this one. I want it for my desk."

"No, you don't."

"Yes, I do. It's so you."

"If that's me . . . Don't even . . . Please."

Vining hugged her daughter around the shoulders and didn't press the issue further.

With her mother still holding on to her, Emily inspected a wet photograph she held between rubber tongs and made a noise of dejection.

Vining looked at it, her chin resting atop Emily's shoulder.

"These are definitely caused by headlights from a car going over the bridge."

Vining stood straight, letting go of Emily who moved to hang up the photo.

"Darn. I just wish—"

"Shhh." It came out of Vining's mouth with an intensity that surprised Emily.

"What?"

Vining held up her hand, ending conversation. She slowly made a fist, as if trying to seize something from the air.

"Mom, what is it?"

Vining searched the ceiling. "It's gone now." Her gray eyes went dark. "You didn't hear that?"

Emily indicated she hadn't.

Vining darted to the CD player and began punching buttons, frustrated by not getting the result she wanted.

Emily came to help.

"Roll it back a little. Roll it back." Vining was breathing through her mouth.

"Mom . . ."

"Emily, play it again. Please."

Vining realized she was using her no-nonsense voice. It was harsh and inappropriate here. She was scaring her daughter. Her rational mind told her to back off.

Emily skipped the CD back and started it playing again.

Vining raised a trembling hand in the air, as if feeling the sound waves. Her eyes grew wide and her mouth gaped. She covered it with her hand, backing up in the small room until she could go no farther.

"Mom, what is it?" There were tears in the girl's eyes. "I don't hear anything except the freeway. Mom . . ."

But Vining heard. Frankie Lynde was speaking to her in the same coarse whisper from the hillside.

"Wear the pearls," Frankie Lynde was telling Vining. "He gave them to you. Wear the pearls."

TWENTY-ONE

Emily followed her mother from the darkroom. "Mom, tell me what's going on. This is not just about you. *I'm* the one who sat in your hospital room day after day. *I'm* the one who almost ended up motherless."

She choked on the last word. It was too horrible to utter. Dejected, she plopped on the edge of the bed.

Vining sat on an overstuffed chair and stared across the room. She listened to her daughter with odd detachment. So much had happened in the past two days. She was overwhelmed.

"Mom!" Emily wailed. "Don't do this to me. *Please.* It's mean. I can't stand it."

Weeping, she slid to the floor and hugged her knees against her chest.

Her daughter's despair roused Vining from her daze. Because of T. B. Mann, she heard corpses talking. She wouldn't let him do this to her. She would not. He had failed at taking her life. Now he was working on her mind, making her alienate her daughter, stripping her of everything that mattered. And she was a willing accomplice.

She went to the floor and cradled and rocked her crying daughter, stroking her hair. Her own tears fell.

"I'm sorry, Em. I'm so sorry. The last thing I want is to hurt you. You're my life."

The girl's crying subsided. "Then tell me what's happening. Don't tell me it's nothing. I won't believe you."

Vining did not want to burden her daughter with her problems, but her behavior already was. The big unknown was worse than the truth. Maybe she was making too much of how Emily would react.

"Okay, Em. I'll be straight with you. No more secrets."

Sniveling, Emily pushed herself up and leaned against the bed.

Vining walked on her hands and knees to grab a box of tissues and returned to sit beside Emily. Her daughter nestled against her neck. She didn't know where to begin. She'd held back so much.

The poetry magnet. She had described the events that had occurred at 835 El Alisal Road to Emily in broad strokes. She'd considered the magnet a meaningless detail. The crazy antics of a madman. She'd decided her daughter didn't need more material with which to embellish her nightmares.

She now told Emily about the magnet. She told her about Frankie Lynde's corpse speaking to her—"I am you. I am not you"—and the panic attack that ensued. She told her about the second panic attack at the Thorne house and the images inside the gemstone in Frankie's earring. She concluded with Frankie Lynde's words on the recording Em had made on the hillside.

"My subconscious is working overtime. That's all it is. Frankie Lynde is not speaking to me from beyond the grave."

"Mom, of course she is."

Vining now regretted saying a thing.

They played the CD again, all of it, and again. At seven minutes in, every single time, Vining heard the admonition about the necklace.

Emily did not. Neither did she discount her mother's perceptions as hallucinations as Vining did. Emily believed in the afterlife and the stages between. She didn't need proof from the scientific establishment. She was building her own proof, ghost by ghost.

"What necklace?" Emily pushed herself taller on the floor.

"There's only one it could be."

"The one someone sent after the Lonny Velcro incident."

Lonny Velcro was the man Vining had shot and killed on duty five years before. She and Emily preferred describing it with the more benign word "incident."

Vining stood and held out her hand to help Emily up. They walked upstairs to Vining's bedroom. The no-frills room had a view of the city and was furnished with the good, simple pieces she and Wes had bought when they were first married.

She opened the dresser drawer where she kept her few pieces of nice jewelry, pulled out a box and removed the necklace. She displayed it on the bed as if around her neck. It was a strand of pearls with a pendant or slide made of a large pearl surrounded by small stones that looked like diamonds.

Lonny Velcro's given name had been Lon Veltwandter.

In 1972, just out of high school in Sherman, Texas, he and his twin brother, Leon, formed the seminal heavy metal group Volume. Volume went on to sell 140 million records worldwide. The band's personal excesses became emblematic of the era. The band broke up in the late eighties and the members went their separate ways. Brothers Lonny and Leon did not speak for years.

Ten years later, after divorcing another wife, Lonny left Malibu and bought a gated mansion in Pasadena. He told friends his sedate new city was the Anti-Malibu, Anti-Hollywood. Even though he claimed to have left his rock-and-roll days behind, he often prowled the Los Angeles club scene with an entourage that always included attractive young women. Forty-six years old, rail thin, weathered, and still wearing his trademark long tresses and bandanna, he remained a player.

Volume was to be inducted into the Rock and Roll Hall of Fame. All the band's original members were to play on stage again for the first time since 1988. Story was fences had been mended, axes buried, and there were rumors of a tour and a new album. Volume's loyal fans around the world were ecstatic.

That June, Vining had been with the PPD nearly seven years. She was on patrol with John Chase, a rookie ten months out of the Academy. At 2:13 on a Sunday morning, she and Chase responded to a call placed by Lonny Velcro, who said a woman had shot herself at his mansion. Vining and Chase arrived to find model and sometime actress Marnie Allegra propped up on an antique church pew in the mansion's foyer, dead from a gunshot wound through her eye.

Velcro stood in the foyer and calmly explained to the officers how he and Allegra were friends and had met that night by chance at Muse, a Hollywood club. After having a couple of drinks together, they decided to party at his house and she followed him in her car. They were making cocktails in the library off the foyer when Allegra said she was going to use the powder room. A minute later, Velcro heard the gunshot.

Velcro took Vining and Chase into the library and stood behind the bar, showing where he had been when Allegra allegedly shot herself.

"Had Miss Allegra talked about suicide?" Vining asked, not believing his story for a second.

"No, she was fine. Kinda drunk, but fine."

"Where did she get the gun?"

"It's mine. I keep it in the commode in the foyer. I like having a weapon near the front door. I've had incidents in the past."

"She knew it was there."

"Obviously. She took it out and shot herself, didn't she?"

Vining pressed him. "You're telling us that out of the blue, this woman goes from having drinks and conversation to committing suicide."

Chase later reported that Velcro again relayed his version of the events, not appearing the least bit troubled, when Vining interrupted him.

"Chase, you realize he's full of shit. When women commit suicide, they rarely use guns, especially in the head. That's basic Academy training."

"You're the one who's full of shit," Velcro countered. "It happened just the way I said."

Vining laughed at him. "You're a piece of work. You killed her and because you're rich and famous, you think you'll get away with it."

"Who the fuck are you to talk to me like that?" Velcro said.

Vining crooked her fingers, calling Velcro from behind the bar. "Step into the center of the room, sir."

"I'm calling my attorney."

"You can call from the station. You're under arrest." Vining loosened her gun in its holster.

"I don't think so. I'm calling him now."

There was the sound of a buzzer.

"Probably your backup at the gate," Velcro said. "The intercom's by the front door. Get it while I make a phone call."

Vining jerked her head to tell Chase to go.

Chase estimated he had left the room for barely a minute when he heard a gunshot. He buzzed the gate open and ran to the library to find Vining leaning over Velcro who was bleeding out onto the carpet from a chest wound. Vining told Chase that as soon as he'd left, Velcro said he was getting a phone from behind the bar but instead pulled a gun.

A .45 was on the carpet in Velcro's open palm. Investigators would later discover that the weapon was unregistered, the serial numbers expertly removed. Velcro had a small amount of gunshot residue on his right hand that was consistent with his handling a gun.

Pasadena Police Department's internal investigation declared the shooting within policy guidelines. PPD's chief engaged the FBI to review the case, seeking to squelch suggestions of bias. The FBI also declared the shooting in policy, but that did nothing to stop the civil lawsuit against the city.

An oddball mixture of antipolice activists and Lonny Velcro fans picketed the Pasadena Police Department for weeks. Volume fan sites on the Net railed against Vining. A top attorney hired by Velcro's heirs claimed he was unarmed and Vining had planted the gun. The attorney attempted to show that Vining had a history of over-reacting when wielding a badge.

PPD investigators turned up a man who claimed to have sold guns to Velcro and had a Polaroid of him posing with a .45 that might have been the one used in the shooting. Several unregistered firearms were found in the mansion. Investigators also tracked down women whom Velcro had threatened with guns. He was known to carry firearms.

The plaintiffs refused to settle. The case went before a jury who found in favor of the city.

A week after the verdict, the pearl necklace was dropped unwrapped into the mailbox at Vining's home. A small card attached by a ribbon had a simple message: Congratulations, Officer Vining.

Most of the letters and cards that Vining received commended rather than condemned her for her actions. Some people had sent small gifts: stuffed toys, balloons, flowers, baskets of fruit, and goodies. These she donated. The pearl necklace stood apart. She had it appraised. It was costume jewelry, although first-rate. The "diamonds" were cubic zirconia. The pearls were imitation, but good quality. It was well made and hard to distinguish from the real thing. The jeweler estimated it was worth around $500.

She hadn't given it away. She told herself someone was generous in rewarding her for a job well done. Still, she could never bring herself to wear it. Now she understood why.

"What's the significance of pearls? It's not my birth-stone. I was born in April. My birthstone is diamond."

"What month is pearl?" Emily asked.

"Don't know."

"Let's look it up."

After a minute on the Internet, Emily had the answer. June.

Em, crafty Em put it together. "Mom, T. B. Mann at-tacked you in June. Didn't the Lonny Velcro incident happen in June?"

"Yes."

"Don't you get it? Pearl is your death stone."

Vining took a pill to help her sleep. She hated relinquish-ing even that amount of control, but her body and mind needed rest. Still, she dreamed. She dreamed her death dream, reliving the vision she'd had when she was dead for two minutes and twelve seconds.

She floated toward a radiant white light and passed a long line of all the dead people in her life. The vision was a classic death experience as reported by many. Vining had read dozens of similar versions on the Internet. That was why she discounted it as meaningless and silly. Its commonness surely proved that the experience was based in physiology. Tonight was the first time she'd had a dream that replicated it.

The line of dead people was long. It included friends and family, even relatives who had passed when she was a kid and whom she had barely known. All the souls she'd encountered during her years as a police officer were there—the traffic fatalities, the suicides, the homi-cides. Many she knew only as corpses. She saw Tiffany Pearson, Marnie Allegra, and Lonny Velcro. She saw the victim of the gang-related shooting she'd investigated right before her assault. Eleven-year-old Denzel Johnson was shot twelve times while riding his bike through an alley on his way home from school. He smiled sweetly at her.

Frankie Lynde was closest to the light. She was standing tall in full dress uniform, brass buttons and belt buckle polished. Her hair was pulled into a tight bun. Her hat was square on her head. Her eyes were clear and knowing.

The dead watched as she passed. They did not convey sadness or anger, not even Lonny Velcro. From them, Vining felt peace. None spoke but they had messages for her, wordlessly imparted as she floated toward the light. Messages she didn't comprehend, but felt she would one day. She moved past Frankie Lynde and took her message as if accepting a mysterious gift wrapped in shapeless tissue paper. Then her progress toward the light stopped. For a brief second, she was suspended, looking into the light, feeling the wonder of it, but knowing she would go no farther right now.

She awakened feeling refreshed but not at peace, not like her dead people. The dream did not comfort or enthrall her. It was just one more confusing pinpoint in her map that was taking her down the road to nowhere except maybe a 5150 lockup. She'd done a fifty-one and a half on a woman before, involuntarily committing her to a mental hospital for seventy-two hours. The woman was stony and quiet the entire trip. Vining now understood. Talking about it gave it validity.

In the early morning while Emily slept, Vining played the CD. After a solid night's sleep and in the warm light of morning, she again heard Frankie Lynde's instructions seven minutes in. Why couldn't Emily hear it? If her subconscious was conjuring messages from Frankie, it was doing so with precision timing. Maybe she was losing her marbles. That was the true explanation.

She stepped back and tried to look at it from a different perspective. What if she did wear the necklace? What harm would it do? Who would know? On the other hand, maybe that step made her certifiably insane, following instructions given by voices in her head. Wasn't that what some of the notorious psychos of all time did? Didn't Son of Sam claim to glean his instructions to murder from a dog?

Dressing for work, Vining put on her second best suit, the navy blue one. Into the slacks, she tucked a dark gray shell with a mock turtleneck. She'd purchased several shells with high necks before she'd returned to work, thinking she'd cover her scar. Today, she was less concerned about that than creating the appropriate background.

From her dresser, she picked up the pearl necklace and put it on.

"I am not insane. I don't know exactly why I'm doing this or what's happening to me, but I know I am not insane."

She admired herself in the mirror. The necklace was striking, dangling precisely inside the V formed by her buttoned jacket. She unbuttoned the jacket and looked at it that way, too. It suited her. That was a creepy thought, but she had to admit the necklace suited her.

She remembered the pair of pearl earrings set with tiny diamonds that Wes had given her one birthday early in their marriage. She used to wear them all the time until he left and she relegated his few gifts of jewelry and her wedding set to the bottom corner of her dresser drawer. She found the earrings and put them on.

She recalled Frankie Lynde's words on the CD, "He gave them to you."

Of all the people who might have dropped the necklace in her mailbox, she never considered it was from T. B. Mann. The Lonny Velcro incident had happened five years ago. She'd put away the necklace and forgotten about it. If it was a gift from T. B. Mann, that meant he had been watching her for much longer than she ever imagined. There was a more reasonable explanation for thinking she heard Frankie's ghostly words on tape. She'd had T. B. Mann on her mind lately, driving by the El Alisal house, getting the case files from Kissick. That's all this Frankie Lynde voice-from-the-grave stuff was— the product of her subconscious mind on overload.

She looked at the card that had accompanied the necklace. The paper stock had a rich texture and a raised border. It looked expensive. Selected by someone who had an appreciation for that sort of extravagance and the time and money to indulge it. The message was scrawled with a fountain pen.

Congratulations,
Officer Vining

She'd never had the handwriting analyzed. She never thought much about it other than people were strange.

He gave them to you. Wear the pearls.

"Okay. Fine. I'm wearing them. Now what?"

TWENTY-TWO

L isa Shipp heard music. Classical guitar. She didn't recognize the tune, but it was beautiful.

Her head throbbed. It felt as if the top of it was going to explode. Trying to turn over, she realized she was restrained. Her arms and legs were tethered to the four corners of the bed or whatever it was she was lying on. Horrible images played on the insides of her eyelids, fueled by her imagination.

Lisa! Open your eyes.

She forced herself to do it. The first thing she saw was herself, nude, splayed out, hands and feet chained to the corners of steel foot- and headboards. There was a mirror on the ceiling above her.

She was whole. She breathed a sigh of relief. She was alive and she was whole. Nearly whole. She squinted at the mirror then pulled up her head as far as she could to see. Her pubic hair had been shaved off.

She shivered.

"You're awake," he said.

The guitar music continued.

She winced as she strained to raise her head and shoulders and climbed onto her elbows. The chains were about two feet long, attached with locked cuffs. She drew her knees up, crunching as tightly as she could, until she could cover herself a little with her legs and arms.

Looking left, she again saw her reflection—this time in a row of large, freestanding mirrors, their frames set with caster wheels at the bottom. Around the bed were several video cameras on tripods. There were lights—around the bed, attached to the ceiling—sufficient to supply a photography studio.

She swallowed. Her throat was bone dry.

What the hell have you gotten yourself into now, Lisa?

He was across the room on a straight-backed chair, one foot propped on a small box, a guitar resting on his elevated leg. He was reading music on a stand in front of him. His other foot tapped the floor, keeping rhythm. He was nude, sitting in profile. His body was taut, tanned, and muscular. She remembered thinking he was handsome when she'd climbed into his car. Dark wavy hair. His nose was a little broad and prominent, but it made his face interesting. Kept him from looking like a sample in a plastic surgeon's picture book. His smile and eyes had been kindly and concerned.

She hadn't been the least bit afraid of him. She realized her judgment had been clouded by her desire to help the drunken woman. Otherwise, she wouldn't have put herself at risk. She thought she was done with risky behavior. Well, just like she'd always be an alcoholic, she guessed she'd also always be a daredevil. She figured she was on number eight of her nine lives. Her luck had held longer than she deserved. Wasn't this poetic justice? She had finally pulled her life together and look what it got her.

She'd trusted him. Believed him. She was raised at the beach and used to being around all kinds of people.

Everyone from all walks of life came to the beach. If he'd been able to put one over on her, who'd seen just about everything, he was good. Real good. Which was bad news. He was a kind of scary she'd never come across before.

"You can raise the bed," he said. "The control is by your right hand."

She found it and elevated the top. It was a full-on hospital bed. She felt the crunching of a plastic lining beneath the sheet.

Where was she? The rectangular room felt damp and musty. The air was cool. The ceiling was low. The walls were finished with unpainted plasterboard. The floor had wall-to-wall, low-pile carpeting. Under and around the bed, plastic sheeting covered the carpet.

The dankness indicated she was underground. Maybe it was a basement. If so, it was a commercial building or a very old house. Houses in California rarely had basements. The houses in the beach city neighborhood where she'd grown up had crawl spaces. She remembered going to a party at an old house in Claremont when her friend was attending one of the colleges there. The basement was such a novelty for her and her friends that they'd traipsed down for a look, to the amusement of others who enjoyed poking fun at Californians anyway.

Maybe she wasn't in California.

Along one side of the room were musical instruments—an upright piano, electric organ, drums, and percussion gadgets. There were guitars and basses, electric and acoustic, in stands around the floor, and amplifiers and recording equipment. The space was comfortably furnished with leather easy chairs, couches, and sturdy coffee tables. A large flat-screen television was the centerpiece on one wall. A full-size refrigerator/freezer and a counter with a sink, microwave, and stacks of disposable plates, cups, and cutlery took up another wall.

She craned her head to look behind. The opposite side of the room was set up as a gym with racks of dumbbells and barbells, workout benches, top-of-the-line cardio equipment, and more rolling mirrors.

To her right was a bathroom that didn't have a door. She couldn't see if there was a tub or shower.

It looked like an upscale frat house.

He paused in his playing to turn the page of music, then resumed.

The sound was muffled and quiet, yet the notes were pure.

She looked around the room again. The unpainted wallboard was caulked along the joints. The ceiling was also covered with wallboard.

The room was soundproofed. The realization alarmed her more than anything she'd seen so far. More than the chained bed. Maybe it was soundproofed because of the music.

Come on, Lisa. Who are you kidding?

Maybe he had a warren of such rooms in which he held women. Maybe he would press her to abduct a girl for him. She wouldn't be able to do it any more than the drunk woman who'd tried to warn her. What had he done to her?

And there he was. Making music without a care.

She ached all over. As her mind cleared, the pain grew more localized, and there was no denying the source. He'd raped her while she was unconscious. The realization made her recoil, jerking against the restraints. She told herself to calm down. It was a blessing that she hadn't known what was going on. She feared she wouldn't be as lucky the next time. Of course, there would be a next time. And a time after that and after that until . . .

You've done it now, Lisa. You've really done it to yourself now.

He looked at her. He seemed oblivious to her chains, nudity, and the way she had contorted herself in a grab for dignity. "Do you like music?"

She nodded. She didn't know if she could speak. She gave it a try. "Yes." Her voice was raspy. She'd been in and out of consciousness for what seemed like days. She didn't even know if it was day or night.

"Where am I?"

He smiled. It was a gorgeous smile, which made it all the more chilling. "A fun place."

"What city?"

"Why does that matter?"

"Are we near Hermosa?"

"Close to it."

"Are we near Los Angeles?"

"Yes." His voice was clipped. He was peeved. "We're near Los Angeles."

She stopped probing. She felt better knowing she was not far from home. She didn't want to die someplace she didn't know. She realized the idea was ridiculous, but it gave her a modicum of comfort. She was born in Southern California. She'd always thought she'd die there. At least she could have that, if it came to that.

He continued playing. He was pretty good, she thought, and couldn't jibe the image of the musician, the sensitive artist, with that of the brutal psychopath who had abducted and raped her.

"It's Bach. Prelude in C Minor. Do you like Bach?"

He didn't wait for her response, but returned to his music. He might as well have been talking to a dog.

Lisa fought the urge to block everything out. To hide. She wanted to close her eyes, but forced them to stay open. She had to be here, in the moment. She had to watch everything. Pay attention. Learn any weakness in her surroundings or in him. She had to look for something she could use to escape. She had no doubt that he intended to kill her. This was too elaborate a setup for any other purpose. But she didn't think he was going to kill her today. She was still a new toy, not yet broken.

He stopped playing then yawned and stretched, holding the guitar by its neck. With a groan, he stood. He placed the guitar onto a stand.

He was magnificent, but the sight of him left her beyond cold. She noticed keys dangling from a leather cord around his neck. "So, you're a musician."

"I have been. Been lots of things."

Sounded like an opening. She'd keep him talking. Make him get to know her. She'd read somewhere that killers turned their victims into objects. Dehumanized them. She wouldn't let him do that to her. She'd make sure he knew who she was, even if he refused to acknowledge it. She'd always been a good talker. It was one of her best attributes, although her father told her that the gift of gab was a double-edge sword: strength and weakness.

"My name is Lisa Leona Shipp."

Her headache pounded behind her eyes. Talking made it worse. Her voice reverberated as if she were inside a steel drum.

"Leona is my grandmother's name on my mother's side."

From the refrigerator, he took a beer and twisted off the cap. "I couldn't care less, sweetheart."

"My name is Lisa Leona Shipp. I'm thirty years old. I grew up in Torrance and I live in Hermosa Beach. I work as a teacher's assistant at a grammar school there. Just started. I did temp office work for a long time. I'm studying for my teaching credentials at night. I'm the first one in my family to have a white-collar job. I come from a family of drunks and—"

"Honey, I don't care about your sad story. Everybody's got one."

Lisa felt her bravado draining away. "I've been sober for a month. I just celebrated my anniversary when . . ." She decided to drop that conversational thread.

He opened another beer and poured it into a plastic cup.

"I've never been married, but I was engaged once. I blew that because of my drinking. I'd like to get married and have a family."

He approached the bed.

She gasped but forced herself to keep talking. The chains reached just far enough for her to cover her breasts with her hands. "My hobbies are surfing, movies . . ."

He bent close to her neck and inhaled deeply.

". . . knitting. I've started knitting . . . It's very calming. I work out. Never used to. The new Lisa works out. I jog on the beach almost every day. I like to read. Mostly history and biographies, but I like a good mystery, too. It keeps me busy."

He closed his eyes as if trying to separate the undertones of a fine wine. He made a small noise of pleasure and moved his head down her body. She felt his breath as he smelled her all over.

She unconsciously pinched her skin as she held herself more tightly. "I have so much more time since I've stopped drinking . . ." She let out a bleat of pain.

He'd bit her on the toe. He leered at her, his head above her feet. "Shut up."

She obeyed.

He grabbed a pair of pants tossed over the back of an easy chair and put them on. Using one of the keys around his neck, he unlocked the cuff on her right ankle.

She flinched when he touched her.

From the floor, he picked up a longer chain and locked this around her ankle. He then unlocked the other cuffs.

She sat up and drew in her knees, dizzy with the effort. She was sore in places she didn't want to think about. She pulled on the chain. It was narrow gauge and about six feet long.

He picked up the cup of beer and held it out to her, a taunting look on his face.

"No thanks." She desperately wanted it, but she could not. To take it would do more than betray her pledge. It would acknowledge that she was lost. She was not lost. She was going to get out of there. Oh, her head hurt. At least the pounding headache made her forget about the rest of her body.

"Honey, I'm not impressed by your sobriety. I make my living off drunks. If I were you, I'd take the drink. I'd take as many as I could get."

She could smell the beer in the cup and on his breath. The cup was full to the brim. A circle of creamy foam lined the edge. It was cold. She could see condensation around his fingers. She knew how it would taste. How icy it would feel going down. She was thirsty. It took every ounce of willpower to shake her head no.

"I would like some water though, if you have it."

"Suit yourself." He chugged down the beer without stopping until it was gone. Then he wiped the foam from his lips and burped. He pressed his fingers against his lips with a sheepish grin. "Excuse me."

"Do you have aspirin or something?"

"Headache, huh? I'll get some." First he took a plastic bottle of water from the refrigerator and handed it to her.

"Are you cold?" he asked.

From a cabinet beneath the counter, he took out a bundle, peeled off a plastic wrapper, and tossed her a brand-new fleece coverlet.

He ascended stairs against the far wall.

She thought she heard him unlock then relock two sets of doors.

She couldn't figure him out. Not that she had any basis for comparison. He had kidnapped and brutalized her, yet seemed concerned about her comfort. She'd witnessed how quickly his polite demeanor could turn menacing. She recalled his dark eyes and sadistic smile when, inside his car, he'd grabbed her and held the cloth over her face. He was a Jekyll and Hyde. The worst monsters live among us, pretending they are one of us. Like that BTK killer, they marry, have families, attend church, are active in the community, and it's all part of their disguise. That's how they get away with rape, torture, and murder for years and years, right beneath our noses.

"Stop it, Lisa. Don't go there. Stay strong."

She twisted the cap from the water and thirstily drank. Clutching the coverlet around her, she stretched her legs over the side of the bed. It was high off the ground. Her toes touched the plastic that covered the carpet. She looked past the bed and saw the sheet she was standing on was still attached to a large roll. Was it there to gather things that might fall on the ground, like hair and blood? Torn off fingernails?

"Lisa, knock it off," she told herself.

She stood and her head swam. She waited until she got her bearings and then walked to the bathroom. The chain was long enough to reach. There was a bathtub with a shower inside. The space was spotless and smelled strongly of bleach. She used the toilet.

A plastic curtain hung from steel tubing over the bathtub. It was printed with a cheerful pattern of fishes and looked brand-new. She slowly drew it back. The shower and bathtub were molded of a synthetic material in one solid piece. It also looked brand-new and like something that could be easily removed. A fresh bar of soap was there along with new bottles of shampoo and cream rinse in brands she didn't recognize but looked expensive. There was a loofah and a nail brush.

She was glad to have access to a bathroom and to find it tidy, but the antiseptic cleanliness unnerved her. More plastic sheeting lay atop the linoleum. She leaned over, making her head pound more, and picked up the edge. The linoleum looked bright and new.

She went to the sink. What she had thought was a mirror was a sheet of shiny metal bolted to the wall, similar to what stood in for glass mirrors at highway rest stops. It dimly reflected her image. Mirrors in the other room abounded, but they could be moved. She could reach this one.

"A suicide would ruin his fun, or maybe he doesn't want someone stabbing him with a piece of broken mirror. Gee, Lisa, you're starting to think like him. Maybe that's good."

A brand-new bar of soap, a large off-white oval, was on the sink. Embossed in its center was a French word. There were high-priced bottles of lotion. The label on one specified it was just for the face. Another only for feet. A third that she guessed was for the rest. A plastic cup held a new toothbrush in a box and a tube of toothpaste. There was a hairbrush, comb, and plastic bottle of mouthwash. There was a stack of skimpy towels in assorted sizes on a chrome hotel rack bolted to the wall. The sink was of the same cheap synthetic material as the bathtub and the fixtures would have felt at home in a Motel 6.

Everything was disposable.

All of a sudden her skin crawled, as if tainted by his touch.

She pulled off a mat draped over the side of the tub and put it on the floor. She turned on the shower. The water flowed cold and she would have settled for that, but then it warmed up and eventually became hot. She climbed into the tub, dragging the chain with her. She didn't care if he didn't want her to do this. The hot water beat on her. She poured on shampoo and clawed her scalp with her fingernails. She wet the loofah and rubbed her skin until it was raw. She scrubbed beneath her nails, hands, and feet, working with a frenzy until the brush cut her skin.

She stepped onto the mat, pulled towels from the rack, and dried herself. She slathered on the lotion and brushed her teeth.

She looked at the mess. Her hair was in the tub. Towels littered the floor. She made a move to mop up with a used towel, then started to laugh. He'd kidnapped and raped her and was probably going to kill her, and she was concerned about being a poor houseguest.

She made a toga of the coverlet and combed out her hair in the pseudo mirror. The sheet of polished metal was a benefit. It was probably best that she could not see herself clearly. Beneath the sink, she found a hairdryer. There were also extra rolls of toilet paper, boxes of tissues, tampons, and sanitary napkins. It was so well thought out and so perverse. She imagined him setting the feminine hygiene products on the store counter, explaining to the cashier, "Just a few things for my torture chamber."

Figures. The most considerate man she'd ever been with was a psychopath.

She started drying her hair. She closed her eyes and tried to imagine she was in her little rented house near the beach.

An old gospel standard entered her head. One she'd latched onto in recovery. "This little light of mine, I'm gonna let it shine . . ."

She finished her hair, turned off the dryer, and whispered the last of the chorus. She tightened the toga, blinked away tears, and returned to the bed. She longed to sit in a chair but they were beyond her reach.

He returned carrying a tray loaded with food—sandwiches, chips, fruit—and six Advil tablets, all on plastic plates. There was a plastic fork and spoon, but no knife.

He opened a tray table, set down the food, and pulled up a chair. He gestured for her to sit.

"Thank you."

"You're welcome." He seemed pleased with the food he'd presented her. "I don't know what you like to eat, but I'm not going to starve you to death." He chuckled and that boyish glimmer again entered his eyes.

"It looks great." She had been a vegetarian for many

years, but didn't complain, picking up a roast beef sandwich and taking a bite. She needed to keep up her strength. The beef was good. She'd forgotten how good. She downed two Advils.

"Um . . . Could I have my clothes?"

"No."

"I would feel more comfortable with my clothes."

"I prefer you naked."

She ate. He sat a few feet away, watching her, a satisfied smile on his lips.

She blurted out the question on her mind, mostly to test him. To see if he wavered. She soon regretted it. "Are you going to kill me?"

"Yes."

TWENTY-THREE

Vining got a ride to the station with Julie Principe, the mother of Emily's friend Aubrey. Vining was picking up her Crown Vic today. Julie worked for a group of general practitioners in an office near Huntington Hospital, not far from the police station. The hospital was yet another monument to the legacy of railroad magnate Henry E. Huntington in the region.

It was the girls' last week of school before summer vacation, and they excitedly chatted about upcoming trips and plans. Emily would go with her father and his family for two weeks at their mountain cabin in Big Bear. Later in the summer, she would join Aubrey and her family for a week in a rental house near the beach in Cambria. Emily and Vining would go camping along the Kern River in Sequoia with Vining's sister and her family. The two of them would spend a long weekend in San Diego and would take day trips on many of Vining's days off. Between sojourns, Emily was taking a photography class.

Vining set out to make Emily's summer busy and fun. The girl had spent enough time with worry and blackness and consumed with her mother's issues. Vining knew firsthand how unfair that was.

Vining tried to participate in the conversation but she was distracted. Almost forty-eight hours had passed since they'd found Frankie's body. They had no solid suspects. She caught herself unconsciously fidgeting with the necklace. She put her hands in her lap and focused on the female gabbing.

Shortly after the girls were out of the car, Vining pressed forward on her personal summer project. She hesitated then blurted it out.

"Julie, can I speak confidentially? I'm still working through issues from the incident—the attack."

Julie shot her a glance and waited.

"It's just . . . I'm still not sleeping well."

"I'm amazed you can sleep at all. That murdered policewoman on top of everything else you're dealing with."

"Right. I was just wondering . . . Could you recommend a good therapist, psychologist, whatever?"

"Of course. There's a woman who has an office in our building. Our doctors refer patients to her. Our biller saw her when she was going through her divorce. I don't know if she's taking new patients, but I'd be happy to call for you."

"Thank you. I appreciate it. Again, I hope we can keep this between us."

"Absolutely."

"I don't want to scare Emily. She's been scared enough."

Julie leveled a gaze at Vining. "Nan, I understand. It's fine."

"Thanks." Vining looked out the window. At least that was over.

"How about that film of the murderers dumping the police officer's body?"

"Excuse me?" Vining couldn't believe it. Had the Thorne security film been leaked? She hadn't had the television or radio on.

"It's all over the news." Julie described the film. "It's awful. Do you think it's a hoax?"

Vining's stomach sank. "It's no hoax."

"Good Lord. I sure hope you catch them."

"Yeah."

Vining got out on Walnut Street alongside the station. She walked to the corner and was about to turn down Garfield when she saw a throng of reporters and TV news vans. She considered dashing back down Walnut, but knew it looked unseemly to be caught running from news cameras. She relaxed. The reporters likely didn't know who she was or that she was working the Lynde case. Lieutenant Beltran had been the face of the PPD during the Lynde murder investigation.

She squared her shoulders and strode into the mob.

She learned their memories were longer than she gave them credit for.

"Detective Vining! Nan Vining!"

Once one sounded the clarion call, the rest swarmed in.

"Detective, what can you tell us about the security tape? Is it a hoax? Was that the woman at the strip club? Are you looking for two people? Do you have any leads? What about the car? Who leaked the film?"

The microphones, cameras, reporters, and their frenetic energy made Vining flash back to the months following the Lonny Velcro shooting. Then, she had only spoken to the media through her attorney. She glanced toward the station and wondered if her team was watching her from the second floor, hiding out until the coast was clear.

Vining muttered "No comment" and "A spokesman will be making a statement." She kept moving, pushing them aside, until a reporter asked a question that stopped her.

"There's speculation that whoever killed Officer Lynde might be the same person who attacked you. Is a killer targeting female police officers?"

Vining should have kept going, but took the bait. "I have something to say about that." She gazed into the camera's shiny eye. "First, we have no evidence indicating the incidents are related." She paused and stared into the lens.

You're out there and you're going to hear me.

"Second, I have a message for any- and everyone involved. My message is: Keep looking over your shoulder because we're coming up on you."

She put up her hand to prevent the woman from again blocking her path and jogged up the station's front steps. A uniformed officer there kept the media from entering.

Vining was glad to enter the elevator. Someone in street clothes darted inside with her. It was Frank Lynde.

It took her a second to reorient herself. "Frank. Hello. I—"

"Nan how are you?" The words tumbled out without punctuation.

The last time Vining had seen him was the day they'd found Frankie's body and he'd shown up at the scene. He looked even worse now.

"I'm okay, Frank. How are you doing?"

He moved in a way that conveyed that things were dicey. The buzz cut he'd worn all the years Vining had known him looked freshly trimmed. He had bathed and shaved, but his face bore several razor cuts. His hand wasn't steady. His eyes were bloodshot and puffy and his skin tone looked as if he'd had too many nights alone with a bottle. He had put on weight over the past couple of years. His posture suggested he had stopped caring.

"You're not back on duty already?"

"No, no . . . They gave me time off until after the funeral." He closed his eyes and smirked. "Found out LAPD's not giving Frankie a fallen hero's send-off. They tell me it's because she wasn't killed in the line of duty, but I know different. It's cuz they think she went over to the other side. But they're sending a wreath and maybe her lieutenant and a commander will stop by." He smiled, but it wasn't because he thought it was funny.

"Seven years, Frankie was with LAPD. She busted a lot of heads for them. This is how they repay her—a couple of fucking brass at her funeral and a wreath. And I'm supposed to be grateful. Now they're showing that thing on TV, with those two dumping Frankie's body like a sack of garbage."

"There's nothing I can say, Frank. It's horrible."

The elevator opened and he held out his hand, inviting her to exit first. "Hey, you have a second?"

She didn't want to be cornered by him but there was no graceful way to turn him down. "Sure."

He ducked into an empty meeting room. She followed.

"I talked to Frankie's friend Sharon and she told me all about this Lieutenant Kendall Moore Frankie was seeing. Course Frankie's aunt Barb had already found out that Frankie was serious with somebody. Frankie never told me anything. We didn't have that kind of a relationship. But this Moore had something to do with what happened to her."

"Why do you say that?"

"Come on, Nan . . . That's the way these things go."

"You know I can't talk about an ongoing investigation. What did Frankie's aunt tell you?"

"Frankie came to a family wedding a couple of months ago and my sister Barb asked why she didn't bring a date. Barb was always on Frankie about getting married and such. Frankie told her she was seeing somebody but wouldn't say who. She said she'd bring him around soon. My sister asked if it was serious. Frankie said she thought so. Barb said, 'You think so?' Frankie said, 'It's complicated.' Barb said, 'Why? Is he married?' Then Frankie turned bright red to her toes. Got all indignant. Said, 'This is why I don't talk to my family about my life. Don't worry about me. I know what I'm doing.' Barb hit the nail on the head. She figured she was hiding him for some reason. He was either married or in jail.

"At the luncheon, I asked Frankie about her boyfriend. Said that Aunt Barbara had told me she was seeing someone. She said she didn't want to talk about it. Frankie was never one to cry, but she looked like she might, so I dropped it. I'm thinking maybe Frankie did something stupid, like threatened to tell the guy's wife. I don't know."

Vining listened sympathetically but did not comment.

"Nan, I want to find out what happened to my daughter."

"We'll find out, Frank."

"That was the last time I saw her, that luncheon. I got my award for twenty-five years of service. Twenty-five years of living by my wits and I couldn't even ask my daughter what was buggin' her that day. She couldn't sit still. Wouldn't tell me what was going on. Why would she? We hadn't had a meaningful conversation in years. Maybe never, to tell you the truth."

"There's always the coulda woulda shouldas, Frank. Everyone has regrets. Frankie cared about you enough to come out that day to celebrate your achievement. Says a lot."

He gave himself a second's respite before resuming his penance. "The autopsy was yesterday."

She knew what he wanted to know. He would find out soon anyway. "She died when her throat was slit."

"Sexual abuse?"

"Yes."

He sucked his teeth and looked away.

"Frank, what are you doing?"

He wiped his eyes.

"Frankie knew you loved her," she said. "And she loved you. Nothing is . . . Lots of us have family relationships that aren't perfect."

"Lots of us could have tried harder, too. Then they're gone and there's no more trying."

She put her hand on his arm. "Go home and get some rest. And I shouldn't have to say this, but I will. Don't do anything stupid."

He raised his hand, telling her to leave. She left him standing there.

In the Detectives Section, Ruiz buttonholed her. "Walked right into it, didn't ya, Ivy?"

She at first thought he was talking about her conversation with Frank Lynde. He was talking about her run-in with the media.

"A simple 'No comment' wasn't sufficient?"

"I scraped my shoes before I came up."

"Where you been, anyway? Having a Starbucks?"

She firmly patted his shoulder, the action calling attention to the several inches in height she had over him. She again restrained herself from patting his head.

"Just talked to your buddy Frank Lynde."

"He's here?" That sobered him. "Why didn't he come in?"

"Left him in a meeting room down the hall." She pressed her lips together, showing the encounter was not good. "No hero's funeral for Frankie."

"He told me yesterday. Poor bastard. He's never getting over this."

Kissick passed by, making a clicking noise with his teeth. He had a shoe box under his arm. "Quick meeting in the war room. You look nice. That's pretty."

"Thank you." Vining ran her fingers down the necklace. *Her death stones.* "Had it for years." That was the truth.

He looked ragged. She suspected he'd had little sleep.

She walked into the conference room on the heels of Lieutenant Beltran and Sergeant Early.

Deputy Chief Dwight Lutz was there, as was Commander Vic Santoro, who was in charge of the Special Operations Division that included the Detectives Section. Caspers, Sproul, and Jones were there. A woman Vining didn't know was also present.

The presence of brass from upstairs showed the pressure to break the case was running downhill. The strain leaped from Early onto her team like an arc of electricity.

Early thumped the table. "Okay, let's get started. Like to introduce Deputy D.A. Mireya Dunn from the CAPOS, or Crimes Against Police Officers Section. Officers Ray Campos and Aaron Faraday have joined the team. We've logged about three thousand leads so far. Thank you, Commander Santoro and Deputy Chief Lutz, for getting us the extra help and taking care of the O.T. we're racking up."

She bowed in their direction.

They nodded in response.

"It seems like the attention of the world is focused on our city," Early said. "After we finish here, Lieutenant Beltran will make a statement about the Thorne security DVD that's all over the media. We were going to release it soon anyway, but not doing it on our terms makes us look like we've lost control of the investigation. Any theories about how it got out?"

"My guy uptown who enhanced it for us said it never left his sight," Kissick said. "I believe him."

Vining said, "Yesterday, when I picked it up from Iris Thorne, the homeowner, she told me someone from her security company had come out to help her copy the sequence onto DVD. My money's on that guy."

"We are where we are," Early said. "Jim, was your

guy able to clean up that DVD enough to make out faces or the make or model of that SUV?"

Kissick said, "He improved it but not enough to see the faces or sex of the two suspects. The view of the vehicle is obscured. It's possibly an SUV but it could be a van. Judging from the builds of the two suspects, they appear to be male and female. The footprint Vining tracked down supports that. Using the model that Forensics made for me and with the help of the manager of the Lady Footlocker over in the mall, I found a match with an athletic shoe."

The shoe he took from the box had thick soles with a band of bright pink in the middle that matched the synthetic leather trim on top.

Ruiz was droll. "Isn't that sweet?"

"New Balance Wind Lass, woman's size seven. It's a new style, on the market this year. Manufacturer says about fifty thousand have been shipped since January. Retails for a hundred and twenty-five dollars. Sold in athletic shoe specialty shops, high-end department stores, catalogs, and on the Internet. Comes in three colors: orange crush, purple haze, or power pink."

"Adorable," Early said.

"This is potentially our Night Stalkers."

Kissick was referring to the nickname law enforcement had given to the Avia brand athletic shoes that serial killer Richard Ramirez had worn while committing murders in the mid-1980s, leaving behind distinctive footprints.

"We'd be lucky if it is," Santoro said. "Footprint could belong to someone drinking beer in the arroyo."

"That's a possibility." Kissick returned the shoe to the box. He was struggling to claim a win. "Still, it doesn't leave this room. We don't want Lolita getting rid of her shoes like the Night Stalker did. After the media got word, Ramirez threw his shoes off the Golden Gate Bridge."

"We can state with a fair degree of confidence that we're looking for a male and a female," Beltran said. "What else does our suspect profile look like as of today?"

Kissick took it. "The female's is based on the woman Frankie was seen with at the strip club. Caucasian. Approximately five feet five inches tall. One hundred ten pounds. Eye color unknown. Hair color unknown. Twenty-five to thirty years old. Our male suspect is easily six feet, judging from how he measures up to Lolita in the security DVD. Medium build. One hundred eighty pounds. Race unknown. Hair and eye color unknown. Making an educated guess, I'd say he's anywhere from twenty-five to fifty. He has plenty of money. And he recently lost a crown off a molar."

Early turned to Ruiz. "Tony, any progress on the dental crown?"

"It's another needle in a haystack scenario, like the strip club limo. The crown may be as unique as a fingerprint but there's no dental crown registry to run it through."

"That's what you *can't* do," Early said. "What *can* you do?"

Vining was glad she wasn't the target of Early's testiness.

"I took it to a dental lab here in Pasadena," Ruiz said. "It's first-rate work. Porcelain overlay. Close to a grand to have it made and set. We're not dealing with someone on public assistance, which we already knew. Whoever lost that crown has probably gone to the dentist to be fitted for a new one and had a temporary put in. Having a jagged crater in your mouth is no picnic. I need a warrant to access dental records. I need a suspect before I even know what dentist to search. Unless someone has a brilliant idea, I don't know where else I can go with this."

He seemed to challenge Early to confront him again.

"Speaking of suspects, what about the good Lieutenant Moore?" Early asked. "Our profile doesn't exclude him. The crown is a way to clinch it or take him off the table for good. Do we have enough for a warrant?"

"What's your fact pattern?" Dunn asked.

Kissick gave her an overview of their history with Kendall Moore.

"It's circumstantial," Dunn said. "Even the most generous judge would have a problem issuing a warrant for dental records."

"What if we just ask Moore?" Caspers suggested. "Hey L.T., how ya chewin' lately?"

There was scattered laughter.

Kissick said, "If Moore is our guy and we start asking questions about his teeth, he'll have a sinking feeling about where he might have left that crown and make his dental records disappear."

"His wife would know," Vining said.

They all looked at her.

Early raised an eyebrow. "Nan's right. The wife always knows. She probably made the dental appointment."

"How do we finesse that out of her?" Kissick asked.

"Bet I can do it," Vining said. "A little woman-to-woman chat."

Kissick raised his chin. "You're on."

"What else?" the deputy chief asked.

"We're fielding leads," Early said. "Tracking down each one that seems legitimate."

She was spreading sunshine, Vining thought. People had called from all over the country and even from foreign cities with Lolita sightings. Lolita could be in there somewhere, among the calls about runaway wives, hitchhikers on the highway, and clerks in Rite Aid drugstores. It sometimes happened like that. The most mundane lead rocked the case open. Or maybe they'd merely collected refuse from the public's overactive imagination.

Early said, "Caspers. Sproul. You make any progress with Randall Mattea or Dustin Lamb?"

Mattea and Lamb were men Frankie had recently arrested who had long and violent criminal histories.

Caspers jumped to respond, grabbing the opportunity to be in the spotlight in front of the brass. "Sproul and I brought them in for questioning. Both have alibis for the early morning of June six. We followed up and the alibis check out."

"We think they're telling the truth," Sproul added.

Lutz distractedly tapped a pencil against the table. "We've got shoes, we've got dental crowns, we've got shadowy security tapes. What we don't got is names. When are you going to produce some names?"

"Nan's working an angle at the Huntington Hotel," Kissick said. "The Police and Citizens Awards Luncheon that was on April fourteenth. Frankie was there to see her dad get his twenty-five-year award."

"What are you saying? She met the couple who killed her at our heroes' luncheon?" Santoro snorted. "That's great for P.R."

Vining defended her theory. "She might have. Frankie's paper trail shows her life took a turn around then. Jones was running down the guest list."

Jones spoke up. "I ran the names that Vining highlighted through NCIC, NCIS, and DMV. Several had criminal records but they were either from years ago or the guys are too old for our profile."

Ruiz said, "That luncheon angle is a dead end. Just because Frankie was text messaging Moore from there, so what?"

Early agreed with him, to Vining's dismay. "We don't need to spend more time on it."

Vining tried to keep it alive. "It'll take me ten minutes to talk to the catering manager today, then it's done."

Early flicked her hand. "Fine."

Jones started sniggering. "You know Officer John Chase?"

Early scowled at him. Her fuse was short. She was in no mood.

Vining knew Chase well. He was the rookie who was with her when she'd shot Lonny Velcro.

Jones continued. "In my background search, I found out that Chase pulled over one of our citizen heroes who got an award that day. Gave him a fix-it ticket because his car windows were tinted too dark."

Caspers broke out laughing. "The Chaser. Gotta love him."

Others who'd worked with Chase, including Vining, laughed along. The young officer had a reputation for aggressive policing, writing citations, and making arrests for minor violations that more seasoned officers would let go. He wanted to show he was tough and working hard as his goal was to move into the street gangs unit.

"Who did Chase cite?" Lutz asked.

"Last name Lesley," Jones said. "Jerry? John?"

"No way," Lieutenant Beltran exclaimed. "Not John Lesley?"

Vining repeated the name to herself.

Beltran indignantly went on. "I sat at the table with him and his wife. He's a great guy. He was the one who saw the elderly couple being robbed in a minimall on Altadena Drive and Orange Grove. Was driving back from a meeting, took a wrong turn looking for the freeway, and encountered this robbery in progress. He jumped out of his car, engaged the suspect in a foot pursuit, tackled him, and held him down until we got there. His wife is as cute as a button." He turned to Lutz. "You remember them, Dwight. You were at our table."

"Right," Lutz said. "Nice guy. Owns a nightclub in West Hollywood."

"I don't know where you're headed with this banquet business, Vining," Beltran said. "Investigating our citizen heroes. I mean, John Lesley. You've got to be kidding. That means his wife is this Lolita you're looking for. Ridiculous, in my humble opinion."

Ruiz hid his smile.

"Lesley fits the broad profile." Kissick defended Vining's pursuit of a lead that he never thought viable in the first place. "We'll wrap it up today."

"You ought to drop it today," Beltran said. "There is no way the Lesleys are involved in this."

Early said, "Vining, tie up your loose ends with that and move on. Okay. Jones and Sproul have been pulled to work the robberies last night at Dinah's Diner and Mack's Chicken. To bring the rest of you up to date, at about twenty-two fifteen last night, six masked and armed gunmen entered Dinah's Diner on Foothill near Sierra Madre, ordered the patrons to the ground, made off with cash and jewelry. Twenty minutes later, the same group, apparently, did the same thing at Mack's Chicken on Mountain near Lake. Thank you for your contributions, Louis and Doug."

The restaurant robberies were horrific crimes and difficult to process because of the number of witnesses and victims, but pulling investigators off to work them signaled that the brass thought the Lynde case was going cold. Inevitably, new homicides would occur, stealing more resources, each one pushing Frankie Lynde's file back even further. In time, Kissick would get to it when he could, following trails that had grown dusty or evaporated altogether, reluctantly putting his faith in luck.

Vining glanced at him. His game face was inscrutable, as always, but he looked weary.

Early stood. "Stay safe."

Outside, Early stopped Vining and Ruiz. "I'm going to need you to put in extra hours tracking down leads tonight and tomorrow. They should start to peter out after that."

"I'll make arrangements at home," Vining said.

Ruiz uttered an abrupt, "Oh-kay."

Early didn't give him a second look but headed to her office.

At her desk, Vining called her grandmother. She didn't like Emily staying home alone again. She realized it bothered her more than it did her daughter.

Ruiz sidled up to her as she was shoving papers into a portfolio.

"What's Early got a bug up her butt about?"

There was nothing like having a difficult supervisor in common to ameliorate hostilities between coworkers.

"She's got a lot of pressure on her from upstairs."

"Because of Ms. Attitude, I'm going to miss my son's athletic awards banquet tonight. I told her about it yesterday. He's a senior. This is his last banquet in high school, he's getting an award, and I'm going to miss it. She could bring in two patrol officers on their regular shift. No overtime. Shows she's not thinking. She's in over her head with this thing."

"It's a tough case." Ruiz had annoyed Vining so much lately, she had a hard time feeling sympathy for him. She didn't know how long ago he'd tripped the odometer and became a jaded cop, but she suspected he could no longer see that milestone in his rearview mirror.

Ruiz hadn't expended his venom. "And Kissick . . . He's milking this for all it's worth. He's building his legacy on this case."

Vining showed no response.

He cussed and retreated to his cubicle. Within a minute, he was bitching on the phone to his wife.

Vining made a promise that she would quit the Job before she turned into Ruiz. She did wonder why Lieutenant Beltran spoke so well of John Lesley. Everyone's a suspect until it's proved they're not. She knew Beltran liked to rub up against celebrities. Whenever Pasadena was used as a location for a movie or TV show, Beltran liked to hang out at the scene. He often spoke of the screenplay he'd written. Everyone knew he'd had his teeth whitened. It wouldn't surprise Vining at all if Beltran had extracted an invitation to John Lesley's club that day at the luncheon.

This put her in a difficult situation because there was

something about Lesley she liked as a suspect and she couldn't express why.

On her way out, she passed Jones's desk. "Did you talk to Chase about the fix-it ticket he gave this John Lesley?"

"Yep. Said Lesley pushed back. Got a little heated. Lesley told Chase, I've just been given an award by the Pasadena police and here you are giving me this boo-shit ticket. Chase said it was no biggie, but he's always pissing off citizens. He's used to it."

"Did Lesley take care of his tinted windows?"

"The next week. Had his ticket signed off by a sheriff's deputy over in West Hollywood near his nightclub. Place called Reign."

"Did you say Reign?" Caspers's head appeared above his cubicle. "He owns *that* place? That's the hottest club in town. I got on their guest list once. My old roommate works with this guy who knows this guy who's on that new TV show about the blended family and some such crap. What a night. They've got these fish tanks with these ultra smokin' chicks swimming in them. They're wearing bathing suits, but barely."

Jones was fascinated. "Like see-through?"

"Ch-yeah. Nearly."

"No men?" Vining faked confusion. "It is West Hollywood."

"Nooo." Caspers grinned. "This club is for guys who love women. There's no mistaking that."

Vining had enough. "Okay. Remember Frankie Lynde? Found with her head nearly cut off? So Lesley is clean other than the fix-it ticket?"

"Matter of fact, he's not. Got a hit on DVROS. His ex-wife got a permanent restraining order against him nearly five years ago. He's married to someone else now. I didn't look further."

The fact that John Lesley was in the Domestic Violence Restraining Order System told Vining that the PRO his ex-wife had put in place was domestic violence related.

Jones added, "His ex-wife is that model, Michaela Michele."

"No way," Caspers said. "What a life that bastard has."

Jones started to hand Vining a sheaf of papers. "Here's your materials back." First, he drew a line across a name with a red pen.

"When were you going to tell us about the PRO, Jones?" Vining asked.

"Didn't think it was a good idea in the meeting, seeing how far Beltran was up Lesley's ass."

"Coward," Vining teased. "Thanks for your help, Louis."

"You're welcome. I may need your help on my two new cases. You were assigned to Robbery when you came back, right? Until this Frankie Lynde murder landed on us."

"Jim needs all the help he can get."

"Case is going cold."

"Right." She looked at the papers he handed her. The red ink line through John Lesley's name looked like a knife cut.

TWENTY-FOUR

*J*ohn Lesley drove his Hummer down Ventura Boulevard with his right hand on the wheel, his left holding a cigar out the open window. The huge vehicle dwarfed others on the boulevard even in the SUV-laden San Fernando Valley. He'd had many cars in his day, but he loved this one best even though the windows were no longer tinted to his preference. The car was still an awesome ride.

He turned onto a small residential street. In Valley parlance, he lived "north of the boulevard." This was a less desirable, less hip address than "south of the boulevard," in the hills and canyons that stood between the Valley and fashionable West Hollywood, Westwood, and Bel Air. But he lived on the remaining five-acre parcel of a once-expansive citrus grove. Acreage in Encino. That said something. It harkened back to a bygone era of weekend house parties, croquet, and Tom Collinses on the lawn and swan dives off the high board in air scented with orange blossoms and night jasmine. He possessed one of the rarest commodities in Southern California: He never heard his neighbors.

In contrast with the congestion on the Boulevard, the quiet, narrow street felt rural. It didn't have a painted line. Giant eucalyptus trees grew down the parkways where sidewalks had never been installed.

Most Valley neighborhoods were a series of yards and tract houses. The Valley was farm and ranch land until after World War II when developers bought out the citrus growers and ranchers. Up went acres of cookie-cutter houses on postage-stamp lots for returning G.I.s and their baby-boomer families. Now developers were tearing down the old homes and building mansions out to the property lines. Larger parcels were being subdivided. This property had been doomed to a date with the bulldozers until Lesley bought it after fierce bidding.

Lesley felt privileged and loved it. To quote a corny movie, he felt like he was king of the world. He'd done many things in his life. Accomplished many milestones. Owning a property like this had been just one of his goals. Having beautiful wives that other men coveted was another. Having the hottest club in town was another. But all those were just window dressing on the way to achieving his ultimate dream. The money gave him the means. The secluded home gave him the place. The beautiful, fragile wife gave him the foil. The nightclub gave him above-the-law celebrity and access. It was all table setting for the main event. Now that he'd accomplished murder, he'd found it more satisfying than his wildest dreams. The release he'd experience had been so powerful, such a high, that he immediately wanted more. It was a physical craving and could not be denied. One hit was sufficient for addiction. Like crack.

He was blessed with many natural abilities, but this was his raison d'être. A dream deferred had now been realized.

He hadn't been certain he'd be able to pull it off. Like

most personal tests and tough challenges, there was that crunch moment, that do-or-die point where he had to face himself straight on and ask the hard question: Can I take it to the next level? The answer was a resounding, *Yes, I can!*

He had his system down. He hadn't achieved success in business by accident. He applied the same hard-learned principles to his new endeavor. Now he was set up to do it as much and as often as he wanted. It was easy for a smart, clear-thinking man to get away with murder. The technology today made it tougher than in, say, Jack the Ripper's day. He had to stay on top of developments in forensic science and investigative procedures. But it wasn't hard to stay ahead of cops, for crying out loud. The hardest part for wannabes was keeping your wits about you and keeping your mouth shut. He'd always been blessed with sangfroid, so that had never been a problem. But as far as using a partner, he had to rethink that big time. He hadn't clearly thought out the Pussycat factor. Then, he hadn't expected that Frankie would be his first. Frankie presented a convergence of circumstances that begged for appraisal with fresh eyes. Then there was Frankie herself. There was irresistible Frankie . . .

He would never do it again like he had with her. He would snatch them off the street with no strings attached. Or track a potential victim until the time was right. He expected repercussions from Frankie. The cops hadn't come sniffing around, but he suspected they would if they were smart enough to follow the minuscule trail he'd left. But that would die down and the cops would go away. He'd taken pains to cover his tracks.

Money. The K-Y Jelly of life. That's what he always said and it was so true. A brilliant observation, if he said so himself, that illustrated the inexorable bond between the two most important things in life: sex and money. Anyone who thought otherwise was a fool.

It had been Frankie's fault. When the three of them had partied those last weeks, she'd become hostile, making broad hints that she was about to end it. He decided he had to act or risk losing her. Couldn't be hotheaded. Had to keep the old self-control. Frankie had always claimed that he and Pussycat were her dirty little secrets. That she had told no one.

"What am I going to tell my friends?" she'd said. "That I'm seeing a high-profile pervert who's paying me to participate in his sex games?"

If someone else knew about them, he would have let her go. He needed proof. He didn't hope for absolute confirmation, but he could look at the evidence and weigh what his instincts told him. Having Pussycat steal Frankie's documents and computer confirmed that Frankie had told the truth. Only then did he make the decision to follow through.

It had been Frankie's fault. So tough, but so vulnerable. He was skilled at picking out female vulnerability. The wounded soul beneath the coat of armor. The fluttering sparrow's heart within barbed wire. All he had to do was peel back the defenses enough to get inside and they were his. Fueled with booze and pot and satiated with sex, he'd slowly gotten Frankie to open up to him, talking about her mother's murder and her distant father. Talking about the aunt and grandmother who raised her but never accepted her. Talking about the married police lieutenant she'd loved but who had only used her. Talking about the abortion she'd had because he'd said it was better for them and how he'd dumped her right afterward. She'd cried. It was the only time he'd seen her cry. She was too tough to cry at the end, but she'd cried talking about the lieutenant who'd done her wrong. As she laid her soul bare, Lesley fell in love with her little by little. She belonged to him and no one else. It had been Frankie's fault.

She was his first kill. That premier position of bittersweet reverie would always be hers, and rightfully so. There would be many more. He was at last, finally, pursuing his true vocation. Once he was old and in failing health, he would confess. But unlike other pussies who let themselves get caught, he would go out differently. He envisioned more of a Butch Cassidy and Sundance Kid exit in a hail of gunfire. Standing. Not strapped to a table waiting for the death juice.

But today he had a more pressing dilemma. Pussycat had become a liability. He had to think long and hard about that one, but for the moment, he had the situation contained.

Midway down the block, he turned into a driveway. Two semicircular walls of rough brick supported an iron gate that swung open when he clicked the remote. He drove down a long, straight lane that cut across a broad lawn. The ever-present background noise of roaring leaf blowers faded as he moved beyond the gates. Soon, he heard nothing but birds chirping.

Surrounding the property was a grove of orange, tangerine, and grapefruit trees. On a long stretch of lawn was an archery target on a stand. A rack holding bows and quivers of arrows was fifty feet away. The equipment belonged to the previous owner, Walter Lemming, a silver medalist in archery at the 1936 Summer Olympics in Berlin, where Hitler sought to demonstrate the superiority of the Aryan race. The four gold medals won by African American track star Jesse Owens and the medal won by Lemming, a Jew, spoke for themselves. Lemming became a sought-after archery coach and built a reputation for training Hollywood stars for roles. He also collected archery equipment. Dozens of antique wooden archery sets decorated the rough hewn walls of a clubhouse on the property. When Lemming died without heirs, the executor of his estate offered the equipment to Lesley. Lesley also asked for the photograph of Lemming posing with Sylvester Stallone, whom the Olympic champion trained for his Rambo movies.

A sprawling ranch-style house was at the end of the lane, about an eighth of a mile away. Lesley had maintained the integrity of the original structure while adding a two-story addition to the back. Terra-cotta pots filled with multicolored flowers descended the brick steps that led to the front door.

In back was a large lawn with a putting green. Beyond it was a pool. To the left were a guesthouse and the clubhouse that looked like a sportsman's lodge with redwood beams and genuine Navajo rugs on the wide-planked floor. Encircling the property were acres of citrus trees with a couple of avocados thrown in for variety.

He pulled in front of the detached garage. An older Toyota was parked where the lane widened at the front of the house. The front fender was painted with gray primer, an unfinished home collision repair job. It belonged to Lolly, his longtime housekeeper.

He went into the house through the back door, which was always open when Lolly was working. He stubbed the cigar in an ashtray on a glass-topped table and left it there. He'd retrieve it later. He liked to smoke cigars but could not abide the smell of smoke in his house. This created a dilemma for him when Frankie had been pleading for cigarettes. Tired of her bitchiness, he'd caved in and let her smoke, only after he'd bought Ionic Breeze air purifiers from Sharper Image. The new one, Lisa Shipp, the dry drunk vegetarian, hadn't asked for cigarettes. He'd nearly gotten her to drink beer, but she'd resisted. No fluttering sparrow's heart there.

"Hey, Lolly Lolly. I brought your favorite pastries from Weby's."

Lolly was a solid and steady, fortyish El Salvadoran who had lived in California for over twenty years. She'd worked for John Lesley since he'd bought this house fifteen years and two wives ago. Lesley knew she wasn't a particularly good housekeeper, but she was reliable, wasn't nosy, and did what he asked.

"Good morning, Mister John. Oooh . . . Look. So good. Thank you." She took an apricot turnover from the box and set it on a paper towel she tore from a roll. She bit in, scattering flaky pastry crumbs onto her chin. "None for you?"

"No goodies for me this week, I'm afraid. I have to watch my figure, or no one else will."

Lolly made a dismissive noise. "Oh, no, Mister. You're in good shape."

"Well, thank you."

"Mister John, Pussycat is still not well?"

"That's right. She has a terrible migraine. She needs to lie still and stay in a dark room."

"But so long? Maybe she should go to the doctor."

"She's been to the doctor, Lolly. He's given her medication. She gets these very bad migraines sometimes. She needs to rest. She's fine. Leave her alone."

* * *

Pussycat was lying in bed with her bichon frise Mignon snuggled beside her. She didn't have the energy to get up. She'd been wearing the same cotton p.j.s for more than a day. They used to be her favorites, now she was sick of them. She should get up, shower, wash her hair, change into street clothes, put on makeup, and fix her hair. If she continued to lie here like this, he had won. She still had some fight left in her. Certainly she did. She tightly held Mignon and closed her eyes. She'd get up later.

She picked at the skin on her arms. Coming off meth made her skin feel like worms were crawling under it. She shoved her hands beneath her.

She'd been locked in her suite of rooms for over twenty-four hours. Only the night before last she'd helped him drug Lisa and carry her into the basement. She'd then climbed to her own rooms and fell deeply asleep, nauseous, still drunk, and crashing down as the meth wore off.

When she'd awakened late the next morning and tried to leave the suite, she discovered she was locked in. There was a small lock on the inside door, but there had never been one on the outside. Now there was one.

She then saw the portable phone missing from its cradle on the end table in the sitting room. Rushing into the bedroom, she found that phone gone, too, the unplugged cord lying across the nightstand. Her purse was where she usually left it, but her cell phone was gone.

She pounded and yelled at the door to the suite, then ran to a window and flung open the heavy black-out drapes. Plywood had been nailed over the windows. The heads of the nails had been cut flush with the wood. She clawed at the panels. Maybe she could find something to pry it off with. Then what? She had no ladder and nothing to use to climb down. Maybe she could tie bedsheets together as she'd seen in movies.

She returned to her purse and took out her wallet. He'd taken her cash and plastic. Her car keys were gone, too. She could still break through the wood and glass, climb out the second-story window, and run to a neighbor's house. She now regretted not attending any of their holiday parties or being more cordial. She didn't know any of them beyond waving hello as she drove out in her Mercedes. She could still run over there. Run to the neighbors, and tell them what? That she'd helped dispose of the murdered policewoman's body? That she'd helped kidnap another woman who was in their basement right now? At least she assumed Lisa was still there.

On the mirror over the bathroom sink, he'd taped a note: Behave yourself and I'll bring Miss Tina to see you later. Take a Xanax and eat something. You'll feel better.

She'd looked inside the cabinet to find he'd left her just two tablets from her recently filled Xanax prescription.

Also missing were the over-the-counter Benedryl she took for hay fever and a bottle of aspirin. In their place were two plastic cups. One held three aspirins. The other had two Benedryls. Her razors were gone, too. And her meth.

He thought she'd try to kill herself. It had occurred to her even before they'd met Lisa. Two Xanax, two Benedryl, and three aspirin would knock her out and give her a terrible hangover when she woke up, but wouldn't kill her.

A few weeks ago, she would have believed he was concerned about her. Now she knew he was more concerned about a suicide bringing the police and their questions to the house. He knew her sister would check on her if several days passed without a phone call.

He'd stocked the small refrigerator with plenty to eat and drink and had left food for Mignon. She'd fed the dog, but couldn't eat a thing herself. Where was Lolly? He must have told her she was sick and not to be disturbed. Knowing Lolly, she'd be happy to have less work to do and would leave it at that.

She felt too sick and drained to cry.

She had loved him once. Always having been a practical girl, Pussycat saw just one solution for him. He would have to kill her. She'd watched enough Court TV to know the best way to dispose of a wife was to make her disappear, have an airtight alibi, and be double damn sure her body never turned up.

He already had the most important part of all nailed. He was a liar par excellence.

On the bed, her dog blinked coal black eyes buried in a cloud of white fur.

Pussycat scooped her up and cradled her beneath her chin. "What are we going to do, Mignon?"

She saw herself in the mirrored closet doors. She looked pathetic.

She set the dog on the floor and got up. Her husband hadn't thought of everything. She yanked open the doors to the walk-in closet. All her clothes and accessories were intact. She opened a drawer full of belts and another of scarves. She grinned with childlike glee at having outsmarted him. She grabbed a handful of scarves. Scarves seemed the best to do the trick. They felt smooth and cool in her hands and she knew from her fashion design courses that silk was one of the strongest fibers there was.

"Where?"

She remembered a story about a rock musician who'd hanged himself with a belt from a closet rod. She'd seen it on VH-1. It was rumored that he was doing that weird sex self-suffocation thing. Yeah. Right. Who was she to talk about weird sex? Then there was the TV mobster's girlfriend who'd hanged herself from an overhead light fixture.

She went into the sitting room and looked at the chandelier. She pulled a long, narrow scarf taut between her hands. She looked at the chandelier, then at the scarf, and again at the chandelier. She drew her fingers across the fine skin of her neck and let the scarf slither to the floor.

Maybe he had thought of everything after all.

If she couldn't kill herself, she could at least slide into unconsciousness for a while. She took one of the two Xanax tablets and set it on the nightstand with a cup of water. She lifted the dog into bed with her and pulled up the covers.

She again pressed her hands beneath her.

This was what her meltdown in Hermosa Beach had brought her. What did he think? That she'd just passively go along with his plan to abduct, torture, and murder women? Hello . . . He'd always been into kinky sex games, but she hadn't seen this coming. Should she have? She was a stripper, not a psychiatrist, for pity's sake. But she was also a person who had always lived by her wits. So far, he'd stayed a step ahead of her. Now, she needed to get a step ahead of him.

Maybe I can cut a deal with the police, she thought. I'll get a good attorney. Someone he doesn't know. He said there's no evidence linking him to Frankie. If the police can't prove he did it, they'll let him go. Then he'll kill me.

It would be my word against his, and who would believe me? He'll make me disappear. Killing him is my only way out. I'll say it was self-defense. Or I'll make it look like an accident. Maybe I'll make *him* disappear. Dear God, is Lisa still alive? I need to get out of here. I need to bust through the windows, make a rope, get out of here, and run to find a phone.

She started to get out of bed, but fell back into it. She felt nauseous and exhausted. Who was she kidding? She was crashing too hard to do anything, except what he wanted.

The door of the suite opened and she heard him singing made-up lyrics to his favorite song: "Pussycat, Pussycat, where are you?"

He stood in the doorway of the bedroom carrying a tray. "There she is." He made room for the tray on the nightstand beside the bed. He raised a silver dome covering a plate to reveal scrambled eggs, toast, and fruit. There was a thermos of coffee, a glass of orange juice, and a red rose in a bud vase.

"You look like shit, my dear." He handed her the orange juice. "Drink this. I can tell you didn't follow my instructions to eat something and take a Xanax. Sit up. Drink this, I said."

She climbed to an elbow, took the juice, and sipped. "How's Lisa?" she croaked.

"She's fine. *She* was wondering how *you* were. Isn't that considerate?"

"I wish I was dead."

"Pussycat . . . Come on, now. I brought a visitor for you." From his shirt pocket, he took a small Baggie. "Miss Tina," he sang.

It was both the last thing and the only thing she wanted. She reached for it.

He pulled it away. "Not so fast. I'll get a bump ready for you while you eat something. Then you're going to wash your face, put on sunglasses, and we'll go downstairs. You're going to tell Lolly you have a migraine and that the light makes your head hurt more. You've been very ill, but you're feeling better and you need to be left alone for a few days. If you can pull that off, you can have the rest of the Baggie."

He handed her a piece of toast and pressed it against her lips.

She took a bite, staring fiercely at him.

"This is your fault, baby. You had to be the drama queen. Here's the deal. As long as you play nice, I'll make sure you stay even. You won't have to feel shitty like this again. And if you don't care about yourself, I know you care about your sister. Fuck with me and I'll snatch her off the street like we took Lisa. I've always wanted to get my hands on her tight little ass. Then I'll put you both in the basement. After I'm done, I'll dump you both in the desert, side by side."

TWENTY-FIVE

Vining hung out in the report-writing room while waiting for her car. A couple of tired officers who had finished their Morning Watch at 8:00 a.m. were still there at computers banging out arrest reports. Some of these would end upstairs in the Detectives Section. Three Latino juveniles, gangbangers or wannabes with hair shorn as short as velvet, gang insignia tattooed on their scalps and across the backs of their necks, were sitting in a glass-walled area on one end of the room, isolated from the adult prisoner population and supervised by officers.

She stuck her head into the Patrol Sergeants' office and asked about the schedule of Officer John Chase, who had written the fix-it ticket to John Lesley. Chase was off until Saturday.

"You have his cell phone number?"

"I do, but I think he went out of town." The sergeant searched for the phone number and gave it to her.

When she was leaving, a female corporal who had overheard the conversation followed Vining from the room and pulled her aside. Vining had become friendly with her while working out at the gym in the building.

"Don't expect a call back soon, Nan. Chase went fishing in Cabo with his buddies. Bachelor party. They might not have cell phone service where he is."

"Do you know where he's staying?"

"He didn't say."

"Thanks."

Jones had already talked to Chase. He reported nothing remarkable about his interaction with Lesley other than normal irritation from receiving a citation. She'd been told to finish the luncheon angle and move on. Still, the name John Lesley rolled around in her head like a ball bearing in one of those maze games she'd played when she was a kid. Rolling into dead ends, searching for the trapdoor—the way out.

After receiving her car keys, she walked down the hall and through the door that led to the parking garage. She went down the stairs and along the uncovered driveway, out of the way of the stream of officers going in and out, finding a private corner where she called Chase's cell phone. He didn't answer. She left a message.

She headed back up the stairs where officers were jiggling a key in the door, bitching about how no one had fixed the lock yet. Someone exiting held the door for them and Vining went upstairs to the Community Services Section. She met with Officer Roberta Ulrick who had coordinated the luncheon. Everyone who'd received an award that day had been photographed with the chief. She wanted to see the citizen hero.

"I remember Mr. Lesley. He was the nicest man." Ulrick found John Lesley's photo. "And not hard on the eyes, either."

Vining admired the shot of the tall, tanned, dark-haired man with the winning smile. He was wearing a well-cut, dark suit and an expensive-looking tie and was firmly grasping the chief's hand.

"Am I right?"

As Vining looked at the photo, the background of the midnight blue stage curtain began to undulate until it looked like troubled water. Lesley's face floated upon it, rippling, breaking up and then becoming clear.

"Don't you think?" Ulrick tried again for a response.

"Absolutely." It was a catch-all answer and rarely a wrong choice.

"Does he have something to do with Frankie Lynde? You're working that case, right?"

"Right. We're talking to people who might have interacted with Frankie at the luncheon. Following up on everything."

"The million tendrils of a life."

"You got it. Didn't Lesley bring his wife?"

"Oh, yes." Ulrick looked through the photographs. "Guess we don't have a picture of her."

"What was she like?"

Ulrick made a face as if she didn't know where to begin. "Also very pleasant. Good-looking as you would expect, being his wife. Some of our guys commented that she was built like a brick you-know-what house."

"What's her name?"

Ulrick looked over the guest list. "They were at table four. Let's see. Pamela Lesley. But her husband called her Pussycat, which the men ate up, of course."

The ball bearing rolled from one side to the other.

While Ulrick ran John Lesley's photograph through the scanner to make a copy, Vining returned to the Detectives Section and logged onto the databases to search for a criminal background on Pamela or Pussycat Lesley. Nothing came up. She was on the phone with her contact at the DMV when Kissick came by.

"What's up?"

"Getting background on John Lesley and his wife."

"John Lesley. The citizen hero who got the fix-it ticket? Why?"

Good question. She didn't have a solid answer. "Following up the luncheon angle."

"Nan, John Lesley and his wife were there with Frankie Lynde and two hundred of their closest friends. So what?"

"An hour ago you asked me about my progress on the luncheon."

"And the sarge said to quickly finish and move on. Frankie Lynde's murderer would not have attended a police event. I don't know why I encouraged you to follow up on it. Not to mention that it became personally embarrassing to me."

"It shouldn't have been. We have sound reasons for checking out the people who were there."

"We have bigger fish to fry, like thousands of leads. I need you elsewhere."

Vining saw the strain in his face. "Okay. You still want me to talk to Kendall Moore's wife?"

"Yeah. See if the SOB has dental issues so we can cross him off the list."

"Will do."

"Without any solid leads, we are in CYA mode—covering our backsides so nothing comes back to haunt us." He managed a smile. "Just so you know, the crap that's running downhill is pooling at my feet."

"I know, Jim. Remember, we're on the same team."

"You said the key word: team. Last thing I need is Cowboy Nan taking off alone into the sunset."

"Got it." She had to check herself. The last thing she needed was to revive her old jacket. She wouldn't have a prayer of returning to Homicide or staying at any desk in Detectives.

"Thanks, Partner," he said. "You okay?"

"Fantastic. You?"

"Never better."

They both grinned at the lies.

Vining checked the fax machine on her way out, wanting to grab her materials before anyone else saw them. The driver's license and car registration information for John and Pussycat Lesley were waiting. They lived in Encino in the San Fernando Valley. Pussycat's photograph showed her to be cute, not gorgeous. Her lips were slightly parted as if she'd been coached on how best to pose. Thick, blond hair framed her face and fell past her shoulders. Twenty-four years old. Brown eyes. Five feet five inches tall. One hundred thirteen pounds. Vining visualized the artist's sketch of Lolita at the strip club. The profile fit.

John Lesley was not smiling in his license photo. His attitude was different from his pose with the police chief. Vining read his gaze as menacing. Someone else would interpret it as annoyance after a long wait at the DMV. He was thirty-eight years old, six-foot-one, one hundred eighty, brown over brown.

He had four cars registered to him. Three were registered to his home address: a new Mercedes S600 sedan, a 1965 Cadillac Coupe de Ville convertible, and a five-year-old Ford F-150 truck. One car, a black Hummer H2, was registered to his business address in West Hollywood. He was driving this car when Officer Chase pulled him over in Pasadena.

As she was leaving, Caspers snatched her as she passed his cubicle.

"Hey, Vining. Listen to what I found out about your boy Lesley. It's like lifestyles of the rich and stupid. He tried to get a restraining order against his wife, saying she stalked him, but it wasn't granted. In the permanent R.O. she got against him, she claimed mental and physical abuse, saying that he once strangled her until she was unconscious and had threatened her with guns. She didn't report any of it to the police, of course. She also said he made her participate in weird sex games with prostitutes. He claimed it was all a ploy to attempt to nullify the prenup. Part of their divorce settlement was an agreement never to disparage each other publicly. This is like eating a steak."

"You got all that from DVROS?"

"Hell no. I Googled John Lesley and Michaela Michele. Got dozens of hits. Most of the material was on this Web site, Stupid Celebrities dot com."

"That PRO still in effect?"

"It's got another year on it."

"Don't let Kissick know you're fooling around with this. He's in no mood."

"I was just taking a break for ten minutes. We've been working twenty-four seven. Kissick needs to lighten up. He's getting on my last nerve, too."

"See you later."

At the in/out board, Vining moved the magnetic dot into "In the Field." Under the terms of the PRO, John Lesley would be forbidden to possess or be in the vicinity of firearms. Guy like John Lesley who owned a nightclub, bound to be a firearm on the premises. She could likely arrest him on a 166, violation of the stay away order.

In Community Services, she picked up the copy of John Lesley's photo with the chief and made photocopies of it and Pussycat's driver's license photo.

The Lesleys were invited to Pasadena to accept an award and had received a fix-it ticket while heading to the freeway. John Lesley had marital difficulties. None of that had anything to do with Frankie Lynde.

Then why couldn't she let them go?

Manda Angeloff, the busy and efficient catering manager at the Huntington Hotel, had already spoken with the staff who had worked the luncheon. Some of them remembered seeing Frankie Lynde with her father, but no one recalled anything noteworthy.

"There were a lot of officers in uniform there. It was a sea of navy blue. No offense, but you kind of look the same."

"Do you have someplace where you could post Frankie Lynde's photograph on the off chance that an employee who wasn't working the luncheon saw something?"

"There's a bulletin board in the employee lunchroom."

"That would be great." Vining wrote her name and cell phone number at the bottom of the flyer. She then showed her the photographs of the Lesleys.

"Remember them?"

"Indeed I do. Especially him. He has that George Clooney thing going on. I walked into the ballroom with him. I thought he was there to act as the emcee. You know how they always get a local TV personality to be the master of ceremonies? Turned out he was getting an award for helping a police officer arrest some guy."

"You walked in with him. Where was he coming from?"

"The pool café. I was checking on another reception we were setting up there. He was walking inside and he held the door open for me." Angeloff's expression showed she was impressed.

"Did he say anything to you?"

"Small talk. Looks like the rain is finally over and such."

"Can you show me where you saw him?"

Angeloff took her down the corridor and they walked outside. The café was busy with the breakfast crowd. Tourists were looking over maps or staring dreamily into the distance. Businesspeople sat stiffly, checking Black-Berrys, nattering into cell phones or at each other.

"At what point during the luncheon was this?"

"I think people were still eating their entrées. That's right. No one had taken the podium yet, so it was before dessert and coffee."

"Why was he out here?"

"I might have smelled smoke on him, but that was two months ago. I can't say for sure."

"Was it raining that day?"

"No, it was beautiful. I do remember that because the people having the reception out here were terrified it was going to rain." Angeloff held her hand toward a man who was passing. "Hector, can you come over here, please? This is Hector, the café manager. He was here that day."

Angeloff explained the situation and Vining showed him the photographs of the Lesleys and Frankie Lynde.

He conscientiously examined them. "I'm sorry, but I don't remember seeing them. That was at the start of our high season. A couple hundred people have lunch here every day."

He flagged down a waitress. "Laura, do you have a second? Laura's here most weekdays."

She was wearing brown slacks and a beige shirt, an apron tied around her waist. Vining thought she was in her thirties. She was trim and tall with blunt-cut black hair. She had several piercings down each ear, but wore diamond studs only in her earlobes. The remainder she likely adorned on her days off. Her eyes brightened when she saw the photograph of John Lesley.

"Oh yeah. I remember."

Vining thanked the others and walked with Laura outside to where she had served John Lesley a beer.

"He said he had escaped the luncheon. They weren't serving alcohol there."

"Why do you remember this?"

"He was a fox."

"I'm sure lots of good-looking men come through here. People who have the kind of money for this place know how to clean themselves up."

"This was more than grooming."

"He flirted with you."

"Maybe he did."

"What about her?" Vining held up the Frankie Lynde flyer.

"I walked away for a second to check on a table and she showed up. Next thing I see, he's lighting her cigarette. She's holding his hand, guiding the flame." Laura rolled her eyes.

"Did they act like they knew each other?"

"No. But she was totally coming on to him."

"Why do you say that?"

"Took his beer out of his hand and finished it. Then she walked back, strutting, flaunting attitude. Nearly shoved me out of the way going through the door. She was big and she was not feminine."

"Police uniforms, Kevlar vests, and thirty-pound equipment belts do that to women."

Chastened, Laura said, "I wasn't talking about all policewomen."

Vining moved past it. "He didn't walk in with her."

"No. I went over to see if he wanted anything else and he was still watching her walk away. He handed me twenty bucks for a six-dollar beer and left."

"She messed it up for you."

"She did. Women like men in uniforms. Maybe it's the same thing in reverse. I still say that she wasn't all that. If that's what he was after, that is not me."

"We found her body by the bridge earlier this week. Maybe you heard."

Laura blanched. "That was her?"

"That *was* her."

Vining handed Laura her card and told her to call if she thought of anything more. She left, satisfied with the waitress's reaction to the bomb she'd dropped. She felt protective over Frankie Lynde and was tired of people talking trash about her.

John Lesley and Frankie had met at the luncheon and flirted. Flirting seemed second nature to him. Frankie was at the end of one bad relationship and was heading into a worse one. She already heard Kissick's response. "So what, Nan?"

TWENTY-SIX

Vining headed west on the 210 freeway that traversed the foothills. It was sparsely traveled compared to the always clogged arteries to the south. She was doing eighty and piqued drivers still passed her. The haze the locals called June gloom hung in the air, muting the edges of the rolling Santa Susana Mountains that had not fully recovered from the last series of fires. She found the barren hills beautiful, their sparseness calming, having the same effect on her as the ocean.

The freeway demographics changed the farther from L.A. she drove. There were fewer imported sedans and more pickups. Flatbed trucks were piled with bales of hay. Craggy sandstone outcroppings appeared in the soft hills. The landscape looked like the background in a western movie, as it should, since many were filmed here. Science fiction, too, the rugged landscape standing in for Mars or the moon.

In Simi Valley, she took the 118, the Ronald Reagan Freeway. Thousands of people had lined that winding road to watch the hearse carrying the body of President Reagan pass by. She'd never been to the library. One Sunday, Wes and Kaitlyn had taken Emily, followed by lunch at an old stagecoach stop that had been turned into a restaurant.

They'd invited Vining to go with them, but she'd used the day to collect overtime. She remembered indulging in reverse arrogance at the thought of Wes and Kaitlyn playing while she had to work. Truth was she didn't have to work. The extra money had probably gone to pay a bill or to buy something Emily wanted that Vining would have managed to take care of somehow.

Why did she have to be so tough all the time? Why couldn't she relax? If she hadn't worked overtime that day, T. B. Mann wouldn't have attacked her. She wouldn't have started on this bizarre path where corpses spoke and strange houses reduced her to an infantlike state. Emily wouldn't have taken on her unhealthy hobby of tracking ghosts. None of it would have happened if she'd been able to enjoy life. If she'd puttered in the yard that day or cleaned out a closet or just taken a walk.

It's not your fault.

With one hand on the steering wheel, she pulled the pearl necklace over her head, opened the glove compartment, and chucked it inside. "T. B. Mann, to hell with you. I'm done. You have no power over me anymore. It's over. Finished. Kaput."

She felt freer. She guessed the feeling wouldn't last, but it felt sweet for that moment.

She exited the freeway. Signage gave directions to both the Reagan Library and the landfill.

Maybe she'd have to accept that T. B. Mann might always be out there. She imagined his face on a helium-filled balloon, a caricature drawn in black marker. She mentally released the balloon and watched as it rose into the sky, higher and higher, growing smaller and smaller until it disappeared.

It was done.

You think it's that easy.

"It is. It is because I say it is."

She opened the glove compartment again, grabbed the necklace, rolled down the car window, and threw it into the meridian, losing it among mounds of oleander abundant with white blooms, thriving in the arid soil.

Simi Valley was a cop-and-firefighter town. Many live in the quiet communities to the north and east of metropolitan L.A. where housing prices are more in line with their means. For the cops, affordability wasn't the only motivation. There they were less likely to run into scum they knew from the streets, people they'd arrested or jacked up, while shopping at Home Depot with their families in tow.

Big-box shopping centers lined both sides of the thoroughfare. She crossed Easy Street and after a mile found the development where Lieutenant Kendall Moore lived. It was a long-established neighborhood of ranch-style homes and cul-de-sacs, built for families, bicycles, and unleashed dogs. The street names were Greek-inspired—Socrates Street, Hercules Court, Plato Court, Aristotle Street—in that oddball juxtaposition that Southern California had mastered. Old Glory was everywhere—painted with house numbers on curbs, decorating pinwheels stuck inside flower beds, hoisted on full-size flagpoles in front yards. Powerboats and RVs were parked in extra-wide driveways.

She turned onto Sparta Court and found Moore's home near the end. The driveway held a new SUV, a powerboat draped with a tan tarp, and a motorcycle. A bicycle lay on the small lawn of St. Augustine. Daylilies bloomed across the front, yellow flowers brightening the green spears. A hibiscus bush as tall as the gutter bloomed pink. An American flag drooped from a post on the front porch. Beneath the flag was another printed with bright flowers that said "Welcome Friends." The porch was furnished with a pair of rocking chairs and a small table of plastic woven to look like wicker. An ashtray had no cigarette butts but retained a residue. A wreath of bent twigs entwined with ribbon and fake berries decorated the front door.

As soon as Vining stepped onto the cement path that led to the porch, two large dogs of indeterminate breed bayed from behind a gate across a side yard. She rang the doorbell.

There was sufficient cuteness to put Vining in mind of Wes's wife, Kaitlyn, who had to hold a record for the greatest number of cloyingly adorable decorative items per square foot. Vining didn't detect any obvious themes here. Kaitlyn collected replicas of frogs. They were everywhere inside and outside her and Wes's manse. Emily once threatened to buy Kaitlyn a real frog as a gift. A disgusting horned toad. Vining would have liked to have seen that, but talked her daughter out of it.

The eyelet curtains moved over the windows off her right shoulder.

Vining held her shield toward the window and then to the peephole in the door.

When a woman opened the door, the fear in her eyes conveyed she expected Vining had come to deliver bad news about her husband.

"Mrs. Moore?"

"Is Ken okay?"

Vining temporarily put her at ease. "Nothing's happened to your husband. At least as far as I know."

She exhaled with relief.

She was not Lolita, although Vining never really thought she would be. Rhonda Moore was three or four inches taller than the strip club description of Lolita and likely fifty pounds heavier. Her hair was done in a curly bob with a reddish rinse, probably to cover gray.

"I'm Detective Nan Vining with the Pasadena Police Department. Do you have a couple of minutes?"

"What's this about?"

"I'd like to ask you a few questions. May I come in?"

"Does this have to do with Frankie Lynde?"

"Yes."

She nodded, as if expecting the visit. "Come in."

Those innocuous two words. The generous gesture of opening one's house to a stranger. This would be the second home Vining would enter since she'd returned to work. Her first, Iris Thorne's home, didn't go well, but that house had put her in mind of the place on El Alisal Road. This house was like the ones she'd grown up around. She understood this house and its people. She felt okay. Had she been in control the entire time? Was that all she had to do to release T. B. Mann and set herself free?

Houses have karma. Lives have karma.

She was going to be fine.

Her conscience again taunted her. *You think it's that easy?*

She stepped over the threshold and looked around, noting the doors and windows, places where people could hide.

"By the way, I'm Rhonda. I was so startled to see you there I forgot my manners. It's never good news when a police officer shows up on your doorstep, especially when you're the wife of one."

She was friendly but not warm.

Breakfast smells hung in the air. Fried eggs, bacon, toast, and coffee.

"Would you like a cup of coffee?"

"That sounds great. Thank you."

The kitchen opened onto a family room dominated by a huge television. It was tuned to a talk show in which four female hosts were badgering a male guest. Rhonda must have been sorting laundry as piles of linens, towels, and clothing were on the floor.

Vining was sure Rhonda cared less about being hospitable to her, but it gave her something to do while she postponed the purpose of Vining's call.

She went about making coffee while Vining strolled around the family room.

There was a coating of dust on an exercise bike near the television. Family photographs covered the walls and flat surfaces. The Moores appeared to have two boys and a girl. There was a wedding photograph. Moore was in a tuxedo, looking about the same but younger and with more hair. Rhonda was in white lace and considerably thinner.

Vining picked up a recent family portrait. The five of them were on the beach, all dressed in blue jeans and white shirts. They were an attractive family. Vining could see Rhonda having the photo made up into Christmas cards she'd mail out with a chatty letter that would state the facts but not the truth. Moore stood in the rear, overseeing his brood. His smile was confident and controlling. The man.

You disgusting rat.

How much did Rhonda know and how long had she known it?

"How old are your children?"

The coffee drained into the pot, filling the air with its homey aroma.

"Sixteen, fourteen, and our girl is twelve."

"I have a fourteen-year-old girl." Vining didn't quite know how to get Rhonda where she wanted her, but talking about family was a place to start.

"Ken adores our daughter, but it's true what they say about boys being easier than girls. Especially lately. Our Meghan has become a handful."

"Emily and I have our power struggles, now more than ever."

The chitchat had superficially broken the ice.

"How do you take your coffee?" Rhonda poured coffee into mugs decorated with teddy bears.

"A little cream or milk and a scant teaspoon of sugar."

That was Rhonda's theme: teddy bears. Now that Vining had gotten it, she saw teddy bears everywhere. Cute and cuddly and nothing like real bears. In reality, they are predators. They kill and eat people.

Vining sensed the tension in this house. Her presence had added to it, but it was there before she had set foot on the front path. The children felt it. Rhonda lived it. And Moore . . . He did whatever the hell he wanted.

Rhonda went to a cabinet for the sugar. She tore open a packet of Equal for her own coffee. She carried the mugs to the family room, set them on coasters on the coffee table, and clicked off the television with the remote. She sat in a deep leather chair and brought her mug to her lips, blowing on the coffee to cool it. She glanced at Vining then back at her cup.

Vining sat on the matching sofa. "Good coffee."

"It's Peets. Ken likes it better than Starbucks. I think they're both too expensive, but I buy it for him."

Rhonda's hair was neat, her makeup carefully applied, her clothes clean and pressed. She wore several pieces of gold jewelry. Her hoop earrings were enameled in a color that matched her outfit. Her figure might have filled out and her husband chased around with other women, but she still made an effort to keep herself up.

"Rhonda, did you know Frankie Lynde?"

"I met her a couple of years ago. Frankie started out in

the Van Nuys precinct. One of the guys had a barbecue. Memorial Day. She was there."

"How long ago?"

"Must have been . . . maybe two years ago. Terrible what happened to her. Made me sick when I heard about it."

She remembered too well a distant, casual encounter that should have been forgotten. It was clear to Vining that Rhonda knew about her husband and Lynde.

"Was that the only time you saw her?"

"Yes."

Vining sensed she was lying. "Why do you remember her? You just saw her once a long time ago."

"I'm sure you've been to backyard cop parties. The wives hang around together and the men stay with the men and the female officers stay with the men. That's where Frankie was. After all, she worked with them and didn't know us. Me and the other wives, we noticed Frankie. She was the kind of woman people notice." Rhonda looked up from her coffee. "Ken was having an affair with her."

Vining reined in her surprise. She hadn't expected Rhonda to come out with it.

"Detective, now you look like you're the one who's had a scare. When I heard about Frankie's murder, I expected one of you from Pasadena to show up. Frankie wasn't Ken's first, but she might have been his longest. No, I don't intend to divorce him. His chasing around doesn't make me happy. It doesn't make me feel good about myself, but he's a great father and provider and a halfway decent husband. I have three kids . . ."

She let the last comment dangle, an underscore to the rest. That summed it up.

"Was he seeing anybody in addition to Frankie?"

"No."

"Why are you so certain?"

"Because I've followed him from time to time."

Vining wondered if Rhonda had friends that fit Lolita's description. They'd focused the investigation on searching for a male/female couple. What if they should be looking for two women? Two women could have beat up Frankie and made it look like a brutal rape. It was far-fetched but not impossible. They could have somehow set Frankie up.

Vining took a sip from the teddy bear mug and knew she was dreaming. This woman did not lash out. This woman bit the bullet and had another piece of cake.

"How long were they together?"

"I think it started before that barbecue, but not much before."

"How did you determine that?"

Rhonda slitted her eyes. "The wives have ways of keeping tabs on the husbands."

"Do you know if Ken gave Frankie jewelry or money?"

"Jewelry or money? You have to be kidding. We have trouble managing our bills as it is. I keep track of the household finances. If he bought anything, I would have known. She had jewelry and money?"

Vining didn't respond.

"If you're thinking Ken stole to give to her, you're wrong. Ken's an honest cop. Check his records. He's had several commendations. He loves being a police officer. He's third-generation LAPD. He would never do anything to discredit his profession or his family."

Rhonda took in Vining as if seeing her for the ogre she

was. She was standing by her philandering husband. Lieutenant Kendall Moore was a jerk, but he was her jerk.

"Ken might be a lot of things, but he's not a murderer. My husband would never do what was done to that woman. He doesn't have it in him. I know that man. I know him inside and out."

Vining made her next comment not to make Rhonda feel better but to grease her enough to keep the woman from shutting down. She could sense Rhonda circling the wagons, withdrawing. "At least he never left you for a bimbo."

The other woman could have a PhD in quantum physics, but in the minds of jilted wives everywhere, she was always a bimbo. The edges of Rhonda's face softened but they wouldn't be grabbing a coffee at Peets together ever.

"Not like my husband, leaving me for a nineteen-year-old hairdresser at Supercuts." That wasn't precisely what happened, but Vining embellished the saga for dramatic impact.

Rhonda tried to gauge if Vining was telling the truth.

After Vining hummed a confirming "Um-hmm," Rhonda made a small moan of sympathy. She then revealed something that Vining had not expected.

"Ken wasn't even seeing her when she disappeared."

"How do you know?"

"He was home when he was supposed to be. When he said he was with his buddies, he was. There's a cop-friendly bar in town. The Maverick. I'd cruise by and see his car parked in front. Sometimes he'd be out on the porch, smoking a cigarette, and see me." She shrugged. "And he was more interested in sex with me."

"When do you think it was over with Frankie?"

"About two months ago. It was my daughter's birthday, that's why I remember. We had a little party. After, I expected Ken to take off because I knew Frankie wasn't working that day. I knew her schedule because I'm friendly with an officer who worked with her. Ken would usually leave after dinner to have drinks with the boys, he said. I knew he'd have one drink and take off, then wouldn't come home until late. That night he stayed home and sulked on the couch. Wouldn't tell me what was wrong. Said he was tired. After that he was always where he was supposed to be. And in a bad mood . . ."

Rhonda winced with the recollection. "I just put up with it. I was happy to have him home."

"When is your daughter's birthday?"

"April fifteen. Ken and I joke that she's our little tax deduction."

"How's Ken been acting lately?"

"Quiet. Not that he's much for talking anyway."

"Frankie Lynde is like an elephant in the room and all these years you've never talked to Ken about her."

She opened her palms as if to say, "There it is."

Vining stood and carried the mug to the kitchen sink. "Thank you for the coffee."

"No problem."

Rhonda looked through the windows over the kitchen sink at a car. It slowed as it passed then circled the cul-de-sac and headed out. Vining saw it was an unmarked detective's car. It was likely Moore.

"I guess that's it." She began walking to the front door as if Vining was a dinner party guest who didn't know when to leave.

On the porch, Vining turned back as if something occurred to her as an afterthought.

"Rhonda, when's the last time you've seen a dentist?"

"Dentist?"

"Dentist."

"I don't know. Six, seven months ago for a cleaning. What does that have to—"

"What about your husband?"

"I'm not getting—"

"Does he go to the dentist?"

"Why are you asking me this?"

"Does he go to the dentist?" Vining gave her the blank eyes she'd learned from Kissick.

"I don't have to answer."

"No, you don't. But it will be easier in the long run if you just answered the question."

Rhonda glared at her. "Ken did not have anything to do with that woman's murder."

"Your life will be easier if you answer the question now, Rhonda. Trust me on this."

Rhonda exhaled noisily through her nose. She gazed beyond Vining, as if seeking divine assistance. Then she gave in. "Ken rarely goes to the dentist, but he's lucky. Has perfect teeth. You want to call our dentist? I'll give you his number. Go ahead and call him."

She could be lying, but Vining didn't think so. This woman would be an inept liar.

"Thank you for your time, Rhonda. Have a good day."

"I hate detectives. You're all the same. Those cold eyes. You hide behind them. I know what you're thinking. Poor thing. Stays married to a serial cheater, but you're not me. Judge not lest ye be judged."

The twig wreath rustled when Rhonda slammed the door.

If Wes hadn't left, Vining wondered if she would have turned into Rhonda Moore. Would she have turned a blind eye to Wes's philandering and crafted a *Better Homes & Gardens* life around a sucking black hole? She didn't know. A lot of years had passed since she'd encountered the young woman she used to be. She was no longer qualified to speak for her.

Judge not lest ye be judged.

Every day she was on the Job she made judgment calls about situations and people. She'd been judged. Plenty. So Rhonda, nine words: *There but for the grace of God go I.*

TWENTY-SEVEN

While sitting in her car in front of the Moore home, Vining called Frankie's friend and fellow LAPD officer Sharon Hernandez. She was off-duty that day but moonlighting as uniformed security part-time in downtown L.A.'s jewelry district. She could meet Vining for a few minutes. She lived in Thousand Oaks, thirty miles north of downtown L.A., but was making a stop at Frankie's condo during her commute. They could meet there in about an hour and a half.

Vining called Kissick and updated him about Rhonda.

When he answered the phone, he had a prickly tone that she hadn't heard in a while. "We can stop wasting time on Kendall Moore."

"Right," she lied.

She told him what she'd learned about John Lesley—

being seen with Frankie at the luncheon, the domestic violence PRO, the nasty interaction with the PPD's John Chase over the fix-it ticket.

"Jim, I know no one wants to pursue citizen hero John Lesley as a suspect, but we have no basis to exclude him or his wife. We're supposed to move off because Beltran thinks Lesley's a nice guy?"

"Nan, we're stepping down because there's no evidence. I don't care about Beltran. You know me better than that. At least I hope you do."

"Sorry, that was out of line." She was angry because she wanted him to leap on the Lesleys, have the same gnawing feeling about them that she did. The facts supported his view. What frustrated her was that they *had* evidence: the dental crown, the New Balance shoe. It was useless unless she could legally link it to the Lesleys.

"Forget it," he said.

There was a pause. "Jim."

"Yep?"

"I know you're under a lot of pressure, but are we having a personal issue?"

"Don't think so."

"Cuz everything was great last night and it's weird today."

"You thought last night was great?"

"I told you that. Come on. Just because I didn't hop into bed with you."

"Like my father used to say, live in hope, die in despair."

She made a small noise to let him know she was smiling. "We'll crack this case, Jim."

"I wish I was as confident. As far as last night goes, I'm mad at myself. You're right. We have to work together.

I've been having doubts about whether we can. Whether it's practical."

That wasn't what she wanted to hear. She tried to be reassuring. "One day at a time."

"Sweet Jesus."

She was about to hang up when he interjected, "Almost forgot. You're on the news."

"Me? Why?"

"This morning."

"Right. The media gauntlet. I forgot. Already?"

"Slow news day, I guess."

"I didn't say much."

"You were fine. They had plenty to say about you. Something to the effect that Officer Nanette Vining was critically injured in a knife attack by an unknown assailant a year ago. Her assailant is still at large, and so on."

"Great. My fifteen minutes of fame has been extended to a half hour. Okay, I'm code seven for an hour or so. Get lunch and run a couple of errands."

She called information for the address of Moore's hangout. His car was the one that had started down the cul-de-sac and retreated. She took a chance on where he might be hiding out. She was confident he didn't kill Frankie, but she wasn't finished with him. Someone had to stick up for Frankie. She might be the only one left who would.

The Maverick occupied a side street corner. The deep wraparound porch was crowded with smokers sitting at resin patio tables or leaning against the porch railing. They were mostly men. The few women wore tight jeans and low-cut tops, whether they had the figure for it or not. A dozen motorcycles were angled against the curb between pickup trucks and Simi Valley PD cruisers. There were sheriff's department vehicles, too. If the cops ate there, it meant good cheap food.

When Vining opened her car door, laughter, country and western music, and the aroma of cooking meat filtered in. The smell made Vining realize she was starving. She drew stares as she climbed the broad, wooden steps. The cops and civilians alike probably made her as law enforcement.

It was a big building, with a bar on the left and a stage and dance floor to the right where a line dancing class was under way.

She spotted Moore seated at the far side of the bar facing the door, hunched over a glass of pale beer. Only his eyes moved as he watched her approach.

The barstool beside him was empty. She didn't wait for an invitation to sit.

"Buy you a drink, Detective?" he asked.

She told the bartender, "Root beer and a menu, please."

The bartender set a red plastic basket of popcorn in front of them and from beneath the bar produced a menu that had a luster of grease. She opened it and closed it after a glance, ordering a cheeseburger with fries. The root beer was cold and had a slight bitter taste that Vining liked. She took another sip before setting it down and grabbing a handful of popcorn. It was a little stale, but she was hungry and ate it anyway.

When she looked at Moore, he bared his teeth at her and opened his mouth wide.

She got the point of his display. She despised him more than ever.

"Got all thirty-two of them. Not a single cavity, although my front teeth are capped from when I broke them playing high school football. Inherited my father's baldness and bad heart, but I got his good teeth."

"Shame. Because of that rotten heart, you'll die before you'll get a full lifetime out of your good teeth."

"Did he leave a tooth in Frankie or something?"

Vining ignored his question and ate more popcorn. "Your wife must have called you right after she slammed the door on me."

His snide laugh degenerated into a racking smoker's cough.

"Rhonda said she figured you and Frankie were together a couple of years."

"Who's counting?"

"Long time to be somebody's back-door woman."

"She wasn't a prisoner."

Wasn't she? Vining thought.

"Maybe the pregnancy was an accident," she said. "I'm sure Frankie thought that after a couple of years together, you'd be more sympathetic. Did she break it to you slowly? Ken, my period's late. Ken, I bought a home pregnancy test. Ken, the test says I'm pregnant. Ken, I did three tests and they all say I'm pregnant. Ken, you promised you'd leave your wife and we'd be together. Ken—"

He whipped his head to face her. "What's your point?"

"She got pregnant and you dumped her."

"Right. *She* got pregnant."

The pregnancy had been speculation until then.

He exhaled a sort of laugh. "Frankie knew the rules. I never told her I would leave my wife."

"Uh-huh. How about those nights when you and Frankie were relaxing after really good sex? There's a little pillow talk. Those dreamy, blue-sky words that just seem to spill out at those times. She's talking about the future . . . You know that master plan women always have for their lives. The Prince Charming, the house with the white picket fence, the perfect assortment of adorable kids. Even women as tough as Frankie want that pretty picture. And not wanting to break the spell, you said, 'Yes, pumpkin, wouldn't that be nice?' Why the hell else do you think she stayed with you? She loved you and you loved her. You loved her, Lieutenant."

The muscles in his cheek pulsed as he clenched his jaw.

"If you didn't love her, you wouldn't have come to our station to try to find out information about her murder. You wouldn't have stood by that hillside after an all-night bender. It took her slaughter to make you realize how much you loved her. She had the abortion because you told her to. Then you decided it was time to end things with her. She had become unpredictable. Emotional. She has to hear through the grapevine that you're seeing someone else. You didn't even have the balls to make a clean break with her, did you? You just stopped returning her calls."

Her voice was low but urgent. She leaned toward his ear. She wanted him to feel her warm breath on his skin. She wanted it to slip beneath the surface and live there, like a fungus.

"Then a sweet seduction falls into her lap, a sexy rich guy who's up front about what she is to him, and she goes for it. No mixed messages there. It's all about sex and money. Problem is, the guy has big issues. He likes to rape and torture women."

Still staring ahead, he blinked rapidly.

"Do you want to hear what he did to her, Lieutenant? He regularly beat her up. She was covered with scratches and bruises, old and new. He'd raped her in every orifice where he could stick his cock. Her vagina and anus had third-degree tears."

She sensed more than saw him begin to writhe. His muscles tensed throughout his body. His back bowed slightly as if his belly had absorbed a blow.

"This asshole was smart, Lieutenant. He used a condom. No semen evidence. After keeping her as his sex slave for two weeks, for some reason known only to him, he decided Frankie's time was up. He made her shave her pubic hair, cut and scrub her fingernails, and wash her hair. Her hair was still wet when we found her. He fed her a steak dinner with salad and wine. He must have tied her up for the next part. He held her neck from behind like this . . ."

She pulled back her head with her fingers. "There were fingertip bruises beneath her chin."

With an imaginary knife in her right hand, she mimed stabbing her neck and pulling the knife across.

He bolted from the stool.

She watched him leave the bar and disappear down the porch steps.

"Cheeseburger and fries, hon?"

A waitress was at her shoulder, carrying a platter of food.

"Yes. Thank you."

The waitress set it in front of her, took bottles of ketchup and mustard from pockets on her apron and set them on the bar.

Vining smacked the ketchup bottle, slathering her fries

and meat. She piled on lettuce, tomato, pickles, and a thick slice of onion, pressed down the other half of the bun, and took a big bite. It was the best meal she'd had all week.

TWENTY-EIGHT

*L*olly *had* worked enough years in other people's homes to know the rules. Rule number one, the rule that went without saying, was "Do your job." The practical interpretation was "Do your job just well enough to keep it." When she'd first started cleaning houses, she used to knock herself out. She soon wised up. The pay and bonuses were not any bigger and the people would still point out things to demonstrate how she wasn't working hard enough. The books on the bookshelves are dusty. The grout behind the sink is icky. She'd learned to say "Yes, Missus," and "Yes, Mister," and fix the problem without argument. She'd then wait for them to bring it up again.

The next unstated rule, as important as the first, was "Never steal." Not even a few cents of spare change. Just dust beneath it, put it in a pile, and leave it.

Rule number three was "If you break something, tell them right away and offer to pay." They would usually be mad, but nine times out of ten would say "Forget it" and not accept her money.

The fourth and fifth rules were "Don't be nosy" and "Don't gossip." Lolly had learned that the richer the people she worked for, the more secrets they had and the less they wanted anyone to know about them. Find butts of marijuana cigarettes in an ashtray—throw them away. Find sex toys in the bedroom—put them in the nightstand drawer. Find bottles of booze hidden—leave them be. Find lingerie that's not the wife's, whatever you do, don't put it with the wife's. You can earn the husband's good graces by giving it to him and acting stupid.

She had worked for John Lesley for nearly ten years and two wives. He was the richest of all her previous employers and had the most secrets. She'd see his picture sometimes in the gossip magazines, especially when he was with the other wife, the famous model. They used to have big parties that Lolly suspected were orgies based upon the women and men in various states of undress she'd find asleep all over the house when she came to work. There would be used condoms everywhere, especially in the great room. She wouldn't touch them even with Playtex gloves and would snatch them up with a pair of steel kitchen tongs she'd later wash in bleach. He would give her big tips when she had to clean up after one of those nights, peeling off $500 from a fat roll of bills. That made it not so bad.

Things grew quieter when Pussycat entered the picture, but in some ways more strange. He finished constructing the recording studio and gym in the basement. He'd have friends down there to play music and party. It was loud when they cranked up the amps. The door to the basement was in an alcove off the kitchen and she'd feel the bass line thumping beneath her feet. The next day, she'd descend the narrow stairs to clean up the usual mess: leftover food, plates, glasses, bottles, and of course condoms. She'd long ago given up trying not to disturb any people she found asleep. Half of them remained out cold while she ran the vacuum around them. She was glad when he'd soundproofed the basement.

She'd helped him test it, standing in different parts of the house while he played music. Once he told her to go down there, scream and yell as loud as she could and he'd see if he could hear upstairs. She did what he asked and didn't think anything about it. She found it curious when the hospital bed arrived, but little surprised her anymore. "Don't be nosy." "Don't gossip."

One morning she'd come to work to find a heavy bolt lock on the door that led to the basement from the kitchen.

"Mister, where is the key so I can clean?"

"You don't need to go down there anymore, Lolly. Okay?"

"Sure, Mister John." Fine with her. Her workload just got lighter. She found it strange that he didn't want her to clean, especially because he was spending more time down there than ever, but she didn't ask and he didn't tell.

Sometimes she wouldn't see him for days, but knew he was home because his car was in the driveway, the big Hummer that Missus didn't like to drive. She wondered if he was living in the basement. Once he was trying to balance a tray of food and had refused her help when she'd approached, but it gave her time to peek past the door. All she could see was a second door farther down that hadn't been there before. It also had a big key lock. Why did he need two doors? She didn't ask and he didn't tell.

Soon after that, he surprised her with a fifty-dollar-a-week raise.

All the years she'd worked for him, she'd gotten used to his peculiar habits, but lately, things were making her uneasy. Missus's behavior confirmed her suspicions that something strange was going on. Missus had always been cheerful and happy. She always asked about Lolly's family and was concerned if one of her kids was sick. Recently, she had dark circles under her eyes and her face was often red and puffy like she'd been crying. She stayed in her rooms a lot and barely ate. She'd lost a lot of weight.

Then in the newspaper and on television, Lolly had seen the pictures of the woman they thought was involved in the policewoman's disappearance. The woman in the drawing had on a cap and heart-shaped sunglasses. Missus had sunglasses like that. After the picture came out, Lolly went looking for them in the drawer where Missus kept dozens of sunglasses. They weren't there. She couldn't find them anywhere.

Lolly didn't say anything to her about it. Shortly after the pictures came out, she heard Missus on the phone with her sister.

"Are you crazy?" Missus said. "You're always trying to do a number on my head. Just because you've never liked John."

Not long after that, Lolly was changing the sheets and Missus was lying on the chaise longue, like she did a lot lately, like she never wanted to get up again. But she got up, opened one of her jewelry cases, and took out a beautiful gold and diamond watch. She stood there holding it by one end, staring at it.

Lolly's dusting brought her nearby and she commented, "Very beautiful."

"Would you like this watch, Lolly? Take it. It's yours."

"Missus, it's so beautiful, but I couldn't take it."

"Please take it. I don't want it." She'd grabbed Lolly's palm and pressed the watch into it.

"Thank you, but—"

"No buts. Here. Take these, too." She picked up a pair of large diamond stud earrings and jammed them into Lolly's shirt pocket.

Lolly was speechless.

"Don't tell my husband. Take them out of the house and never bring them back. Never, ever bring them back or mention this to him or me. *Ever.*"

"No, no. Of course."

Missus had collapsed onto the tufted chaise. She looked so sad. "I can't stand them around me. You're doing me a favor."

Lolly's husband had a friend who worked for a jewelry wholesaler. The friend had the pieces appraised. The watch was a Patek Philippe and was worth $25,000. The earrings were not as grand, but the stones were good and worth about $1,500.

Lolly tried to close her eyes to the strange occurrences and carry on as she always had, but the coincidences were piling up. There was the work done to the basement, the murdered policewoman, the pictures that looked like Missus in the news, Missus's depression, her giving up the jewelry, and Mister locking her in her rooms. She didn't recall having seen the policewoman at the house, but a lot went on after she went home at five and on the weekends when she didn't work. Mister and

Missus were night owls, usually not rising until after noon or later.

Her conscience started to get the better of her and she thought about calling the police, but her husband talked her out of it.

"You're crazy, Lolly. You call the police and they go over there and bother him for nothing, he'll fire you. Then what are you going to do? Who's going to hire you? Word will get out that you're trouble. You know how they talk to each other."

He was right.

Lolly resumed looking the other way until today.

Mister had left for the club around two p.m. like he did every day except Monday, when the club was closed. She knew he'd left the property because she'd heard the "blump blump" noise that happened whenever someone drove over the loose slab of cement in the driveway that tree roots had pushed up.

On the kitchen counter, he'd left keys attached to a leather cord that Lolly had never seen before. She didn't touch it and continued her work. It was her day to clean the big picture windows in the great room. There were televisions in most of the rooms and she usually had them tuned to her favorite telenovelas on the Spanish language stations so she could follow the story as she moved through the house. She carried her plastic carryall of cleaning products and utensils into the great room and was about to turn on the television when she heard tapping.

She left the house through the patio doors. She saw nothing outside that could be making the noise. She poked around the flower beds that abutted a row of narrow windows that led to the basement. The windows were covered with soundproofing material and she could not see inside. On her hands and knees in the dirt, she pressed her ear to the glass.

Did she hear someone yelling "Help"? It was muffled and faint, but she swore she'd heard it.

She ran back inside the house, grabbed the keys, and tried to find one that fit into the lock on the basement door. She'd gone through three when she jumped within an inch of her life as Mister came through the back door. She hadn't heard the warning blump blump of the loose cement block in the driveway.

She hid the keys behind her.

"Hey, Lolly Lolly. Whatcha doin'?"

"I was cleaning the windows in the great room, Mister John."

"You don't look like you're cleaning the windows in the great room. Whatcha doin'? Tell the truth."

She cringed when he came nearer. He could be so nice, making jokes and everything, but he could also get scary. His face would change. His eyes especially. He was scaring her now. She didn't resist when he pulled her arm from behind her back and took the keys.

"I heard noises down there. Maybe rats?"

"Oh, I remember. I was watching television while I was working out. I must have left it on." He put the keys in his pocket. "Didn't I tell you not to bother with anything in the basement?"

"Yes, Mister, you did."

"Didn't I give you a nice raise this month?"

"Yes, Mister."

"You know what housekeepers in this neighborhood earn. You earn more than any of your friends, don't you? A lot more."

"Yes, it's true. You pay me good."

"Okay then. So we don't have any problems, right?"

"No, never. Everything's great. I'm very happy here."

"Good. I like having you here, Lolly. You're a great gal."

She saw through the kitchen windows that he had not pulled up by the garage but had left his car in the driveway. That was why there had been no blump blump. He was still looking at her in a way that made her uncomfortable.

"Lolly, do you have anything else on your mind? Anything you want to ask me about?"

"Um . . . No. Well, maybe. It's just, the Missus. She can't get out of her rooms."

"She told you herself that she hasn't been feeling well and wants to be left alone. She asked me to lock her in for her own good."

"Okay."

"Did she ask you to let her out?"

"No."

"Does she seem like she's not being well cared for?"

"No."

"Okay then. Clearly she's fine and you have nothing to worry about, right?"

"I didn't mean—"

"I know you didn't." He grabbed her by the shoulders with both hands. She tried not to flinch, but she was afraid of him, especially the way he was smiling now.

"Lolly, just stick to your knitting and you and I will get along just fine."

"Knitting? I'm sorry, I—"

He chuckled. "That's one of my mother's old sayings.

It's a polite way to tell someone to mind their own business. You understand that, don't you?"

"Yes, yes. Oh, yes. I understand, Mister John. Okay. I'll clean the windows now."

TWENTY-NINE

Vining made her way to the 118 East, passing the spot where she'd tossed the necklace out the window. Let it sleep with the lizards. She took the 118 to the 405 to the 101, exiting at Laurel Canyon in Studio City. She parked on the street in front of Frankie Lynde's condominium complex. The front gate was locked. The keypad still listed Frankie's name. Vining pressed the button beside it and almost immediately the gate buzzed.

The door to Frankie's condo was open. A man was going around the place with a tape measure and making notes on a pad of paper.

The dismantling of Lynde's life was in progress. First her corpse, now her possessions.

She knocked on the door and called out.

Sharon Hernandez walked briskly into the living room from the rear of the condo. She was wearing a security firm's uniform and wasn't what Vining expected. She was about five-foot-four even with her thick-soled work shoes, her stature diminutive but solid. Five sparkling stud earrings descended the perimeter of each ear. Her thick, dark brown hair was streaked with red highlights, French-braided, looped behind her head, and tightly pinned. She had a pretty face. Energy seemed to spark from her. She had likely learned that she might as well dress as girly as she wanted as clothing or hairstyle would never dilute her basic appearance as a cute, petite female. Vining suspected she overcompensated by being a hellion in uniform.

She gave Vining a firm handshake. "Nice to meet you. I'm glad a female D is working Frankie's case. Two Ds from Pasadena came to talk to me already. Tall and short."

"Kissick and Ruiz."

"Right. Ruiz came a second time. I don't know why he bothered. Didn't ask me anything new. It was like he made the trip for something to do. Got the impression he's punching his time card until retirement."

Vining didn't comment. "What's going on here?"

"Gerardo's going to paint the place. Gerardo Rincon, this is Detective Nan Vining from Pasadena."

They shook hands.

"Gerardo's retired LAPD. Was a field sergeant."

Vining had made him as law enforcement. "Yeah? How long were you in?"

"Twenty years and twenty seconds." He scratched the side of his nose. "Started helping a buddy with his painting business on my days off. Five years later, I have my own crew and I've never been happier."

"No one shooting at you on this job," Vining said.

"Yeah." He smiled past her, reflecting. "What it came down to was the betrayal, not the bullets. That's what got to me. Firing cops for doing their jobs. Offering us as sacrifices to the media and the politicians."

Hernandez weighed in. "I've got lots of years before I can retire, but I'm going to be out the door twenty seconds after. The politics have gotten ridiculous. If you get in a situation and your actions deviate one iota from policy . . ."

"Instead of backing you, the brass will cut off your head and hand it over," Gerardo said. "Reason I retired was I got into a situation. Got called before the review board."

The two women groaned.

"They're sitting around the table asking me, why this, why that. Then it came to me. Today is my twentieth anniversary. I can retire. So I did."

"Right then?" Vining's face showed she admired his decisiveness.

"Twenty years and twenty seconds."

Hernandez nodded. "Civilians will never understand what it's like to be out there on the street, to have some guy whaling at your head with a brick or driving a car straight at you or trying to bite off your ear. The decisions I make on the spot with the pressure on will be put under a microscope by people who have no clue what it's like to be in those circumstances."

"And whose agenda has nothing to do with fairness," Vining said. "Been there, done that."

"Hiring William Bratton raised morale for a while," Hernandez said. "Now we're starting to 'smile and wave' like we did under Chief Parks. Avoid confrontation."

"Pasadena's hiring," Vining said. "There's politics everywhere, but Pasadena's smaller. Family. I love it."

"I've thought about that, especially now that Frankie's gone." Hernandez gave Gerardo's arm a slap. "Enough bitching. I'll let you get back to work. I've gotta take off soon. Nan, let's go in here."

She walked into Frankie's bedroom and Vining followed.

Hernandez surveyed the room. "It's still weird, being in Frankie's place with her gone. The first week she went missing, I knew it was over for her, that she was dead. But it's still weird."

Vining thought, *This was where Frankie lived, but she never found her place.*

"Frankie hasn't even been buried yet and her father's putting her condo on the market already?"

"Frankie left everything to me." Hernandez responded to Vining's expression. "Shocked me, too. She didn't say anything. This attorney calls, says to come down. They're reading Frankie's will and I need to be there."

"When did they read it?"

"Last night."

Vining recalled her encounter with Frank Lynde at the station that morning and how troubled he was. Frankie's will was the last nail in the coffin of their relationship.

"The department advises that we put all our documents in order, in case . . . I didn't expect Frankie to leave me anything. Maybe pieces of jewelry I'd admired. But everything? Then I realized it made sense. Her aunt and grandmother always treated her like she was trash. She and her dad were getting along better at the end, but she never got over the way he abandoned her after her mother was murdered. Why should she? Some things people do are so bad, you should *never* get over them. That's what I think. Why give them any peace that it's all okay when it's never gonna be okay? Know what I'm saying?"

Vining couldn't disagree.

"Her leaving me all her stuff was a big F U to her family, in my opinion."

Hernandez picked up a bottle of cologne from the dresser and spritzed herself. "You know what's creepy, Frankie just recently put all her affairs in order. Had been on the force for seven years without even writing a will. A month ago, she pulled it all together. I mean everything—cemetery plot, funeral arrangements, flowers. Even the music she wanted played."

"A month ago."

"Yeah."

"Sharon, what was going on with Frankie those last months?"

"It's like I told the other two Ds, I don't know. I knew she broke up with Ken Moore and I can't say I was sorry about that. She even told me, 'You'll be happy, Sher. I'm not with Ken anymore.' "

"Did she say why?"

"It ran its course. Whatever. I used to tell her, 'Frankie, he's married. What are you doin'?' So she stopped talking about him to me. I should have known not to confront her. She wasn't one to talk about herself anyway. I worked side by side with her for years before she told me her mother had been murdered. She was the kind of person—We'd all be out at a bar, having a good time, talking, laughing, then you'd think about it later and realize the rest of us were doing the blabbing. All Frankie did was ask questions. Don't get me wrong. She was great. She'd do anything for her friends. She was a standup gal. I loved Frankie. I miss her a lot. She was my sister. She was my girl."

Her eyes reddened.

Vining didn't tell her about Frankie's abortion. Frankie had her reasons for keeping it a secret. Vining would preserve Frankie's wishes.

Sharon sighed and rolled open a mirrored closet door. "I'm glad she took care of the funeral. I have enough to deal with. Look at all this stuff."

She started flipping through the hangers. In front, easiest to get to, were casual clothes including expensive leather jackets. Shoes overflowed a rack onto the floor. In the middle, harder to reach behind the closet doors, were a navy blue suit and strappy cocktail dresses.

Hernandez took out a halter dress in a green silk print. "Frankie wore this to a wedding a couple of weeks ago. She looked hot. She liked it when men looked at her. Liked nothing better than everyone turning when she came in. That was Frankie. Guess she craved the attention of men because she was always looking for her father's love or some such psychobabble crap."

She gathered the fabric between her hands and pressed her face against it. "Still smells like her. Cigarettes and that Escada perfume she liked."

She closed the door and slid open the one on the opposite side, revealing Frankie's uniforms in dry cleaner's plastic.

"Check this out."

Hernandez made suggestive noises as she displayed a series of bustiers, tube tops, miniskirts, clingy dresses with deep slits, boots, and sky-high platform shoes. Wigs on head forms lined the shelf above.

"Her work clothes from vice prostitution. She'd put

on this stuff and we'd laugh. She'd tell me, 'Sher, men are so simpleminded. They'll risk being arrested just to rub up against a miniskirt, garter belt, and high heels.' "

"You think she went over to the dark side?"

"It's the only explanation that makes sense. She was in a weird place those last weeks."

"Weird how?"

"All bipolar. Happy, but crazy happy. Then depressed. She'd call me, 'Sher, let's go to Vegas. Let's go to Tahoe. Right now.' The next week, she'd be, 'Sher, I'm not going out today. Staying in bed. Tired.' I was like, 'Hey, Frankie, what's goin' on wit' ju?' And she was, 'I'm fine. You worry too much. Worry about yourself.' My boyfriend and I were just getting together then, you know, building, so I wasn't spending as much time with her. Don't get me wrong. I loved her, but she could be exhausting. Sometimes I had to get away for a little while. Look at this . . . Frankie loved this thing."

She took down the long silver wig Frankie had worn the last day she'd worked the street, according to Detective Schuyler's M.P. report. She put her hands around the foam neck and shook the fake head.

"Frankie, what did you get yourself into, girl? If you were here, I would slap some sense into you. I should have kicked her ass more. Maybe she'd still be here."

"You did the best you could."

Hernandez smoothed the wig. "That's what we tell ourselves, isn't it? Every day on the job. So is the asshole who did that to her gonna get away with it?"

It was a test.

"Not on my watch," Vining responded.

"We'll get him, Frankie." Hernandez squared her

chin. "We'll get him good." She set the wig form on the dresser.

Vining took the photographs of John and Pussycat Lesley from her portfolio. "You recognize these people?"

Sharon scrutinized them and shook her head. "Sorry. Who are they?"

"People who might know something. Call me if you think of anything." Vining put the photos away. "So what are you going to do with this place?"

"I might move in. It's closer to work and my boyfriend. We're talking marriage already."

"Congratulations."

"Neither of us can believe it. We're pretty in love. We get along good. But I'm not cohabitating until we get married. I don't need that kind of aggravation."

"I heard that. What does he do?"

"He's a cop, what else? Deputy sheriff over in Malibu. Freaking cushy job. Hey, I know it looks harsh, Frankie's not even buried yet and I have a guy here measuring for paint. I called Gerardo last night, thinking it would be a week before he'd have time to come by. He had a cancellation and was able to fit me in this morning. I had Frankie's keys, so what the hell. Knowing Frankie, she'd tell me to get on with it. Now I have to decide what to do with all this stuff."

She swatted at the clothing, then crouched down, spying something at the rear of the closet. "Ah-ha!"

She pushed clothes out of the way and dragged out a cardboard box. Kneeling on the carpet, she raised the lid to reveal vinyl record albums crammed inside. She pulled out a dog-eared Monkees album followed by a Beach Boys album. She flipped it over and read the back.

"Good. Found it. 'California Girls.' Frankie wanted that played at the service and she wanted it played off *this* album. These were her mother's albums and that was her mother's favorite song. Frankie wasn't sentimental about anything except when it came to her mother."

Vining was looking at the photographs on the dresser. Still stuck beneath the mirror frame was the toothy school photo of Frankie that she'd noticed the first time she'd visited Frankie's home.

Vining pulled it out. There was handwriting on the back in a feminine script. "Says Frances Ann 11 years."

"That's the year her mother was murdered. See? I told you she was sentimental about her mother."

"May I keep this?"

"Sure. Go ahead."

Vining slipped the photograph into her jacket pocket.

Gerardo called for Hernandez from the other room.

"I've gotta get out of here and take off for my other job. Let me finish with him."

Alone, Vining looked around for the last time. She picked up the wig from the dresser. The head form was molded into a rudimentary face, blank and white. She touched the synthetic hair.

I am you. I am not you. Wear the pearls. Frankie, if you are really talking to me, why don't you give me something I can use to arrest him?

Semis traveling the 101 freeway that ran behind the building rumbled the ground.

It's just voices in my head, isn't it? I'm following instructions from voices in my head. Me and Son of Sam.

She spoke out loud. "Stress. Stress is a killer. But I'm in charge now. Everything's good."

She returned the silver wig to the shelf and rolled the closet door closed.

Before she left the complex, she knocked on the door opposite Frankie's unit where Mrs. Bodek lived. She showed her the photographs of the Lesleys.

"That gal, she could be the one who was here that day. She had the hat and sunglasses and all, but it could be her. Can't say for sure."

It was a common affliction. No one could say anything for sure.

Sitting in her car, she called Kissick.

"I'm confident the dental crown isn't Moore's. He confirmed Frankie had an abortion not long before she met John Lesley."

"She met Lesley?"

"Yeah. Found a waitress at the Huntington Hotel who saw them talking and smoking on the patio. Flirting. Good witness. Clear memory of it because she was ticked off at Frankie for moving in on Lesley before she could."

"Let's go have a talk with Mr. Lesley."

Vining feigned a shocked tone. "But he's our citizen hero. Hands off."

"We're just personally delivering Lieutenant Beltran's greetings."

"I'll meet you in West Hollywood at Lesley's club," she said.

"I'll be there in a bit. I need to get a tattoo and my eyebrow pierced first."

THIRTY

Kissick hated West Hollywood. Too much traffic and too self-conscious. There was a shortage of ordinary people going about their business, not thinking about how they looked every five seconds or where they were going to dine now that the fabulous chef with the hyphenated name had left for Orange County. Orange County! And what was with the gunk that the men put in their hair to make it stand up? Gel heads, he called them. Caspers was into the male personal products. Must be a generational thing. Kissick wasn't quite forty, but he was feeling the trends passing him by. He'd already caught himself talking about the way things were when he was young. He was turning into his father. Maybe that was the real reason he hated West Hollywood. He didn't get it. It made him feel old and out of step.

He'd found a parking spot across the street from John Lesley's club, Reign. The art deco building had zigzag plaster friezes descending each side and was painted lighter and darker shades of chocolate brown. A silver awning extended from the front door. A shiny silver sign high on the façade had the club name in script within an oval.

He was willing to follow Vining this far, to West Hollywood to talk to a wealthy gel head who had flirted with

Frankie Lynde, according to the hazy memory of a wait-ress, and who had verbally and physically abused his ex-wife. He wasn't in a position to discount any angle.

He'd seen Vining instinctively work a case. Latch onto something that no one else thought was important, find-ing the pony in the manure pile. He'd seen it backfire on her, too. Not often, but it had. Lieutenant Bill Gavigan had saved her bacon a couple of times. Kissick didn't think Sergeant Early would let Vining twist in the wind, but Lieutenant Beltran would if it benefited him. Kiss-ick had observed Beltran becoming more political over the years. The lieutenant had always been mindful of appearances. Now it seemed he filtered every action through a lens to assess the impact upon his upward mo-bility. Kissick had gotten a load of Beltran's venom that morning. He knew it was all about Beltran having mud on his face because the Thorne security DVD had been leaked.

He saw Vining drive past and turn onto a side street. He crossed the street and waited for her. A Latino worker was power washing the sidewalk in front of the nightclub.

He watched Nan walk toward him. She had a long, de-termined stride. She was a tall woman but did not com-pensate by hunching. The tight line of her jaw softened when she saw him, which made him soften.

"Hey," he said.

"Hi. Thanks for coming out."

"Have you eaten yet?"

"I have but I could eat again after we're done here."

"That's my girl."

"I know what you want."

He smiled crookedly. "Yeah . . ."

"Don't start. You're the one who's saying how we maybe can't work together. I'm not the one who went to that place."

"I was thinking about a Pink's chili dog. What are you thinking about?"

She gave him a close-lipped smile.

"And an order of chili fries."

"And Zantac on the side. Advancing age . . . Gives a whole new meaning to doing drugs with your friends."

"Indigestion will at least distract the hound dog in me." He pinched her arm.

She held up her index finger. "I warned you."

"You love it."

She did, but she wouldn't give him the satisfaction of admitting it.

"So, Corporal Vining, how do you want to handle John Lesley?"

"I'll do the talking, if that's okay."

"See if he has issues with women."

"*All* men have issues with women."

He raised his eyebrows. "That's a sweeping comment."

"It's that womb thing."

"If you say so."

"I know so."

"Oh-kay. You're in charge."

"I like being in charge."

"Ooh . . . Yes, you do. I've never forgotten that."

"Easy, big stallion."

"See? You do love it." He stepped over a soapy puddle and reached for the door.

She gave him a coy look over her shoulder as she walked inside.

They were both temporarily blinded when walking into the poorly lit place. The June gloom hadn't yet burned off and the sunlight reflecting off the haze magnified the brightness outdoors.

Vining didn't like the joint. It put her on edge.

"Can I help you?"

After blinking a few times, Vining located the source of the voice. He was in his twenties with a beard that looked like a Brillo pad stuck to his chin. He was unloading a case of Bohemia beer into a refrigerated case.

She and Kissick badged him. "Pasadena Police. I'm Detective Nan Vining and this is Detective Jim Kissick."

He didn't give the credentials a second glance, making Vining wonder if detectives were a common occurrence there.

"What's your name?"

"Aaron Black."

"How long have you worked here?"

"Over a year."

"What hours do you work?"

"Depends. Five to three. Noon to ten. Four nights a week. What's going on?"

From her portfolio, she pulled out a photograph of Frankie Lynde in street clothes at a family barbecue. She had selected that shot from Frank Lynde's collection as it had not been broadcast around the globe. "Ever see her here?"

Aaron took it from her and scrutinized it. He raised a shoulder. "Lots of women come through here. I don't remember her specifically."

Vining put the photo away. "John Lesley around?"

"Yeah, John's here." Turning his back to them, Aaron

picked up a phone behind the bar, punched at the keypad, and had a quick conversation.

"He'll be right down."

"Thanks, Aaron."

"No problem."

Vining crabbily corrected him. "You're welcome."

"Huh?"

"It goes, thank you, you're welcome. Not thank you, no problem."

"Nhn." His raised eyebrows conveyed he was humoring her. He resumed working.

She grimaced and turned away.

"You're in rare form," Kissick observed.

"Somebody's gotta tell this generation how to behave. I thought our generation was bad, raised by hippies. This new one was brought up by computers and Xboxes. They'd have been better off raised by wolves."

He didn't respond but his body language communicated that he was keeping his distance.

This place *had* gotten under her skin. Bitchiness was her smoke screen.

They strolled around. Dim overhead lights revealed stains in the carpet, nicks in the furniture, and scratches on the bar and dance floor.

"Caspers claims this dump is the peachy keen joint in town," Vining commented.

"Seeing a nightclub during the day is like picking up a woman you thought was beautiful and the next morning realizing it was all makeup."

"Common occurrence for you?"

"Hardly ever. Two, three times a week. I've cut back."

She shot him a glance.

He surveyed the aquariums lining the walls. "No fish?" he asked Aaron.

"Not the kind with gills," the bartender responded.

"Female humans, according to Caspers. Surgically enhanced, I bet." Vining patted Kissick on the sleeve. "You ought to get John Lesley to put you on the guest list. You'd have new standing with Caspers and the younger guys. I can see it. You and Beltran at the bar, knockin' 'em back."

"Bar, hell. VIP room. I suspect Lesley's a guy who knows how to treat law enforcement. Good for business."

A rectangle of light shone as the front door opened. The fresh air seemed like an alien intruder. Silhouetted in the doorway was the workman from outside. He lugged in the power washer and rolled it to a storeroom.

Aaron tossed an empty box into a pile and ripped open a case of Sam Adams.

The lights in the aquariums went on, bathing the room in blue. The water sloshed as the workman cleaned the inside of the glass with a long-handled squeegee.

A door at the top of the stairs in back opened and a man descended. He had a confident bearing, moving quickly but not hurriedly, as if he wouldn't rush for anyone or anything. He crossed the dance floor that was cast in a blue patchwork from the aquariums. He almost looked submerged underwater, rising toward the surface as he drew near.

Vining thought of the fragmented, indistinct image of a man she'd seen that day in the conference room while peering into Frankie's aquamarine gemstone. With each step that Lesley took, the facets of the image in her mind shifted as the bits of colored glass in the kaleidoscope turned and turned, taking form, becoming clearer.

He was upon her. Lesley's image clicked into place.

A chill tingled her spine.

"Hello, I'm John Lesley."

He offered them both a disarming smile but beamed at her a beat longer. It was the subtle flirtation of a skilled seducer, who knew a hint of heightened interest was more powerful than overt flirting.

She swallowed drily, briefly at a loss for words. The fluttering beneath her ribs unsettled her. "I'm Detective Nanette Vining and this is Detective Jim Kissick from the Pasadena Police Department."

"Aaron told me. Welcome. I'm an avid booster of the PPD. Lieutenant George Beltran and I are friends. Maybe you know that. We just played golf last week. Great guy. A real asset to your organization."

"I understand you're one of our citizen heroes," Vining said.

"Oh, that." He raised his hands in a what-else-could-I-do gesture. "Right place, right time. It was terrific for the PPD to honor me, but I only did what anyone would have. At least, I hope anyone would have."

"Chase down and tackle a man who had robbed an elderly couple? I think not."

"Guess I've always been a bit of a daredevil."

"Have you?"

He was flirting with her. And she flirted back. Being with John Lesley made her tremble deep within, yet it was titillating. She recalled T. B. Mann's arm around her waist, tightly pulling her against him so he could feel the blood draining from her. Now, she completely understood. In just the same way, she craved John Lesley's death.

Lesley again held her eyes for a second. Could he read her mind? She hoped so.

He rubbed his hands together. "How can I be of assistance to the PPD today?"

"Do you have someplace where we can talk?" Her mind was in chaos but she managed the right words.

"Let's go to my office." Lesley started back the way he'd come.

She followed him as she had followed T. B. Mann in that house. She didn't feel panicked. Rather, she felt cool and in control.

She heard Kissick's solid footsteps behind her. He was there, silent and appearing bored, but ever watchful.

Lesley stopped and hooked a thumb toward the bar. "Can I get you anything?"

She said, "No thanks."

They climbed the back stairs. At the top, they went through a door with a small window and entered a private lounge. The wall that overlooked the club was of floor-to-ceiling one-way glass. A long bar was on one end of the room. Scattered around were cocktail tables and chairs and conversation nooks of couches, armchairs, and coffee tables. The décor was several notches above that of the lower level but nothing to write home about. Just being let past the door was reward enough. The windows gave a bird's-eye view of the goings-on below.

"Our VIP room," Lesley explained.

Behind the bar, he slid open a pocket door camouflaged with wainscoting and wallpaper. A peephole was barely detectable. They entered an expansive and plush room. A desk, bookcases, and business equipment were on one side. The remainder was decorated like a living room with a small bar and a baby grand piano. The outer wall was the same floor-to-ceiling one-way glass.

To Vining, the undeniable theme was seduction. If he had brought Frankie here, it would have been after hours. He had hatched his plan early, kept it in his back pocket, just in case there was that perfect solar eclipse of the moon and the night went pitch black.

Lesley invited them to sit in austere chairs while he positioned himself in a leather chair behind a hefty walnut desk.

Kissick's attention was distracted by a large portrait on the wall behind the desk of a voluptuous nude blonde in a provocative pose with a wooden chair.

The small hairs on the back of Vining's neck stood up. She recognized the woman as Pamela Lesley from the DMV photo.

Noting the object of their attention, Lesley proudly announced, "My wife, Pussycat."

"Pussycat?" Vining repeated.

"Her given name is Pamela, but Pussycat suits her better. You have to agree." Lesley leaned back in the chair and laced his hands behind his head. The gesture caused the knit golf shirt he was wearing to hug his muscular physique.

His appearance wasn't lost on Vining, nor was she taken in by it. She understood how he would be a sweet diversion for brokenhearted Frankie Lynde.

The wall was covered with photographs of John Lesley with luminaries. Some included his wife du jour. In a large black frame with regal navy blue matting was his award from the Pasadena Police Department and the photograph of him accepting it, shaking hands with the chief.

"So, how can I help you?" He waited, looking from one to the other, meeting Vining's benign smile with his own.

She leaned across to place Frankie Lynde's photograph on the desk in front of him. "Do you know her?"

Not changing his expression, he picked it up. "Attractive female. I might know her."

"What does that mean?"

"Detective Vining, I own a nightclub. Six nights a week, five hundred people come through here. I'm an affable host."

"She should look familiar because you were seen talking with her at the Huntington Hotel poolside café the afternoon of the awards luncheon."

He looked again. "Oh yes. I remember now. The police officer. I was there having a beer and she came out to smoke a cigarette."

"And then what?"

"We talked."

"About what?"

"The weather."

He returned the photo, his eyes inscrutable.

"A witness said the two of you looked like you were flirting."

He chuckled. "Flirting? I'm a married man, Detective."

"Anything happen on your way out of Pasadena that day?"

"One of your finest gave me a ticket because the windows on my Hummer were tinted too dark. I had that taken care of weeks ago."

"You argued with the officer."

"I had a few choice words for him. It was a bullshit ticket written by an overzealous cop."

He said to Kissick with a wink, "Letting the little lady run things, huh?"

Vining was not deterred. "Where's your wife?"

He gave a languid shrug. "Home or shopping or having her nails done . . . Whatever wives with plenty of money and time on their hands do."

He looked over his shoulder at the portrait. "She's my queen. As long as she's happy, I'm happy."

"Does she know about your past?"

"Would you care to be more specific?"

"Your first wife has a restraining order against you."

"That nonsense. She did that to get her picture back in the gossip rags. She's a publicity hound and has a hard time dealing with the cruel fact that she's no longer the hottest woman in the room. What you don't know is the judge who signed off on the restraining order is the friend of a friend of hers."

"A year ago, you were sued for sexual harassment by two cocktail waitresses who worked for you."

"Both settled out of court. They only did it for the money. Which they got." He frowned at the desk as if thinking. "Wait a minute . . . That woman you're asking about. The one I talked to by the pool that day. She's the police officer who was murdered, right?"

"That's correct."

"Cops." Movement of his chest showed he was laughing, but he didn't make a sound. "I got crosswise of a couple of women who had it in for me and someone accuses me of flirting with a police officer who got herself killed. That's all it took to bring you all the way from Pasadena to my place of business and imply that I'm a rapist and a murderer. Maybe it's just me, but don't you think you're making a stretch?"

Vining didn't answer.

"All I can say is I feel sorry for that poor dead woman if I'm the best suspect you've come up with."

He left an opening for them to respond but they remained silent.

He laughed aloud. "I'm a hero in Pasadena. There's a picture of the chief shaking my hand." He gestured toward the framed photograph. "First, I get a ticket on my way out of your fair city because of the dangerous crime of having my car windows too dark. A complete waste of my time and money. Now, you two show up. One thing's for double damn sure, I'm not *ever* setting foot in Pasadena again."

He gave them a questioning look. "Did Lieutenant Beltran approve this interview? If he doesn't know about it, he will in about five minutes."

He stood and they followed. "If there's nothing more, Detectives, I have things to do. Would you mind seeing yourselves out?"

"Thank you for your time," Vining said.

"The pleasure was all mine. Good luck on your investigation. In my humble opinion, you're gonna need it."

"Smooth son of a bitch," Kissick said. He and Vining were standing beside his car across the street. "What's wrong with that picture?"

"We didn't announce to the media that Frankie was raped."

"Interesting choice of words he used to describe Frankie: The police officer who got herself killed."

"Like it was her fault." Vining looked at the sign on the club's roof. "Cocky bastard. Reign. Thinks he's the freaking king. Calling his wife 'my queen.' Did you catch that?"

She was pacing back and forth.

"Calm down, big girl. You're breathing through your mouth."

She inhaled deeply. "He did it, Jim. I feel it."

"He's definitely worth a closer look."

"I'm telling you he murdered Frankie." She spun on her heel and walked away. After a few steps, she returned. "I know, I know. There's that little issue called probable cause."

"I'll try for warrants for his dental records, the night-club, and his house."

She stared across the street at the club, her hands planted on her hips. "There's bound to be a gun in that joint. Arrest him on a violation of the stay away order while we get the warrants in place. Bet we could get one of his employees to cop to the presence of a gun. Send out a cute female undercover, get somebody talking."

Kissick unlocked his car. "I'll call Early about the warrants while we head out to the Valley to visit Mrs. Lesley."

"My thoughts exactly."

Vining walked to her car. The trembling beneath her ribs would not subside.

THIRTY-ONE

Pussycat opened her eyes and saw sunlight filtering through cracks around the plywood covering the windows. The clock on the nightstand said it was one p.m. She had slept for eleven hours. She felt a weight on her chest and looked down to see her dog lying there, watching her with shiny doll's eyes.

At her mistress's glance, Mignon leaped up and began licking Pussycat's face.

"Hi, sweetie. Mommy slept late. I'm sorry. Did you go pee pee on the newspapers? I hope so. Daddy will kill you if you did it on the rug."

Pussycat's offhand comment gave her pause. She remembered Lisa Shipp and her stomach roiled. It wasn't a bad dream. It was real.

She sat up in bed and rubbed her eyes. The door that separated the bedroom from the sitting room was open. Her mind was still hazy, but she thought she'd closed it when she'd gone to bed.

She saw a tray on the console in the sitting room. On it was an insulated coffee carafe and a silver dome. A spray of small white roses was in a bud vase. She'd been so deeply asleep, she hadn't awakened when he'd entered. She was certain her husband had brought the tray and not Lolly. The housekeeper would have been told not to go near Pussycat's suite of rooms, and she would obey. Lolly wouldn't even question it.

Pussycat pushed herself up in bed. The dog nudged her hand to be petted. Pussycat gave in.

"What would I do without you, Mignon? You're my only friend."

She threw back the bedcovers. Her hand flew to her mouth at what she saw there.

Laid out on the bed beside her was the shirt from Frankie Lynde's uniform, buttoned to the neck, the brass shield and name badge still in place from the last time Frankie had worn it.

Pussycat scurried off the bed. The dog began sniffing the shirt and Pussycat lurched to grab her up into her arms. She had wondered what he had done with Frankie's clothes. Cradling the dog against her with one hand, she circled the bed, stretched forward, grabbed the bed-covers, and flung them all the way back.

The uniform was presented as if Frankie were wearing it, complete with the equipment belt buckled around the waist. The gun was in the holster. Stuck beneath the belt buckle was a folded sheet of paper.

Pussycat set down the dog and tugged out the paper, not wanting to touch the uniform. It was a note from him written in longhand. She always had a hard time de-ciphering his spidery handwriting.

"Good morning, Sunshine. Hope you had a good rest. I miss seeing that beautiful smile I fell in love with. I brought you coffee and your favorite breakfast—eggs Benedict. Fresh strawberries, too. They were so beautiful at the farmer's market, I had to buy them for you. And I spiked the coffee for you—the way you like it. I want you to eat, ma chérie. I worry about you.

"I'll bring dinner from the club. Put on Frankie's uni-form and be waiting for me. The three of us will have a bite to eat and then we'll party. I'll bring Miss Tina, too. Whether you get to party with her has to do with how you behave today. Even if you don't care what happens to you, I know you care about your sister and your little niece and nephew and, of course, our sweet Lisa."

She opened her hands and the letter fluttered to the ground. She collapsed onto the bed and began to sob, her hands convulsively grabbing the bedcovers and the uni-form. The dog began yipping, responding to her distress.

Pussycat writhed and moaned, the uniform crumpling

beneath her. She felt something hard beneath her thigh, something cold and dense. She recoiled, realizing she was on top of Frankie's gun.

Wiping tears from her face, she sat upright and tentatively touched it, wrapping her fingers around the butt. Her hand felt feverish against the soothing cool steel. She tugged. The holster securely held it in place. She took hold of the holster in her left hand and pulled with her right. The gun came free. It was lighter than she thought it would be.

Pussycat knew how to shoot guns. Her father was a hunter and gun collector. She'd been handling guns since she was ten. She looked inside the base. He'd taken out the clip of bullets. Of course he had.

She looked at the empty slot at the bottom of the handle and started to cry again. She put the gun to her head anyway. Suddenly, she pulled it away. She had to stop thinking that way. It was a blessing that he'd taken the bullets. What would killing herself accomplish? Who would save Lisa if she weren't around? Who would tell the story about what happened to Frankie?

She spotted a framed photograph of him on the dresser across the room. He was the one she should direct her venom against. He was the source of her problems, including that monkey on her back, that bitch Miss Tina.

She took aim and squeezed the trigger.

The gun felt like it exploded in her hands when it went off, shattering the glass and hurling the photograph to the floor. The kick jerked the gun from her grasp.

She screamed and buried her head under her arms.

He'd taken out the clip, but hadn't cleared the chamber.

She dared to peek at his shattered face. It was only a photograph, yet she was shaking.

She fell to her knees and prayed.

Vining and Kissick drove to the Lesley home in Encino, but no one answered the gate. They were debating their next move when John Lesley drove up in his black Hummer.

"Hello again, Detectives. What part of, 'I didn't have anything to do with your dead cop' don't you understand?"

"Where's your wife?" Kissick asked.

Lesley put his hand to his ear. "I believe I hear Lieutenant Beltran calling you home. Back to sweet, stupid Pasadena. Home to the Rose Parade, the Rose Bowl, and a police department that doesn't know their rosy asses from their elbows."

"You finished?" Kissick asked. "Get it all out? Feel better?"

"Where's your wife?" Vining asked.

"I told you she is not well."

"You told us she was shopping or having her nails done," Vining said.

"Whatever."

"Why don't we go inside and talk?" Kissick said.

"Where's your warrant?" Lesley smirked.

Vining sidled closer to him. She detected his scent. The way it made her heart beat faster both disgusted and encouraged her. "Why won't you let us inside just to talk, John? There are no secrets. There's nothing to hide. We don't know our asses from our elbows anyway, so what difference does it make?"

"You're on my property and I'd like you to leave before I call the real cops. And oh, by the way, I have friends there, too."

Kissick and Sergeant Early briefed Caspers and Jill Hendricks, a vice detective, who would go undercover to Reign that night to attempt to learn whether Lesley possessed firearms. Two officers were dispatched undercover to surveil Lesley's home. If any of them saw Pussycat Lesley, they would take her into custody for questioning. Same thing went for Lesley's domestic help.

Vining and Ruiz would drive to Pomona to talk with Pussycat Lesley's family.

Making a quick stop by her desk, Vining glanced at memos that had landed there in her absence. She retrieved Frankie's grade school photo from her pocket and was looking at it when Ruiz came by.

"Ready?" His lips were set in a line.

Vining didn't know if it was the trip to Pomona in traffic or the amount of time he'd be confined in a car with her that had ticked him off. Probably both.

She stuck Frankie's photo on top of Emily's school portrait and left to join Ruiz, who was already standing by the elevators.

Vining didn't want to make the two-hour round-trip drive in stony silence. She offered to drive and that slightly defrosted Ruiz. The freeway traffic was light, which helped, too.

"Tony, how did you make out tracking down Frankie's arrests?"

"Other than those two guys Caspers talked about who had alibis, everyone's either in jail, dead, moved out of state, or are honest taxpaying family men who got caught soliciting prostitution."

"It's the only time I've ever done this, Officer." She affected a distraught voice. "My wife has cancer—"

"My wife left me."

"My wife had a sex change operation."

They laughed.

"Then you call up their rap sheet and see this is the twentieth time they've gone down for solicitation."

"But you live for this, Vining."

"I do. You grind through hundreds of hours of bullshit living for the day when those cuffs go click. It's like childbirth. You forget the pain the moment they put that little baby in your arms."

"That's beautiful, Nan."

"Didn't know I had a poetic side, did you?"

"No, I didn't."

"How's Caspers doing?"

"Pretty good, as long as he can keep his dick in his pants."

"I heard he dated a couple of girls he arrested."

Ruiz imitated Caspers. "I pinched them for misdemeanors. Nothing big."

"Glad to know he has his standards. It's not just about having two legs and a hole." Vining shrugged. "Maybe he doesn't care if they have two legs."

Ruiz chortled. "There was this time we were all at Manny Wilson's retirement party. Caspers was all over Wilson's daughter. Wilson got pissed and Chase and a couple of guys had to separate them. Course, we'd all had plenty to drink by then."

"Did she have two legs?"

"Who? Wilson's daughter?" Ruiz guffawed. "Yeah. She did."

"Speaking of John Chase, you ever roll with him?"

"The Chaser. Yeah. A couple of times."

"I was his FTO. I haven't ridden with him since. Does he still carry a micro recorder on the street?"

"Hell yeah. He's the CYA man."

"Sure would like to know if he got John Lesley arguing with him on tape. Heard Chase is in Cabo until Monday. No cell service where he is."

"Call him at his hotel."

"I don't know where he's staying."

"I bet Caspers knows. He runs with that group."

Ruiz called Caspers on his cell phone. John Chase was staying at the El Conquistador. Caspers offered to give Chase a call.

Pussycat's parents and two younger brothers lived in a modest, neat home in a nice area of Claremont. Her mother was petite and had likely been pretty but had aged early and not well. Her father was overweight with slicked-back hair and a beard. He volunteered that he was on disability from an accident at his job as a warehouse foreman. He spent his time restoring and showing classic Chevrolets and was delighted to show Ruiz the cars in his garage workshop. Her brothers seemed typical good high school kids growing up in difficult circumstances. Vining knew something about that.

"You call her Pamela, not Pussycat?" Ruiz asked.

The mother became grim. "That's her stage name. She's Pam to us."

The family hadn't noticed anything unusual about Pam over the past weeks. But then she called a couple of days ago.

"She seemed upset," her mother confided.

Her father waved off the comment. "She was fine.

You're always looking for trouble. John Lesley was the best thing that happened to Pam. He gives her everything. She's living large. Have you seen that house? The land alone is worth a mint."

He frowned and shook his head as if it was too much to comprehend.

Vining looked around at the high-end electronic equipment and noted the new cars in the driveway.

"Does Pam help you out financially?" Vining asked.

All her father would admit to was, "It's happened."

On the way back to Pasadena, they stopped at Pussycat's sister's house in West Covina. Rosemary was three years younger than Pussycat and similar physically, but not as pretty. They didn't need to press her for opinions.

"Something is very wrong with Pam, but she wouldn't tell me what it was when I had lunch with her last week. She was teary. She said her dog was sick, losing weight, and not eating, and the vet can't figure out why. I told her I didn't believe her. That there was something going on with her, not the dog. I asked, 'Is he hitting you?' I know he tries to keep her from seeing me."

"What did she say?" Vining took notes.

"She said, 'Oh no. John would never do that. John's great to me.' " Rosemary showed her disgust.

"When did you last talk to her?"

"Day before yesterday. She called. Sounded like she'd been crying again. Said she had a cold."

"Why did she call?"

"To say hi. To let me know she was okay."

"Does she normally call just to let you know she's okay?"

"Not really. There's usually more to the conversation.

What are you doing? I'm doing this. When do you want to get together? You know, like that. It was strange. She definitely didn't sound right."

"Could you call her for us? Just sound normal without mentioning that we're here?"

"Right now?"

"Yes."

"Umm . . . Sure."

Rosemary tried both Pussycat's private line and cell phone. She left messages.

"See, that's what's weird. Pam lives by her cell phone. She always has it with her and leaves it on."

"Is there anyone else who might be in the house besides John Lesley?"

"Their housekeeper, Lolly. She's worked for John for years. Long before John hooked up with Pam."

"She live-in?"

"No. She's there from seven in the morning until four or so. Monday through Friday. Pam always said Lolly was sort of clueless, or pretended to be."

"Do you know where she lives? Her phone number?"

"I don't. I know she's married and has a couple of teenagers. I don't know her beyond that."

Vining handed Rosemary her business card. "If your sister calls you back, please call me right away?"

At the station, Ruiz took off for home and Vining went upstairs.

Kissick was in the conference room working on the search warrants with Mireya Dunn, the deputy district attorney from CAPOS. Everyone else was gone.

Vining stuck her head in the door and filled Kissick in on her and Ruiz's progress.

On her way to her desk, Vining noticed a new flyer on the bulletin board—a missing person notice issued by the Hermosa Beach Police. Hermosa resident Lisa Shipp was last seen leaving a meeting at Pier Avenue and Tenth Street just over a day ago. A photograph showed a smiling Lisa standing against a tree, long hair pulled over one shoulder. Her eyes were deep-set and sparkling. The description said she was twenty-six years old. Five feet five inches tall. One hundred twenty pounds. Blond hair. Brown eyes.

"Kinda soon," she mused aloud.

Maybe that's the response he expected.

She took down the flyer, made a photocopy, and tacked it up again.

At her desk, she organized for the next day. It was eight p.m. Sixty hours had passed since they'd found Frankie's body. She had an unsettled feeling in the pit of her stomach that wasn't entirely bad. It was that same tense anticipation and excitement with a hint of dread that accompanies a joyous yet life-altering event, like one's wedding or a child's departure to college. Something was about to happen, about to change. She didn't know what, but she felt it like a breeze blowing past, leaving its mark in her hair and on her skin.

Her eyes landed on Frankie's school photo that she had stuck in the corner of a framed snapshot of Emily. Vining plucked it from beneath the frame and again looked at the handwriting on the back, written diagonally across the photo. The script slanted to the left and was done in blue ballpoint with light pressure so as not to damage the photograph: "Frances Ann 11 years."

That inscription may have been one of the last things that Frankie's mother wrote. That was why it was the only childhood photo Frankie had displayed. It was her "before" photo. Before, when her life had been normal.

Vining looked at Frankie's bright eyes and genuine smile—innocence that was about to be scrubbed. She slipped the photo into her jacket pocket and grabbed her portfolio to leave when her phone started ringing.

"Detective Vining."

"Is this Nan Vining?"

"This is Detective Nan Vining. How can I help you?"

"My name is Richard Alwin."

She sat. She knew the last name.

"I saw you on the news tonight. I put off calling, then decided I had to. My wife was Johnna Alwin. She was a detective with the Tucson Police Department."

Johnna Alwin. Vining had turned up Alwin's ambush murder when conducting her off-the-books investigation about female police officers killed while on duty. She'd spoken with the lead investigator at the Tucson Police Department, who'd told her the case was closed.

"I'm calling because of the necklace you were wearing on television. A year before Johnna was killed, someone gave her a necklace very similar to the one you had on."

Vining was silent.

"Hello?"

"I'm here, Mr. Alwin. Go on."

"I wouldn't have thought anything of it but for the similarities between your story and my wife's. See, Johnna had been involved in a high-profile shooting while on duty, just like you. It was all over the news. We had reporters camping out in our yard. I'm sure the same thing happened to you. Shortly after, the necklace showed up in our mailbox. It was loose in a manila envelope with a card that said: Congratulations, Officer Alwin."

THIRTY-TWO

Vining got Alwin's phone number and said she'd call him back. She told Kissick good night and left.

She pulled her car out of the police lot, parked on the street around the corner, and called Alwin on her cell phone.

He asked, "Where did you get your necklace?"

She deflected the conversation. "I'd rather talk about what happened to your wife."

He told her how Johnna was found stabbed multiple times in a storage closet of a medical building.

"Detective Owen Donahue was in charge of the investigation," Alwin said. "He was only too happy to hang Johnna's murder on her informant Jesse Cuba and call the case closed. No doubt the evidence pointed to Cuba. Johnna had enlisted him as a confidential informant a couple of years before her murder. He was on parole for heroin possession and she caught him with drug paraphernalia. He said he could help her out, claiming he knew about illicit activities in the medical building where he was a part-time janitor. He got the job through this do-gooder, help your local ex-con program. To Cuba's credit, he stayed clean the whole time he worked for Johnna, passing all his drug tests. Johnna felt she had a role in that."

Vining found something soft and too willing to please in Alwin's voice. In her experience, that indicated a passive-aggressive personality.

"Johnna had a big arrest based on Cuba's information about the owner of a medical equipment supply store in the building who was selling stolen wheelchairs. Then Cuba tipped Johnna off about an internist in the building. The good doctor was in over his head, selling prescription drugs to cover his lifestyle. When Cuba called Johnna that Sunday and asked her to meet him, she had no problem going to the medical building alone. She'd worked with Cuba for years by then. It bothered me, but I knew that Johnna didn't take unnecessary chances. She told me sports gambling had replaced Cuba's heroin addiction. He probably wanted twenty bucks to bet that day's game."

"So why did he stab her seventeen times?"

"Good question. Cuba had never been arrested for a violent crime. Not even a fistfight. Detective Donahue brushed it off, saying, 'Guess that was the day he snapped.' But I always felt it went deeper than that."

"Why?"

"You've heard of Louie Louie Lucchi."

"The Mafia turncoat."

Louie Louie Lucchi was the underboss of a New York mob family whose testimony brought long prison sentences for the family's leaders, including the Don. At the time, Lucchi was the most highly placed mobster the FBI had flipped. The once publicity-shy gangster came out of the shadows of the Witness Protection Program to write a book and make the rounds of talk shows. Charming, handsome, and oozing bravado, Lucchi enjoyed celebrity and the public couldn't get enough of him.

Vining didn't have a fascination with the Mafia like many people did. She had never seen *The Sopranos* and thought *The Godfather* movies repulsively glorified what she considered to be a bunch of thugs.

"After Louie left Witness Protection, he came to Arizona because of the weather and because it was relatively mob-free. The mob never got a foothold here and considered Arizona open territory—not belonging to any of the families. Lots of associates and exiles moved here and made new lives, but they were still dangerous people. Louie bought a house in a nice development in the Catalina foothills and lived there with his wife, daughter, and her husband."

"Wasn't the wife's nephew one of his hits?"

"Yeah, and she still stuck with Louie. She opened a beauty supply store and Louie started a company that installed swimming pools. From all appearances, they were businesspeople. Citizens. I'm the assistant manager of the Arizona Inn and Louie drank in our bar a couple times a week, holding court at a corner table. He loved it when people came by to shake his hand or ask for an autograph."

Vining shook her head.

"It was because of Louie that I met Johnna," Alwin said. "This all happened about five years ago. She was working vice undercover with another TPD detective, posing as students at the UA. They were living in the dorms and attending classes like real students. Plan was to entice Louie into a deal to distribute Ecstasy at the university."

Vining remembered that Louie was now back in prison, charged with operating an Ecstasy drug ring.

"The police and feds had the Arizona Inn under surveillance and we had no idea. Johnna spent a lot of time at the hotel bar, hanging with Louie. He liked her. Johnna had a wonderful personality. I told Louie that I thought she was great. He kept pressing me to ask her out, so I did. I thought she really was a UA student. Was that a shock when I found out her real job.

"Louie was close to Crispin Oakley, one of the founders of a white supremacist gang here called the Devil Dogs. Louie put Oakley in charge of distribution of his drugs. Oakley started coming on to Johnna. He thought she was a student, right? She tried to keep her distance but he wouldn't back off. One night he nearly raped her in the parking lot across the street. Businessmen leaving the hotel happened by, giving Johnna an opening to kick Oakley in the nuts and get away."

Vining recalled her solo confrontation with Lonny Velcro in his library.

"Oakley later showed up at Johnna's dorm room and forced his way inside. In the struggle, she grabbed a gun she had hidden and shot him. Louie later claimed that Johnna called Oakley, asked him to come over, and killed him to keep him out of the picture and throw the mob into turmoil, making it easier for the law to sweep in. The story was ridiculous. All Johnna wanted was to keep a low profile and her cover intact. Instead, she ended up in the news for weeks."

Like me, Vining thought.

"Johnna was exonerated, of course. No one gave a rat's behind about Crispin Oakley. Everyone in Tucson was glad he was gone. Johnna made a lot of fans. And she made enemies, not the least of which was Louie Louie. Oakley was like the son he never had."

"You think Lucchi orchestrated Johnna's murder."

"Jesse Cuba was found dead in his motel room on Miracle Mile, which is Tucson's skid row. The coroner said the death was due to an accidental overdose. He had a packet of high-grade heroin in his room. He also had Johnna's purse with her blood on it. She usually carried about a hundred bucks in cash and it was gone. Cuba had been clean for over a year. One day, he decides to use again and slaughters my wife for a hundred bucks?"

"When does the necklace come in?"

"A few months after Johnna shot Crispin Oakley, things settled down. Louie and his gang were in prison. The story faded from the news. Johnna and I got married. One day, the necklace showed up in our mailbox."

"Did she have any idea who might have given it to her?"

"She thought maybe a local businessman who had been shaken down by Oakley's gang was being generous."

"What was the card like?"

"It was one of those panel cards people have done up for announcements or receptions. The message was handwritten in ink. It's been a long time, but I remember what it said."

"Do you have it?"

"I threw it out."

"Where's the necklace now?"

Alwin had been animated during his recitation of the events. Now Vining sensed him withdrawing.

"The police have it. She was wearing it when she was murdered."

Vining was dubious. "She was wearing an expensive necklace on duty."

"She wasn't on duty. We were heading out for dinner.

It was her birthday. Johnna was ready to go when Cuba called. She told me, 'I'll just be a few minutes. I'll meet you there.' She left and . . ." He let out a long sigh.

Vining thought of the necklace she'd kept yet had never considered wearing, finding the idea repellent without knowing why. "She was wearing that necklace to a birthday dinner. Sounds like it had meaning to her. Sentimental value."

It clicked into place. "You gave it to her as a birthday gift from you."

He let out an exasperated huff of air. "I know how this looks."

She hadn't liked him from the moment he'd called. Her instincts had never led her astray. Too bad she hadn't learned to pay attention to them earlier in her life.

"Let me get this straight. You steal your wife's mail and present it to her as a birthday gift from you."

She heard rustling noises as he squirmed.

"I was jealous, okay? After the Oakley shooting, Johnna received a lot of attention. It hadn't blown over. It looked like it would never blow over. Johnna was a local hero. Girl detective takes on the mob. Guys sent drinks over to her when I was sitting right there. She was even on TV talk shows. That necklace wasn't the only gift she'd received, but it was the most expensive. I thought about not giving it to her at all, and then thought that would be a waste."

"Your marriage was already on the rocks."

"We'd been happier."

Vining pressed on. "The case is closed. You never requested her effects?"

"Sure I did. I have her wedding rings and the earrings

she was wearing. I didn't ask for the necklace. Didn't want it. I always felt creepy about it."

She appreciated how he felt, but it did nothing to melt her opinion of him.

Instead of going home, Vining got on the 210 freeway heading west. At the far end of the Valley, she merged onto the 118 and got off at the exit for the Reagan Library. She retraced her route to Kendall and Rhonda Moore's home, driving slowly, pulling over to let cars pass, as she tried to remember where she'd tossed the necklace into the meridian.

Panic welled inside her. It was pitch dark and the streetlights were widely spaced. All she remembered was that the meridian had large oleander hedges. She made a turn and found the hedges, but the boulevard stretched for blocks. Where had she tossed the necklace?

She decided on a spot and parked in the traffic lanes, turning on the light bar inside the car. Fortunately, the streets rolled up early in that city and traffic was light. With a flashlight, she picked her way through the tall shrubs, moving a block from her car. She returned to it, drove farther, and began searching anew, knowing that her chances were about as good as finding the proverbial needle in a haystack.

A short time ago, Vining had wanted to destroy the necklace, to forget it existed. Now it was precious, a prized trophy that linked the attack on her with the murder of a Tucson detective. She had to get it back. It was proof that the attack on her had not been random. She had not been the first and she probably was not the last.

She'd walked a good half mile from her car. Burrs and stalks of wild wheat stuck to her slacks and abraded her ankles. She'd knocked so many pebbles from her shoes she'd given up. She was starting to feel desperate and tried to comfort herself with the knowledge that she could get the television station's videotape of her wearing the necklace. That might be the sole evidence she'd ever owned it.

The arc of the flashlight hit something that glimmered back at her. She bent double to creep into the bushes, nearly twisting her ankle when she landed on a gopher hole. The faux diamonds glittered under the beam, like a beacon, guiding her.

She gathered the necklace into her fist and clutched it against her chest.

Emily came up from her room as soon as Vining entered the house through the garage.

"Hi, sweetheart. How was your day? What are you doing up so late? School project?"

"School's out tomorrow, Mom. There's no more homework."

"School's out?"

"Tomorrow. You knew that."

"Right. Already."

"What's going on? You seem all . . . distracted."

Vining took off her jacket and followed her nightly procedure of taking off her shoulder holster and storing her Glock. "I am, sweet pea. I've had a long day."

From the kitchen counter, she picked up a green leafy plant in a small pot. "What's this?"

"Basil."

Vining pulled out the business card wedged into a plastic spear stuck into the dirt. It was from another local realtor. "I get it. To go with the tomato plant the other realtor left. Not to be outdone."

She opened the refrigerator and looked inside. "I'm famished."

"I made dinner."

"*You* made dinner?"

"Lemon chicken cutlets."

"Chicken cutlets?"

"*Lemon* chicken cutlets." She moved her mother out of the way and took a covered plate from the refrigerator. "I pounded boneless chicken breasts, dredged them in breadcrumbs mixed with lemon zest, and browned them for a few minutes on each side in a little olive oil. I got the recipe from the Food Network."

"When did you start watching the Food Network?"

"I was channel surfing and saw this guy cooking. He was doing something interesting and I thought I'd give it a try. It's fun." Emily warmed the cutlets in the microwave. "I'm expanding my skill set."

Vining broke off a sample with her fingers. "This is really good, Em."

She shrugged. "Wasn't hard."

"Cooking's a good skill to have."

"I also bought spinach salad in a bag." Emily retrieved it from the vegetable bin. "You should have some. You're not eating enough vegetables."

"Yes, ma'am. This is a feast. What a wonderful surprise. Thanks. You made my day." Vining felt her eyes glisten. Her becoming emotional over small things was a sure sign she was overtired.

Emily piled spinach on a plate and sprinkled on the dried cherries that had come with it. With a fork, she laid on two cutlets. "You're welcome." She took a bottle of salad dressing from the fridge and plunked it on the table. "Raspberry vinaigrette. I'm going to bed."

She put her arms around her mother who held on after Emily tried to let go. She kissed Emily's head. "Good night. Sleep well."

"You, too. Don't stay up late," her daughter said.

"I won't. I promise."

Vining drizzled salad dressing over the spinach, poured a glass of skim milk, sat at the dinette off the kitchen, and ate. The folded newspaper was on the table, but she didn't look at it. The remote control was within reach, but she didn't click on the TV.

The Food Network? A fun new hobby. Emily hadn't talked about ghost hunting in a while. Maybe it was that simple. Maybe there was a lesson for her.

She put her dishes and utensils into the dishwasher, picked up her jacket from the back of a chair where she had draped it, and headed to her bedroom.

She took the necklace from her jacket pocket and put it away in the dresser drawer inside the box where she had stored it for years. She removed and hung up her clothes and sat to unfasten her ankle holster, putting the Walther beneath her pillow.

She spied the thick notebook on her desk. Her name, the date of the crime against her, and the case number in black marker were on the spine in Kissick's printing. His personal file of documents and photographs from her case. She didn't open it. She didn't know how many more nights would pass before she did.

THIRTY-THREE

Pussycat sat on the bed for over an hour, holding her sleeping dog on her lap, a towel protecting her clothing from fur. Her husband hated the dog and would especially hate white fur on this particular outfit. She was wearing Frankie's uniform, as he'd requested. The top three shirt buttons were undone and her breasts billowed from the opening. The remaining buttons strained to remain closed. Her feet swam inside Frankie's heavy-soled, lace-up shoes, even with thick gym socks. She'd had to fold up the pants hem. The equipment belt had most of the pieces intact. Missing were the spare clip, the pepper spray, and the cherrywood baton that Frankie told her had belonged to her father and his father before that. Of course, John had removed the weapons.

Wearing Frankie's clothing, she tried to draw upon Frankie's strength. Unlike herself, easily wooed by romance and hearts and flowers, Frankie had always known the score. Her mistake was miscalculating the endgame.

Pussycat had seriously misjudged her husband's motives regarding Frankie. What was she supposed to think when she had to sit there and smile as he gave Frankie the watch that was supposed to be her birthday gift? That same night, the night they'd picked up Frankie at the strip club, he'd told Pussycat to leave the basement so he and Frankie could be alone.

Jealous, she refused to go. He dragged her all the way to her rooms by her hair and shoved her inside. Her dog Mignon yipped at him and tried to bite his ankles. He picked up the dog and threw her against the wall, then swung around and gave Pussycat a right jab in the ribs for trying to stop him. Pussycat feared he'd killed Mignon but, miraculously, the dog was all right. As for her, she was certain he'd broken a rib. He had definitely pulled out locks of her hair. She took a Vicodin and managed to fall asleep.

Pussycat was despondent when she'd come down for breakfast the next morning, expecting any minute for him to tell her to pack her bags. Through the kitchen windows, she saw John walking down the driveway to pick up the newspapers. Pussycat peeked and saw he'd left both doors to the basement open. He was more careless about that when Lolly wasn't working.

Pussycat felt a dull ache in her ribs. While taking another Vicodin with a cup of coffee, she heard Frankie's voice coming from the basement. She was shouting and cursing John. He was muttering profanities in that disjointed way that told Pussycat he was approaching orgasm.

Pussycat crept down the stairs. Playing on the flat screen was a movie of her husband sexually brutalizing Frankie.

"Turn it off," Frankie said.

She was handcuffed to the bed.

Pussycat stared at her, stunned.

"Turn the fucking thing off."

Her husband was yelling, "Scream, bitch. Scream louder."

Pussycat grabbed the remote and silenced the television.

"That bad?" Frankie asked in response to Pussycat's horrified expression. Frankie's lip was split and her eye was black. Blood streaked her thighs and torso.

"He's never hit me in the face before. He's never kept me locked up down here. You getting a picture of what he plans to do?"

Pussycat gaped at her. She didn't want to accept Frankie's interpretation. "But he loves you. I'm the one he's getting rid of."

"Oh, honey. We both underestimated him. Get me out of here. We can take him."

"I don't have the keys."

"Then get the fucking keys!"

"He wouldn't do that. I know him." She winced and held her ribs.

"Did he beat you up, too? Pussycat, what are you waiting for?"

Her eyes darted to the side and Pussycat turned to see him behind her. She recoiled as he reached for her, but his hand on her arm was gentle.

"Come on, sweetheart. You're my wife. She's not worth worrying your pretty head over."

Frankie shrieked, "You think you're done with me? You'll *never* be done with me. Ever!"

Now Pussycat looked down at Frankie's uniform that she wore. She turned the nametag so she could see it. She wished she'd done what Frankie had asked and gotten the keys. Her husband was careful about where he kept them after that, but she could have found a way.

Who was she kidding? Her husband and Miss Tina called the shots in her life these days. And her husband knew how to get Tina to speak in just the right way.

Frankie continued cursing them long after she heard both doors bolted. She had hoped for Pussycat's help. She should have known she couldn't count on a meth tweaker. This was what her mother would have called a come-to-Jesus moment. Frankie knew she was as good as gone. She accepted that fact with a serenity that surprised her. She'd always wondered about people who realized they were about to die. Wondered how they handled it. Now she understood. There was a certain peace in knowing. Sort of like watching a movie you've seen before. The suspense falls away and you have time to pick up on details that had slipped by because you were absorbed in the story.

At that moment, the detail Frankie noticed was the silence in the soundproofed basement. It no longer felt like the absence of noise, but she recognized it as an entity unto itself with its own character and substance. It surrounded and caressed her. Infiltrated her. She closed her eyes to take it in. After a while, she opened her eyes. She felt not sad, but wistful. And angry. Above all, she was angry. He might just get away with what he had done and would do to her, and that made her more upset than the thought of her impending death.

While she was thinking about that, something near the pillow caught her eye. She reached to pick it up, the chain on her wrist rattling. At first she couldn't figure out what it was. Then she remembered. It was a crown that had fallen off his tooth. He had been sitting cross-legged on the bed, eating one of those stinky cheeses with which he was so impressed, conversing like they were sitting across a dinner table, like a normal couple, when he'd jumped up, spitting out a chewed-up mass in his hand. Losing that crown had really pissed him off. She didn't remember what he'd done with it. There it was.

Frankie measured the heft of it in her palm. Then she had a tremendous idea. She set the crown on her tongue, like a communion wafer, then rolled it back into her mouth and swallowed it.

"I've got you now, you prick."

THIRTY-FOUR

The next morning, as Vining made her short drive on the 110 into Pasadena, she received a call from Rosemary, Pussycat's sister.

"Pam just called me."

"What did she say?"

"She said she was feeling better but was still in bed. I told her I wanted to come out to see her tonight and she said not to bother. She'd try to get together with me later this week. I said that she should go to the doctor because migraines don't last this long. She said John had taken her yesterday and the doctor told her she needed to rest."

"How did she sound?"

"Sort of out of it. I asked her if she'd taken a tranquilizer or something. She said she'd taken Xanax. I think she goes to this pill doctor who'd prescribe anything. Course John, in that business he's in, can get anything. I'm thinking of driving out to their house."

"That's not a good idea. Let us take the next step."

"What's the next step?"

"We have a plan. That's all I can say."

A thought occurred to Vining. "Rosemary, do you have the name of an old friend of Pussyca—ah, Pamela's? Maybe someone from school who might try to get in touch with her? A voice from the past?"

Rosemary gave her a name and promised to back Vining's story.

Vining parked in the lot of the minimarket on Walnut and Los Robles. At a phone pod there, Vining called the Lesley residence. She had no doubt that a man like John Lesley would have caller I.D. and possibly contacts who could trace her cell phone number. A woman with a Spanish accent answered.

"Lesley residence."

"Who am I speaking with?"

"This is Lolly the housekeeper. May I help you?"

"I'd like to speak with Mrs. Lesley, please."

Lolly hesitated. "She can't talk right now. May I take a message?"

"Is she there?"

"She's here." The inflection of her voice ascended. Vining guessed she was under stress, but being truthful. "But she can't talk right now, okay?"

A male voice came on the line. "This is John Lesley. Can I help you?"

A chill tickled Vining's spine. She carried on, pitching her voice higher than her normal contralto. "This is

Debby Selvig. I'm an old friend of Pamela's and Rosemary's from high school. Is she there?"

"She's resting. I'll take your number and have her call you."

"Rosemary said that Pam wasn't feeling well. I'm sorry to hear that. I'm in town for a few days and wanted to come by and see her."

"Rosemary gave you this number, I bet."

"Yes, she did. I can stop by this morning."

"Pamela is not well enough for guests. If you talked to Rosemary, she should have told you that. Pamela has exerted herself enough today. I'm sorry but she can't come to the phone. Good-bye."

Vining entered the second-floor Detectives Section and passed Lieutenant Beltran and Sergeant Early, who were in the conference room with the door closed. Through the windows, Vining saw that the interaction was tense. They were both standing. Early leaned on the table on both hands, her eyes shooting daggers at Beltran.

Ruiz was in but Kissick and Caspers were not.

"Where's Jim and Alex?" Vining stood in the opening to Ruiz's cubicle.

"Jim's at the courthouse with Mireya Dunn trying to get approval for the search warrants. I don't know where Caspers is."

She jerked her head in the direction of the conference room. "What's going on?"

"Don't know. They were in there when I got here. Must be serious. They didn't want to talk in front of Cho and Taylor. I do know that Lesley made our team that was surveilling his house last night. He drove up about half past midnight and knocked on the car window."

"Son of a bitch." Vining went to the Detective Sergeants' office where Sergeant Cho was at his desk. "What's the deal with Early and Beltran?"

Cho was going through reports. He looked up at her without moving his head, his eyes almost lost in his fleshy face. "Your surveillance got snuffed."

"What?"

"Order from on high."

"Why?"

He hiked his shoulders. "You know what I know."

Vining went back to Ruiz who was standing in his cubicle. "Cho says our surveillance got snuffed."

"Huh?"

Early and Beltran were still at it.

Caspers showed up. "What's going on?"

"Were you pulled off your surveillance at Reign last night?"

"Yeah. I was there with Jill Hendricks. She was chatting up the bartender. I was hanging out. John Lesley passed by, started shaking hands with people at the bar. I was like, 'Hey, howyadoin'?' That was around midnight. An hour later, Early calls me on my cell and sends me and Hendricks home."

Early jerked open the conference room door and stormed out with Beltran on her heels. He left the area. Early agitatedly waved at the group, calling them into the conference room.

She worked her mouth, as if struggling to find words. "Beltran called me around one this morning and told me to shut down the Lesley surveillance." She held up her hands, forestalling comment. "That's just the way it is. If Kissick gets his warrants, we'll be back in there. Otherwise, hands off the Lesleys. We still have plenty of leads to follow up."

She left the room.

Vining, Ruiz, and Caspers looked at one another.

"You know what that's about," Caspers began. "John Lesley is farther up Beltran's ass than we thought."

"Lesley made you and Hendricks last night," Ruiz said. "Probably went home to see if we had a car on his house. Called his buddy Beltran. Beltran thinks he's a Hollywood player. Wasn't he trying to sell a screenplay?"

"Yeah. 'Death in a Blue Uniform.' " Caspers snickered.

"We should have seen this coming," Vining said. "At his club yesterday, Lesley didn't just brag to Jim and me about how he's friends with Beltran, he taunted us, saying he's got contacts in the local law."

"West Hollywood is covered by Sheriffs, isn't it?" Ruiz asked.

Caspers nodded.

"What the hell?" Ruiz added. "We didn't have anything solid on Lesley anyway. We're on to him only because he might have beat up his ex-wife and he was seen talking to Frankie."

"It's not much," Caspers agreed.

Vining ground her teeth. They were wrong, and she couldn't tell them why. "Jim decided on the surveillance after we interviewed Lesley yesterday. He found enough to take a closer look."

"He's got his reputation on the line," Caspers said. "He's getting desperate. Frankly, I'll be surprised if Kissick gets those search warrants."

Vining glumly stared at the ground. She looked up at

Caspers. "Did you and Hendricks find out anything when you were at Lesley's club?"

"Nothing. Hendricks worked over the bartender, talking about how she'd been robbed, was thinking of buying a gun, did he know anything about them."

"Not exactly subtle," Ruiz said.

"We didn't exactly have a lot of time to build this thing. Couldn't get the bartender to talk."

"Lesley must have warned them if anyone asked about a gun," Vining said. "His ex-wife probably tried to get him on that before."

"I heard from Chase," Caspers said. "He did record his encounter with the Lesleys. He remembered it well. It got nasty. He threatened to pull Lesley in on a one forty-eight. If we want the tape right away, it's at his house. His housemate will let me in."

"We want it right away," Vining said.

"I'll take off."

"Guess I'll keep dialing and smiling," Ruiz said. "Tracking down harebrained leads. If anything good was coming in, it would have come in by now."

Vining put her hands in her jacket pockets. She wore a different pair of slacks but the same jacket she had on the day before and was surprised to find Frankie's school photo that was still there.

She picked up her purse and went into Early's office. "Sarge, I'm going to work some leads in the field, if that's okay."

Early waved her on. Everyone was in a funk, in a holding pattern, waiting for Kissick to return with news of the warrants.

Vining grabbed a two-way from the charger in the sergeants' office. She moved the magnet on the in/out board to show she was out. She had a job in mind and she didn't want to hear anyone's opinion about its viability.

In Hermosa Beach, Vining found a rare parking space a block from the American Legion Hall where Lisa Shipp was last seen at the A.A. meeting. There she met Josh Pierpont, the detective in charge of Lisa Shipp's missing person case.

To Vining, Pierpont's name evoked the beach and so did he. He was about Vining's age, lean and tanned with sun-streaked hair. A perforation in his earlobe hinted at an earring that he did not wear on duty.

"Shipp left the meeting on foot around eleven-thirty that evening after telling friends there that she was heading home," Pierpont said. "She probably would have walked this way after leaving the hall."

They followed what might have been Shipp's route to the tiny, rented house four blocks from the water that she shared with two other girls. The house was shabby yet cute in the manner that an earnest realtor would describe as "beachy." Like everywhere else in Southern California, the old neighborhood was being gentrified. Some of the 1920s cottages had been bulldozed and two-story homes overwhelmed the small lots.

They walked to the strand. It was a bright morning and joggers, bicyclists, and Rollerbladers jockeyed for space on the cement bike path. People out for a stroll were finding the activity more stressful than they anticipated.

Vining took off her sunglasses, breathed fog on the lenses, and cleaned them on her jacket sleeve. "Any chance Lisa went away for the weekend without telling anyone?"

"Her friends and family say it's unlikely. Lisa was a free spirit and adventurous, but she wouldn't have wanted anyone to worry about where she was."

"Any boyfriends? Anyone angry with her?"

"There was a guy she had been seeing, but they parted friends. I tracked down the last few men she dated. I couldn't find anyone who had anything bad to say about her."

He was watching surfers riding the waves a short distance from the pier.

"You surf?" she asked.

"Yeah. Those guys don't know what they're doing. You have to be in the water by six in the morning for decent waves here. This time of day, you need to go on the other side of the Peninsula, where Marineland used to be. But it's risky to surf the beaches down there. The locals are territorial. The police spend their days breaking up fights."

Vining showed Pierpont the photographs of the Lesleys and the artist rendering of Lolita at the strip club, wearing the heart-shaped sunglasses.

After a glance, he returned them to her.

"If someone was looking to pick up girls around here at around eleven o'clock on a Tuesday night, where would they go?"

He pointed. "You've got The Mermaid on the strand down there. Gato's Cantina up the block. And The Lighthouse. That's it for Pier Avenue. There are places along Hermosa Avenue."

Pierpont's sunglass lenses had a metallic yellow coating that reflected Vining's image back to her. It was another thing that annoyed her about him.

"You have a few minutes to walk with me?" Vining asked.

"Sure."

They headed down a broad street perpendicular to the water that was lined with small businesses. She had no luck at The Mermaid or Gato's Cantina.

They passed a surf shop and then reached The Lighthouse. Vining stepped over a large dog curled on the pavement outside the open door. It was only ten in the morning, but a couple of people were sitting at the bar with beers in front of them and empty shot glasses. The jukebox was blasting an old Bruce Springsteen tune. A spattering of sand covered the linoleum floor. Vining surveyed the Hawaii-on-crack décor.

Pierpont and the bartender slapped hands and held on, as if each was saving a man overboard.

"Hank, how's it goin', man?"

"Goin'. Goin' good." Hank acknowledged Vining with "Howyadoin'?" in a manner that suggested he'd confused her with one of Pierpont's female companions.

"Josh, you keepin' our streets safe for the citizens?"

"You got it, buddy."

Pierpont crossed to the rear of the bar where he grabbed a handful of popcorn from a cart.

Hank leaned across the bar toward Vining, his confidential message delivered in a loud voice. "Still can't believe they gave this guy a gun and a badge."

Pierpont returned, draining popcorn from his fist into his mouth. He swatted his hands clean. "This is Detective Vining from the Pasadena Police Department."

"Oh, hi." Chastened, Hank extended his hand to her. "Good to know you."

Vining showed him her photographs. "You see these people in here earlier this week?"

He set John Lesley's photograph on the bar. "Not this guy." He tapped Pussycat's photo. "This girl. I remember her. Yes, indeed. Cutie pie. She got pretty wasted."

"How certain are you that she's this woman?"

"If that's not her, that's her sister."

"Was she here with anybody?"

"Nope. All by herself."

"Any estimate of her height and weight?"

Hank held his hand level against himself to show how tall she stood. "Five-five or something? Had a smokin' body on her. Big boobs. Sorry. I should say she had a generous bosom. No fat on her that I could see. What she was wearing didn't leave much to the imagination. Had on this stretchy, low-cut top. Short jean skirt. Real short." He lapsed into reverie.

"Hair?"

"Not like in your picture. Red. Straight. Down to her shoulders. Had to be a wig. I mean, it was red, like fire engine red."

"Eyes?"

"Eyes. Yeah." He looked away as he thought about something. "That's right. She had those funny contact lenses. You know. The hypnotic eyes with the circle, spiral things in them."

Vining thought about the heart-shaped sunglasses and the chauffeur's outfit at the strip club. This time she shows up nearly nude with costume contact lenses. She crafted her outfits to be distracting so she could hide in plain sight.

Vining lost track of Pierpont and saw him in an adjacent room talking to a heavyset, bearded man who was shooting pool.

"She in trouble?" Hank asked. "I remember her blowing out of here all of a sudden right in the middle of having a hell of a time."

"By herself?"

"She was doing some kissy-face with one of our regulars. He might have followed her outside. Yeah, I think he ran after her. Who wouldn't?"

"One of your regulars. What's his name?"

"Speak of the devil . . . Hey, Pollywog."

Pollywog made his way to the bar, the soles of his flip-flops barely clearing the floor, the rubber worn down until it was compressed into a wafer. He took a corner stool and ran his hands through long oily hair. He wore a plaid shirt with the sleeves cut off and the buttons open to reveal a tanned and tight midsection. A tattoo of vines and flowers covered his right arm from shoulder to elbow. A sprinkling of hair on his chest thinned out as it trailed beneath the waistband of his shorts beyond his belly button. He was still young enough to pull off the grungy look and come off as seedily handsome. In ten years, he'd be a broken-down wreck with a vein roadmap on his face and a beer gut.

He rubbed both hands over his face. " 'Sup, bro'?"

Without being asked, Hank set in front of him a bottle of Corona with a lime wedge stuck in the neck. "This is Detective Vining from Pasadena."

Pollywog angled his head back to get a better look at her. His bloodshot eyes conveyed that he liked what he saw.

"She's asking about your hottie the other night."

"Oh, yeah." Pollywog became dreamy with the recollection. "Thought she was gonna give me some mud for my turtle. Some honey for my . . ." He frowned. "For my what, Hank?"

"Scone?" Hank suggested.

"Right. Honey for my scone."

They both thought that was hysterically funny.

"No . . . Wait, wait . . ." Pollywog paused for effect, hands out. "Honey for my poppin' fresh dough."

"Poppin' fresh dough!" Hank slapped the bar and they started up anew.

Vining shifted her feet and was about to put an end to the frivolity when Pollywog became somber.

"But, alas . . . It was not to be." He poked the lime wedge down the bottleneck. "My little honeybee in trouble?"

Hank dipped glasses into a hot bath and dried them with a towel. "Remember how she blasted out of here?"

"Yeah. I went after her."

"Sir, I'll ask the questions," Vining said.

"Oh, right. Sorry." Hank took a damp rag and retreated to the other side of the bar.

"What's your real name and where do you live?"

Pollywog told her. His speech was slow and deliberate, as if he was focusing on getting the words right.

"What can you tell me about that night?"

"First off, I was dumbfounded she gave me the time of day."

"You were dumbfounded, all right," interjected Hank.

"Hey," Pollywog cried. "I'm talking to the detective. I was dumbfounded because Honeybee was acting like she wanted to pick up a chick. She had her eyes on all the women in the room. Really checkin' 'em out."

He detailed his entire encounter with the woman Vining was certain was Pussycat Lesley, how he'd followed her outside where another woman told him to beat it. Pollywog may have been drinking elsewhere this morning or maybe this was as sober as he ever was. Still, his recollections were clear. He confirmed the nutty contact lenses. He observed that her boobs were fakes, but he was quick to add that he didn't care; he liked them big, fake or natural. Her tattoos were fakes, too. He professed expert knowledge in both arenas.

"So why did she take off like that?" Vining asked.

"Hell if I know. We were getting hot and heavy. She was into it, too, when she split. I think she saw something on TV."

Vining glanced around at the televisions that were mounted everywhere. "Hank, would you have had the news on?"

"I put it on at eleven when I work nights."

She wanted to pump her fist but instead tried to look bored as she took notes.

Pierpont sauntered back as Vining was leaving with Pollywog.

"You done?"

"No." She walked out. Pierpont was cute but she found him useless.

Pollywog retraced his steps with Honeybee on her drunken journey. They ended up in the alley.

Vining showed him the flyer with Lisa Shipp's photograph. "Was this the other woman?"

"That's her. Definitely. Honeybee starts hurling and this one comes up out of nowhere. She gets all in my face, all 'Leave her alone.' And I'm all, 'I'm helping her.' And she's all, 'Get out of here.' So I was like, have a good life, and I beat it. You know what I'm sayin'?"

"Yeah. Hold up. We're not finished yet," Vining said to Pollywog as he started to head down the street.

"I'll be at The Lighthouse. Got a beer there that's half-full. Or maybe it's half-empty."

"Stand right there, please," Pierpont said. "I'll buy you a fresh beer, all right?"

Vining walked inside the alley. It was off a quiet residential street. Late on a Tuesday night, it would be an ideal location for abduction.

She leaned over to look at a crusty splotch that could be vomit.

Pierpont came up behind her. "Some drunk lost his cookies. We saw that when we searched this area."

Vining squatted for a closer look.

Pierpont veered away to stand at the mouth of the alley with his back to her and his hands shoved into his pockets.

"We searched this area," he reminded her again.

Vining pulled her digital camera from her pocket and took shots of the vomit and the surroundings. Putting the camera away, she took out her spiral notebook and ripped sheets of paper from it. Using a twig she found on the ground to pry up the dried substance, she moved a sample onto the papers. Holding it in front of her, she approached Pierpont.

"Not just any drunk. *My* drunk. See that?"

He squinted at the paper and gave her a "so what" smirk.

"Look again." She moved it closer. "See that little plastic chip? Dried up contact lens. The bartender and Pollywog both said Lolita was wearing contacts with spirals in them. Guess you didn't hear. You were in the back room playing pool."

Pierpont's gaze hardened and he pulled his chin up a millimeter. Vining knew she'd ticked him off and was glad. He was playing hail-fellow-well-met around his beach berg while one of his citizens was missing and, Vining feared, being sexually tortured if she wasn't already dead. Vining imagined Lisa Shipp's mother with her stomach in knots as she waited for news.

"He made her go to the club to pick up a girl."

Vining carefully folded the paper into an envelope.

"She couldn't do it. She couldn't let him do to another woman what he did to Frankie Lynde. She fled. He found her. Poor Lisa Shipp showed up at the wrong place at the wrong time."

Tearing more paper from her notebook, she scooped a larger hunk of the vomit.

Pierpont took Pollywog by the arm, attitude gone. "Let's go down to the station and take a statement." They were ultimately the same, he and Vining. A bad guy was out there who needed to be caught.

THIRTY-FIVE

*T*ough girl, huh? Doesn't want to give in. Thinks she's not going to give in. Won't cry. Boo hoo, Officer Lynde. Boo, hoo, hoo."

He was nude. He stood in front of Lynde and made a quick biting gesture near her nipple as if to snap it off between his teeth.

Not flinching, Lynde glared at him.

"You piece of shit. I'll make you scream, bitch. You'll scream for me. You'll scream for your fucking life before I'm through."

Lynde worked her jaw. A wad of spittle shot onto his face.

He wiped it into his hand and rubbed it over her face, mashing her mouth and nose.

"You'll scream and scream until I slit your throat and then you'll try to scream and you'll sound like this." He made a gurgling noise at her.

She again spat at him and he backhanded her across the face.

Lisa Shipp's four limbs were chained to the hospital bed. The top was elevated enough for her to see the room.

The DVD continued to play even though he had finished abusing her for the moment. The remote control was just beyond her reach. He'd moved it from its usual spot in a pocket attached to the side of the bed where she could reach it. He subscribed to all the premium channels. She passed the time mostly watching the news for word of herself and any mindless entertainment she could find. Her story had appeared steadily on the local news until a bigger story blew it off. It probably received more press in the *Daily Breeze,* the South Bay's local newspaper. The public wasn't much interested in a missing teacher's aide, part-time student, and reformed drunk.

Watching television not only helped Lisa pass the time, but also helped her keep track of it. There was only artificial light in the basement. A row of narrow windows near the ceiling were plugged with soundproofing mats sealed with caulking. There was a spot above the piano where the seal was warped. A tiny ray of light shone through. When he left her alone with the longer chain on her ankle, she'd stretched as far as she could but was not able to reach the windows. The chain was long enough to allow her access to the bathroom but everything else was out of reach. The bed was bolted to the floor.

She closed her eyes to try to shut out the DVD. He never tired of watching himself torture the police officer he'd eventually murdered. He reenacted the abuse, demanding she take Frankie's role, saying Frankie's words along with the DVD. He slapped and punched her as he had Frankie. Lisa learned what was coming based upon the section of the DVD playing. She'd learned to steel herself, to project her mind elsewhere. She meditated. She visualized. Her favorite visualization was an experience she'd had in Alaska where she'd walked on a glacier. Bright blue water flowed between cracks in the feet-thick ice, rushing clear and cold. That was her pain. That was her fear. Rushing beneath the ice. The bright blue, frigid water doused its sting. Rendered it clean. Swept it away, leaving her mind and soul glacier white and pure.

He'd played the murder DVD over and over. The first time she'd watched it, she'd barely made it to the toilet before getting sick. She tried closing her eyes, but he'd held a gun to her head. Her stomach still roiled at the sight.

"Watch," he ordered, panting, his eyes wide.

The murder excited him. He relived his rage, jumping around, shouting profanities at the recorded images. Excited him sexually, too. After he was spent, he'd lapse into depression. Curled on the floor in front of the flat screen, he'd cry, "Frankie. I love you, Frankie."

He now lay beside her, nude and snoring, smelling of booze and sweat. A ring of keys dangled from a length of leather fastened around his neck.

His wife was sitting in a recliner across the room.

Pussycat had pulled her legs to her chest and circled her arms around them. She rested her head against her bent knees. Unlike Lisa, she had not attempted to cover herself. The police officer's uniform Pussycat had been wearing was crumpled on the floor. He'd had them switch off wearing it, making them both assume Frankie's role. He was obsessed with Frankie.

When he had brought Pussycat with him that day, Lisa was relieved. She'd feared the woman was dead.

Introducing Pussycat into the mix took his sex games to a new level. Pussycat went through the motions like a robot. He had broken her. Lisa took comfort in the knowledge that she was not broken. She had plenty of life left. She'd decided upon a strategy early. She would not fight him. The longer she stayed alive, the greater the odds that something might happen and she'd escape. The only currency she had was time. When her wits failed, she put herself onto that glacier. Cold, blue water, rushing free and clear.

She had kept her pledge even though wine, spirits, and drugs flowed in that gussied up dungeon. It was tough at first to turn down the booze, but she knew it would get easier. Just say no today. She needed every single one of her wits intact.

That afternoon, he and Pussycat had polished off two bottles of red wine, with him drinking most of it. He made a big deal of swirling it in the glass and holding it to the light, announcing it was a Château so-and-so from nineteen something. He'd bought a case at auction. A steal at seven thousand dollars. To Lisa, a drunk was a drunk, no matter if they consumed the finest wine or Thunderbird. She was glad to see him drink though, and drink he did. Now he wasn't so much asleep as passed out. He'd wake up in a while then leave for the club. She'd have at least twelve hours before he came down again.

Lisa had helped herself to the cheese, fruit, and crackers he'd brought down. He never starved her, but that could change. She looked at Pussycat and wondered if she had enough marbles left to attempt an escape. Watching Pussycat hold herself, staring into space, she had her doubts. Pussycat clearly hadn't been any use to Frankie. Lisa knew she was on drugs.

Her stare roused Pussycat from her reverie. She met Lisa's eyes, rubbed her hands down her arms and shivered. Her mouth formed the words "It's cold."

Lisa didn't know if she vocalized them because of the sound that blared from the DVD.

Pussycat stood and put on the police uniform, sitting to roll up the pant legs.

Lisa raised her hand from where it was chained to the top corner of the bed frame. The pillow supporting his head lay across her other arm that was chained to the bed's opposite corner. Her fingers there had gone numb.

She pointed at the television screen and mouthed "Turn it down." She pointed in the direction she wanted the volume to go.

Pussycat walked to the bed and grabbed the remote. She took in her husband, made a face, and clicked off the DVD. "He's out. He's not going to wake up." She still kept her voice low.

Lisa whispered, "We have to get out of here. He's going to kill us." She couldn't guess his plans for his wife, but thought it best to scare her.

Pussycat's eyes welled.

"Go call the police. Do it, before he wakes up."

"I can't. He locked us in. What do you think those keys are around his neck? You think I'm sitting here for my health?"

"Didn't you know I was down here?"

"Of course I knew."

"Why haven't you called the police? He's going to kill you, too. You're a fool if you think he's not."

"Hey, missy, he's kept me locked up in my rooms upstairs ever since you've been here. He nailed the windows shut and took the phones. Please don't treat me like an idiot. I know he'll get rid of me, too. He'll make it look like a suicide. I know him better than you do. He thinks of everything. There's no hope for us."

Pussycat broke down. Still mindful of her makeup, she drew her fingertips beneath her eyes, trying to avoid smearing her mascara.

"Don't say that. Don't ever say that. As long as we're alive, there's hope. We have to hold it together or else we'll be lost for sure." Lisa rose onto one elbow, her other arm pinned beneath his head. "Doesn't he have a phone down here?"

Pussycat walked to a table across the room, reached to the floor, and picked up the end of a phone cord. She waved it at Lisa and hissed, "Of course he has a phone. He took it. I told you, he thinks of everything."

"No one thinks of everything. There's no such thing as a perfect crime."

Lisa looked around and her eyes fell upon his clothes that he'd tossed onto a chair. "Does he carry a cell phone?"

Pussycat's eyes widened. She went to the chair and rummaged through his clothes pockets, beaming when she produced the prize. She turned it on, both of them wincing while the start up tones played, keeping their eyes on him.

Pussycat's smile faded when she looked at the display. "No signal. I told you. He thinks of everything. He's always making lists and keeping track. It's a game for him. He reads up on the law. Knows what the police can and can't do. He loves those forensic shows. All that autopsy stuff . . ." Her face became grim.

"What?"

"Nothing."

"What's on your mind?"

Pussycat looked away and twirled a lock of hair. "It doesn't matter."

"Tell me." Lisa's voice was louder than she intended and his snoring stopped.

They both froze and stared at him. After a couple of breaths, the wet sawing resumed.

"I'll mess you up with him, Pussycat. I swear I will. Don't screw with me."

"It's just . . . He's so careful about not leaving evidence. He made Frankie cut and scrub her nails and wash her hair before he killed her. Then when he touched her, he wore a cap over his hair and rubber gloves. He didn't want to leave any piece of himself behind."

"That's why he shaved my pubic hair."

"I don't know about that. That's just his thing." Pussycat fell silent and bit her lip.

"Okay. So?"

Pussycat sighed. "So, what I'm trying to say is, he always used condoms with Frankie."

Lisa collapsed onto the bed. He'd never used a condom with her. She knew what it meant. "He left Frankie Lynde's body in plain sight. That's why he took pains to remove all traces of himself. But he's going to make sure no one ever finds a trace of me."

Lisa started to cry. She'd vowed to stay strong, not to waver, but the thought of her parents and brother waiting for word of her that would never come was overwhelming. At least Frankie Lynde's family had a body. At least they knew.

Pussycat went to the bed and stroked Lisa's hair. "Don't cry, Lisa. Please don't cry. We'll figure something out."

"I wish that gun was loaded. I'd shoot him in the head. I won't even kill a spider in my house, but I could kill him. I swear to God I could."

He snorted and his snoring stopped.

The women both stared at each other, eyes wide. After what seemed like eternity, the snoring resumed.

Lisa lay her head back down. Her eyes fell on the remnants of the cheese and crackers on a table across the room. She gasped. "The cheese knife. Go get it. Get it and stab him in the heart."

Pussycat hesitantly walked to the table.

"Go on!"

She picked up her pace, as if she might lose her nerve. She snatched up the knife from the cutting board.

"It's not very big."

"It's big enough to pierce his heart."

She inched toward her husband, slowly moving closer until she stood beside him.

His snoring was deep and even. His mouth sagged open and his cheeks had a pink flush.

"You do it," Pussycat said.

"The chains don't reach. I could only stab him in the side. It wouldn't kill him right away. Then we'd be done for. It has to be one stroke. Right through the heart."

"Okay."

Lisa held her breath as Pussycat grabbed the knife handle between both hands and raised her arms above his chest. She'd dreamed of this. Planned what she would do if she ever had the chance. The moment was here.

Pussycat wavered as she looked at his face, at the fringe of dark eyelashes. Her hands trembled.

"Do it," Lisa growled. "You said he was going to kill you."

Pussycat's trembling grew worse. She veered from the bed, dropping the knife onto the carpet.

"What's wrong with you? You're an idiot."

Pussycat whirled to face her. "Hey, you're not the one standing here thinking about stabbing a man in cold blood. He's still a human being. And be careful who you're calling an idiot. I'm the only friend you've got."

"Okay. I'm sorry. You're right. I don't know if I could do it, either."

"Damn straight, you don't know." Pussycat retrieved the knife from the floor and returned it to the cutting board. "I'm sick of people thinking I'm stupid because of the way I look. Get over it already."

"I said I'm sorry. I am."

Pussycat dropped onto the chair.

"Think he'll wake if we try to get the keys?" Lisa asked.

"Yes."

"He's hardly budged the whole time we've been talking."

"Talking is one thing. Touching him is something else.

He's ticklish. Why else do you think he put the keys around his neck?"

"I can cut the leather with the knife."

"He'll wake up."

"Take the phone by the windows. The seal isn't good there, above the piano. I can see daylight. Maybe you'll get a signal."

Pussycat picked up the cell phone, threw her husband's clothes from the chair, and carried it to the wall. She climbed on top, looked at the phone's display, and shook her head.

She clawed at the rubber seal around the thick mat, sliding her fingers beneath. She pulled it up and a bright ray of sunlight shone in.

Lisa nearly cried when the light hit her face.

Pussycat took the phone from her pocket, looked at the display, and nodded excitedly. "Three bars." She punched in 9-1 . . .

Lisa yelped and darted her free hand over his face. The sunlight bathed him as well, right in the eyes. He was stirring.

"Pussycat," Lisa warned. "The light."

John Lesley staggered to his feet, and flung himself headlong at his wife, knocking her off the chair and onto the piano. She hit the keys and then the floor, hard. The phone flew across the room. He picked it up and cleared the number she'd started to dial.

"You want to make a call, huh? You want to make a call?"

He ground the phone against the side of her face and mouth, breaking the skin on her lips.

"Make your call. Go ahead."

He smacked her in the head with it.

She curled into a ball and whimpered, shielding her head with her hands and tucking her elbows tight, warding against a kick.

"And you . . ." He sprang toward the bed and grabbed Lisa's throat between his hands. "You put her up to it, didn't you?"

Lisa writhed against the restraints that bound her wrists and ankles, bowing her body.

"You're the fucking survivor." He kept squeezing.

Lisa's eyes bulged and her face turned purple.

Pussycat tucked her head between her hands against the floor and moaned.

"Keeping her sobriety vows. Praying. I heard you. Where's your God now, huh?"

Lisa went limp.

Pussycat wailed, the sound feral.

"Relax. She's not dead."

He slapped Lisa's face. She choked and began gasping, pulling against the restraints.

He gave Pussycat a smug look. "See?"

He went to her, pulling her up from the floor by her hair. "I expect something like that from her. But you. I expect a little loyalty from my wife. Everything I've done for you and this is the thanks I get."

He cinched her hair more tightly in his fist.

She cried out.

"You could just go along, but no. You have to make trouble." He dragged her by her hair to the bed.

"Look at her," he said to Lisa. "This woman had everything. Didn't I give you everything you wanted? Didn't I?" He shook Pussycat by her hair.

"Yes, baby. Yes." She grimaced with the pain.

"All I ask is a little loyalty. All you had to do was go

along. Go along to get along. It's not hard, Pussycat. Everybody has to die sometime. Everybody has to endure pain. I'm just speeding it up for these girls and having a little fun, but you can't freaking get it!"

He threw her down. She hit the carpet and started to crawl away.

He grabbed the handcuffs from Frankie's equipment belt on the floor, roughly grabbed Pussycat's wrist and locked on the cuff. He dragged her and looped the other cuff around the same O ring where Lisa's left hand was bound.

"I'm sorry, baby," his wife cried. "I was just confused."

"Poor Pussycat. She was just confused. You do some pretty dumb-ass things when you're confused." He began putting on his clothes. "Pull yourself together. Your sister's been calling. I'm bringing you a Xanax. You're going to chill out, then you're going to call your sister and have a nice conversation. I don't want to give the police any reason to keep nosing around. I'm already into that Beltran down there for his buddy's bachelor party in the VIP room. I already passed his piece of shit screenplay to one of the top agents in town. Now I owe that guy a favor, too.

"Then I'm going to the club, like normal. You're going to stay down here and think about the rest of your life, Pussycat. You have exactly one day to decide because I can't milk this migraine excuse any longer. You are the weakest link. You can either pull yourself together and we can have a nice life doing what we want, or you're going to have a car accident or meth overdose that you won't survive."

He turned back. "Something to tuck away, Pussycat. You're thinking I'm the bad guy, you'll rat me out to the police and get off with a slap on the hand. You're thinking you're the poor abused wife and the jury will give you a break. No, darling. You aided and abetted. You are guilty of the same crimes I am. And no one's going to be sympathetic to an ex-stripper meth hag who married a rich nightclub owner and helped him with his hobbies."

He counted off on his fingers. "Kidnapping, murder, torture. Two counts."

He leered sadistically at Lisa. "You heard right: two counts. Think about it, Pussycat. Clock's ticking."

THIRTY-SIX

It was late afternoon by the time Vining returned to Pasadena from Hermosa Beach.

Kissick, Ruiz, Caspers, Sergeant Early, and Deputy District Attorney Mireya Dunn were in the conference room listening to a recording on a microcassette that Caspers held.

On it, Officer John Chase and John Lesley were having a heated exchange.

"Sir, if you don't get back inside your car and let me write the citation, I'm going to have to arrest you for interfering with the duties of a police officer."

"I don't like the way you're looking at my wife. Give you a fucking badge and you think you can do anything."

His wife's voice was farther away. "John, please just take the ticket and let's go."

"Did I ask your opinion, Pussycat?"

Chase interjected. "If you keep doing what you're doing, Mr. Lesley, you're going to jail."

"I just had my picture taken with the chief and you're taking me to jail because my car windows are too dark. I stopped a robbery in progress in your city. I'm real glad I put myself at risk for you idiots. What are you looking at?"

"What's in that box on the floor, sir?"

"None of your fucking business."

"Can I search your car?"

"Search my car? The answer's not only no, it's hell no."

"What's the problem? You've got nothing to hide, right?"

"You think I was born yesterday, Officer?"

There was strained silence. Then Lesley said, "Give me the fucking thing."

"Vujaday," Pussycat whined in the background. "This is so vujaday."

"You call yourself a police department." Lesley's voice faded. Chase was apparently returning to his cruiser.

"Is this how you keep busy because you don't have real crime in this berg?" Lesley continued to rage. "Writing bullshit tickets and giving yourself awards."

There were sounds of Chase opening the door of his vehicle. "Have a good day, sir." He uttered a soft chuckle.

"If you had a real crime to solve, you guys would fall—"

The recording ended.

Caspers said to the recorder he still held, "My man, the Chaser."

Early looked dubious. "Could be a motive to mess with us by dumping a body in Pasadena."

"A crack defense attorney would shoot holes through everything we have," Dunn said. "John Lesley can afford to hire the biggest gun in town."

"What have you been up to?" Kissick asked Vining.

"I'll tell you in a second. Alex, would you please play the last part again? From where Chase asks to search the car."

The recording reached Pussycat's final words.

"Stop it there, please," Vining said. "Vujaday. What is she saying?"

"Vujaday." Caspers looked incredulously at her. "Come on. Everyone knows that."

"I don't know what it means," Kissick said.

Vining tried to remember where she had recently heard those words. She closed her eyes.

"It's the opposite of déjà vu," Caspers said. "Déjà vu means you think you've been in this place before. Vujà dé means you never want to be in this place again."

Vining snapped her fingers. "Mrs. Bodek. Frankie's neighbor. That's where I've heard that. The woman Mrs. Bodek saw leaving Frankie's condo told her the same thing. It was Pussycat. This is great. Mrs. Bodek will be priceless as a witness."

She became animated. "Let me tell you about my conversation with John Lesley and what I found out in Hermosa Beach."

She brought them up to date and tossed statements from Hank the bartender and Pollywog onto the table.

"I've already booked the vomit and contact lens into evidence."

"Good work, Nan," Early said.

Everyone gave her atta girls, even Ruiz.

"We need Pussycat Lesley's DNA to match against the vomit and contact lens," Kissick said. "How fast can we get DNA run?"

Dunn responded, "We can get preliminary results in twenty-four hours, but it's expensive."

"Lieutenant Beltran will push it through for us," Ruiz said sarcastically.

"Our buddy," Caspers said.

Early warned, "Watch it."

Kissick moved past the Beltran-bashing. "Lisa Shipp's missing person case is collateral to the Frankie Lynde homicide. But it places Pussycat at the scene of a second woman's disappearance. Maybe we can find witnesses who saw Lesley or his Hummer in Hermosa Beach that night."

"So we get samples of Pussycat's DNA when we serve the warrants." Vining noted the lack of enthusiasm in the room. "What?"

"No warrants," Kissick said. "Judge Ralston shut us down." He mocked, "Corporal, if we're going to examine someone's highly confidential medical records and invade their home and workplace, we'd better have sound reasons, and I don't see that you've fulfilled that requirement."

Early spat, "Yeah, highly confidential and personal dental records."

"Ralston's notorious for blowing warrants out of the water," Dunn said.

"Didn't he cut his teeth as a public defender?" Early asked.

"Guess he never left," Kissick said. "We're still the enemy."

Dunn picked up the statements Vining took in Hermosa Beach and the microcassette recorder. "With this new evidence, we can rewrite the affidavits and hope we get someone other than Ralston."

Ruiz spread cheer, as usual. "The way our luck's been going, I wouldn't count on it."

"If John Lesley is our guy," Early said. "I'm not convinced."

"All due respect, Sarge," Vining began, "but what's not to like about him?"

"Vining, if you can't convince me, how are you going to convince a jury?" Early rubbed her eyes.

"So where does that leave us?" Kissick asked.

"Surveil the Lesley house, wait for the missus to leave, and grab her off her property," Ruiz suggested.

"Therein lies the problem," Kissick said.

"He appears to be holding her captive at home," Vining said. "That's probably where Lisa Shipp is and where he held and likely killed Frankie. That property is large and isolated. He forces Pussycat to call her family so they don't report her missing. The parents don't question because they're afraid he'll shut off their gravy train. He's got Lolly the housekeeper backing him up. No doubt she knows more than she's telling."

"We don't have the P.C. to enter Lesley's home," Dunn said. "To get the probable cause, we need the warrants."

"I'm going to be damn sure I've covered my ass on this one." Early scowled. "I've already had one of my decisions slapped down from on high."

"I'd like to know the story behind that," Ruiz said.

"Doubt we ever will," Caspers said.

"While we're spending time trying to get warrants signed, Lesley knows we're on to him," Vining said. "I'd like to try to get inside the Lesley house now. Maybe the housekeeper will let us in. I've already set up the long-lost school friend scenario. My husband, Jim, and I could have decided to drop by. Lolly doesn't know us. Neither does Pussycat."

Dunn reminded her, "Even if you get the consent of the housekeeper or Pussycat to go inside, your evidence must be in plain sight for an exigent circumstances exception to the search warrant. Else, any evidence you find will be considered fruit of the poisonous tree at trial. It and anything learned from it is inadmissible."

"Get ready for the lawsuit against the city," Early said.

Vining's body language betrayed her emotions. Her words left no doubt. "Sarge, at the risk of being insubordinate, have we turned into the LAPD? More afraid of betrayal than bullets. Stay under the radar. Don't make waves. Don't bend the rules. Just smile and wave. While we're here figuring out how to appease judges who fret over the privacy of criminals and second-guessing brass in our own department who have delusions of grandeur, two women are being held captive and possibly tortured and murdered and no one cares."

Vining had always admired Early, but her stock had diminished in Vining's eyes.

Early sighed. "Let's take it to the next step with the Lesleys, but I don't want to be caught with our backsides hanging out. Let's bring in Pussycat for questioning."

"We don't need to trouble Lieutenant Beltran with every detail of this case, do we, Sarge?" Kissick asked.

"Beltran's a busy man," Early said. "A need-to-know basis is sufficient."

Vining was pleased that Early had stepped up.

Kissick was energized. "John Lesley goes to his club in the late afternoon until closing. Let's send a team over there to monitor his actions and keep him from going home."

"He doesn't know me," Ruiz said. "I'll pretend I'm selling something and ask for five minutes of his time. If he won't see me, I'll say I'll wait and sit by the front door. Caspers can wait in his car by the back entrance."

Caspers offered, "I can make fake business cards for you. What are you selling?"

Ruiz raised his shoulders.

Caspers snapped his fingers. "Security services."

Kissick added, "If you can't keep Lesley there and he leaves, it'll take him at least half an hour to get from West Hollywood to Encino. Plenty of time for Vining and me to take the housekeeper and Pussycat into custody."

"Procedurally, we should notify the police agencies in the two jurisdictions where we'll be operating," Early said. "Last thing we want is a police response to a disturbance that pits our folks against officers from another jurisdiction. Encino is the LAPD's West Valley Area. Lesley's nightclub is covered by West Hollywood's sheriff's station. That said, if Lesley has connections with the law in Pasadena, he undoubtedly has his claws in the local law."

"He bragged about it to Vining and me," Kissick said.

"Let's do this," Early said. "Wait until you're on site, then call the watch commander of the local jurisdiction and ask for confidentiality. Ruiz and Caspers, not as critical for you since you're just doing surveillance, but things could get dicey at the Lesley house. Jim, if you don't want to risk notifying the local law, best to wait until Lolly or Pussycat leaves the house, follow her until you're out of the West Valley jurisdiction, and then make contact."

"We'll communicate by cell phone," Kissick said. "I don't want someone with a scanner, especially Lesley or his cop friends, listening in."

"Stay safe," Early said.

THIRTY-SEVEN

K issick and Vining approached the gates to the Lesley home. The street was quiet, as on their prior visit. An occasional car passed. A leaf blower wielded by an unseen gardener droned in the distance. Both the heat and smog had increased as the afternoon dragged on.

Vining rolled down the driver's window and pressed the call button on the keypad. After several rings, an automated male voice sounded through the speaker, "No one is available to take your call . . ."

After the beep, she left a message. "Hi, Pamela! This is Debby Selvig. Long time, no see. I'm in town on business and thought I'd stop by. I called earlier. Your husband said you weren't feeling well, but you know me, I decided to stop by anyway. I'll just stay a few minutes. I promise. Just buzz—"

The message recorder shut off.

"Crap. I'll try Pussycat's cell." Vining got out of the car and made the call. When Pussycat didn't answer, she left the same message as on the house phone.

Kissick was surveying the property through binoculars.

"There's a car in the driveway," he said. "I think it's a Honda Civic. Beige. Home repair job on the left front fender. I can make out the license plate."

Vining took out a notepad and pen. "Go."

He read off the plate.

Vining pressed speed-dial numbers for PPD dispatch.

"This is Nan Vining on cell phone. Jim Kissick and I are code six at one-seven-two Encino Avenue in Encino. The property belongs to John Lesley. Mr. Lesley is not present but his wife and a housekeeper may be. Run this plate for me, please."

Dispatch returned that the car was registered to a Mauricio and Dolores Nunez at a Pacoima address. After another minute, dispatch told her that the couple had no wants or warrants and no priors.

"You have a phone number at that address?"

She wrote it down. "Ten four." She punched in the number on the phone keypad.

"Hello. This is Debby Selvig. I'm a high school friend of Pamela Lesley. You probably know her as Pussycat. May I speak with Mauricio or Lolly Nunez, please? Mr. Nunez, hello. Pussycat gave me your phone number. I'm waiting at the front gate of the Lesley's home to see her and no one is answering. I'm visiting from out of town. I know Pussycat is sick in bed, but she said Lolly would let me in. Did Lolly come to work today? What time did she leave this morning? Does she drive the Lesleys' cars to run errands? That's probably where she is, at the grocery."

While Vining made her call, Kissick speed-dialed Caspers's cell phone. Caspers reported that Ruiz called him from inside the club. The bartender dialed an in-house extension to talk to Lesley, then told Ruiz to wait. That was forty minutes ago. Caspers was parked in the alley that ran behind the club and had a visual of Lesley's Hummer. He contacted the watch commander at the sheriff's West Hollywood substation, but only after a deputy sheriff on a motor had tapped the window of his unmarked car and asked what was up.

"Interesting timing," Caspers commented.

"You haven't seen Lesley yet?"

"Nope. Ruiz says he hasn't come down. Don't worry. Ruiz has the front and I've got the back. Unless Lesley's walking to Encino, he won't be coming up on you."

"Keep me posted."

"Keepin' it real here in WeHo."

Kissick then made a call to the local LAPD watch commander to let him know what was going on. He requested confidentiality.

He resumed surveying the property.

Vining continued her conversation with the housekeeper's husband. "Is there anyone else usually in the house this time of day? Does Lolly keep the doors locked? Does she set the alarm when she's working? How have things been for Lolly, working for Mr. and Mrs. Lesley? Has everything been going okay? I'm just wondering because when I spoke to Pussycat she said that Lolly seemed stressed out lately. Pussycat said her husband can be kind of demanding."

Kissick noticed the archery range on the side lawn that lined the driveway. Arrows protruded from the bull's-eye of a target supported on a stand.

Vining persisted. "Does your wife have a cell phone number? May I have that, please? I'll call her and maybe she can hurry back from her errands so I can see Pussycat before I have to catch my plane. Thank you very much, Mr. Nunez. When I see Lolly, I'll tell her to call you."

She was distracted by Kissick's frantic waving. "Mr. Nunez, can you hold on for a second, please?"

"Black limo," Kissick said, peering through binoculars. "Lincoln limo in a turnabout in front of the garage."

"Mr. Nunez, I see a black limousine parked in the driveway. Ahh . . . It belongs to your nephew." She widened her eyes at Kissick. "Your nephew has a limo service and Mr. Lesley lets him park his car here. How nice for Mr. Lesley and Pussycat if they can drive it. Oh, they *do* drive it. Mr. Lesley pays him? Perfect for your nephew. He gets the money and he doesn't have to work."

Kissick clenched his fist.

"Thank you, Mr. Nunez. Good-bye."

"Limo in his driveway," Kissick said. "Smells like probable cause to me." He climbed onto the car hood, clambered atop the stone wall, and jumped to the ground on the other side of the gate. He found the release to open the gate, then brushed off his clothes.

Vining drove the car inside and Kissick got in.

"Want to try Lolly's cell for me?" She handed him the number.

He did, then closed his phone and slipped it into his pocket. "No answer."

"She was here when I called for Pussycat this morning. Her husband says she drives that Civic to run errands."

"So where is she?"

"Good question. Lolly's husband says she's usually the only one home this time of day. The gardeners come on Tuesdays. When Lolly's working, she locks the doors but doesn't set the alarm. Did you contact West Valley watch commander?"

"Yep. I think I woke him up."

Vining parked sideways, blocking the driveway.

Kissick grabbed a two-way radio and shoved it inside his jacket pocket. They both got out.

He tried the limo's doors. They were locked.

The doors of the Civic weren't. Vining found little. On the front passenger seat was a juice box pierced with a straw. On the backseat were an adult's sweater and a brightly hued tank top from a high school athletic team. The glove compartment and trunk held the usual junk.

They crossed the grass and ascended flagstone front steps. A steel placard from a home security firm was in the flower bed. Vining flattened against the wall while Kissick pressed his ear against the door. Not hearing anything, he peered through a narrow paned window that ran the length of the door.

He shook his head at Vining, signaling he didn't see or hear anyone.

He tried the brass door lever. It was locked. He glanced at Vining.

"Go for it."

He pounded the heavy brass knocker. "Police. Lolly Nunez. Pussycat Lesley. Open the door." He knocked again. "Police." He again listened and heard nothing from inside.

Vining crept along a flagstone walkway across the front of the house, reaching a row of picture windows.

She craned her neck to look inside, then again concealed herself, shaking her head at Kissick.

He drew his weapon and she did the same. He pointed toward the rear of the house. They crouched as they cleared the windows above the walkway. Reaching the detached garage, they flattened themselves against each side of the walk-through door. Kissick listened at the door before flinging it open. After a beat, he peered inside the dark interior. He ran his hand along the wall and flipped on a switch. Fluorescent lights flooded the room.

Guns front, they cleared the area. The garage had spaces for six cars. Parked there were a Mercedes S600 sedan, a 1965 Cadillac Coupe de Ville convertible, and a Ford F-150 truck.

They left the garage, turning off the lights and closing the door. They faced the patio and pool bounded by a lush lawn. Beyond the lawn, a citrus grove bordered the property, surrounded by a chain-link fence. The house was to their right. A short distance past the garage on their left was the clubhouse—a long, low structure with wood-framed sliding glass doors.

Kissick tipped his head in that direction, but Vining was looking elsewhere. He followed her gaze and saw that several windows near the rear of the house were covered with plywood on the inside.

They headed toward the clubhouse. They crossed the patio to stand on either side of the sliding doors. Vining held her gun in both hands against her chest while Kissick held up his thumb and two fingers and began counting down by folding each one. At "three" they pulled open the doors and swung inside the room with guns in front. Backs to the wall, they skirted the perimeter of the room, moving quickly, scanning right and left.

The large space was furnished with plump couches and chairs upholstered in Native American blankets and leather. Well-worn, heavy wood tables filled the spaces between. Navajo rugs and woven baskets were displayed along the walls. One wall was covered with bows and arrows in all shapes and forms, from simple wood versions to titanium crossbows. More Navajo rugs covered the broad-planked wood floor.

They were both briefly distracted by a photograph on the wall of an older bald man with Sylvester Stallone in his Rambo costume.

Vining cleared one side while Kissick worked the other. She was unpleasantly aware of her heart beating. Perspiration seeped through her shirt. She tightly grasped her weapon with both hands but couldn't stop them from trembling.

I'm in control.

A pass-through off one end of the room allowed her to look inside a small kitchen. She sidestepped to enter the enclosure, stopping when she reached a doorway. She spun inside, gun first. It was a bathroom and it was empty. She made her way to a door on the opposite wall that looked like a supply closet or pantry.

She peeked into the pass-through to see Kissick across the room bending down to pick something off the porch outside. She resumed clearing the last of the kitchen. With her weapon in hand, she grasped the doorknob. The pantry in the El Alisal house flashed into her mind. She had crawled there, trailing blood, a knife embedded in her neck, in search of the word he'd left for her. The word he'd wanted her to see.

It's just a space in a house.

Her right hand was shaking and she barely maintained

her grip on her weapon. She reached for the door with her left. Something on the floor drew her attention.

A ribbon of blood oozed from beneath the door.

She blinked.

It's an illusion. It's not real.

She blinked again. It was still there. She touched it with the toe of her shoe and drew back a red smear.

"Jim, there's something here."

She flung the door open, jumping when a can of tomatoes rolled out. Canned goods and cartons knocked from the shelves were strewn about.

Crumpled on the floor was the body of a Latina. Her throat was slashed.

She heard Kissick shout followed by the retort of a gun. She instinctively knew it was his gun. She should take cover, get down, call out to him, but she stood mesmerized. The aroma of burnt gunpowder filled the air. Was he moaning? It might as well have been a television broadcast.

That familiar yet dreaded fluttering in her chest took over. There was no air. Surely it had been sucked from the room. Her ears buzzed, the noise building until it took over, drowning out Kissick's agony and her pounding heart. Was that her bloody body lying there? No. She was standing here. Wasn't she?

She grabbed the door frame as the room whirled. She squeezed her eyes shut to block at least that one sensory input. The snap of passing seconds slugged like hours.

"Nan . . ."

Kissick could barely get it out. She felt his distress.

Open your eyes, she commanded herself.

She did. In the pantry was a dead woman lying in blood.

"I am *not* you."

The declaration shook the demons from her. Her fear drained from her and oozed through the seams in the plank floor with the dead woman's blood, a melding of essences. All the ghosts of her past and present. One by one, they left. She felt at once lighter and more solid. Just like that, her long hangover was finally cured.

Her mind was icily clear.

A window near her shattered and an arrow whizzed by her head, brushing her hair, embedding in the doorjamb.

She hit the floor as a second arrow hit where her head had been. She discharged her weapon at John Lesley standing in the window. She heard him cry out as he released another arrow from his crossbow.

THIRTY-EIGHT

Vining leaned against a cabinet on the kitchenette floor, holding her Glock between both hands. She was sitting in broken glass and smeared blood. It only faintly repulsed her. She heard a moan and labored breathing.

"Jim?"

"Here."

He struggled to voice that single word.

She threw herself against the wall beneath the window, crept up until she could glance outside and again concealed herself. Lesley was gone but she saw drops of blood along the patio.

Crouching low, she crossed the room. Another trail of blood led from the open sliding glass doors and disappeared behind a sofa.

"Jim," she said again.

"Hhh . . ."

She followed the direction of his voice, darting past the open doors to the cluster of heavy furniture and found him on the floor leaning against a sofa. An arrow protruded from his chest. He managed to turn his grimace into a labored smile. The portable two-way radio on the floor was broadcasting three sharp tones as someone on the other end tried to raise him.

She squatted beside him. "Jim. My God."

"Got . . . my lung, think."

Vining picked up the two-way and radioed their location and circumstances.

"They'll be here like five minutes ago."

Looking at Kissick, she helplessly spread her hands.

"Looks worse . . ." he said, talking about the arrow.

He cradled his gun against his chest in one bloody hand, but had something else clutched in his other. She started to pry it from his fingers and he let go. It was a pink athletic shoe. The logo said New Balance. The lining told her the style was Wind Lass, size seven.

Picking up the shoe had distracted Kissick for the second it took Lesley to line him up between the sights of his crossbow.

Lesley took advantage of a new opportunity.

An arrow hit Vining in her left bicep.

She muffled her cry as she jerked out of view, falling over Kissick's legs.

"Motherfu . . ." She rose up from behind the sofa and released a volley of gunshots at the receding figure.

" 'Kay?" Kissick asked.

She pulled out the arrow and threw it across the room. She rose to head out, but Kissick latched onto her.

"Backup."

"One minute is all the time he needs to escape. He's not getting away. Not this time."

Keeping low, she ran from the clubhouse and followed drops of blood that led through the open back door of the house.

She heard a noise that sounded like tapping against glass. She traced the sound to a row of small windows along the base of the house. They were blocked out on the inside. As she drew near, the tapping turned frantic.

She stepped into a flower bed filled with rosebushes, snagging her slacks on thorns. Checking for Lesley, hoping she wasn't in his sights, she squeezed behind the roses and dropped to her hands and knees. She rubbed the glass to clear mud splatter over an area where the inside covering was pulled away. She heard a faint "Help!"

She squinted through the glass and saw Pussycat. She was wearing an ill-fitting LAPD uniform. In her outstretched hand, she held what looked like a drumstick. Her other arm appeared tied to something. Beyond her in the dim light she saw Lisa Shipp, splayed out on a bed, her four limbs tethered to each corner.

Vining worked her hands around the window. There was no way to open it as the latch was on the inside.

She shouted, "Stand back," looked to make sure Lesley wasn't around, and then shattered the glass with the heel of her shoe.

The women shielded themselves the best they could.

Once Vining had broken through, Pussycat started screaming and crying. Lisa was calmer, but trying to talk over Pussycat. The result was near hysteria.

"Pussycat. Lisa. Calm down," Vining said quietly. "You need to be calm for me, okay? Where's the entrance to this room?"

"Through the kitchen," Pussycat managed through her tears.

"Where is he?"

"We don't know," Lisa said.

"He's not in there?"

Lisa responded, "No."

"Does he have guns in the house?"

"Lots of 'em." Pussycat was sobbing and could barely speak.

"I'm going to get you out of there. There's dozens of police coming. Hear the sirens? Stay calm. Stay quiet."

Vining's left arm was bleeding and she only now started to feel pain. She decided to wait there in the flower bed, pressed against the side of the house. Backup was on the property. She heard the cars approaching. It was a good plan and it shortly went to hell.

Pussycat and Lisa began screaming as John Lesley burst through the door into the basement. His shirt was soaked with blood.

Vining took aim at him through the window but he pulled Pussycat in front of him. He held a gun to her head.

"I'll make a trade, Detective," Lesley said. "Them for you. You have ten seconds to decide. I mean business. I have nothing to lose. Both of them for one of you. Ten seconds, starting now. One thousand one. One thousand two . . ."

Vining clutched her badge in her hand as she crawled between the rosebushes and rolled clear of the basement window. A swarm of LAPD uniforms and SWAT team officers fanned out across the property. Guns aimed at her were lowered at the sight of her badge.

"Pasadena PD," she announced. "Detective Vining," she blurted to a field sergeant who approached. "Detective Jim Kissick is injured in that outbuilding behind the garage. He needs medical assistance."

"We're taking care of it."

Lesley inside the basement shouted, "Vining! One thousand seven . . ."

Vining started toward the house, telling the sergeant, "I'm going inside. He's trading the female hostages for me."

"Wait for a hostage negotiator."

The SWAT team was taking positions around the basement windows and clearing the house.

Pussycat appeared in the broken window with Lesley behind her. He yelled, "This is the only deal that's on the table. Detective Vining for Pussycat Lesley and Lisa Shipp. Take it or leave it. I'll give you ten more seconds then I start the executions. One thousand one . . ."

He began shoving pillows into the opening.

Vining jogged toward the rear of the house with the sergeant. "When Pussycat Lesley comes out, arrest her for the murder, kidnapping, and torture of Frances Lynde and kidnapping and torture of Lisa Shipp."

"I'm not letting you go in there," the sergeant said.

"John Lesley will kill those women, Sergeant. No doubt." She met his eyes.

After a pause, he said, "Detective, you're sure you know what you're doing?"

They entered the kitchen. Vining moved toward the

open door to the basement, saying to the sergeant, "Yeah. I'm getting the bad guy."

Lesley continued his countdown, "One thousand five . . ."

At the top of the stairs, she shouted, "John Lesley, I'm here." She saw the second door a few steps beyond where she stood. It was also open.

"Take off your jacket and gun. Walk down with your hands up."

"Send out Lisa Shipp first."

"That's not the deal."

"You said you'd trade me for the women. Send out Lisa."

"Pussycat first."

"Look, John. I'm the one you want. I'm the one who tracked down your sorry ass. I'm the reason you're bleeding to death in a basement. Who better to take with you than me? Send out Lisa now."

"I'm sending out Pussycat."

Lisa wailed, "Please let me go. Please . . ."

Lesley said, "Here she comes. Once she's out, come down with your hands up."

"Put your hands behind your head, Pussycat," Vining said.

"Don't shoot." Pussycat rounded the corner and faced a sea of firearms pointed at her. "Please don't shoot me."

As she pranced up the stairs, sounds of dismay and disgust went up at the sight of her in Frankie Lynde's uniform. The LAPD officers did not handle her gently as they arrested and Mirandized her.

Vining fished her hands into her jacket pockets and shoved her cell phone and anything else she found into her pants pockets. She stripped off the jacket and handed it and her gun to the sergeant. He and a SWAT team captain blathered instructions and strategy to her, but she knew nothing would likely go as planned. All she could count on was training, instinct, and luck. She felt calm, confident in the knowledge that this was what she had to do. She wasn't worried about her daughter. She wasn't even worried about being late for dinner. For the first time in a year, she was completely without fear.

"I'm coming down, Lesley."

Lacing her hands behind her head, she started down the stairs, passing the interior door and stepping onto the carpet.

He'd unchained Lisa from the bed. The sheet she had wrapped around her was mottled with his blood where he held her against him with one arm. His other hand held a gun against her head. He leaned heavily against her, needing her for support.

Lisa began to weep at the sight of Vining.

"Come closer," he ordered Vining.

She approached a few steps then stopped. "Let her go."

Holding Lisa ahead of him, he shoved her to the inner door, pushed her out, slammed it closed, and slid a metal bar into place across it. He staggered back into the room, reeling and catching his balance against a chair.

"It's just you and me, Detective Vining. You, me, and eternity."

Vining still stood with her hands laced behind her head. The noises she heard beyond the pillow shoved into the broken window fell away. She knew they were out there, waiting.

"We're both too arrogant for our own good, wouldn't you say? Balls to the wall. Look where it's gotten us." He smiled, revealing teeth smeared with blood.

She didn't respond.

"How about some music?" he asked. "I think better

when music's playing. Plus they're trying to listen to us. I can hear them rustling around, like rodents in the wall."

He grabbed a remote control and started the DVD of him brutalizing Frankie Lynde, turning the volume up loud.

It took Vining a second to absorb what she was seeing and hearing. Frankie Lynde was prone while he savaged her, holding a knife to her neck.

"You say it's not music?" Lesley grinned sadistically as he turned up the volume again. The sound of Frankie trying to stifle a moan filled the room. "It's music to *my* ears."

He extended one arm, holding on to a chair back with the other. "Look at this. I had a harem. Once I had a dozen women in here at once. All for me."

Shaking his head with delight at himself, he slipped his gun into the front of his waistband against his bloody shirt. He stumbled to one of the giant mirrors and admired himself.

"Look at me. Like one of those gangster rappers." He turned back to her. "And you're my ho. My ho." He repeated the slang, accompanying it with a gang hand sign probably pilfered from a music video.

He pulled the gun from beneath his belt, pressed off the safety, and came close to her.

She didn't flinch when he held the barrel against the side of her head.

"What do you have to say now, Detective Vining?"

The gun felt cold and hard. It was the first time she'd had a gun against her head. She'd never even dared it with an empty gun. The cold steel was a powerful sensation and sparked a surprising reaction.

John Lesley, you're going to die.

"What do you have to say *now*?" He repeated the question slowly, tapping the gun against her with each word.

She turned to face him. His hand remained in place and the gun barrel traced a path around her head. It was now pointed at her forehead between her eyes.

"Speak."

She looked at him, not blinking. Her stance was steady, as was her heartbeat. One thought possessed her.

You're going to die.

"Speak. Woof, woof."

She sensed more than saw the tension on his finger tighten on the trigger.

She said, "If you pull the trigger, twenty SWAT team members are going to burst through those windows. Unless you're prepared to die right now, I wouldn't do it."

"Ya think?" he chortled. "This is fun and all, but I've got a little piece of business to take care of before we say the big adios. Turn around."

She complied.

On the DVD, Frankie shouted in pain and cursed him as the sounds of his sexual ecstasy escalated.

He patted Vining down. Searching one pants pocket, he found her cell phone and threw it across the room. Sticking his hand into the other pocket, he took out a stiff rectangle of paper.

Vining turned to see him looking at Frankie's school photograph, his expression wistful. He flipped it over and read the writing on the back.

A voice blasted the room. "You think you're done with me?"

It was Frankie on the DVD, the volume abruptly spiking louder.

"You'll *never* be done with me!"

It startled John Lesley. He glanced at the television screen, his expression bewildered.

Vining dropped and grabbed her Walther from her ankle holster just as Lesley regained his composure and took aim. Too late. She squeezed off all eight bullets.

The room exploded with breaking glass, gunfire, and heavy boots.

Vining scrambled to get to John Lesley first.

He gurgled blood. His eyes shifted to focus on her.

She jammed her fingers against his carotid artery. His blood covered her hands. She didn't care. She held his gaze as she felt his pulse grow weaker and weaker. Soon, there was no pulse at all. The life went out of his eyes. She watched. She didn't miss a thing.

THIRTY-NINE

*V*ining came up from the basement to see Sergeant Early, Ruiz, and Caspers waiting. They fell upon her, high-fiving, hugging, and slapping her back. Caspers picked her up and paraded her around the lawn.

"You the man, Nan," he cried.

Early exclaimed, "No, she the wo-man."

LAPD officers joined in the accolades. Caspers lost his balance and they both went tumbling onto the grass.

Vining rolled onto her back and looked at the sky where news helicopters were making a racket.

Ruiz grinned down at her. "Poison Ivy. Quick Draw. They're your jackets, girl. You earned them. You wear them with pride."

"Thanks, Ruiz." Vining stared at the copters. "I've got to call home. My family's gonna see this and flip out."

She borrowed Caspers's cell phone. She let Emily know she was okay and asked her to tell Granny and to broadcast the news to the rest of the family. When she'd finished, she asked, "Anyone know how Jim is?"

Early sat on the grass beside her. "He's been transported to the hospital. He was talking, telling us not to worry. I think he's going to be okay."

Someone handed Vining a bottle of water.

"You need a doctor, too, Vining." Early pointed at her bloody left sleeve.

"Bastard got me with an arrow." Vining looked at herself. "Crazy freak."

A paramedic approached and Vining brushed him away. "I'll catch up with you in a minute, okay? It's not too deep. I'm fine."

"It's just a scratch," Caspers taunted.

"Shaddup."

Ruiz kneeled beside her, his tone contrite. "Nan, we're sorry for letting Lesley give us the slip. Turns out there's an exit from Lesley's club through the restaurant next door. Lesley borrowed a car from one of the cooks."

Caspers chimed in. "Really, Nan. We're embarrassed."

Vining patted Ruiz on the leg. "It turned out for the best. Otherwise, we'd be putting that asshole on trial. He could be on the street again, the way juries think these days."

"Word is, you got all the shots right into John Lesley's sweet spot," Early enthused.

Vining climbed to her feet as they brought out the gurney that held Lesley's body. It was covered with a sheet to thwart the photographers aloft in helicopters.

"Hold up." She raised a corner of the sheet. She wanted to see Lesley's face. He was the third corpse she'd seen since her return to duty. His eyes were open. Blood trailed from his mouth. To her he was a hunk of cooling, dead flesh and nothing more. She thought of the line of dead people in her white-light dream. He would now occupy the head, standing beside Frankie. She didn't like it, but he was part of her now and there was nothing to be done about it.

Caspers had gotten up to see as well. Looking at the corpse, he said, "John Lesley has left the house."

"Yes, he has."

She went inside and into the basement where the photographers and crime scene techs had taken over. A young man was setting numbered plastic tents beside spent bullet casings and blood splatters. He bent over to examine Frankie's school photograph that was immersed in the gore.

"That's mine," Vining said, surprising him. "I dropped it in the struggle. Can I have it back, please?" When he hesitated, she said, "It won't add anything to your investigation. It has sentimental value and I don't want it booked into evidence where I can't get it back."

He picked it up and handed it to her.

It was splattered with John Lesley's blood. Vining stuck it inside her pants pocket.

Outside, the LAPD SWAT team captain told her, "We made an audio recording of the entire incident between you and Lesley in the basement. Put a microrecorder in through the broken window. Everything came through good. Will be important once they start the investigation of the shooting, which they will."

"But of course. Thanks for covering my back."

"If we don't do it for each other, who will?"

She shook his hand. "Can I listen to that tape?"

"Sure." He handed her the small digital recording device.

She sat in an LAPD cruiser and played it through twice. She pulled Sergeant Early over to listen.

"Right before the shooting starts, what do you hear on the DVD that's playing in the background?"

Early rubbed her eyes as she listened. "Frankie Lynde moaning in pain. John Lesley, the creep is getting off. Ugh."

"I'm gonna play it again. You don't hear Frankie saying anything?"

Early paid closer attention then shook her head. "I just hear a woman who's in serious distress. Should I hear something else?"

Vining shook her head. "Just wondering." She had clearly heard Frankie's threat to Lesley: "You'll *never* be done with me!" Curiously, Lesley seemed to hear it, too. Maybe Frankie had already latched onto him. Maybe in doing so, she'd released her grip on Vining.

Vining had her arm attended to at the hospital, then joined the PPD team to wait for Kissick to come out of surgery. He was awake but groggy, so they didn't stay long. The surgeon assured them that his injuries were not too serious and that he would recover. His two sons were there as was his mother and his ex-wife.

Vining had seen photos of the ex but they had never

met. The vibe that Vining got suggested that the ex knew about Vining's relationship with Kissick and thought it was ongoing. Vining found this curious. Maybe there was something in the way she and Kissick interacted, even as ill as he was, that suggested romance. Romance had persisted, like a willful child, unresponsive to her efforts to keep it in line. Maybe she should let it run free.

After leaving the hospital, the PPD team went for drinks and appetizers at Outback to celebrate.

Vining ordered two beers, finishing half of the second one. The men were talking steaks. She didn't want to be the first to leave, but felt the need to be home with her daughter. Emily had promised reheated spaghetti with meat sauce, and nothing had ever seemed more appealing to Vining. She trailed out shortly after Sergeant Early.

FORTY

The funeral home was in a trim older house set back on a sprawling lawn shaded by an expansive oak tree. A thatch of clivia grew beneath the oak, stalks with pompoms of orange blossoms standing like fire torches above verdant sword-shaped leaves.

Frankie's wake was in a large room with stained-glass windows. A scant dozen people were scattered among rows of folding chairs. Many were police officers in uniform, their hats in their laps. Vining pegged some in street clothes as law enforcement. Voices were subdued. The air was heavy with the scent of flowers.

Frankie's family was standing in a loose circle near the entrance, their black garments making them look like crows resting in a leafless tree.

Frank Lynde broke away from the group and warmly embraced Vining. "Hello, hero."

"Please. Just doing my job. You would have done the same thing. Howyadoin', Frank?"

"Better. Each day, better. You and I know that closure stuff is bullshit. It's all about learning to live with what happened. I do feel like maybe Frankie's finally at peace."

She gave him a small smile.

He seemed to want to talk. "I don't blame ~~Frankie~~ for anything. Sometimes we hurt people we love on purpose. Sometimes it happens by accident, when we're doing what we need to do to get by."

"Guess we all do what we need to do to get by."

Sharon Hernandez, Frankie's buddy on the force, came over. She was in uniform. "Hi, Nan. Thanks for coming."

They hugged.

"That was amazing what you did. Everybody's talking about it."

Vining shrugged. "Thanks, but I'm looking forward to life returning to normal. Whatever that is."

Mostly police officers came and went. It was the typical slow erosion, Vining thought. Old friends, who didn't understand the demands and pressures of the Job, faded away to be replaced by new friends who carried a gun, badge, and a decidedly different view of the world.

They turned as Kendall Moore entered. He gave them

a brief nod and did not speak, but went straight to the casket, halting before he got too close. He dared to lean in and made a small movement as if he might touch Frankie. His hand again dropped to his side and he quickly left.

Frank Lynde watched Moore retreat and read Vining's mind. "What would be the point of jacking him up? Can't say I haven't thought about it."

"Hell, *I've* thought about it." Sharon touched Vining. "Say good-bye when you leave."

Vining approached the casket. Frankie was in uniform, her hat between her hands. Her makeup was heavy. Her blond hair was curled and stiffly sprayed. The uniform's collar was buttoned high, obscuring the gash on her neck.

Vining hated what morticians did to corpses.

On an easel was a display of photographs of Frankie throughout her life.

Vining reflected that she knew everything about the dark side of Frankie's world, but nearly nothing about the joy. She didn't know her favorite color, food, or ice cream flavor, her favorite time of day or the movies that made her cry. That was not part of Vining's job.

They would soon put Frankie's casket into the ground. Her case files would go into storage, eventually buried beneath files and more files until the case of Frances Ann Lynde was forgotten.

Vining and Frankie had made the same journey. They were sisters, bound by their calling, by violence and their own spilled blood. Vining had made it back. She couldn't explain everything that had happened. She accepted that some things had no logical explanation.

From her pocket, Vining took out Frankie's school

photograph splattered with John Lesley's blood. She slipped it beneath the hat Frankie held and placed it between her cold fingers.

So this is good-bye.

Vining snapped her hand to her forehead in a salute.

She found Sharon Hernandez in the lobby where the funeral director was helping her with a vinyl record album.

As Vining left, the opening riff of the Beach Boys' "California Girls" began to play.

FORTY-ONE

*I*t was the Fourth of July. Nearly a month had passed since the violent resolution of the Frankie Lynde affair. Later in the day, at the Vining home, there would be hot dogs and hamburgers on the grill and viewing of fireworks shows around the city from the bird's-eye perch off the back deck. Granny, Vining's sister, Stephanie, and her family, and Vining's mother and her new beau were coming by. Jim Kissick, enjoying the last weeks of his leave, was bringing his boys by for the fireworks.

Emily and Granny were at the market picking up last-minute supplies and Vining was enjoying some quiet time to herself. She sat at the kitchen table, drinking the last of a cup of ginseng tea Emily had pressed on her. The girl's dogged expansion of her skill set had led her to explore the organic food store. Vining followed the tea with a chaser of dry Count Chocula cereal to dilute the tea's bitter aftertaste.

She refolded the cereal's inner liner and shoved the box aside. Now the only thing before her was Kissick's thick binder about her assault case. She ran her fingers around its plastic edges, now feeling strong enough to open the book, but reluctant nonetheless. She reflected back to the Frankie Lynde case.

It had been quiet in Pasadena since then. Even the gangbangers seemed to be taking R&R. The stunned city needed time to recover.

There had been changes in the Detectives Section. Alex Caspers had returned to patrol and was delighted to get back on the streets. Vining had Kissick's desk in Homicide, working with Ruiz, until Kissick returned. After that, Sergeant Early promised Vining a desk in Detectives, but she couldn't say where.

It was fine with Vining. She was through sweating the small stuff.

There had been developments since John Lesley's bloody demise in his basement playhouse. Pussycat Lesley's attorney, fresh from helping her last celebrity client beat a child molestation rap, was trying to cut the best possible deal for her notorious new client. DDA Mireya Dunn vowed that while Pussycat might be able to keep herself off death row, she'd never get out of prison.

Lisa Shipp was out of the hospital, recovering at home with her parents and fielding phone calls from a William Morris agent about a book and movie deal.

Lieutenant Beltran had taken every opportunity to heap praise on Vining. He now claimed that his comments about being friends with John Lesley were taken out of context and misconstrued. Vining didn't know whether to respect or be horrified by the machinations of guys like Beltran. Teflon-coated jerk. Still, she dutifully saluted the uniform, not the man.

Her thoughts turned to Frankie. At the wake, Frank Lynde said he felt his daughter was at peace. Vining wondered what it would take to find peace for herself. She feared there was just one way: bring T. B. Mann to justice by whatever means necessary.

She opened the binder. The first thing she saw was a photo of the pantry smeared with her blood. As she looked at it, rage surged just beneath her skin. She closed the binder and stood, crossing to the living room where she opened the sliding glass door. A blast of hot July air hit her. She walked onto the terrace and looked at the foothills. Below, the giant city crept across the basin until it melted into the smog.

He's out there, she thought. *He's free while I'm in prison.*

She clenched her fists and whispered, "Game on, T. B. Mann. Game on."

Read on for a thrilling preview of
Dianne Emley's next book

Cut to the Quick

the white-knuckle sequel to *The First Cut*!

Nothing bad ever happened to Oliver Mercer. He hadn't
followed Mercer long before he'd figured that out. Nothing really bad. Having your teeth kicked out bad. Watching
someone slit your girlfriend's throat in front of you bad.
Watching someone slit your girlfriend's throat while you're
gurgling through your own slit throat bad. Or losing all your
money. A guy like Mercer probably thought that was the worst
thing that could ever happen to him. Or handing over his Rolex
to a robber. Or finding his girlfriend in bed with his best friend.
The fool.

Mercer had all the advantages. Born into money. While following Mercer around Pasadena, he'd heard people call it "old
money," like that made it even more important and special.
Dough was dough as far as he was concerned. No better cushion from life's problems than a mountain of cash. If at all, real
trouble had just skimmed the surface of Mercer's life, its misery
lasting as long as a tiny baby's frown. And when his troubles
were over, those little tears and that wrinkled brow melted
away, leaving nothing behind. It took decades of worry for
those frown lines to dig in. That's what Mercer was, as far as he
was concerned: a big, fat baby acting like he's something special because he has money he didn't earn. Having airs and looking down on people. He'd seen Mercer do it. He'd gotten that
close. He'd worn his favorite disguise, but Mercer would have
looked right through him anyway. He was one of the little
people.

He smiled. Sometimes little people had big plans that could
whip around and bite a guy like Mercer right in the ass.

He'd heard Mercer go on about a billboard company he'd

bought into. "Outside advertising," he'd called it, like that dressed it up or something. Guess it made Mercer feel like he had a real job. A well-placed billboard, Mercer had said, like the ones along the Sunset Strip, could earn fifty grand a month in rent. Billboards, for crying out loud. Who knew? Mercer's partner had been having problems with the law for allegedly poisoning some expensive trees, city property, that were blocking his signs. Personally, he thought that was funnier than hell and had to hand it to the guy, if the story was true. Mercer had used unkind words when speaking of his business partner. Well, you gotta know who you're getting in bed with, so to speak.

One thing's for double damn sure, Mercer wouldn't have gotten his girlfriend if he was a working stiff. Babe like her wouldn't have given him the time of day. That's all anyone needs to know about life right there.

Bad things did happen to good and to so-so people too, for no apparent reason. Mercer hadn't learned that life lesson yet. He was about to show Mercer a different view of the world.

Looking through binoculars from his vantage point across the Arroyo Seco, he caught himself holding his breath. He let out a small sigh when all the lights in Mercer's glass-walled home turned on at once, as they did the same time each evening. The house, designed by the much-discussed Spanish architect, Santiago Torres, was striking on the hillside. The lights spectacularly set it off. He was sure that's why Mercer turned them all on. That was okay. Then everyone could enjoy it a little bit. The worker bees commuting on the 210 freeway could look up at the big house shining on the hill and have their spirits raised. It was like looking at a faraway castle. Sometimes just the suggestion that life can be different is enough to get you through another mean day. That was another astute observation, if he said so himself. Astute meaning "smart." And if life was being difficult, sometimes you take things into your own hands.

He was grateful for Mercer's attention to appearances for another reason. The lights made watching Mercer easier. The lights could pose a problem later, but he'd deal with it. He tapped ash from his cigarette into the car's ashtray.

The globes on the antique lampposts along the Colorado Street Bridge near where he was parked also turned on. That was a pretty view from the freeway too. It was the first Saturday of September, the middle of the Labor Day holiday weekend. The evening was just how he liked it—clear, warm, and not too smoggy for the city. Not much traffic or people. It would be a fine weekend to go fishing, but the payoff of the sport he was engaged in now would ultimately be more satisfying.

Mercer walked out onto one of the terraces, holding a martini. The man was a creature of habit.

"Look at him up there, acting like he's master of his domain," he nearly shouted to no one. "King of the hill. What's that old Beatles song? The fool of the hill. No, on the hill. That's it. Fool on the hill."

He hummed a few bars of the tune. Grinding out his cigarette, he said, "Showtime."

He craned his neck to look at himself in the rearview mirror, then turned the key in the ignition. He circled the cul-de-sac and headed for the bridge to cross the arroyo.

At Mercer's driveway, he punched in the code to open the gate. He'd gotten it by watching the housekeeper when she came to work. Even the stupidest criminal wouldn't have trouble getting into this place. And he was not a stupid criminal.

He rang the doorbell, impressed with the pleasing musical notes it emitted. He turned his back to the peephole, knowing that Mercer would open the door for a blonde. He could almost count the steps it took Mercer to get to the door from the terrace. He'd look through the peephole and wonder what the intrusion was about. Then he'd open the door, still holding his martini.

The door opened and there was Mercer, holding the martini.

"Hello, Oliver. I love it when people fulfill my expectations."

Mercer blinked at his visitor, as if having trouble taking it all in.

"Such an ugly scowl, Oliver. Not very hospitable."

"Who the hell are you? Maybe I should ask *what* are you? A man dressed like a woman?"

"I hate when people criticize things they don't understand."

Before Mercer could close the door on him, he kicked it open, knocking Mercer to the floor, the high heels doing a good job. The hunting knife was out, and he started stabbing and stabbing.

Later, after whacking off another piece with the chain saw, he cut the motor and stepped back to admire his work, taking a drag on his cigarette. If he had it to do over again, he would have rethought the chain saw. It made such a mess, splattering bits of meat all over him and everything else. He took a bottle of Miss Dior from the pocket of his plastic apron and dabbed more beneath his nostrils.

The doorbell rang, followed by rapid knocking. Still holding the chain saw, he wiped a gloved hand against the apron in a wasted gesture. He was covered in blood and gore. His dress was ruined. He had figured it might be, so he hadn't worn one of his favorites. He looked through the peephole and *tsked tsked*.

Standing behind the door, he opened it a crack.

Lauren Richards tentatively pushed it and leaned inside. "Oliver? Are you playing games with me?"

She gasped at the trail of blood in the marble entryway and took a step toward it in spite of herself. Her mouth twisted in horror, her eyes fell upon the corpse of Oliver Mercer on the living room floor. At least, she thought it was Oliver. His arms and legs were in pieces, disassembled at the joints, the hands and feet cut off. The severed body parts were rearranged.

She made strangled squeaking noises through her palms pressed against her mouth.

A hand snatched her arm and flung her inside, where she slipped on the blood-slick marble. The door slammed closed. She looked up from the floor to see him and the bloody butcher's apron, women's clothes, and blond wig. She didn't know if his mouth was covered in blood or smeared lipstick.

He still held the chain saw. A burning cigarette dangled from his lips.

He shook his head.

"Oh, honey. Talk about wrong place, wrong time."